CAPTURING THE SINGLE DAD'S HEART

BY
KATE HARDY

DOCTOR, MUMMY...
WIFE?

BY
DIANNE DRAKE

MILLS &
BOON

Kate Hardy always loved books, and could read before she went to school. She discovered Mills & Boon books when she was twelve and decided this was what she wanted to do. When she isn't writing Kate enjoys reading, cinema, ballroom dancing and the gym. You can contact her via her website: katehardy.com.

Starting in non-fiction, **Dianne Drake** penned hundreds of articles and seven books under the name JJ Despain. In 2001 she began her romance-writing career with *The Doctor Dilemma*, published by Harlequin Duets. In 2005 Dianne's first Medical Romance, *Nurse in Recovery*, was published, and with more than 20 novels to her credit she has enjoyed writing for Mills & Boon ever since.

CAPTURING THE SINGLE DAD'S HEART

BY
KATE HARDY

Published in Great Britain 2016
By Mills & Boon, an imprint of HarperCollins*Publishers*
1 London Bridge Street, London, SE1 9GF

© 2016 Pamela Brooks

ISBN: 978-0-263-91501-3

Printed and bound in Spain
by CPI, Barcelona

Dear Reader,

I'd got to that stage of life where I'm really fascinated by gardens—and then my friend Michelle told me about a news story of a sensory garden for spinal patients. What a perfect setting, I thought. Especially when I kept seeing stories about spinal patients in the news.

But who would get involved with a sensory garden? And who would think it was a bad idea?

Meet Erin, who has a lot of shadows in her past, and Nate, who has a lot of shadows in his present.

The sensory garden starts by keeping them apart, and then it is very instrumental in bringing them together. Add in a troubled teen—who reminds Erin very much of herself at that age—complicated families and the whole idea about how love happens when you least expect it…and you have what happens with Erin and Nate.

I hope you enjoy their journey—and that the garden inspires you as much as it did me.

I'm always delighted to hear from readers, so do come and visit me at katehardy.com.

With love,

Kate Hardy

To Michelle Styles, with love and thanks for the lightbulb

Books by Kate Hardy

Mills & Boon Medical Romance

Dr Cinderella's Midnight Fling
Once a Playboy...
The Brooding Doc's Redemption
A Date with the Ice Princess
Her Real Family Christmas
200 Harley Street: The Soldier Prince
It Started with No Strings...
A Baby to Heal Their Hearts
A Promise...to a Proposal?
Her Playboy's Proposal

Mills & Boon Cherish

A New Year Marriage Proposal
It Started at a Wedding...
Falling for Mr December
Billionaire, Boss...Bridegroom?
Holiday with the Best Man

Visit the Author Profile page at
millsandboon.co.uk for more titles.

Praise for
Kate Hardy

'This was a truly stunning, heartfelt read from Kate Hardy. She
blew me away with the intensity of the heartache in this read.'
—*Contemporary Romance Reviews* on
The Brooding Doc's Redemption

'*Bound by a Baby* moved me to tears many times. It is a
full-on emotional drama. Author Kate Hardy brought this tale
shimmering with emotions. Highly recommended for all lovers
of romance.'

—*Contemporary Romance Reviews*

***Bound by a Baby* won the 2014 RoNA
(Romantic Novelists' Association) Rose award!**

CHAPTER ONE

WHY WOULD YOU turn down every single invitation to a team night out when you were new to the department? Erin wondered. Surely you'd want to get to know your colleagues and help yourself fit in to the team more quickly, rather than keep your distance?

Nate Townsend was a puzzle.

As a colleague, he was fine; she'd done a few ward rounds with him, and had been pleased to discover that he was good with their patients. He listened to their worries, reassured them and explained anything they didn't understand without showing the least bit of impatience. The team in Theatre had all been thrilled to report that, unlike the surgeon he'd replaced, Nate was precise with his instructions and always bothered to thank the nursing staff.

But he didn't socialise with the team at all. There was always a polite but guarded smile, a rueful shrug of the shoulders, and, 'Sorry, I can't make it,' when anyone asked him to join them. No excuses, no explanations. Just a flat no: whether it was a drink, a meal, going ten-pin bowling or simply catching the latest movie. He didn't even have lunch or coffee with any of his colleagues in the spinal unit; he grabbed a sandwich at his desk instead and wrote up his notes so he could leave straight at the end of his shift.

Erin knew that some people preferred to keep themselves to themselves, but she'd been working at the London Victoria since her first year as a junior doctor, and the friendliness of her colleagues had always made even the most harrowing day more bearable. Why did Nate rebuff everyone? Did he have some kind of complicated home life that meant he needed to be there as much as he could outside work and just didn't have the energy to make friends with his colleagues?

Not that it was any of her business.

Then she became aware that Nick, the head of their department, was talking to her.

She really ought to be paying attention in the monthly staff meeting instead of puzzling over her new colleague.

And it wasn't as if she was interested in Nate anyway, even if it turned out that he was single. Erin was very firmly focused on her career. She'd let her life be seriously derailed by a relationship when she was younger, and she was never going to make that mistake again. Friendship was all she'd ever offer anyone from now on. 'Sorry, Nick. I didn't quite catch that,' she said with a guilty smile.

'No problems. Can you bring us up to date on the sensory garden?'

Erin's pet project. The one that would help her make a real difference to their patients' lives. She smiled and opened her file. 'I'm pleased to report that we're pretty much ready to start. The hospital's agreed to let us transform the piece of land we asked for, the Friends of the London Victoria are working out a rota for the volunteers, and Ed's finalised the design—the committee just has to approve it. But they liked the draft version so it's pretty much a formality and we're planning to start the ground work in the next week or so.'

'Hang on,' Nate said. 'What's the sensory garden?'

'We're remodelling part of the hospital's grounds as a sensory garden, and making sure it's accessible to our patients,' Erin explained.

He frowned. 'That kind of project costs an awful lot of money. Wouldn't those funds be better spent on new equipment for the patients?'

This was Nate's first monthly team meeting, so he wouldn't know that Erin had been working on the garden project for almost a year in her spare time. She was sure he didn't mean to be rude, so she'd cut him some slack. 'I know that sensory gardens have a reputation for costing an arm and a leg, but this one's not going to cost anywhere near what you imagine,' she said with a smile. 'We already have the grounds, and the designer's working with us for nothing.'

'For nothing?' Nate looked sceptical.

'For publicity, then,' she said. 'The main thing is that he's not charging us for the actual design.' Like Erin herself, Ed the garden designer had a vested interest in the project. This was his way of giving something back, because the spinal unit at the London Victoria had treated his younger brother after a motorcycle accident. But it wasn't her place to tell Nate about their former patient. 'Actually, I hope he gets a ton of clients who respond to his generosity.'

'Hmm.' Nate's blue eyes were so dark, they were almost black. And right at that moment they were full of scepticism. Did he really have that bitter a view about human nature?

'The labour isn't costing us anything, either,' Erin continued. 'Ayesha—she's the chair of the Friends of the London Victoria—is setting up a rota of volunteers from across the community. So that's everyone from students who want some work experience for their CVs through to people who just enjoy pottering around in the garden in their spare time,' she explained. 'It's going to be a true community garden, so it will benefit everyone. And the rota's not just for planting the garden, it's for maintaining it as well.'

'What about the cost of the plants and any other materials used in the design?' Nate asked.

'Some things have been donated by local businesses,' she said, 'and the staff here, our patients and their families have been raising funds for the last year. We have enough money to cover the first phase of the project.'

'And you really think a sensory garden's the best way to spend that money?' he asked again.

Just who did the guy think he was? He'd been here almost a month, kept himself completely aloof from the team, and now he was criticising a project that had been months and months in the planning without having a single positive thing to say about it? Erin gritted her teeth in annoyance and, instead of letting her boss deal with it—the way she knew she should've done—she gave Nate Townsend her most acidic smile. If he wanted an answer, he'd get one.

'Actually, I do, and I'm not alone,' she said crisply.

'As you know, most of our patients have just had a massive and unexpected life change. They have to make a lot of adjustments—and they can be stuck inside in a clinical environment for months, just staring at the same four walls. A garden will be a restful space for them to sit in and have some quiet time with family and friends, chat with other patients, or even just sit and read in a space that's a bit different. It'll help them start getting used to their new lives rather than just feeling that they're stuck inside the same four walls all the time with no greenery. A sensory garden has scent, sound, texture, colour and even taste—all things that stimulate our patients and can help with their recovery.'

'You said a restful space,' Nate repeated. 'How are you going to find that in the centre of London, with traffic going past all the time?'

'Fair point,' she conceded, understanding his scepticism on that particular subject, 'but we're using hedging to lessen the impact of the traffic noise. You're very welcome to have a copy of the plans.' She looked him straight in the eye. 'Constructive comments from someone with relevant experience are always welcome.'

His eyes widened slightly to acknowledge the point of her comment; clearly he understood that she didn't think he was being constructive at all or had any relevant experience.

But that didn't stop him asking more questions. 'So what about the fact that some of our patients have problems regulating their temperature and can get either too hot or too cold in a garden?'

'Phase two,' she said, 'will be a covered space to help those particular patients. But we're beginning the first phase now so our patients and their families can start to benefit from the garden as soon as possible, rather than having to wait until we have all the money for the second phase. And, before you mention the fact that our patients are usually confined to wheelchairs, we're making sure that the pathways have no bumps and are smooth-running for anyone in a chair. Actually, Ed— the landscape designer—even spent a few hours being wheeled about the grounds in a chair so he could see for himself where the problems are.'

'Right.' But Nate still didn't look convinced.

She sighed. 'I did a lot of research before I suggested the project. And I've visited sensory gardens both in England and in Scandinavia.' The glint in his eye made her add, 'At my own cost, during my annual leave.'

'Very public-spirited of you,' he drawled.

She was really starting to dislike him now. How dared he judge her?

Though there was some truth in his barb. The whole reason she'd thrown herself behind the sensory garden project was because she'd seen the difference it had made to her brother. And helping to make that same difference to their patients might go some way towards lessening her guilt about what had happened to Mikey.

Might. She knew that her brother had forgiven her a long time ago, but she still couldn't forgive herself.

'It's important,' she said quietly. 'From a medical point of view, exposure to nature helps with pain management, reduces stress and increases feelings of calm and relaxation.'

He shrugged. 'That's a bit New Agey, don't you think?'

'Apart from the fact that garden therapy has been

used as far back as ancient Greece,' Erin pointed out, 'in modern terms you can actually measure the effect on the patient's blood pressure and heart rate. Plus a change of scene makes a mental difference. It might be a very small thing to you and me, and we all probably take it for granted, but for a patient who's been stuck inside for weeks it's a *massive* thing to be able to go outside.'

Finally, to Erin's relief, Nick spoke up. 'As the project's already been agreed, perhaps we should all just agree to disagree on the use of funds and what have you.'

'Sure,' Nate said easily. 'And, as the new boy, I know I shouldn't make waves. But my sister's a deputy headmistress, and she tells me that the thing she likes best about having a new governor on the team is that you get a critical friend—someone who looks at things from the outside with a fresh pair of eyes and asks questions. I guess I was trying to do the same thing here.'

'You're very welcome to a copy of the file,' Erin said again, 'if you want to check the costings and make sure I haven't missed anything.'

'I'll take you up on that,' he said.

Erin simmered through the rest of the meeting. Critical friend, indeed. There was nothing *friendly* about Nate Townsend. He might be easy on the eye—on his first day, several of her female colleagues had declared him one of the sexiest men they'd ever met, with his Celtic good looks of dark hair, pale complexion and navy blue eyes—but in her view character was much more important than looks. And she really didn't like what she'd seen of Nate Townsend today.

And of course she *would* have to do the ward rounds with him after the meeting.

'Do you have a particular way you'd prefer to do the ward rounds this morning?' she asked, knowing that she sounded snippy but not being able to stop herself.

'I'm quite happy to follow the normal protocol here,' he said mildly.

'That's not the impression you gave in the meeting.' The words were out before she could hold them back.

'I apologise if I upset you,' he said. 'Why is the garden so important to you?'

He seriously thought she was going to tell him that— so he could go ahead and judge her as harshly as she judged herself? No way. 'I've been working on the project for a year,' she said instead. 'And I've seen the difference it's made to patients elsewhere. Phase one is the garden, phase two is the covered area, and maybe we can have some raised beds in phase three and a greenhouse so the patients can grow plants. If it proves to them that they can still do something, that they can still contribute to life instead of having to be looked after every second of the day and feel like a burden to everyone, it'll help them adjust to their new life and the prospect of having to change their career.'

'I think Nick's right,' Nate said, his expression inscrutable. 'For now we'll agree to disagree.'

She inclined her head. 'As you wish. Though I'd be interested to know why you're so against the project.'

'Because several times before now I've seen funds raised to help patients and then wasted on people's pet hobbyhorses,' he said.

Deep breath, she told herself. He might be right about

it being her pet hobbyhorse, but the rest of it was way off the mark. 'I can assure you that what we're doing isn't a waste of funds. And it's not just about the patients. As I said, it's a community garden, with local volunteers helping. That's everyone from older people who've moved into a flat and miss having a garden through to young mums who want just a couple of hours a week doing something that's not centred around the baby, and the local sixth form's involved, too. It's a project that gives extra credit towards exams for some of them, and others can talk about it on their personal statement when they apply to university. It's getting everyone working together to make a difference and absolutely everyone involved gets some benefit from it. I'm sorry if you see a garden as a waste of money, but the rest of us really don't.'

Erin was really passionate about this project, Nate thought. Her face had been full of animation when she'd talked about the garden and what she thought it could do for their patients.

Then he shook himself mentally. Yes, Erin Leyton was pretty, with her curly light brown hair caught back at the nape of her neck, clear grey eyes and a dusting of freckles across her nose. But, even if he were in a place where he could think about having a relationship—which he most definitely wasn't, with his life being in utter chaos right now—it would be way too complicated, given that they had such opposing views on fundamental things.

Though maybe he was only being scratchy with her because he was so frustrated with how things were going outside work, and that wasn't fair of him. It wasn't Erin's fault that his ex-wife had dropped a bombshell on him only a week before he'd started his new job and he'd been running round like a headless chicken ever since, trying to sort everything out. And it definitely wasn't Erin's fault that he hated himself for being such a failure.

'I'm sorry,' he said. 'You're right—it's like the new boy stamping everywhere to try and make an impression.'

'I didn't say that.'

'You were thinking it, though.'

She gave him a rueful smile. 'Can you blame me?'

'No—and actually, it isn't that at all. I apologise. I shouldn't bring my baggage to work.'

The hostility in her grey eyes melted in an instant. 'Apology accepted. And sometimes,' she said quietly, 'it helps to have someone to talk to—someone who isn't involved with the situation and won't judge you or spread gossip.'

She was offering him a shoulder to cry on, even after he'd been combative towards her in a meeting involving what was clearly her pet project? That was unbelievably generous. Then again, he wasn't that surprised. He'd already noticed Erin's name at the top of all the internal memos organising a team night out or a collection for someone's birthday or baby shower. He had a feeling that she was one of life's fixers.

Well, his life couldn't be fixed right now. He wasn't sure if it ever could be. 'Thanks for the offer,' he said, 'but I don't really know you.'

She shrugged, but he could see the momentary flash of hurt on her face. 'Fair enough. Forget I said anything.'

He felt like a heel, but he couldn't even offer anyone friendship at the moment. Not until he'd sorted things out with Caitlin and established a better relationship with her. And he had no idea how long that was going to take. Right now it felt like it was never going to happen.

'Let's do the ward rounds,' he said. 'We have Kevin Bishop first. He's forty-five, but he has the spine of a sixty-five-year-old—it's a really bad case of stenosis.'

'Is that from normal wear and tear,' she asked, 'or is it job-related?'

'Probably a bit of both. He's a builder. He has two worn discs, and the sheath around his spinal cord has narrowed,' Nate explained.

'Which would put pressure on his spinal nerves—so it sounds as if the poor guy's been in a lot of pain,' she said, her face full of sympathy.

'He's been taking anti-inflammatories,' Nate said, 'but he says they don't even touch the pain any more.'

'So you're looking at major surgery and weeks of rehabilitation?' she asked. 'If so, Mr Bishop could be a candidate for the sensory garden.'

'No, no and no,' Nate said. 'He won't be here for long. I'm planning to use an interspinous spacer device this afternoon rather than doing a laminectomy.'

'I've read about that,' she said. 'Isn't there a larger risk of the patient needing to have surgery again in the future if you use a spacer rather than taking a slice of bone off the area putting pressure on his spinal cord?'

'Yes, but there's also a much lower risk of complications than you'd get from taking off the bit of bone that rubs and causes the pain, plus it's just a small incision and he'll be out again in a couple of days. I'd normally use the procedure for older patients or those with higher risks of surgery,' Nate said. 'Kevin Bishop is still young but, given that he's overweight and has high blood pressure, I think he's higher risk.'

'Fair enough. So how exactly does the spacer work?'

Nate could see that she was asking from a professional viewpoint rather than questioning his competence; he knew that Erin was a neurologist rather than a surgeon. 'We'll put a spacer into his lower vertebrae. It'll act as a supportive spring and relieve the pressure on the nerve. It gives much better pain relief than epidural steroid injections, plus the spinal nerves aren't exposed so there's a much lower risk of scarring.' He paused. Maybe this would be a way of easing the tension between them after that meeting. 'Provided Mr Bishop gives his consent, you can come and watch the op, if you like.'

'Seriously?' She looked surprised that he'd even offered.

'Seriously.' Was she going to throw it back in his face, or accept it as the offer of a truce?

'I'd really like that. Thank you.' She smiled at him.

Again Nate felt that weird pull of attraction and reminded himself that this really wasn't appropriate. For all he knew, Erin could be in a serious relationship. Not that he was going to ask, because he didn't want her to think that he was interested in her. He didn't have the headspace or the mental energy right now to be interested in anyone. His focus needed to be on his daughter and learning how to be a good full-time dad to her.

'Uh-huh,' he said, feeling slightly awkward, and went with Erin to see his patient.

He introduced her swiftly to Kevin Bishop.

'I've reviewed the scans of your spine, Mr Bishop, and your blood tests are all fine, too, so I'm happy to go ahead with surgery today,' he said. 'Would you mind if Dr Leyton here sits in on the operation?'

'No, that's fine,' Mr Bishop said, looking relieved. 'I'm just glad you're going to do it today. I'm really looking forward to being able to tie my own shoelaces again, and to stand up without my legs tingling all the time.'

'It's been that bad?' Erin asked sympathetically.

Mr Bishop nodded. 'The pain's been terrible. Rest doesn't help and the tablets don't seem to work any more. My doctor said I'd have to have surgery—I was dreading the idea of being stuck in hospital for weeks, but Mr Townsend said that I'd only be in for a few days.' He gave her a weary smile. 'I just want to be able to play football with my kids again and get back to my job.'

'The surgery will make things much better,' Nate promised. 'I know we talked about it before, but I'd like to run through the situation again to make sure you're happy about what's happening.'

Mr Bishop nodded.

'Basically what happens is that the nerves in your spine run down a tunnel called the spinal canal. You've had a lot of wear and tear on your spine, and that makes the spinal canal narrower; that means it squeezes the nerves when you stand or walk, which is why you're getting pain. What I want to do is put a spacer between two of the bones in your spine, and that will relieve the pressure and stop the pain. Now, you haven't eaten anything since last night?'

'No, though I'm dying for a cup of tea,' Mr Bishop admitted.

Nate smiled. 'Don't worry, you'll get your cup of tea this afternoon. I'll get the pre-op checks organised now and I'm going to operate on you at two. The operation's going to be under a local anaesthetic, but you'll also be sedated so you won't remember anything about it afterwards. You'll be lying face down during the operation on a special curved mattress; that will reduce the pressure on your chest and pelvis, and also give me better access to your spine.'

'How long will the operation take?' Mr Bishop asked.

'It should be about an hour or so, depending on what I find—but from your scan it looks pretty straightforward.'

'That's great.' Mr Bishop smiled. 'I still can't believe I'll be able to go home again in a couple of days. I thought I'd be stuck in here for weeks.'

'You're not going to be able to go straight back to work or to drive for the first few weeks after the operation,' Nate warned, 'and you'll need to do physiotherapy and exercises. They'll start about four weeks after the op—and in the meantime it'll be better for you to sit on a high, hard chair than a soft one with a low back.'

'And no bending or lifting?'

'Absolutely. Listen to whatever the physiotherapist tells you,' Nate said. 'This is a newish procedure, Mr Bishop. I do need to tell you that, because it's so new, there's a very small possibility the spacer might move in the future or need replacing.'

'If it takes the pain away, I can cope with that.'

Nate talked Mr Bishop through the likely complications and all the possible consequences of the operation, then asked him to sign the consent form. 'I'll see you later this afternoon,' he said with a smile.

Later that afternoon, watching Nate perform in Theatre, Erin was spellbound. His instructions to Theatre staff were clear, he was polite as well as precise and he talked her through every single step of the operation, explaining the methodology and what it would do for the patient.

With their patient and in Theatre, he was a completely different man, she thought. Not the cool, critical and judgemental stranger he'd been in the meeting. This man had deft, clever hands and really knew his stuff— and he treated everyone around him as his equal. She noticed that he made the time to thank every member of the team at the end of the operation, too.

This Nate Townsend, she thought, was a man she'd like to get to know.

And she understood now why so many of her colleagues had dubbed him the sexiest surgeon in the hospital. The only bit of his face she could see clearly was his eyes—a gorgeous, sensual dark blue. And the combination of intelligence and clever hands made a shiver of pure desire run down her spine.

Which was totally inappropriate.

She was here to observe, not to go off in some ridiculous, lust-filled daydream.

'Thank you for letting me observe, today,' she said when they'd both scrubbed out. 'That was really useful. I can talk to patients with spinal stenosis about their options with a lot more authority now.'

'No problem. And if you have any questions about the procedure later, come and find me.'

He actually smiled at her, then, and she caught her breath. When he smiled like that—a smile that came from inside, more than just politeness—he was utterly gorgeous.

And he was probably involved with someone. Given that he kept everyone at a distance, she'd bet that his home life was full of complications. And none of those complications were any of her business.

'See you tomorrow,' she said, feeling slightly flustered.

'Yeah.'

Once Nate was happy that Kevin Bishop and his other patients from Theatre that afternoon had settled back on the ward and there were no complications following surgery, he finished writing up his notes. And then he braced himself for the drive to his mother's house.

Guilt flooded through him. What kind of a father was he, to dread picking up his own daughter? But being her full-time parent—the one with total responsibility—was a far cry from being the part-time dad who saw her for a few snatched days in school holidays and odd weekends. Before Caitlin had come to live with him, they hadn't spent long enough together at a stretch to run out of things to talk about. Now, it was the other way round: he had all the time he could've wanted with her, and not a clue what to say.

As he'd half expected, Caitlin wasn't in the mood for talking.

'How was your day?' he asked as he pulled away from the kerb.

Her only answer was a shrug.

Great. What did he ask now? Clearly she didn't want to talk about school or her friends—he didn't even know whether she'd made friends, yet, because she always sidestepped the question whenever he asked.

Food would be a safe subject, surely? 'Do you fancy pizza for dinner tonight?'

A shake of her head. 'Your mother already cooked for me.'

As part of her protest about being forced to move from Devon to London, Caitlin had shut off from Sara, her paternal grandmother; she avoided calling Sara anything at all, just as she'd stopped calling Nate 'Dad'. He had no idea how to get round that without starting another row—and he was trying to pick his battles carefully.

By the time he'd thought of another topic, they were home. Not that Caitlin considered his house as her real home, and he was beginning to wonder if she ever would. Though neither of them had any choice in the matter.

'Do you have much homework?' he tried as he unlocked the front door.

'I've already done it. Do you have to be on my case *all* the time?' she demanded.

It took her five seconds to run up the stairs. Two more to slam her bedroom door.

And that would be the last he saw of her, that evening.

He didn't have a clue what to do now. Stephanie had made it clear that it was his turn to deal with their daughter, and being a full-time dad was as much of a shock to the system for him as it was for Caitlin. Of course he understood that it was hard starting at a new school and being away from the friends you'd known since you were a toddler, but Caitlin had been in London for a month now and things still hadn't got any better.

He'd rather face doing the most complicated and high-risk spinal surgery for twenty-four hours straight than face his teenage daughter. At least in Theatre he had some clue what he was doing, whereas here he was just a big fat failure. He didn't know what to do to make things better. When he'd tried asking her, she'd just rolled her eyes, said he was clueless, stomped upstairs and slammed her bedroom door.

Why was parenting a teenage girl so much harder than the job he'd trained for more than ten years to do?

And how was he ever going to learn to get it right?

He grabbed his mobile phone and headed out to the back garden. Hopefully Caitlin would be less likely to overhear this particular conversation if he was outside; he didn't want her to misunderstand and think he was complaining about her. And then he called his ex-wife.

'What now?' was Stephanie's snapped greeting.

He sighed inwardly. Caitlin had definitely inherited

her mother's hostile attitude towards him. 'How are you, Steph?'

'Fine.' She sounded suspicious. 'Why are you calling?'

'Because I need help,' he admitted. 'I'm absolutely rubbish at this parenting business.'

'You can't send her back here,' Stephanie said. 'Not after the way she's been with Craig.'

'I know.' Caitlin had been just as hostile towards Nate's now-ex-girlfriend. Though, if he was honest with himself, the relationship with Georgina had been on its last legs anyway. If the final row hadn't been over Caitlin, it would've been about something else, and he was pretty sure they would've broken up by now. Maybe Stephanie's new marriage had slightly firmer foundations. For her sake, he hoped so. 'I don't know what to say to her. How to get through to her. All she does is roll her eyes at me and slam her bedroom door.'

'She's a teenage girl.'

'I know, but they're not all like that. Not all the time. And she wasn't like that when she visited me or I came down to Devon.'

'So it's my fault?'

'No. I don't want to fight with you, Steph.'

'But you're judging me for putting my relationship before her.'

'No, I'm not,' he said tiredly. 'Who am I to judge, when I put my career before both of you?'

'I'm glad you can see that now,' Stephanie said.

Nate told himself silently not to rise to the bait. It was an old argument and there were no winners.

'Well, you'll just have to keep trying. Because she

can't come back here,' Stephanie warned. 'She's your daughter, too, and it's your turn to look after her.'

'Yeah.' Nate knew that asking his ex for help had been a long shot. Given that Stephanie had spent the last ten years hating him for letting her down, of course she wouldn't make this easy for him now. And he knew that most of the fault was his. He hadn't been there enough when Stephanie had been struggling with a demanding toddler, and he hadn't supported her as much as he should have... It wasn't surprising that she'd walked out and taken the baby halfway across the country with her.

Maybe he should've sucked it up and gone after her. Or at least moved closer so that access to their daughter wasn't so difficult. Even though he had a sneaking suspicion that Stephanie would've moved again if he'd done that.

In the end they'd compromised, with Nate doing his best to support his daughter and ex-wife financially by working hard and rising as fast as he could through the ranks. He'd called Caitlin twice a week, trying to speak to her before her bedtime even when he was at work, and then as soon as video calling became available he'd used that—though Steph had made pointed comments about him being the 'fun parent' buying their daughter expensive technology. But without that he would've been limited to the odd weekend and visits in the school holidays. He hadn't bought the tablet to score points or rub in the fact that he was making good money—he'd simply wanted to see his daughter as much as he could, even though they lived so far apart.

'Thanks anyway,' he said, hoping that Stephanie would take it for the anodyne and polite comment it was rather than assume that he was being sarcastic and combative, and ended the call.

Being a new single dad to a teen was the most frustrating, awkward thing he'd ever done in his life.

But he'd have to find a way to make this work. For all their sakes.

CHAPTER TWO

NATE HAD DARK shadows under his eyes, Erin noticed.
And, although he was being completely professional
with their patients, she could see the suppressed misery in his eyes.

I shouldn't bring my baggage to work.

His words from the previous day echoed in her head.
Right at that moment, it looked to her as if he was fighting a losing battle. Clearly whatever was bothering him
had stopped him getting a decent night's sleep.

OK, so he'd rebuffed her yesterday when she'd offered to listen. But that didn't mean she should give
up on him. Erin knew what it was like to be in a bad
place—and she'd been lucky enough to have her best
friend's mother to bat her corner when she'd really
needed it. Maybe Nate didn't have someone in his life
like Rachel. So maybe, just maybe, she could help.

Which would be a kind of payback. Something to
help lessen the guilt that would never go away.

At the end of their rounds, she said, 'Can we have
a quick word?'

He looked confused, but shrugged. 'Sure. What can
I do for you?'

'Shall we talk over lunch?' she suggested. 'My shout.'

He frowned, suspicion creeping in to his expression. 'Is this anything to do with the sensory garden?'

'Absolutely not. No strings,' she promised. 'A sandwich and coffee in the staff canteen. And no haranguing you about my pet project. Just something I wanted to run by you.'

'OK. See you in my office at, what, half-past twelve?' he suggested. 'Though obviously that depends on our patients. One of them might need some extra time.'

She liked the fact that even though he was clearly struggling to deal with his personal life, he was still putting his patients first. 'That'd be great. I'll come and collect you.'

Erin spent the rest of the morning in clinic, and to her relief everything ran on time. Nate's pre-surgery consultations had clearly also gone well, because he was sitting at his desk in his office when she turned up at half-past twelve.

'I'll just save my file,' he said, and tapped a few buttons on his computer keyboard while she waited.

In the staff canteen, she bought them both a sandwich and coffee, plus a blueberry muffin, and directed him to find them a quiet table in the corner.

'Cake?' he asked when she turned up at their table.

'Absolutely. Cake makes everything better,' she said.

'So what can I do for you?' he asked, looking slightly wary.

'Yesterday, you said that you didn't know me.'

He winced. 'Sorry. That was rude. I didn't mean it to sound as mean as that.'

'I'm not trying to make you feel bad about what you

said,' she said. 'What I mean is that we all go through times when we can't see the wood for the trees, and sometimes it helps to talk to someone who's completely not connected with the situation—someone who might have a completely different viewpoint.'

He didn't look convinced.

'So I guess I'm repeating my offer from yesterday,' she finished.

'That's very kind of you, but—' he began.

'Don't say no,' she broke in. 'Just eat your lunch and think about it.'

'Why are you being so kind?' he asked. 'Because you don't know me, either.'

'I don't have any weird ulterior motive,' she said. 'It's kind of payback. You know—what goes around, comes around. In the past, I was in a tough situation when I really needed to talk to someone. I was lucky, because someone was there for me. So now it's my turn to be that person for someone else.'

'As in me?' He looked thoughtful. 'Got you.'

Though she noticed that he still looked worried. And she could guess why. 'For the record,' she said gently, 'I'm not a gossip. Whatever you say to me will go nowhere else. And right now I think you really do need to talk to someone, because you look like hell.'

He smiled, then. 'And you tell it like it is.'

She shrugged. 'It's the easiest way. So just eat your cake and think about it, yes?'

Nate knew that he really didn't deserve this. But, oh, it was so tempting to take up Erin's offer. If nothing else, she might help him to see things from Caitlin's point of view so he could understand what was going on in his daughter's head. Since Caitlin had come to live with him, he'd never felt more alone.

He believed Erin when she said she wasn't a gossip. He'd never heard her talk about other people in the staff room in their absence. Besides, the kind of people who organised departmental evenings out and collections for gifts for colleagues weren't the kind of people who took pleasure in tearing people down.

Even though he barely knew her, he had the strongest feeling that he could trust her.

And maybe she had a point. Talking to someone who didn't know either of them might help him see his way through this. Then maybe he could be the father Caitlin so clearly needed. 'You're sure about this?' he asked. 'Because it's a long story and it's not pretty. I...' He dragged in a breath. 'Right now, I don't like myself very much.'

'Nothing's beautiful all the time, and if you have regrets about a situation then it's proof that you're willing to consider making changes to improve things,' she said. 'And it might not be as bad as you think. Try me.'

'Thank you.' But where did he start? 'It's my daughter,' he said eventually.

'You're a new dad?' she asked. 'Well, that would explain the shadows under your eyes. Not enough sleep, thanks to your newborn.'

He gave her a wry smile. 'Yes to the sleepless nights bit—but it's complicated.'

She simply spread her hands and smiled back, giving him space to make sense of things in his own head rather than barging in with questions. Funny how that made it so much easier to talk to her.

'I'm sort of a new dad, but Caitlin's not a newborn,' he explained. 'She's thirteen.'

Nate had a thirteen-year-old daughter.

So did that mean he was married? Well, good, Erin thought. That would make him absolutely out of bounds. Any relationship between them would have to be strictly platonic. She was aware that made her a coward, choosing to spend her time with people she knew were unavailable so were therefore safe: but she'd turned her life round now and she wasn't going to risk letting everything go off track again.

But then again, he'd just said he was a new dad. How? Was he fostering the girl?

Giving him a barrage of questions would be the quickest way to make him close up again; but silence would be just as bad. 'Thirteen's a tough age,' she said, hoping that she didn't sound judgemental.

'And she doesn't get on with her mother's new husband.'

New husband? Oh, help. So Nate wasn't married, then—or, at least, he wasn't married to the mother of his daughter.

'She didn't get on with my now ex-girlfriend, either.'

Meaning that Nate was single. Which in turn meant he was no longer safe. Erin masked her burgeoning dismay with a kind smile.

'And I have absolutely no idea how to connect with my daughter.' He sighed. 'Anyone would think I was eighty-five, not thirty-five.'

So if Caitlin was thirteen now, Nate had been quite young when she was born. Not even fully qualified as a doctor, let alone as a surgeon.

Clearly her thoughts showed in her expression, as he sighed again. 'I'm sure you've already done the maths and worked out that we had Caitlin when we were young. Too young, really. Steph was twenty-one and I was twenty-two. We hadn't actually planned to have Caitlin at that point, but we didn't want the alternative, so we got married. We thought at the time it would work out because we loved each other and we'd manage to muddle through it together.'

Yeah. Erin knew that one. Except loving someone wasn't always enough to make things work out. Particularly when the feelings weren't the same on both sides. And particularly when you were too young to realise that it took more strength to let go than to hold on and hope you could change the other person, instead of making the sensible decision to walk away before things got seriously messy. She'd learned that the hard way.

But this wasn't about her baggage. It was about helping Nate.

'It's pretty hard to cope with normal life when you're a junior doctor,' she said, 'let alone a baby.'

'Tell me about it,' he said ruefully. 'I was working— well, you know yourself the hours you work when you're a junior doctor. So I was too tired to take over baby duties from Steph when I got home from work. She'd had to put her plans on hold. Instead of doing a postgraduate course to train as a teacher, she was stuck at home with the baby all day and every day, so I totally understand why she was fed up with me. I should've done a lot more and supported her better.'

'You were working long hours and studying as well. All you can do is your best,' Erin said.

'I tried, but it wasn't enough. Steph left me in the end, when Caitlin was three. They moved away.' He grimaced. 'I should've moved with them instead of staying in London.'

'You're a spinal surgeon,' Erin pointed out. 'There aren't spinal units in every single hospital in the country, and you were, what, twenty-five when she left?' At his nod, she continued, 'Back then you would still have been studying for your surgeon's exams. Even if you'd found another spinal unit close to wherever Steph and Caitlin had moved, there's no guarantee they would've had a training place for you. It's not like working in an emergency department or in maternity, where there's a bit more flexibility and you can move hospitals a little more easily if you have to.'

'It's still my fault. Maybe I specialised too soon, or I should've just stopped being selfish and realised I couldn't follow my dreams. Maybe I should've compromised by moving specialties and working in the emergency department instead,' he said. 'Steph and Caitlin ended up living in Devon, a five-hour drive from me. So I got to see her on the odd weekend, and she used to come and stay with me sometimes in the holidays, but that's nothing like living with someone all the time. I feel as if we're almost strangers. And she hates living with me.'

'So why is she living with you? Is her mum ill?'

'No.' He winced. 'As I said, she didn't get on with

her mum's new husband. Steph said Caitlin's a night-mare teenager and it was about time I did my share of parenting—so she sent Caitlin to live with me.'

Erin went cold.

A difficult teenager who didn't get on with her mother's new man, kicked out of home by her mother and sent to live with her father. Erin knew that story well. Had lived through every second of it in misery herself, thirteen years ago. 'When did this happen?'

'Just over a month ago.'

A few days before he'd started his new job. Not great timing for either of them. And now Erin understood exactly why Nate didn't socialise with the team. He needed to spend the time with his daughter and build their relationship properly.

'So she's moved somewhere she doesn't know, miles away from all her friends and everyone she's grown up with, and she's got to settle in to a new school as well.'

'Which would be a huge change for anyone,' he agreed, 'but it's harder still when you're thirteen years old. And I'm clueless, Erin. I don't know how to deal with this. I'm way out of my depth. I asked Steph what to do, and…' He stopped abruptly.

Clearly his ex hadn't been able to help much. Or maybe she hadn't been willing to offer advice. Erin knew that one first-hand, too. Erin's mother had washed her hands of her, the day she'd kicked Erin out. And even now, all these years later, their relationship was difficult.

But Erin liked the fact that Nate was clearly trying hard to be fair and shoulder his share of the blame for things going wrong, rather than refusing to accept any responsibility and claiming that it was all his ex's fault. 'It sounds to me as if you need a friend—someone's who's been there and understands thirteen-year-old girls,' she said carefully.

He blinked. 'You're telling me you have a thirteen-year-old? But you don't look old enough.'

'I'm not.' Though she flinched inwardly. If things had been a little different, she might have had a thirteen-year-old daughter herself right now. But things were as they were. And she still felt a mixture of regret and relief and guilt when she thought about the miscarriage. Regret for a little life that hadn't really had a chance to start, for the baby she'd never got to know; relief, because when she looked back she knew she hadn't been mature enough to be a mum at the age of sixteen; and guilt, because she had friends who'd be fantastic parents and were having trouble conceiving, whereas she'd fallen pregnant the very first time she'd had sex. The miscarriage had been her wake-up call, and she'd turned her life round. Studied hard. Passed all her exams, the second time round. Become a doctor. Tried to make a difference and to make up for her mistakes. Not that she would ever be able to make up for the biggest one.

She pushed the thoughts away. *Not now.* 'I was a thirteen-year-old girl once. Although I was a couple of years older than your Caitlin when my parents split up, my mum got involved with someone I loathed and it got a bit messy.' That was the understatement of the year. 'So I ended up living with my dad.' Because her mum hadn't believed her about Creepy Leonard, Erin had gone even further off the rails—and then she'd made the terrible mistake that had ruined her brother's life.

Maybe, just maybe, this could be her chance for pay-back. To help Nate's daughter and stop Caitlin making the same mistakes that Erin herself had made.

'So you've actually been in Caitlin's shoes?' Nate asked, looking surprised.

'From what you've just told me, pretty much,' Erin said.

He sucked in a breath. 'I know this is a big ask—because you don't know me, either—but, as you clearly have a much better idea than I do about what she's going through, would you be able to help me, so I don't make things even worse than they are for her right now?'

'I'm not perfect,' she warned, 'but yes, I'm happy to try. Maybe we could meet up at the weekend and do something together, so Caitlin can start getting to know me and I can try and get her talking a bit.'

'Thank you.' He looked at her. 'And what can I do for you in return?'

She flapped a dismissive hand. 'You don't need to do anything.'

'If you help me, then I need to help you. It's only fair.'

She couldn't resist teasing him. 'So if I asked you to do a stint in the sensory garden with a bit of weeding or what have you, you'd do it?'

'If that's what you want, sure.' He paused. 'Why is the garden so important to you?'

It sounded as if he actually wanted to know, rather than criticising her. And he'd shared something with her; maybe he'd feel less awkward about that if she shared something in return. Not the whole story, but enough of the bare bones to stop him asking more questions. 'Because I know someone who had a really bad car accident and ended up in a wheelchair. He was helped by a sensory garden,' she said. 'It was the thing that stopped him going off the edge.'

'Fair enough,' he said. 'Don't take this the wrong way but, if you're going to help Caitlin and me, I need to ask you something. Is there a husband or a boyfriend who might have a problem with you doing that?'

'No.'

'OK. I just…' He blew out a breath. 'Well, I've messed up enough of my own relationships. I don't want to mess up anyone else's as well.'

She smiled. 'Not a problem. There's nothing to mess up.'

'Good.' He grimaced. 'And that sounded bad. I didn't mean it like that. I'm not coming on to you, Erin. I split up with my last girlfriend nearly a month ago, a few days after Caitlin arrived, and frankly I don't have room in my life for a relationship. All my time's taken up learning to be a dad, and right now I'm not making a very good job of it.'

'I know you're not coming on to me,' she said. Besides, even if he was, it wouldn't work out. Love didn't last. She'd seen it first-hand—her own parents' marriage and subsequent relationships splintering, her brother's girlfriend dumping him when he needed her most, and then none of her own relationships since her teens had lasted for more than a few months. She'd given up on love. 'I'm focused on my career and I'm not looking for a relationship, either. But I can always use a friend, and it sounds as if you and Caitlin could, too.'

'Yes. We could.' He looked at her. 'I ought to warn

you in advance that most of her communications with me right now involve slammed doors or rolled eyes.'

'You need a bit of time to get used to each other and to get to know each other better,' Erin said. 'As you say, seeing someone at weekends and holidays isn't the same as living with them all the time. She needs to find out where her new boundaries are. Her whole life's changed and she probably thinks it's her fault she's been sent to live with you. Especially if she was close to her mum and now they're not getting on so well. What's the problem with her mum's new man?'

'He seems a bit of a jerk,' Nate said. 'Which isn't me saying that I'm jealous and I want Steph back—we stopped loving each other years ago, and the best I can hope for is that we can be civil to each other for Caitlin's sake. But he doesn't seem to be making a lot of effort with Caitlin.'

'If you get involved with someone who has a child, you know they come as a package and you have to try to get on with your new partner's child if you want it to work,' Erin said. 'If Steph's new man doesn't bother doing that, that makes it tricky for you. You can't take sides, because whichever one you pick you'll be in the wrong. If you take Steph's side, Caitlin will resent you for it; and if you take Caitlin's side, Steph will resent you for it. So your best bet would be to tell them both that you're staying neutral, that the bone of contention about Steph's new man is strictly between them, and absolutely refuse to discuss it with either of them.'

He leaned back and gave her a look of pure admiration. 'How come you're so wise? Are you twice as old as you look?'

'And have a portrait of an ageing person in the attic, like Dorian Grey?' she asked with a grin. 'No. I'm twenty-nine.' But if she'd had a portrait in the attic, it would've been very ugly indeed. A portrait of sheer selfishness. She'd spent the last thirteen years trying and failing to make up for it.

'Twenty-nine. So you're just about young enough to remember what it was like, being thirteen years old.'

'And a girl,' she reminded him. 'You're at a disadvantage, you know, having a Y chromosome.'

'Tell me about it.' He rolled his eyes.

She laughed. 'I think you might've learned that particular move from your daughter. I hereby award you a gold star for eye-rolling.'

'Why, thank you,' he teased back.

Nate hadn't felt this light-hearted in what felt like for ever. Not since that first phone call from Steph, informing him that Caitlin was coming to live with him permanently as from that weekend and he had to sort out her new school immediately.

'Thank you,' he said. 'And I'm sorry we got off on the wrong foot.'

'Over the sensory garden?' She shrugged. 'We agreed to disagree. And we're fine as colleagues. I like the way you explain things to patients, and I like the fact you don't look down at Theatre staff.'

'Of course I don't. I couldn't operate without them,' he said. 'Literally.'

'Which isn't how your predecessor saw things, believe me,' she said. 'You'll be fine. It's hard enough to settle in to a new team, but to do it when your home life's going through massive changes as well—that's a lot to ask of anyone.'

'Maybe. I'm sorry if people think I've been snooty.'

'Just a little standoffish. Shy, even.' She smiled. 'They're a nice bunch. And they don't judge. Obviously I'm not going to tell anyone what you've said to me, but if you feel like opening up at any time you'd get a good response. There are enough parents in the department who could give you a few tips on handling teenagers, though I think the big one is to stock up on cake and chocolate. That's what my best friend's mum did, anyway.'

'And do you get on with your parents now?'

Tricky question. Erin knew that her mother still didn't believe her about Creepy Leonard, and blamed Erin for the break-up of that relationship as well as for what had happened to Mikey. 'We get along,' she said carefully. Which was true enough. She and her mother managed to be coolly civil to each other on the rare occasions they accidentally met. But neither of her parents had been there for her when she'd needed them most; her father had been too cocooned in feeling guilty about leaving his family for someone else, and her mother had already thrown her out. And her brother, Mikey, was already paying the price for helping her earlier.

She'd never forgive herself for it. If she hadn't called him in tears, hadn't confided in him about what had happened to her, he would never have come to her rescue— and he would never have had the accident and ended up in a wheelchair.

'You just do your best,' she said with a bright smile.

'So. You said you saw her at weekends and she stayed with you in the holidays. What sort of things did you do together?'

'Things she finds too babyish now—building sand-castles, or going to the park or the zoo.' He spread his hands. 'And how bad is it that I don't have a clue what my own daughter likes doing?'

'The teen years are hard. You're growing up and you don't want people to treat you as if you're still a kid—but at the same time you feel awkward around adults. It's not all your fault,' Erin said. 'You said your sister was a deputy head. Can she help?'

'Liza's too far away. She lives in York and Caitlin's only seen her half a dozen times in her life. Though obviously Liza deals with teens every day at work, so I asked her advice. She just said to take it slowly and give it time.'

'That's really good advice.' Erin paused. 'What about your mum?'

He sighed. 'She tries. Caitlin goes to her place after school until I've finished at work and can pick her up. But there's quite a generation gap between them and Caitlin doesn't really talk to her, either.'

'It sounds like a vicious circle—the harder you try, the more distance you end up putting between you all.'

'Yeah. You're right. We need help.' He looked bleak. 'Though I feel bad about burdening you.'

'You're not burdening me. I asked you what was wrong, and I offered to help. I wouldn't have done it if I didn't want to,' she pointed out. 'I remember what it was like for me. And I was difficult at fifteen. Rude, surly, wouldn't let anyone close. I was the original night-mare teenager.'

'And it got better?'

With her dad, at least; though they weren't that close. 'Yes.'

'Thank you,' he said. 'It feels as if you've just taken a massive weight off my shoulders.'

And, oh, when he smiled like that… It made Erin's heart do a funny little flip.

Which was completely inappropriate.

If they'd met at a different time in his life, things might've been different. But he didn't need the extra complications of a relationship—especially with some-one who had baggage like hers and didn't believe in love any more.

So platonic it would be. It was all she could offer him. 'That's what friends are for,' she said. 'Though, be warned, you might think the weight's back again plus a bit more, when I've had you weeding and carting heavy stones about and then muscles you've forgotten you had suddenly start to ache like mad.'

'As you say—that's what friends are for.' He smiled again. 'Thanks for lunch. My shout, next.'

'OK. But I'm afraid I have to dash, now—I have clinic,' she said, glancing at her watch.

'And I have Theatre.'

'Want to walk back to the unit with me?' she asked.

He gave her another of those heart-stopping smiles. 'Yes. I'd like that.'

She smiled back. 'Right then, Mr Townsend. Let's go see our patients.'

CHAPTER THREE

WEREN'T FAIRY GODMOTHERS meant to be little old ladies with baby-fine white hair pulled back into a bun, a double chin and a kind smile, who walked around singing, 'Bibbidi, bobbidi, boo'? Nate wondered.

But the one Fate seemed to have sent him was nothing like that. Erin was six years younger than he was. Although she wore her hair caught back in a ponytail at work, it was the colour of ripe corn and the curls that escaped from her ponytail made him think more of a pre-Raphaelite angel's hair, luxuriant and bright. She definitely didn't have a double chin; and, although her smile was kind, it also made his heart flip.

Which wasn't good.

If he'd met Erin at a different time in his life—before Caitlin had come to live with him, perhaps, or maybe after he and Caitlin had established a workable relationship— then he would've been interested in dating her. Very interested.

But right now, all he could offer her was friendship. And it was a relationship where Nate was horribly aware that he was doing most of the taking.

That evening, he said casually to Caitlin, 'We're going out on Saturday.'

She looked at him. 'Why?'

'I'd like you to meet a friend of mine.'

She rolled her eyes at him. 'I don't need to meet the women you date.'

'She's not a date,' he corrected. 'She's a friend. And I think you'll like her.'

Caitlin's expression suggested that she didn't think she would. At all.

'Have a think about where you might like to go,' he said.

'I already know that. Home,' she said.

The word cut him to the quick—the more so because he knew she hadn't said it to hurt him. She really did want to go back to the place where she grew up, where she knew everyone around her. 'I'm sorry,' he said softly. 'That's not an option. And I know it's hard for you to settle in to a place you don't know, living with someone you don't really know that well, and to leave all your friends behind and start all over again in a new school—but I'm trying my best to make it as easy as I can for you, Caitlin.'

Tears shimmered in her eyes. 'It isn't fair.'

'I know. Sometimes life's like that. The only thing you can do is try to make the best of it.' Awkwardly, he tried to hug her, but she wriggled free.

'I have to do my homework.'

'OK. But if you want me for anything, I'm here. I'm your dad, Caitlin. I know I haven't been there enough for you in the past, and I regret that more than I can ever explain, but I'm here for you now. And you come first.'

She made a noncommittal noise and fled.

Had he started to make some progress? Or was this how it was going to be for ever? he wondered.

He just hoped that his fairy godmother would be able to work the same magic on his daughter as she'd worked on him, and could persuade Caitlin to open up a little. To let him be there for her.

'Erin, it's the Emergency Department for you,' Ella, the receptionist, told her.

'Thanks, Ella.' Erin took the phone. 'Erin Leyton speaking. How can I help?'

'It's Joe Norton from the Emergency Department. I've got a patient who came in for an X-ray—but the department sent her through to us because when they'd finished she couldn't stand up, and she can't feel anything from the middle of her chest downwards. I think it might be a prolapsed disc or a spinal cord problem, but we really need a specialist opinion. Would you be able to come down and see her?'

'Sure. I'm on my way now,' Erin said. She put the phone down, grabbed the pen to write on the whiteboard and smiled at the receptionist. 'I'm stating the obvious here—I'm going down to the Emergency Department.' She wrote her whereabouts next to her name on the whiteboard, and was just about to leave the unit when Nate came round the corner.

'Just the man I wanted to see. Are you up to your eyes, or can I borrow you?' she asked.

'What's the problem?'

'The Emergency Department needs our specialist opinion. Our patient might have a spinal cord problem, which would be me; or she might have a prolapsed disc in her neck, which would be you.'

'I'll come with you,' he said.

'Thanks.' She smiled at him and scribbled 'ED with Erin' next to his name on the board.

Downstairs in the Emergency Department, she found Joe Norton and introduced Nate to him. 'Depending on the problem, it could be either one of us, so we're saving a bit of time,' she said.

'Thank you both for coming,' Joe said, looking relieved, and took them through to the patient. 'This is Mrs Watson,' he said. 'Mrs Watson, this is Dr Leyton and Mr Townsend from the spinal unit.'

Erin noticed that Mrs Watson's face was ashen and she was trembling slightly. Clearly her sudden inability to walk had terrified her and she was fearing the worst.

'Dr Norton called us down as we're specialists in the area where he thinks the problem lies—so please don't be scared, because we're here to help,' Erin said gently. 'Mrs Watson, we know some of your medical history already from Dr Norton, but would you like to tell us in your own words about how you've been feeling?'

'Call me Judy,' Mrs Watson said in a shaky voice.

'Judy. I'm Erin and this is Nate. He's a surgeon and I'm a neurologist,' Erin explained, 'so hopefully between us we can sort everything out for you.'

'I'm so scared,' Judy burst out. 'It must be really serious for them to have called you. Does this mean I'm never going to walk again?'

'Not necessarily, so try not to worry,' Erin said.

'I know that's easier said than done,' Nate added, 'but tell us what's been happening, and that will help us to work out what the problem might be and how we can help you.'

'It started a few months ago,' Judy said. 'I kept waking up with my right hand all numb and tingling. I thought I was just lying on my arm in my sleep, so I didn't want to bother the doctor with it. But then I woke up last week feeling a bit fluey—and after that I started getting real pain in my neck and shoulders. I took painkillers, but they didn't do a lot.'

The symptoms were starting to add up for Erin; she glanced at Nate, who mouthed, 'TM?'

She gave the tiniest nod—she'd been thinking transverse myelitis, too—but said to Judy, 'That must've been worrying for you. Did you go to see your doctor about it?'

'Yes, and he said he thought it might be carpal tunnel or it might be a problem with my neck, so he was going to refer me for an X-ray.' Judy bit her lip. 'That's why I came to the hospital today. I thought I was just going to have an X-ray and then everything would be sorted out—but then, when it was over, I couldn't stand up, and I can't feel anything from here down.' She pointed to the middle of her chest. 'Dr Norton said it might be inflamed nerves in my neck, or it might be a prolapsed disc.'

'That's very possible,' Nate said, 'but we need to carry out some more tests to help us narrow everything down. I want to do an MRI scan of your spine—that's a special kind of X-ray using magnets and radio waves, and it doesn't hurt but you do have to lie as still as you can in a kind of tunnel for a few minutes, and it can be a bit noisy. Depending on what the scan shows us, I'd like Erin here to do a lumbar puncture.'

'That's a lot less scary than it sounds,' Erin said. 'It means I'll ask you to lie on your side and I'll put a needle into the space between two bones at the bottom of your spine and draw off a little bit of fluid from around your spine so I can run some tests on it.'

'Does it hurt?'

'No. I'll numb the area with a local anaesthetic first,' Erin said. 'It takes about half an hour, and you can have someone with you if you like.'

Judy bit her lip again. 'Dr Norton said he'd call my husband.'

'Good. I'll make sure the department's contacted him,' Erin said, 'and if you'd rather we waited until he's here before we do any of the tests, that's absolutely fine.'

'I'd like James to be with me, please.' She dragged in a breath. 'I'm so scared I'm not going to walk ever again.'

'I know it's pretty frightening for you right now,' Erin said, squeezing Judy's hand, 'but until we've done some more tests we can't give you any proper answers about why you can't stand up at the moment or what we can do to treat you. What I think we should do now is take you up to our department and settle you in with a cup of tea, and then we'll wait for your husband to arrive before we do the tests. Is that OK with you?'

Judy nodded.

Erin had a quick word with Joe Norton to explain what they were going to do, and the Emergency Department reception confirmed that James Watson would be there in half an hour and they'd direct him up to the spinal unit.

Once James had arrived and Erin had explained the situation to him, they sent Judy for her scan.

Nate looked at the results on his computer. 'I can't see any signs of a prolapsed disc or any compressive lesions,' he said to Erin.

'I'll need to do a lumbar puncture, then,' she said. 'Obviously I'll get the lab to test for signs of lupus, neurosarcoidosis and Sjögren's as well, but it's looking more and more like TM to me.'

Nate was in Theatre when the results of the lumbar puncture came back. Just as Erin had half expected, Judy's white blood cell counts were elevated, and so was her immunoglobulin G index. So she and Nate had been right from the start. She knew that her patient was waiting anxiously for a diagnosis, and anyway this particular condition was her area rather than Nate's, so she decided not to wait for Nate to come out of Theatre to break the news.

Judy and James looked up anxiously when she walked into the room.

'So do you know what's wrong?' Judy asked.

'Yes. It's something called transverse myelitis,' Erin explained. 'Basically it's a problem caused by inflammation of your spinal cord. It's quite rare so your GP probably hasn't even seen a case before, so I quite understand why he thought it might be a problem with your neck or your carpal tunnel. It's called "transverse" because the swelling's across the width of your spinal cord, and "myelitis" because it's to do with the myelin sheath that covers the nerves in your spine.'

Judy looked stunned. 'How did I get it?'

'Sometimes it's caused by a virus,' Erin said, 'and you did say that you'd felt a bit fluey, so it might've been that. But sometimes there's no reason for it—it just happens.'

'Will she get better?' James asked. 'It's not—well…?'

'The good news is that it's not fatal,' Erin reassured him, guessing what he was worrying about. 'And the even better news is that we can treat the condition. I'll give you a five-day course of steroids, Judy, and that will reduce the inflammation and stop the pain.'

'Steroids? Aren't they the things you hear about sportspeople taking when they cheat?' Judy asked.

'No—those are anabolic steroids, which are a totally different type,' Erin explained. 'The steroids I'll prescribe are the sort that occur naturally in the body and help to beat inflammation—actually, they're the same kind that people take for treating asthma. They'll reduce the pain and swelling, and if they don't help enough we can look at a couple of other treatments as well.'

'How long will it take her to get better?' James asked.

'It does take time and you need to be patient,' Erin warned. 'Usually you start recovering in a couple of months.'

'Months?' Judy looked horrified. 'But we were going on a swimming holiday in Greece in four weeks' time.'

'I'm sorry—you're not going to be well enough for that,' Erin said gently. 'It might be a couple of months before you're back on your feet, and then we find that between three and six months after the episode you'll recover more rapidly. And I do need to warn you that it can take up to a couple of years to make a full recovery.'

'A couple of years?' James blew out a breath, look-ing shocked. 'OK. Could Judy get it again?'

'Usually TM is a one-time thing,' Erin said. 'About a third of patients make a really good recovery, and a third find they have a slight permanent disability.'

'Which means a third don't recover at all?' Judy asked. 'Do you know which one I'll be?'

Erin squeezed her hand. 'I'll be honest with you— right now, it's too early for us to tell how you'll respond to the treatment. But, as I said, we can start with ste-roids, we have some other treatments that we can try and we'll get you some physiotherapy with a specialist in neurological cases. The exercises will help you get back on your feet and improve your condition, and it's important that you keep doing them—but you will find that you get tired a bit more easily than usual, so you'll need to build up to things.'

'I can't get my head round this,' Judy said. 'So if this thing's caused by a virus, does that mean James could get it as well?'

'No. TM isn't infectious and it's not hereditary,' Erin said. 'I can put you in touch with the local support group, so you can talk to other patients who've had the condition. They can help reassure you that this isn't going to be the end of the world.'

'It feels like it,' Judy said. 'Right now, I can't walk. We can't go on holiday next month—and we were going to start trying for a baby after the holiday. We can't do that now, either, can we?'

'It's not ruled out for ever,' Erin said, 'but, yes, you will need to put that on hold for now.'

A tear trickled down Judy's cheek. 'I feel so useless.'

'You're not useless,' James said immediately. 'It's not your fault you're ill.'

'It's nothing that you did wrong,' Erin reassured her. 'But try not to worry. My best friend's mum always used to say, "Never trouble trouble till trouble troubles you." Right now it's very early days and we need to see how you respond to the initial treatment—and, as I said, if the steroids don't help, there are other treatments we can try. Remember, there's more than a sixty per cent chance you'll either make a full or a partial recovery.'

'And what if I don't recover?' Judy asked quietly.

'Then you'll learn to adapt,' Erin said. 'You'd be surprised how quickly people adapt to a new situation.'

'I guess you see a lot of that, here,' James said. 'With people who've broken their back and what have you.'

'We do,' Erin confirmed. 'I'm not saying it's going to be easy, and a lot of people on this unit do suffer from depression as well as from the physical problem that brought them here in the first place, but we're here to help you as much as we can. We can give you lots of support and help.' She smiled at them. 'And you have each other.'

'But this isn't what you signed up for,' Judy said to James.

'Yes, it is. "In sickness and in health",' he corrected. 'You're still the woman I fell in love with and married. And we're going to get through this, Jude. Together.'

'I'll leave you to talk,' Erin said. 'But if you have any questions, please come and find me. That's what I'm here for, OK?'

Judy nodded, clearly too upset to speak, and Erin left the room.

She sat in the office, writing up her notes, but it was so hard to concentrate. Judy was clearly worried that she wouldn't recover and then her husband would leave her. And, although James had reassured her, the whole thing had brought back a lot of painful memories for Erin. The early days after Mikey's accident, when his girlfriend had walked out, leaving him devastated...

At the rap on the door, she looked up. Nate was leaning against the door jamb. 'Are you OK?' he asked.

'Sure,' she fibbed.

He raised his eyebrows. 'I need a word. Can I borrow you for a bit?'

'OK.'

'Let's go to the canteen.'

She frowned, but closed her file and followed him. He bought them both a coffee and cake, and found them a quiet table.

'What's the cake for?' she asked.

'You look as if you need to talk—and someone very wise once told me that cake makes everything better.'

She smiled at him, recognising her own words. 'Thanks. I probably just need cake.'

'So what's sauce for the gander isn't sauce for the goose, then?'

He had a point, she supposed. But the words stuck in her throat.

'For the record, I don't gossip, either,' he said gently.

She gave him a wry smile. 'I'd pretty much worked that one out for myself.'

'So what's upsetting you?'

She took the easy way out. 'Judy Watson.'

'The lumbar puncture showed more than inflammatory markers?' he asked.

She shook her head. 'No, it's definitely TM. I talked her through the prognosis, but she's not adjusting very well to the idea of not being able to walk, even for a few weeks. She thinks her husband's going to leave her.'

'People adjust to their situations—and sometimes they surprise themselves by how well they cope,' he said.

She had a feeling that he was talking about his own situation, too. 'I'm going to put her in touch with a support group. But this is the really hard bit, coming to terms with what's happened and what it might mean for the future—and for her relationship.'

'This sounds personal, not just about a patient,' he said softly. 'Am I right in guessing that you've been here before?'

'Not with TM.' Maybe she could tell Nate some of the truth. 'My older brother, Mikey, has a T5 injury from a car accident.' She knew Nate would know exactly what that meant: that her brother's trunk and legs had been affected by the injury and, although his arm and hand functions were normal, he needed to use a wheelchair and special equipment.

'Is he the one who you said was helped by a sensory garden?'

She nodded. 'And, yes, before you ask, this is exactly why I work in a spinal unit now. I want to make a difference to other people, the way Mikey's team made a difference to him.'

'When did it happen?'

She couldn't quite bring herself to tell him that. Nate

was bright enough to work it out for himself. If she told him it had happened nearly fourteen years ago, he'd make the connection. And if he worked out that that accident was all her fault, he wouldn't let her help him with his daughter. She wouldn't get the chance to make something right.

'Mikey was twenty,' she said instead. 'He was in the second year of his degree in politics. He lost an awful lot of things that mattered to him—being on the university rowing team, his girlfriend, his planned career.' And she knew she'd never stop feeling guilty about how much she'd taken away from her brother.

'Did he finish his degree?'

'Yes, though he changed career—he's a journalist now. Mainly politics. Unsurprisingly, he's usually the one on the magazine who covers the disability stories.' And she'd been the one to nag him into it. If she could turn her life round and ace her exams, then so could he. She'd visited him every single day—when her mother wasn't there, by mutual agreement—and nagged him until he gave in and agreed to go back to finish his degree.

'So where does the garden fit in?'

'I'd been doing research into spinal injuries and treatments, and I came across something about gardens. One of the rehab places had a project involving a garden, and patients were encouraged to help grow things. According to the early research findings, it made a real difference to the patients' mental attitudes. I talked to Mikey's rehab place to see if they could get him involved with the project or maybe become part of it themselves, and they thought it was a good idea. They arranged for him to go and stay at the other rehab place for a few weeks. I didn't get to see him while he was there, because he was too far away to visit, but we talked on the phone every day and we had email. And I could hear the difference in him, every time we talked. Working on the garden gave him hope that he could still do things and his life wasn't over. It made him think about what he *could* do instead of what he couldn't.'

'Now I get why the sensory garden is so important to you,' he said.

'Yes, though you're right, too, about checking costs—because if it's a pet project, you really want it to work and that's more important to you than how much it costs,' she said. 'Which means you're not always getting the best value for money.'

'Well, hey. Get this. We're almost agreeing about something,' he said with a smile.

'It's the sugar talking,' she retorted.

'Cake makes everything better. You're right.' He eyed the crumbs. 'I might try that on Caitlin.'

'Or get her to help make it. She might be into baking.' She paused. 'Did you talk to her about the weekend?'

'Yes.' He winced. 'Let's just say she wasn't very forthcoming.'

'We can play it by ear. I'll have a think about some different places we could go to, and maybe text you a few ideas to run by her?' she suggested.

'That sounds great. Thank you. I'll do the same and run them by you before I try them out on her.'

'OK.' She paused. 'Thanks for making me come here and eat cake, Nate. I try to keep my personal life separate from work, but sometimes a case brings back the early days with Mikey and it gets to me,' she admitted. 'Judy's worried about her husband leaving her if she can't walk—and that's exactly what happened to Mikey. His girlfriend said she couldn't cope with his disability and she left him.'

Nate winced. 'I'm assuming his girlfriend was around the same age that he was when the accident happened—she was in her second year of uni?'

'Yes.'

'Then she still had a lot of growing up to do.' He paused. 'James Watson seemed pretty supportive when I saw them together. I think Judy's worrying over nothing.'

'Me, too, and I've told her that,' she said. 'But thanks. You've made me feel a bit better.'

'Any time. You've made me feel better, too.'

For a moment, their gazes met; again, Erin felt that funny little flip in the region of her heart. But nothing was going to happen. Nate had too much going on in his life to offer her anything more than friendship. Even if his circumstances had been different, she had too much baggage for a relationship to work between them.

If only she'd made some different choices, all those years ago. If only she hadn't gone to that party with Andrew. If only she'd left when he started pushing her. If only she hadn't called Mikey to come and get her and had called her best friend's mum instead…

But you couldn't change the past. You could only learn from it.

'I'd better finish writing up my notes,' she said. She scribbled her mobile phone number down on a scrap of paper and handed it to him. 'Text me later and I'll send you some ideas.' And maybe thinking up things to do to help Nate bond with Caitlin would help her to smother her guilt again.

'We could go on the London Eye on Saturday,' Nate suggested. 'Or the cable car over the Thames.'

Caitlin remained impassive. Obviously neither of those suggestions appealed to her.

'Or shopping. Apparently there are good shops on Oxford Street.' He named the clothing stores Erin had mentioned as being popular with teenage girls.

'I used to go shopping with my friends,' she said.

Meaning that she didn't want to go shopping with him? OK. He could see that it wouldn't be cool, hanging round clothes shops with your dad. 'How about a speedboat ride on the Thames?'

Her expression clearly said, *Really?*, with only the scorn a teen could muster.

'I'm very happy to hear your ideas,' he said.

She shrugged. 'Whatever.'

He knew she was hurting, so he wasn't going to make it worse for her by yelling at her. He wanted to get closer to her, not push her away. But how?

She hates all the ideas I suggested, he texted to Erin later.

OK. How about this? It's an escape game. You're locked in a room and you have sixty minutes to get free—you have to work as a team to solve the clues and puzzles. There's a countdown clock.

She sent him a link to the company's website. The more Nate read, the more he liked the sound of it.

That looks like fun, he texted back. But you have to book in advance. I just checked and they're not free on Saturday. Can we do that another time?

Or was he presuming too much, hoping that Erin would spend more time with them?

Definitely do it some other time, was her immediate response. Then his phone pinged with another text.

What about food? We could do Camden Lock—the street market there has something for everyone and we could see who can find the most unusual food stall. Or go and spot movie locations, if you find out what her favourite movies are. Or we could go to Abbey Road and do THAT pose on the crossing.

All things he'd love to do. Georgina had only really liked posh restaurants and parties where he'd been just a tiny bit bored. And she definitely hadn't had the patience to deal with a troubled teen.

But Erin was his friend, he reminded himself. Even though he'd like her to be more than that, it wasn't going to happen. He needed to sort his life out, first, and he really didn't have the right to ask her to wait for him.

I'll check with her, he texted back. Maybe we could go and see a movie. Or a show.

Or Madame Tussauds™, she suggested. Depending on what sort of music and movies she likes. She could take great selfies with the waxworks to send to her friends at home.

Clearly she realised her gaffe as soon as she'd sent the text, because a second one swiftly followed.

I didn't mean it like *that*. I meant to her friends. Her home's with you.

I knew what you meant, he texted back.

The problem was, what she'd written was true. Caitlin didn't think of London as her home. And he didn't know if she ever would. Talk to you later. And thanks.

CHAPTER FOUR

AFTER SEVERAL MORE false starts, Nate and Erin decided to take Caitlin trampolining on Saturday morning. 'Even if she's not in a good mood to start with,' Erin said, 'bouncing about will get her endorphins going. And it's not just jumping on a trampoline. There's an obstacle course and an airbag, and you can play dodgeball—so she can enjoy chucking a ball at you. In fact, she can have a competition with me about who can score the most hits on you.'

'You're a big kid at heart, aren't you?' Nate accused with a grin.

'Oh, yeah.' She grinned back at him. 'And if the trampoline place is as good as I think it's going to be, I'm so organising a departmental night out there.'

'Sounds good. We'll meet you at the Tube™ station tomorrow at ten,' he said. 'What do you have to wear?'

'Anything you can bounce in, so jeans would be a good bet,' she said. 'No jewellery, and you have to wear special jumping socks for safety reasons.'

He grimaced. 'That might be a sticking point.'

'Nope. No socks, no chucking a dodgeball at you.

That's the rules,' she said with a wink. 'Trust me on this. She'll do it.'

But when Saturday dawned bright and sunny, Erin was filled with doubts.

Was she doing the right thing?

OK, so this wasn't a *date* date. This was helping out a friend.

But would it help Nate to bond with his daughter, or would she be making things worse?

There was only one way to find out. And please, please, let this work out, she begged silently.

She changed into jeans, a neutral T-shirt and flat shoes, tied her hair back in its usual ponytail, and decided not to bother with make-up. By the time they'd bounced round on the trampolines for an hour, she'd be red-faced and glowing; besides, this wasn't the same as if she was dressing to impress a boyfriend. She didn't need to impress Nate. She knew he wasn't interested in a relationship. Even if he was, she was the last person he needed in his life.

Nate and Caitlin were already waiting at the Tube™ station when Erin arrived. It was the first time she'd seen him dressed casually—at the hospital he was always in a suit or scrubs—and her heart skipped a beat. Right now he looked younger. More approachable. *Touchable.*

Oh, for pity's sake. How inappropriate was that? Today was friends only, not a date, she reminded herself sharply.

Like her father, Caitlin was tall and had dark hair, but her eyes were deep brown rather than blue and she had a slightly olive complexion, which Erin guessed she'd inherited from her mother.

'Caitlin, this is my colleague Dr Leyton. Erin, this is my daughter, Caitlin,' Nate introduced them formally.

Erin held out her hand. 'Good to meet you. Call me Erin,' she invited.

Caitlin said nothing and didn't take her hand. But Erin wasn't in the least put out by the teenager's lack of manners; she could remember only too well feeling awkward, out of place and totally miserable, at that age. Right now she thought Caitlin needed someone to cut her some slack.

'Thanks for agreeing to come trampolining with me,' she said with a smile. 'I've wanted to try this new place for the last two months, ever since it opened, but all my friends say I'm insane and refuse to go with me.'

'I didn't agree. He made me come,' Caitlin said, jerking her head to indicate her father.

'And you think it sounds like hell on earth?' Erin spread her hands. 'Well, I can't guarantee that you'll like the music they play, and I might not either, but I can guarantee that you'll feel good after you've been on the trampolines for a few minutes.' She smiled. 'I could give you a really long lecture about why endorphins are the best thing ever when you're having a bad day, but I'll be kind and spare you the science. Let's just say that I'm looking forward to the dodgeball section, and I was going to challenge you to a competition to see who can score the most hits on your dad.'

'Hmm,' Caitlin said. 'So did you ask me along just so you could get close to him?'

Nate looked horrified. Just as he opened his mouth,

clearly planning to tell his daughter off, Erin forestalled him. The last thing he and Caitlin needed right now was a fight.

'Are you asking me if I fancy your dad?' she said, looking Caitlin straight in the eye.

The teenager had the grace to blush. 'I suppose so.'

'Nuh-uh,' Erin said, shaking her head. That wasn't strictly true, but Nate wasn't in a position to start any kind of relationship and even if he was then Erin was the last person he should get involved with. Her relationships never lasted, and with his daughter living with him for the first time in years he needed something stable, not something that was bound to go wrong. 'Walk with me, Caitlin, because I need to explain something to you. Nate, you're not allowed to listen, so you have to walk at least ten paces behind,' she said.

'Why?' he asked, still looking horrified.

'Because this is girl stuff. But if you really want to talk about period pains and things like that...' She waited for him to blush. 'Then be our guest,' she finished, waggling her eyebrows at him.

'Got you. I'll walk ten paces behind,' Nate said swiftly.

'Good boy,' Erin said with a grin, and patted his shoulder before shepherding Caitlin through the barriers to the escalator leading to the platform. 'Now, there are some people in the hospital,' she told Caitlin, 'who call your dad Mr McSexypants.'

'They call him *what*?' Caitlin looked horrified; but to Erin's relief she also caught a glimpse of amusement in the younger girl's eyes.

'Mr McSexypants,' Erin repeated. 'And yes, I know he's not Scots. Don't make me explain that bit.'

'All right, but why Mr? I thought he was a doctor?'

'He is. But he's a surgeon—and when you're a surgeon you can go back to being called Mr or Ms,' Erin explained. 'So. Now you know. A lot of our colleagues fancy your dad and they think he's one of the most gorgeous men in the hospital. But I don't call him Mr McSexypants.'

'What do you call him?' Caitlin asked, looking interested.

Erin laughed. 'I don't think I should tell you. Not yet. But he's not my type.' Again, that wasn't strictly true, but she was working on a need-to-know basis. Neither Caitlin nor Nate needed to know anything about her feelings right now. 'Now, if you made him blond with longer hair, gorgeous biceps and superhero powers, then we'd be talking.'

'Oh, you mean like…' Caitlin named one of the actors in a popular sci-fi movie series. 'He's nice,' she added, almost shyly.

'Isn't he just?' Erin named a couple more from the same movies. 'Actually, any of them would do nicely. I think some of them might have a waxwork in Madame Tussauds™, if you want to go and have a look some time.'

'Maybe.' Caitlin frowned. 'So if you don't fancy him, why do you want to go out with us?'

'Obviously your dad hasn't told you what I told him in confidence,' Erin said gently, hoping that the girl would pick up that it meant she could trust her father, 'so I'll tell you myself. The reason why is because I've been exactly where you are. I was a couple of years older than you when it happened, but my parents split up and then my mum got involved with a real creep. Things got a bit messy, and she sent me to live with my dad—and then I had to start all over at a new school.'

'Just like me.' Caitlin looked at her. 'So you're here because you feel sorry for me, then?'

'No. It's empathy, not pity. I know how it feels to move home and school when you're a teenager. It's hard to fit in and make friends. You feel lonely—like an alien who doesn't belong. And you feel that everyone you left behind is going to forget you so you won't fit in at home any more, either.'

'Yeah,' Caitlin said feelingly.

'They won't forget you,' Erin said. 'It might feel like it right now, but I promise you I've been there and they won't. You just have to learn to juggle a bit. And I was lucky because, although I wasn't getting on very well with either of my parents at the time, I could talk to my best friend's mum, Rachel. I'm guessing that right now that might not be an option for you.'

'It's not,' Caitlin admitted.

'I'm seeing this as my chance to pay forward what Rachel did for me and stop someone else feeling as lonely and miserable as I did when I was fifteen,' Erin said. 'If you want a friend, someone who's going to listen and let you moan to them when things get you down, but who won't let you wallow in misery—then hello, my name's Erin, I work with your dad and I'm very pleased to meet you.'

'And that's it? You're just being kind to me because

someone was kind to you?' Caitlin looked as if she was having difficulty getting her head round the concept.

'That's it,' Erin said. 'But if you'd rather do something for me in return so you don't feel that you owe me anything, then you can always nag your dad about what a great idea the sensory garden is.'

'Sensory garden? Like a little garden where you have plants that rustle and smell and are all different colours?' Caitlin asked, suddenly looking interested.

'And textures and tastes,' Erin added.

'We had one of those at my junior school. We used to have story-time out there in summer and watch all the butterflies. It was brilliant.'

Erin gave the girl a high five. 'Oh, yes. That's *exactly* what I'm talking about.'

'But why do you need a sensory garden?' she asked. 'Aren't you a surgeon?'

'No. I'm a neurologist,' Erin said. 'I work in the spinal unit. Your dad does the surgery side of things and I do the other side, looking at the way our patients' nervous systems work.'

'But don't all your patients come in because they've had an accident and broken their neck or their spine and it needs fixing?'

'Nope. There are lots of other spinal conditions not caused by accidents—some are just caused by people getting older, and some are caused by viruses. Sometimes we can help patients go back to a normal life without any pain. Sometimes we can't get rid of all the pain or they might end up in a wheelchair because the damage is a little bit too much for us to fix, but then we can help them to adjust to a new life.' Erin smiled. 'That's where my sensory garden comes in.'

'So it's your garden?'

'Strictly speaking, it's a community garden that belongs to the hospital, but it's my pet project and that's where a lot of my spare time is going at the moment,' Erin explained. 'I know it makes a real difference to my patients, being able to be outside in a garden after they've been stuck inside in a bed for months.' She glanced over Caitlin's head at Nate and mouthed, 'Catch us up—you need to hear this.'

'Did you have much to do with your sensory garden at junior school?' she asked Caitlin.

'We had a gardening club and we were allowed to do little bits. We had a tree nursery,' Caitlin said, 'where we planted acorns. When the trees were three years old someone would come and take them to a local woodland to be planted.'

Nate said, 'I didn't know you liked gardens.'

Caitlin rolled her eyes at him. 'You never asked. Anyway, you're never home and you never talk to me.'

Erin said, 'Hey, truce. When communications break down, there are always faults on both sides. Right now we're agreeing to disagree, OK?'

'OK,' Caitlin muttered.

'OK,' Nate echoed.

'Good. Caitlin, would I be right in thinking you like plant biology?' Erin asked.

The teenager looked at her father and scowled, and then nodded at Erin. 'If my new school actually *lets* me do biology.'

'I'll make sure they do,' Nate said.

Caitlin looked as if she didn't quite believe that he'd fight her corner for her, but to Erin's relief this time she didn't argue.

'You know what—it's really nice and sunny today, and it'd be a shame to spend a morning like this stuck indoors,' Erin said. 'We could give the trampolining a miss and go and look round Kew Gardens instead, if you like.'

'But you said you wanted to go trampolining,' Caitlin said, looking surprised.

Clearly she wasn't used to her views being taken into account, poor kid. Erin shrugged. 'We can do trampolining another time—maybe when it's raining. I haven't been to Kew for ages. If you haven't been there before, I think you might enjoy the greenhouses. There's one with about ten different climates—it's amazing.'

'I like the biodomes at the Eden Project,' Caitlin said. 'I've been there on a couple of school trips—we live not far away, in Devon. *Lived*,' she corrected herself, looking miserable.

'London's really not so bad, and there are some amazing gardens in the city,' Erin said. 'In fact, there's a garden right next to the Thames where they have banana trees growing in the middle of a bed of sunflowers. We could go and look at them some time, too. And the Sky Garden. I haven't been there, yet, and it'll be nice to have someone to go with.'

'What's the Sky Garden?'

'How good's your phone?' Erin asked.

Caitlin just sighed.

'That bad? OK.' Erin took hers from her pocket and handed it over. 'Look it up on this. Your job today—

apart from eating cake with me, talking plants and making your dad see that sensory gardens are totally awesome—is to make a list of gardens in London that you want to go and see. Then we'll work through your list together over the next few weeks.'

Caitlin's eyes grew round as she looked at Erin's phone. 'But this is the latest...'

'I know. I'm a total tech junkie,' Erin admitted with a grin. 'They give me a hard time about it at work because I always get the newest version on the very first day it comes out. I have been known to queue up outside the shop at stupid o'clock to make sure I get one.'

'But if I drop it...' Caitlin looked worried.

'Then, yes, the screen would probably crack and I'd have to get it fixed, which would be a pain. But I'm trusting you not to drop it. You're thirteen, not a baby,' Erin said briskly. 'OK. We're going to Kew instead of trampolining, so we're taking a different route from our original one. You're looking for the District Line, which is the green one. Go and have a look at the map on the wall and tell me which station we need to change at to get there.'

'OK.' Caitlin carefully put Erin's phone in her pocket to keep it safe, and went over to look at the map of the Tube™ lines on the wall.

'Oh, my God. She's talking to you like I've never heard her talk to my mum or to me—even in the days when she was little and seemed to like being with me. How did you *do* that?' Nate asked, looking impressed.

'I was straight with her,' Erin said. 'I told her I'd been in the same place as her, so we've got something in common. And I just hit lucky with the garden thing.' She wrinkled her nose. 'Sorry. That's going to be a bit difficult for you. I promise I didn't do it to score points off you—it was just the first thing that came into my head.'

'I know you're not scoring points, and it's fine. More than fine.' Nate looked relieved. 'You've just given me something I can do for her. She can have her own patch in my back garden—and my mum loves gardening, so it gives her something in common with my mum as well. You're amazing, Erin.'

She lifted both hands in a 'stop' signal. 'I'm not amazing. I'm just me. And it's very early days. It's not all going to be plain sailing and you're still going to have fights. But this is a good start and you can build on that—because now you both know you're on the same team, right?'

'Yeah.' Nate swallowed. 'You have no idea how good this feels.'

'It's good for me, too, knowing that I can stop someone feeling as bad as I did at that age,' she said. 'So you don't owe me anything, OK? This is a situation where everybody wins.'

Caitlin came back and recited directions about where they had to go and where they had to change lines.

'Great. You're in charge of getting us there,' Erin said.

'But—' Caitlin looked shocked.

'The best way to learn your way about on the Tube™,' Erin said, 'is to just do it. If you miss your stop, don't worry—all you do is get off at the next station, cross to the other platform and go back the other way. There's only one rule.'

'Rule?' Caitlin looked wary.

'I don't have many rules,' Erin said, 'but they're not negotiable and they're not breakable. If you get on the train and you end up separated from me or your dad, then you get off the train at the very next station and you stay right there on the platform where you get off. Then we can find you easily. Same as if I get on first and I'm separated from you, then you stay where you are on the platform and you get on the next train in exactly that place—then when you get off at the next stop you'll see me as soon as you get out of the doors. Got it?'

'Got it,' Caitlin said.

'Good.'

On the Tube™, Caitlin looked up the Sky Garden and started making a list of other gardens. Then she handed Erin's phone back to her. 'Thanks.' She gave Erin a shy smile.

'No worries. I'll text the list to your dad later, and you as well. Put your number in my phone, then I can text you and you'll have my number.' Erin handed the phone back.

'OK.' Caitlin tapped in her number. 'You're not like I thought you'd be.'

'What, a boring old doctor?' Erin teased.

Caitlin shook her head. 'Not that, but...' She spread her hands. 'You're cool.'

Erin laughed and gave her a high five. 'Thank you. So are you.'

Nate paid for their tickets at Kew, refusing to let Erin go halves, and they wandered round until they found the conservatory with the ten different climates.

In the wet tropic zone, Caitlin went all chatty and

told them about a school project she'd done in Geography on rainforests and mangrove swamps. And Nate was stunned to realise that his daughter said more to him in the last quarter of an hour than she had in the whole of the previous week.

Finally, Caitlin was connecting with him again. Better still, she shared his love of science—even if her preference was for plant biology rather than human biology. He'd had no idea because he'd never really talked to her about his work, and he knew he had Erin to thank for this. He caught her eye; she smiled at him and gave him a wink, as if to tell him to relax and say that everything was going to be just fine.

It gave him an odd feeling in the pit of his stomach; but he knew she was doing this for his daughter's sake, not for his. He needed to keep that in mind and not let himself get carried away. The attraction he felt towards her was totally inappropriate.

Caitlin was fascinated by the carnivorous plants. 'Are you using anything like that in your sensory garden, Erin?'

'No, because it's all outdoors at the moment and these kinds of plants wouldn't survive the winter outside,' Erin explained.

'They'd be interesting to look at, though, if you did an inside garden.'

'Could Caitlin be involved with the sensory garden?' Nate asked.

'Sure,' Erin said. 'I can take you to meet the garden designer, if you want, Caitlin. His name is Ed, and he's a really nice guy. He's designed a couple of gardens for the Chelsea Flower Show before now.'

'Is that why you chose him to design your garden?' Caitlin asked.

'Not just because he's a good designer. It's a charity thing so we have to think about costs as well. Ed offered to do the design for nothing, because his brother had a motorcycle accident and broke his back, and he spent a while in our unit before he got a place in rehab,' Erin explained.

Caitlin looked confused. 'Rehab, because he was on drugs?'

'Rehab, as in teaching him how to adjust to life in a wheelchair and helping him with his physiotherapy,' Nate said.

Caitlin looked at him. 'Did you fix his back?'

'That particular accident happened quite a while before I went to work at the London Victoria,' Nate said, 'but if it happened now then, yes, I would probably be the surgeon.'

'So that's what you do all day, fix broken backs?'

'And necks—though not all of them are fractures. Some are where I take off a bit of bone in the spine to take the pressure off the nerves and stop my patients being in pain.' Nate could hardly believe that Caitlin actually seemed interested in his job. If anyone had suggested that to him even a few days ago, he would've scoffed. But now... Now, it felt as if Erin really was a fairy godmother and was fixing his life.

They enjoyed looking round the waterlily garden, and Erin looked something up on her phone. 'Did you know that the leaves of the giant waterlily span two metres across, and they can take the weight of a baby without sinking?'

'They're amazing,' Caitlin said. 'I'd like to sk—'
Then she stopped abruptly.

'You'd like to do what?' Erin asked.

Caitlin shook her head. 'It doesn't matter.'

'Were you going to say "sketch"?' Erin asked.

Caitlin shrugged. 'Mum says art's a waste of time.'

'I don't want to fight with your mum,' Nate said, 'but I often have to draw things to explain to my patients what I'm going to do. Without the drawing, it'd take a lot longer to explain and they might still be worried.'

'So you don't think art's a waste of time?'

'No, and if you're thinking about a career in plant biology you'll probably need to be able to draw for your exams,' he pointed out. Why had he never guessed that she liked art?

'So are you good at drawing?' Caitlin asked.

'I can show you some of my student notes later, if you like,' Nate suggested. 'Then you can tell me whether I'm any good. And if you like looking at art, there are loads of good galleries in London. Maybe we could go some time together.'

'All right,' she said, and Nate felt as if the sun had just come out after a long, lonely winter.

They stopped for a toasted cheese sandwich and a milkshake in the café for lunch.

Nate teased Erin. 'I just know you're going to choose cake and claim it's one of your five a day.'

'Of course it is. Blueberry muffins count as fruit,' Erin retorted. 'Right, Caitlin?'

Caitlin looked bemused. 'But you're a doctor. You're supposed to tell people they're not allowed to eat cake and stuff because it'll make them fat and rot their teeth.'

'Cake,' Erin said, 'is absolutely fine in moderation. And in my professional opinion it makes a lot of things better.'

'Trust her. She's a doctor,' Nate said in a conspiratorial stage whisper.

And Caitlin's grin made his heart feel as if it had just cracked. He thoroughly enjoyed watching his daughter blossom. He knew there was still a long way to go, but for the last month he'd failed badly at being a full-time dad, and now finally she was responding to him; they could build on this. For the first time, he really felt as if there was hope for him as a parent.

After lunch, they wandered round the gardens to find some of the oldest and biggest trees.

By the hawthorn, Nate said, 'Did you know years ago they used to think it was unlucky to take hawthorn indoors because it meant someone in the household would die?'

'But that's not true, is it?' Caitlin asked.

'No—but there is some science behind it. Did you know that the same chemicals in the scent of hawthorn are also present in decaying corpses?'

'Oh, that's so gross!' But she didn't look appalled; she was actually laughing. Laughing *with* him. Just the way she had as a young child when he'd told her terrible jokes and pushed her on the swings.

This was going to be all right, he thought.

He noticed that Erin was really relaxed with Caitlin, too, in a way that Georgina never had been. And Erin seemed to be blossoming as much as his daughter in the garden environment. Her grey eyes were almost luminous. Beautiful.

He caught his thoughts and gave himself a mental kick. Yes, he was really attracted to her, but he couldn't act on that attraction. If it went wrong between them, he'd be letting his daughter down again and it would make things awkward between him and Erin at work. He'd already discovered that he liked working with her; he liked her kindness with their patients, the way she was always good-humoured and always seemed to bring out the best in people. Just as she was bringing out the best in his daughter right now.

How could he possibly risk losing that?

And even though an insidious little voice in his head suggested that maybe dating Erin would make his life even better, he squashed it ruthlessly. He couldn't take the risk. So he kept things light and chatty, coming up with outrageous facts that made both Erin and his daughter laugh.

At the end of the day, Caitlin actually let Erin hug her goodbye.

'We'll sort out our garden list,' Erin said, 'and maybe we can do some other stuff together as well.'

'The trampoline thing?' Caitlin asked.

Erin nodded. 'And there's a place where they put you in a locked room and you have an hour to escape. You have to work as a team to sort the clues. It's kind of like a console game, but better. I'm dying to try it out. What do you think?'

'That,' Caitlin said, 'sounds like a lot of fun.' She looked at Nate, as if checking that he wasn't going to scoff at the idea.

'I agree,' he said with a smile. 'We'll have to think up a good team name for us.'

'That's settled, then. We'll add it to the list,' Erin said. 'Oh, and we have to go for a proper afternoon tea.'

'Because cake makes everything better,' Caitlin chorused.

Erin laughed. 'Indeed it does. You're a fast learner. See you soon, Caitlin. I'll see you at work, Nate.'

'Yeah, see you—and thanks for today.' So what did he do now? Shaking hands would seem too formal. He wasn't really the kind of person to give her a high five. Should he hug her? Or would that be too forward?

Right at that point, he thought his social skills were quiet a few rungs lower than his teenage daughter's were.

As if Erin guessed at his awkwardness—or, more likely, it stood out like a beacon—she stepped forward and gave him a hug. 'We can't leave you out of the hugs,' she said. 'You can be an honorary girl today. Right, Caitlin?'

The feel of Erin in his arms made him tingle all over. But her teasing comment was just enough to keep him on the right side of self-control.

'Hmm. My dad as a girl. With very short hair,' Caitlin said.

'And guyliner,' Erin suggested.

'Guyliner?' he asked, totally lost.

Caitlin collapsed into giggles.

'Eyeliner. For men,' Erin explained, her eyes full of mischief. 'Blue would look great with your eyes.'

'I am not wearing eyeliner,' Nate said. 'Blue or any other colour.'

And he wasn't sure whether he was more worried or amused by the conspiratorial look they shared. Or distracted by the fact that Caitlin had actually acknowledged him as her dad.

They'd come what felt like a million miles, today. And it made him feel on top of the world.

Hugging Nate goodbye had seemed like the right thing to do at the time, Erin thought on the way home, but it had left her antsy. She'd been so aware of the warmth of his body and his clean masculine scent.

Worse still, she was really attracted to the man Nate was outside work. The one who could admit his vulnerabilities and shortcomings, but who tried so hard to make it right rather than making everyone else fit round him. It was frighteningly easy to imagine herself with him.

But they were doing this for Caitlin's sake. She couldn't afford to start anything with Nate. If it went wrong—*when*, she amended, because she hadn't made a relationship really work since Andrew—there would be way too much collateral damage. She'd simply have to keep reminding herself that they were friends. Just friends. And she couldn't offer him anything more.

CHAPTER FIVE

On Monday, Nate caught Erin in the staff room at lunch-time. 'Do you have time for a quick update?'

'Over a sandwich in the canteen? Sure.' She smiled at him.

'So how's Judy Watson doing?' he asked when they were settled in the canteen.

'She's starting to feel a bit better, though she's not on her feet yet. I've arranged physio, and spoken to some people from the support group—they're coming to see her this week,' Erin said. 'And James is still reassuring her that they won't split up over her illness.'

'That's good to know.'

'So how's Kevin Bishop doing? Did the spinal spacer work in the way you hoped?'

'Yes—he's walking again, out of pain and full of smiles. Though I've warned him that playing football with his kids has to wait until the physio gives him the go-ahead.'

'You can't blame the poor guy for being impatient, though,' Erin said. 'He's been in pain for so long—and now he can actually move again, of course he'll want to run before he can walk. Anyone would.'

'I guess.' He paused. 'Things are quite a bit better with Caitlin, thanks to you. She showed me her sketch-pad yesterday. And it turns out that she really likes my mum's cat, Sooty. It never occurred to me she'd like animals—Steph always refused to have a pet because they caused too much mess, and I guess when Caitlin stayed with me in London we tended to stay at my place, so my mum visited us and Cait never saw the cat. She's drawn a few pictures of the cat—and they're good.' He smiled. 'And I had a word with her school, this morning. She won't be choosing her exam courses until next year, but apparently there's a gardening club and the head of the science department is going to have a chat with her today.'

'That's great,' Erin said, meaning it.

'It's still early days,' he said, 'but I actually feel there's a light at the end of the tunnel and we've got a chance of making it work.' He looked her straight in the eye. 'And it's all thanks to you.'

'Hardly. You're the one actually *making* it work. I'm just helping to facilitate things,' Erin protested.

'If you hadn't hit on gardens as her favourite thing, I don't know if she would ever have started to open up to me,' Nate pointed out. 'I was really sinking, Erin.'

'It was a lucky break, and you might've got there on your own.'

'Seriously. You've made a real difference,' he said quietly, 'and I appreciate it.'

'Any time. She's a nice kid.' Much nicer than Erin herself had been. 'I had a word with Ed, the garden designer. He's here on Thursday. If Caitlin wants to drop in after school, he can talk her through what we're doing here.'

'I'll check with her.' He gave her a wry smile. 'Considering that you and I fell out over that same garden, it's pretty ironic that it's made such a big change to my life.'

'Hey. You've come round to my way of thinking because you know now that I'm right,' she teased. 'Actually, Caitlin's texted me a couple of times. Obviously I'm not going to betray any of her confidences and I'm certainly not going to discuss her with you, but she seems to be settling in a bit more.'

'I wish I'd been a better dad to her in the past instead of focusing on my work. If I could do things differently, I would,' he said, his face sombre. 'I wish I could go back and change things.'

So would I, she thought. *So would I.* 'You can't change the past, Nate,' she said instead. 'You can only learn from it. And you did what you thought was best at the time.'

'I guess.' He lifted his mug to her in a toast. 'To you. Because you've made a massive difference, whether you admit it or not.'

'And to you. Because you're the one making the effort.'

Early on Tuesday afternoon, Nate was called down to the Emergency Department to see a patient who'd crashed while driving without wearing a seatbelt, and had been thrown seventy metres from his car.

'I can't believe the guy could even move his arms and legs after a crash like that,' Doug, the lead paramedic, told Nate. 'He didn't show any signs of serious spinal injury, but given what had happened to him we were very careful when we moved him and we put him on a long spinal board.'

'Good call,' Nate said.

'I sent him for an X-ray and it's unbelievable,' Joe Norton said. 'He's got a broken shoulder and ribs, and punctured a lung. But just look at this. I've never seen anything like this before.'

Nate stared at the picture on the computer, stunned. 'I don't think I've ever seen a fracture dislocation as severe as this. Usually a patient who presents like this is paralysed. And you're telling me that this guy can actually move his arms and legs, Doug?'

'Yes. We've assessed him and he can move all his different muscle groups. His sensation is all intact, too. We're all wondering if he's a secret superhero,' Doug said with a grin. 'I've never seen anything like this in twenty years as a paramedic.'

'He'd better hope that I'm in superhero mode in Theatre,' Nate said. 'I can fix the fracture and realign his spine, but the operation's really high risk and there's a chance that it could cause further neurological injury. If any damage occurs to his spinal nerves during the operation, we're looking at paralysis.' And the patient would definitely be a candidate for Erin's garden. 'Is he up to talking?'

'Yes.' Joe took him over to Barney Mason and introduced him swiftly. 'Barney, this is Nate Townsend, our spinal surgeon consultant. He's the guy who's going to fix your back.'

'You can really fix me? So I'm going to be able to walk again?' Barney asked.

'Right now, we're all amazed you've got any movement at all,' Nate said, showing Barney the X-ray. 'You've fractured your spine and it's dislocated as well, so it's a bit on the complicated side.'

'Can you fix it?'

Nate nodded. 'I'm going to send you for some MRI scans—that just gives me a little bit more detail than the X-rays do—and then we'll take you up to Theatre. But I do need to warn you that your spine is in a serious condition right now, and the operation carries a high risk that you could end up paralysed.'

'But if I move at all while my back's like this, I'll be paralysed anyway,' Barney said. 'Is that right?'

'Yes.'

'As it is, I'm lucky I'm still alive. The way I see it, I have nothing to lose. Go for it,' Barney said. 'Do whatever you have to do.'

'Can we get in touch with anyone for you so they're here when you wake up?' Nate asked.

Barney grimaced. 'Right now, I can't face the idea of all the nagging.'

'Nagging?' Nate asked, not understanding.

'What idiot drives a car without wearing a seatbelt?' Barney asked. 'I'll never hear the end of it.'

'What happened?' Nate asked.

'I was in a rush to get to a meeting. I was having a screaming row with my girlfriend on the phone at the same time because I had to cancel our date for tonight, so I didn't hear the car beep at me to put my seatbelt on. And then...' He blew out a breath. 'I know I'm lucky to be alive,' he said again, 'let alone in almost one piece. I can't believe I'm even here. I thought I was going to die when I went through the windscreen.'

'I could ring your girlfriend or your mum for you,' Nate suggested. 'And I can tell them as your surgeon that you need calm, peace and quiet to help you recuperate.'

'I guess. But no tears. Please. I hate tears.'

Nate was sure that half of this was bravado and Barney Mason was completely terrified at the idea of becoming paralysed, but he squeezed Barney's hand. 'Got it. Now, I'll need you under a general anaesthetic during the op, and the op's going to last for a few hours.'

'Hours?' Barney looked shocked.

'Hours,' Nate repeated, 'because as well as repairing the damage we'll put a special monitoring system in place to make sure we minimise the risk of causing any damage to your spinal cord while we're fixing you. What I'm going to do is put screws above and below the fracture to act as a kind of scaffold, realign your spine, and then insert rods and a titanium cage so you have a strong structure.'

'So I'm going to have a metal spine, then?'

'In part, yes. The cage and rods will be there permanently. I also need to tell you that you're looking at a few weeks to recover from the op, you'll need to wear a supportive brace around your midriff for three months afterwards, and you'll need a lot of physio to help you get back on your feet. Overall I'd say it'll take about six months to get you back to normal.'

'Six months?' Barney blew out a breath. 'I know I

should be grateful I'm not dead, but that sounds like weeks of being stuck staring at the same four walls.'

Nate had heard that before. But now, thanks to Erin, he had an answer for it. 'Not necessarily. There are rehab places where you can go out in the garden and even do some work out there. Yes, you'll be in a wheelchair for at least some of the time, and you're going to have to learn to pace yourself. And you need to do whatever the physio team tells you, or you'll set your progress back and it'll take even longer before you're completely back on your feet.'

'I'm not so good with orders,' Barney said.

'It's your call,' Nate said. 'I guess it depends how quickly you want to get mobile again.'

'Yesterday?' Barney asked hopefully.

Nate smiled. 'I'm pretty good at what I do, but I'm afraid that one's beyond even me. It'll take as long as it takes, and I know how frustrating it is for you that I can't give you a definite answer, but no two people heal in quite the same way.'

While Barney was being prepped for Theatre, Nate organised his team of specialists and ran through exactly what he wanted to do, then called Barney's girlfriend and his mother to fill them in on the situation and explain that Barney was going to be tired and groggy after the op and would need quiet support, but Nate himself would be there to answer any questions they might have. He called his own mother to warn her that he was going to be in Theatre for a complicated op so he'd be late picking up Caitlin, but he'd call as soon as he was about to leave the hospital.

Finally he scrubbed up, ready for the operation.

'I know the monitoring system's a bit unusual—it's what we'd usually use for scoliosis cases—but we need to make sure there isn't any damage to the spinal cord during the op,' he told his team. 'So I want monitors on his brain, electrodes on his spinal cord, and we stimulate the muscles of his foot at regular intervals so we can measure his response and see if anything's affecting his spinal cord—if it is, then we stop and think about how to tweak whatever we're doing. Everyone OK with that?'

'Sure,' they chorused. 'You're the boss.'

'I'm just the one with the scalpel. This is a team effort, and everyone plays an important role,' he reminded them.

The monitoring system worked perfectly, to Nate's relief, leaving him to work quietly and methodically to realign Barney's spine and repair the damage. He inserted the screws, rods and titanium cage.

'Thanks, everyone,' he said when he'd finished the last suture to close the incision site. 'You were all great. Between us, we've given this guy a fighting chance to get back on his feet.' They'd made a real difference to Barney's life. Which was exactly what Nate had trained for; but had the price been too high? Or would he get a chance to fix his relationship with his daughter, the way he'd just fixed a complicated dislocated spinal fracture?

The operation had taken time and patience, which was also what Erin had counselled for fixing things with Caitlin. So maybe the situation with his daughter would work out, too.

And he wasn't going to let himself think too closely

about his growing feelings for Erin. He couldn't have it all. He needed to be grateful for what he did have instead of wishing for more.

On Thursday morning, just before ward rounds, Nate took Erin to one side. 'Have a look at this.'

She looked at Barney Mason's X-ray and blinked. 'Ouch—that's really nasty. A fracture *and* a dislocation. I don't think I've seen anything as bad as that before.'

'It's probably the worst one I've seen, too,' Nate admitted.

'Is he going to be OK?' Erin asked.

'Come and see him and tell me what you think.'

She blinked. 'You mean you've already fixed that?'

'With screws, rods and a titanium cage,' he said. 'Actually, it's a shame you were off duty on Tuesday afternoon or I would've asked you to be on the neurophysiological team in Theatre. But actually that's not why I want you to see him. I want you to talk to him about rehab places.'

'Oh.' She grinned as the penny dropped. 'Would that involve sensory gardens, by any chance?'

He rolled his eyes. 'Yes, Dr Leyton. And, yes, I admit that you were right about all the garden stuff. I've been reading up about it, too, and it surprises me how much difference it does make.'

'Excellent.' She punched his arm. 'I'm glad you're finally admitting it. By the way, speaking of gardens, is Caitlin still OK to meet Ed after school in our garden today?'

He nodded. 'Though I'm in Theatre, so if there are

any complications when I'm operating I might not be able to make it.'

'That's not a problem. I'll be there to introduce them to each other anyway, and I can always stay a bit longer if you need me to.'

'Are you sure?'

'Very sure,' she said. 'I don't have anything planned for this evening.'

'Thanks. I owe you one,' he said.

As he'd half feared, there were complications in Theatre, but Nate knew that Caitlin would be safe and happy with Erin. When he finally scrubbed out and had made sure his patient was settled, he called Erin's mobile phone to find out exactly where they were and went down to meet them.

'Good to meet you, Nate,' Ed said, shaking his hand. 'Your daughter here's got a real affinity with plants. She's made some really good suggestions about the design.'

'That's good,' Nate said with a smile. How did he deal with this? Singing Caitlin's praises would probably embarrass her and make her back away; but at the same time he didn't want her to feel that he was just dismissing her.

Erin came to his rescue. 'We were wondering if Caitlin could join the volunteer team, Nate. Provided it doesn't interfere with her homework or what have you.'

'And it'd look great on her CV if she decides on a career in horticulture,' Ed added. 'Being involved in a hospital sensory garden is a really big thing.'

Caitlin's eyes were wide with longing. 'Can I?' she asked.

Damping down the wish that she'd call him 'Dad', Nate nodded. 'Sure. Provided you stay on top of your homework.'

'I will,' she promised. And then, to his shock, she hugged him. 'Thanks.'

The combination of that hug and the look of pure approval on Erin's face completely floored him. Nate was relieved that Ed picked up the slack by chatting away about what they could do. He didn't pay much attention to what the garden designer was saying, because all his focus was on Caitlin and Erin: his daughter, and a woman who was growing more important to him by the day.

Was he simply being selfish, wanting to have everything? Or was there a possibility that Erin might see him as more than just a colleague whose life needed fixing? Plus he had no idea how she felt. Did she feel the same attraction towards him? Or did she think that the situation was way too complicated for her to want to take their relationship any further than friendship?

At the weekend, it was raining, so Nate, Erin and Caitlin headed out to the trampoline place. As Nate had half suspected they would, Erin and Caitlin ganged up on him in dodgeball and took great delight in throwing the ball at him and bouncing it to each other for another shot at him.

But then Erin tripped and he caught her.

For a moment, he held her close. He could feel the warmth of her body and the softness of her skin, and she smelled of vanilla and chocolate. Edible.

His mouth went dry as he imagined kissing her.

And when she looked up at him, he could see that her pupils were huge.

So did she feel this same pull towards him? Could anything come of this?

He was just about to dip his head and brush his mouth over hers when he remembered where they were—and that his daughter was standing right next to them. Much as he wanted to kiss Erin, he knew it really wasn't a good idea to do it right here and now. So he set her back on her feet with a grin. 'Given how many times you've hit me with that ball in the last ten minutes, you're very lucky I didn't just let you fall flat on your face, Dr Leyton.'

'Yeah, yeah,' she said, and bounced a ball against his chest with a cheeky grin.

'So much for gratitude,' he grumbled.

Erin threw the ball to Caitlin. 'Actually, I think we're about done now,' she said. 'And, as trampolining burns about a thousand calories an hour, I reckon we've burned enough to have afternoon tea.'

'Bring on the cake,' Nate said. 'And scones. I have a ton of calories to replenish.'

She smiled at him, and his heart felt as if it had done a somersault. Ridiculous. He really needed to keep himself under control. But when they were settled in the café with a platter of sandwiches and a tiered stand full of scones and cakes, he found himself staring at her mouth.

Oh, help.

'Dad?'

Then he became aware that Caitlin was talking to him.

'Sorry. Miles away.' But his daughter was bright and he didn't want her to guess why he was wool-gathering. Thinking swiftly on his feet, he said, 'I was wondering how many of these sandwiches I can eat before you notice that I've scoffed your share.'

'I was saying, Erin's tea is actually nice. She just let me try it.'

'It's passion fruit tea,' Erin added. 'My favourite, after pomegranate.'

It was bright orange and it smelled gorgeous.

'Want to try some?' she asked.

'I think I'll stick to my good old-fashioned breakfast tea,' he said. Because the idea of drinking from a cup where her lips had just touched sent a shiver of pure desire running through him, and he needed to stop this right now.

But it got worse when they started some teasing bickering about the proper way to eat scones, and whether the cream or the jam should go on first. Because then Nate and Erin reached for a scone at the same time and their fingers brushed against each other. Nate's skin tingled where they'd touched, and his whole body felt incredibly aware of hers. Maybe he should've sat next to her instead of opposite her—because then he wouldn't have to look at her and wonder what it would be like to touch his mouth to hers. Then again, sitting next to her would've been just as bad, because then his foot might've ended up brushing against hers...

He needed a cold shower.

But for now, concentrating on his cup of tea would have to do.

* * *

The following Tuesday morning, Erin let herself into her brother's flat. 'Hey, Mikey.'

He looked up from his computer. 'Hey, it's my favourite sister.'

'Your only sister,' she corrected.

'But you're still my favourite.' He smiled at her. 'Would that be a box of freshly baked cookies I spy in your hand?'

'I made most of them for the bake sale at work later today, but I earmarked these ones for you,' she said. 'Though you have to save at least one for Louisa. And I've already texted her to say I made cookies, so she'll know if you scoff the lot.'

'True. I'll make us some tea to go with them.' He saved his file, wheeled himself into the kitchen and made tea.

Yet again Erin noticed how matter-of-fact Mikey was about his situation. He didn't let his disability get in the way. Then again, she supposed he'd had fourteen years to get used to being in a wheelchair.

'How's the sensory garden doing?' Mikey asked.

'Really well. The structure's almost there, and we're going to start planting things, next week.'

'Has the new guy at work stopped giving you a hard time about it?'

Erin squirmed. Why had she opened her mouth to her brother about that in the first place? 'Uh-huh.'

'Spill,' he said.

She tried for innocence. 'Spill what?'

'I've known you since you were two hours old,' he

reminded her, 'so you can't flannel me. What's the deal with this guy?'

'There's no deal.' That bit was true. 'Nate and I are friends.'

'As in "just good"?' Mikey asked wryly.

Erin nodded. 'We can't be any more than that.'

'Why not?'

'Because his ex-wife has just sent their thirteen-year-old daughter to live with him.'

Mikey winced in sympathy. 'Ah. I take it you're seeing yourself, from the time when Mum kicked you out?'

'Yes and no. Caitlin's a nice kid, actually. Her mum's new husband isn't quite as bad as Creepy Leonard was. It seems that he just doesn't want the bother of having a teenager around or having to share her mother's attention.'

'And she gets on OK with her dad?'

'It's getting better. We found some common ground between them.' Erin laughed. 'Ironically, it was the sensory garden. So I guess that's why he's had to come round to my way of thinking on the subject.'

Mikey wheeled his chair over to her and gave her a hug. 'Erin, you don't have to rescue everyone, you know.'

'I'm not trying to rescue anyone,' she fibbed.

'You can't change the past,' he said, 'but you've more than learned from it. I know Mum blames you for what happened, but I don't, and as the one who's actually in the wheelchair then I outrank her in the validity of my opinion.'

'And the political journalist goes back into using

long words and a fancy sentence structure,' she teased, wanting him to change the subject.

'Erin.' He took her hand. 'When are you going to forgive yourself, sweetheart?'

She couldn't answer that. Mainly because she was pretty sure the answer was 'never'.

'Look at you. Think how many lives you've made a real difference to at work,' Mikey pointed out. 'If I hadn't had the accident, you might not have become a doctor, let alone a neurologist. The way you were going when you were fifteen, you might have ended up drifting from dead-end job to dead-end job, never settling to anything for long.'

She knew he was right, but she still thought that the price had been too high. And the fact that he'd been the one to pay it was unacceptable.

'And,' he added gently, 'you might have been the mother of a thirteen-year-old yourself right now—which is another reason why I think you're stepping in to help. This girl is the child you could've had.'

'Mikey, I'm not trying to replace the baby. I came to terms with the miscarriage a long time ago. And you and I both know I was too young anyway to be a mum, back then. I wouldn't have given my daughter a good life.'

Her little girl.

Would her daughter have looked like her? Would she have had the same unruly fair hair, the same dusting of freckles across her nose? Would they have clashed as badly as Erin and her own mother did, or would they have been friends as well as mother and daughter?

When she'd first realised she was pregnant, Erin had

been horrified, unable to believe it was true. She'd gone into denial about it and pretended it wasn't happening until her best friend had found her crying in the toilets and taken her home to talk to her mother—and Rachel had really helped her come to terms with it and see that the baby was maybe a gift, a chance to have the parent-child relationship she didn't have with her own parents. Losing that had devastated Erin; once she'd accepted the idea of being pregnant, she'd planned to put her child first, to give her child a feeling of importance and security that she'd never had herself.

It had taken a lot of hard work for her to come to terms with the miscarriage and realise that maybe it was her own second chance, and she could turn her life around.

'You don't know for sure that it would've gone wrong,' Mikey said, 'and things are never that clear-cut. Yes, having the miscarriage meant that you could go on to concentrate on your studies instead of having to drop out; but at the same time you missed out on having a child. I think you're still missing out, because you don't let anyone close enough to date you for more than a couple of months, and settling down really doesn't seem on the cards for you.'

She suppressed the ache. 'Maybe. But be honest about it, Mikey. Relationships don't work for me.'

'Because you don't give them a chance.'

She scoffed. 'You and Rachel are the only people who've ever been there for me. And look what I did to you.'

'I was the one driving,' he reminded her, 'and it was an accident. Have you told this Nate guy what happened?'

She shook her head. 'He knows you had an accident, but he doesn't know it was my fault.' She dragged in a breath. 'And he doesn't know about the baby.' She never talked about the baby to anyone nowadays—except when her brother made her talk about it.

'The accident wasn't your fault,' Mikey said again, 'but maybe you should tell him what happened, and he can make you see that.'

'Or he might run a mile in the opposite direction because he'll see me as a bad influence on Caitlin,' she countered.

'Or,' Mikey said, 'more likely he'll see what a brave, strong woman you are, how you've turned your life around and what a great role model you are for his daughter.'

Erin flapped a dismissive hand. 'That stuff is all on a need-to-know basis, and right now Nate doesn't need to know.'

'So you're scared of his reaction?' he asked perceptively.

Petrified. 'No,' she fibbed.

'So he's *that* important. Interesting. And he's the first man you've actually talked to me about in a long time.' Mikey finished making the tea and handed her a mug. 'Open up to him, Erin. If he deserves you, then he'll understand. And if he doesn't understand, then he's not good enough for you anyway.'

She gave him an awkward hug. 'I love you, Mikey.'

'I love you, too, Erin—but you need to start really living your life.'

'I *am* living my life,' she protested.

He scoffed. 'No, you're not, because you won't let

anyone close—partly because of what that bastard Andrew did to you.'

'I had counselling,' she reminded him. 'I came to terms with it. Not all men are rapists. I've dated since then. I've had sex since then.'

But trying to embarrass her brother into shutting up didn't work. 'You still don't let anyone close,' he pointed out.

She sighed. 'Mikey, love doesn't last. So what's the point in looking for it?'

'Love *does* last,' he said. 'And I can prove it.'

'How?

'Grab your diary, because Louisa and I are taking you out to dinner.'

'Dinner? That sounds good. What's the occasion?'

'Double celebration. I got promoted to editor at the magazine,' he said.

'That's fabulous news! Then I'm buying the champagne at dinner—no arguments,' she said.

'Accepted,' he said with a smile.

'You said double. What's the other bit?' she asked.

'That's the proof I was telling you about. We're looking for a chief bridesmaid,' he said. 'Know anyone who might be interested?'

It took a second for the penny to drop. 'You're getting married?'

He grinned. 'I asked Louisa at the weekend and she said yes. And you're our first choice as chief bridesmaid. Actually,' he confided, 'we're hoping to make it a triple celebration, because we've been accepted for the IVF programme.'

'Mikey, that's wonderful news.' Tears welled in

her eyes as she realised that she hadn't quite taken everything away from her brother. He was going to get married to the woman he loved and who loved him in return, and with luck they were going to have a child together.

'So,' he said softly, 'I understand about turning your life round, being brave enough to risk loving someone and letting them love you. And if I don't let being unable to walk get in my way and stop me doing things, then you shouldn't let anything get in your way and stop you doing things, either.'

'I'm not. I'm too busy at work to date.'

'Busy? Sweetheart, what that means is you don't have to take any risks. Working hard and helping others means you're able to hide how vulnerable you are and bury your fears.'

Mikey was too perceptive for her comfort. Which went with the territory of being a political journalist, she supposed—he wasn't afraid to tackle difficult subjects and he didn't let people back away from the truth.

'I'm not one of your interviewees, Mikey. You don't have to give me a hard time. Anyway, I brought you cookies. And they're still warm. Don't let them get cold while you keep yakking on.'

'Hmm. But just think about this, Erin: if you carry on keeping people at a distance, Andrew keeps winning. Is that what you want?' he asked.

'No, but we're not talking about me. We're talking about your wedding.' She lifted her mug of tea. 'Congratulations, Mikey. I'm so pleased for you and Louisa. And if you need any help organising anything at all…'

'You're my wing woman,' he said. 'You always have

been. If it wasn't for you, I wouldn't have gone back to finish my degree or had the confidence to apply for my job—or to start dating Louisa.'

'I guess.' But if it hadn't been for her, he would've finished his degree two years earlier and had a completely different life. Why didn't he hate her for taking so much away from him?

'Think about it. Talk to Nate. If he's worthy of you, he'll understand.'

'Yeah.' She finished her tea and kissed him. 'I have to go. The bake sale starts in an hour and a half and I need to set up the stall.' And she knew she was being a coward. Mikey had a point. Taking the risk of a relationship with someone wasn't something she wanted to do. Taking the risk that it would break down, that happiness would be snatched away and yet again she'd lose someone she loved. She couldn't face it. Better not to risk her heart. Better to keep herself busy at work and helping other people, so she didn't have time to think about what she might be missing.

'Go get 'em, kiddo.' He punched her lightly on the shoulder. 'Talk to the guy, and let me know how it goes.'

'I will,' she said, having no intention of doing either. Nate was her friend. And she didn't want to risk losing that—or the chance to help Caitlin and make sure she didn't repeat Erin's mistakes.

CHAPTER SIX

AT THE HOSPITAL, Erin set up her bake stall in the atrium, where everyone visiting the hospital would be able to see it. Her colleagues on the spinal unit had contributed cakes or cookies, whether home-made or a glitzy one bought from a bakery, as had staff from other departments who knew her well. Volunteers from the Friends of the London Victoria had also brought in cakes and were helping her to man the stall.

'Caitlin sent these. She made them last night,' Nate said, coming along to the stall with a plastic box filled with home-made brownies.

'Awesome. I'm definitely buying one of these,' Erin said with a smile.

'And my mother says to thank you.'

'What for?'

'Because Caitlin asked her if she could bake something, and she wanted to use one of Mum's recipes. Thanks to you, Caitlin's starting to open up to her as well.' He swallowed hard. 'She actually called Mum "Gran" last night, for the first time in months. And she's started calling me "Dad" instead of avoiding the word.'

Erin felt a lump in her throat. 'That's so good to hear.'

'Yeah.' He rested a hand on her arm. 'We owe you.'

Her skin tingled where he touched her, and she had to remind herself that it was inappropriate.

She was busy with the bake stall all afternoon and didn't really have the time to think about Nate, but the question went round and round in the back of her mind: was Mikey right, or would Nate run a mile if she told him the truth about her past? Telling him risked losing his friendship—and she'd lost enough in her life. But at the same time she knew she'd held so much back that their friendship was based on a lie—on who he thought she was, rather than who she really was. That wasn't healthy, either.

She was just packing up when he came over.

'I've finished in Theatre and written up my notes, so I wondered if you need a hand with anything?' he asked.

'I'm just returning the tables I borrowed from one of the meeting rooms. Don't you need to go and pick up Caitlin?'

'She'll be fine with Mum for a while.'

'Then if you've really got time, sure, you can give me a hand.'

It was fine until they both reached for the same table at the same time and their fingers touched. Erin felt that same prickle of awareness as when their hands had touched over the scones; but this time, instead of avoiding eye contact, she looked him straight in the eye. Nate's pupils were dilated to the point where his eyes looked almost black.

Oh, help. It looked as if this attraction she felt towards him was mutual, then. What were they going to do about it? Because this situation was impossible.

His face was serious. 'Erin.' He reached out and cupped her cheek in his palm, then brushed his thumb over her lower lip.

She felt hot all over and her skin tingled where he touched her.

'Nate. We're right in the middle of the hospital,' she whispered.

'And anyone could see us. I know.' He moved his hand away. 'Erin, I think we need to talk.'

She knew he was right. 'But not here.' It was too public.

'Where? When?' His voice was urgent.

'You said Caitlin would be all right with your mum for a while.' She took a deep breath. Maybe she needed to be brave about this, as Mikey had suggested. Do it now. Tell him the truth. And if he walked away—well, it just proved that she'd been stupid to let him matter to her. 'My place, right now?'

He nodded. 'I'll drive you.'

'No, we need to go separately. We don't want people to start gossiping about us,' she said quickly.

'I guess you're right,' he said.

'I'll text you the address on my way to the Tube™,' she said.

'OK. I'll, um, see you soon, then.'

His eyes were full of longing—the same longing that she felt. But, once he knew the truth about her, would he look at her in a different way?

There was only one way to find out. And it scared the hell out of her. But he'd find out in the end, so she knew it would be better to tell him now. Before either of them got hurt.

Though she had a nasty feeling it was already too late for that.

Nate walked back to his car to wait for Erin to text him her address so he could put the postcode into his satnav, feeling as nervous and excited as a teenager on his first date—which he knew was crazy. They weren't actually dating. They might not ever date. After all, what did he have to offer her apart from a very complicated life?

But the kind of pull he felt towards her was rare, and the way she'd just reacted to him made him think that it might be the same for her. Between them, could they find some kind of compromise?

He really hoped so. Because, the more he got to know Erin, the more he liked her. She was serious when she needed to be, and yet she had a sense of fun and an infectious smile. She was sweet and kind and funny. She was straight-talking and not afraid to face things head-on. And physically he was more aware of her than he had been of anyone since he'd split up from Stephanie ten years before. He wanted her more than he could ever remember wanting anyone.

Erin realised that she was actually shaking with a mixture of nerves and excitement as she got on the Tube™. She wanted this so much—and yet if she thought about it she knew it made no sense at all. Where could their relationship possibly go from here? Nate came as a package, and his relationship with his daughter was still so new and so fragile that he couldn't afford to take his focus away from it. Plus they worked together at the hospital, so if things went wrong between them—given her track record, she amended, that was more likely to be 'when' than 'if'—it could be awkward between them in the department.

So, even if he felt that same pull of attraction, they were just going to have to pretend that it didn't exist. Because this couldn't happen. Once she'd told him the truth about her past, he would realise for himself that she wasn't a good bet and he'd back away. Though, at the same time, part of her didn't want to tell him the truth because she didn't want to risk losing his friendship.

Yet she knew that the longer she left it to tell him, the closer she got to him, the harder it would be to find the words. So she needed to be brave. Tell him. *Now.*

Her flat was reasonably tidy, but she whizzed the Hoover round while the kettle boiled—more to stop herself from thinking than because her flat needed cleaning.

And then the doorbell rang.

Nate.

Erin felt almost sick with nerves, and her heart was beating so hard as she walked to the front door that she was sure people in the street outside could hear it. She took a deep breath, and gave Nate her best and brightest smile. 'Perfect timing. The kettle's just boiled—tea or coffee?'

'Whatever you're having.'

'Coffee,' she said. It would take longer to make and it might buy her enough time to slow her pulse rate and get her common sense back. 'Come and sit down. I won't be long.' She ushered him in to the living room, intending to be all bright and breezy and chirpy—but then he stopped in the doorway and dipped his head to kiss her.

When he lifted his head again, she was shaking.

'Nate, I...' She didn't have a clue what to say. That kiss had just blown her mind.

'Me, too,' he whispered. 'I wasn't expecting this and I know it's unfair of me to do this because I come with complications.'

So did she. And, if this thing between them was to stand even the slightest chance of growing into something good, she needed to be honest with him right from the start. 'Coffee,' she said, and fled to the kitchen.

When she returned with two mugs, he was browsing the photographs on her mantelpiece.

'I take it this is your brother?' he asked, gesturing to the picture of her with Mikey. They were sitting in her father's garden, laughing together, and Mikey's wheelchair was very obvious.

'Yes,' she said quietly. She handed him one of the mugs and took a deep breath. 'I told you that Mikey's in a wheelchair. What I didn't tell you was that it's my fault he's in a wheelchair. So I guess I owe you an explanation.'

He frowned. 'You don't owe me anything.'

'I think I do—before things between us...' She swallowed hard. 'Well.' Too late to go back, now. She just had to hope that he wouldn't hate her the way her mother did or think that she'd be a bad influence on Caitlin. 'I should probably have told you this before. And, once I've told you the truth about me, I'll understand if you want me to stay out of your life.'

His frown deepened. 'But I do want you in my life, Erin. That's the whole point of us talking now.'

'You need to know the truth about me, first. You know I said my parents split up when I was a couple of years older than Caitlin?' At his nod, she continued, 'When Dad left us, I went off the rails pretty badly and I got in with a rough crowd. I might have found my own way back out of it again—but then my mum started seeing this guy. Mikey and I called him "Creepy Leonard."' Even thinking about the man made her feel sick.

'Why was he creepy?' Nate asked.

'I always felt that he was watching me. And it wasn't just teenage awkwardness or paranoia. The way he looked at me…' She shivered. 'Let's just say I discovered that he thought that dating the mother meant that he had the same rights over the daughter.'

Nate looked truly shocked, his eyes widening in horror. 'You mean he…?'

'He *tried*,' she said grimly. 'When he touched me inappropriately, I told him to take his disgusting hands off me or I'd scream the place down. Then I kicked him hard enough in the shins to make him let me go.' For a second, she gritted her teeth. Remembering the older man's lecherous behaviour still made her angry. 'He called me a tease, and I told him I was nothing of the kind. I also told him that my boyfriend would beat him up if he ever laid another hand on me.' Considering what had actually happened with Andrew, that was so ironic. But at the time she'd thought that her boyfriend would protect her from all harm. It hadn't occurred to her that Andrew was where the real danger lay.

'Did you tell your mum what he did?'

She nodded. 'But Leonard had got there before me. He'd convinced her that I was trying to stir up trouble so they would split up—and she didn't believe me when I told her what really happened.'

Nate looked as if he couldn't take it in. 'That—that's *appalling*, Erin. Why would she believe the word of a guy she obviously didn't know very well rather than her own daughter?'

'Remember, her life had just fallen apart,' Erin said. On her counsellor's advice she'd tried so, so hard to see it from her mother's point of view; she'd gone over it again and again, trying to work out what her mother had been thinking. 'Her husband of twenty years had just left her for someone else. She felt ugly and useless and old and betrayed, and then this guy flattered her and made her feel good about herself again. Of course she was going to listen to him.'

'Even though he'd just tried to touch her fifteen-year-old daughter very inappropriately?'

'I blamed Mum for Dad leaving us,' Erin said, 'so we weren't getting on very well. She thought I was trying to spoil things for her—that I was trying to get my revenge on her for Dad leaving, by breaking up her relationship with her new man. From a distance of fourteen years, I can understand why she thought that.'

'It's still appalling. You were a child. Why on earth didn't she listen to you and put you first?' Then he looked at her in horror. 'Oh, my God. Erin. You don't think Steph's new husband…?'

'Tried to touch Caitlin inappropriately?' she asked, guessing what was worrying him. 'No. I think he just wants Steph to himself and doesn't want to share her attention with her daughter. Caitlin's opened up to me about some things, and I think she would've told me if there was any more to it than that—which isn't saying you're a bad father,' she added swiftly, 'just that it's a lot easier to tell something difficult like that to someone who isn't your parent.'

'That sounds like personal experience talking.'

'It is.' She blew out a breath. 'My best friend Gill's mum, Rachel—I told her what Creepy Leonard had done, and she said I needed a lock on my bedroom door to keep me safe. She got her husband to fit it for me that same evening. Mum was really angry when she found out. She said I was attention-seeking and trying to cause trouble for Leonard because I was jealous.'

'You were pretty much understating it when you said your relationship with your mother was tricky,' Nate said, still looking shocked.

'Just a bit,' she admitted. 'Anyway, the lock worked, because it kept Creepy Leonard out. But things got even worse between me and Mum after that, and I started spending more and more time with the crowd who accepted me for who I was—even though they weren't good for me and deep down I think I knew that.' She closed her eyes for a moment. 'Nate, I mean it when I said I went off the rails. It was really bad. I started skipping school and hanging out with them instead, and going to parties that were way too old for me. Let me spell it out for you—I was running around with a crowd who drank and smoked and did soft drugs.'

'Did you do what they did?' he asked.

'Not the smoking or the drugs. But I did start drinking vodka when I wasn't old enough, just so I fitted in with them,' she admitted. 'I was fifteen, but I looked old enough to be eighteen, so I got away with it. And one of my new friends got me some fake ID for when we went clubbing. Let's just say we went to the kind of places where they didn't check the ID that closely.'

'I take it your mum was too caught up in Creepy Leonard to notice what was going on?'

'To be fair,' Erin said, 'even if she had been looking out for me, she wouldn't really have known what was going on because I covered my tracks pretty well and we were barely speaking to each other.' She bit her lip. 'And then one night I went to this party. I wish now I'd never gone in the first place, but I guess it's easy to see things in hindsight.'

'And you were still very young,' he said gently.

'I made some really bad decisions, Nate, and my brother was the one who paid the price for it. I don't think I can ever forgive myself for what I did.' She swallowed hard. This was something she almost never spoke about. 'Nobody at work knows about this.'

'They're not going to hear anything from me,' Nate promised.

'Thank you.' Though that didn't make it any easier to tell him. Every word felt as if it ripped another layer off the top of her scars. But if they were to have any chance of a real relationship, he needed to know who she really was. What she'd done. 'Andrew, my boyfriend, had decided that night was the night we were going all the way.' She closed her eyes for a moment. 'I wasn't ready. I didn't want to do what he wanted, because I wasn't even going to be sixteen for another couple of months, but he was nineteen and he expected me to behave like the rest of the girls in his crowd. He didn't want to wait any longer.'

And she'd been so, so shocked by his reaction at her refusal. By the way he'd pushed her into one of the bedrooms, locked the door behind them and thrown all the coats off the bed. Shoved her onto the mattress. She could still feel the weight of his body on hers, his hands gripping her wrists and holding them above her head. The panic when she'd realised that nobody would be able to hear her scream—and, even worse, that nobody was going to come to her rescue even if they did hear her.

'He said age was just a number and it didn't matter. I said I didn't want to do it, but he wasn't listening. He wanted to have sex with me.' She swallowed hard. 'So he pushed me into one of the bedrooms, locked the door and took what he wanted.'

Nate took the mug from her hand and placed it on the low coffee table next to his own, then drew her over towards the sofa and scooped her onto his lap, holding her close.

'Oh, honey,' he said, his voice gentle. 'What a horrible, horrible thing to happen to you.'

'I guess it was my own fault. I knew what that crowd was like. And we'd—well—I'd let him touch me more intimately than I should've done at that age, and I'd touched him. Even though I knew I wasn't ready... It was good to be accepted by someone. To feel loved again—because I didn't think either of my parents cared about me any more. I really thought Andrew loved me, Nate. He'd been pushing me to go the whole way with him for a while, but I'd held off, and...' Bile rose in her throat, and she grimaced. 'Maybe Creepy Leonard was right and I was a tease who deserved what I got.'

'Absolutely not,' Nate said, and kept his arms wrapped round her. 'No means no, and Andrew should've accepted that and waited until you were ready.' He stroked her cheek. 'Violence doesn't solve anything, but I'd quite like to flatten the guy, right now.'

'Violence *really* doesn't solve anything,' she emphasised. 'That's why Mikey ended up in a wheelchair. After Andrew finally unlocked the door and let me out of that room, I called my brother and asked him to come and get me. I didn't say what Andrew had done, but when Mikey took me home I realised Mum and Creepy Leonard were out, and I just broke down and told him. He said I had to call the police, but first he was going to make absolutely sure Andrew never did that to another girl—and he drove off before I could stop him.' She dragged in a breath. 'On the way back to confront Andrew, Mikey had the accident.'

Nate stroked her hair. 'Erin, it was an *accident*. It wasn't your fault.'

'No? According to my mother, if I hadn't been an attention-seeking whore, Mikey wouldn't have been driving, let alone anywhere near the crash site.' Erin swallowed miserably. 'And she was right.'

'No, she wasn't,' Nate said. 'Erin, we deal all the time with patients who've been paralysed in accidents, and we talk to their relatives. You know how many of the relatives find it hard to accept what's happened and the consequences. Blaming someone for the accident is the only way they can start to come to terms with it. It sounds to me as if that's what your mother was doing, and because you were the closest person to her you were the one who copped the flak.'

Why wouldn't he understand? 'But it's *true*,' Erin said again. 'If I hadn't gone to that party, Andrew wouldn't have forced me to have sex with him, I wouldn't have called Mikey afterwards to rescue me and Mikey wouldn't have ended up in the crash.'

'It's a chain of circumstance, and you can't know that the crash wouldn't have happened anyway. Mikey could've been driving anywhere, at any time, and still had that crash.' He stroked her face. 'Did you tell your mother about what Andrew did?'

It was another memory that made her flinch. 'I tried.' Erin closed her eyes. 'She said I was making it up, trying to get attention away from Mikey in his hospital bed.'

Nate couldn't suppress a curse. 'What about your dad?'

'Mum sent me to live with him because she couldn't bear the sight of me—because it was my fault Mikey was never going to walk again, and every time she saw me it reminded her of what I'd done.'

'Did you tell your dad about Andrew?'

Erin shook her head. 'I didn't think he'd listen, either. Not that Dad had fights with me, the way Mum did, but he felt guilty about having the affair and leaving us, and he avoided talking about anything emotional. Dad's one of those men who just can't deal with emotional stuff. He simply looks away, mumbles, "All right," and changes the subject.'

'So you were all on your own? What about your friend's mum? Did you tell her?'

'No.' At least, not then. She'd talked to Rachel later, when it was way, way too late. But she couldn't bring herself to tell Nate about that. Telling him this much had drained her emotionally. She didn't have the strength to tell him the bit that had finally broken her.

'So Andrew got away with it?'

'I guess.' She bit her lip. 'I feel bad about that, too, because I hate to think he might have gone on to do the same thing to someone else.'

'Erin, it really wasn't your fault. You were still a child yourself and you needed someone looking out for you, not blaming you.'

She could guess from his expression what he meant. 'Don't judge my mother too harshly,' she said softly. 'She was really upset about what happened to Mikey. And I can see where she was coming from.'

'Has your mother ever seen the situation from your point of view?' Nate asked.

The crunch question. 'No,' Erin admitted. 'But that doesn't matter because I can see hers. And I can't forgive myself for what happened to Mikey, because he wouldn't have been in his car that night if I hadn't asked him to rescue me.'

'What does Mikey say about it?'

'Pretty much what you do,' she said. 'Actually, he's the one who told me I ought to tell you about this.'

'He was right. I'm glad you did.'

'Even though you know now how—' she caught her breath '—how *bad* I am, deep down? You don't think I'm going to be a bad influence on Caitlin?'

'You were young and you made some mistakes,' he

said. 'Just because you've made some bad choices, it doesn't mean that you're a bad person.'

Was that true? For the first time ever, Erin thought that maybe there was a chance. Maybe the way she'd lived her life ever since had started to make up for her actions as a teen.

'If you were talking to someone who'd been in your situation, would you judge them as harshly as you judge yourself?' he asked.

She thought about it. 'Maybe not.'

'Definitely not,' he said, 'because you'd see that circumstances played a big part in what happened. It's very clear to me that you can see similarities with Caitlin's situation and your own,' Nate continued. 'You've persuaded Caitlin to talk to you and trust you, so you can guide her into not making the same kind of mistakes that you did.'

She looked away. 'So you think I'm using your daughter to try and stop myself feeling guilty?' Which she was, in a way. Which made her hate herself even more.

'No. I think you're being a strong, kind woman who's using her experience to stop someone else going off the rails in a similar situation. Isn't it time you stopped beating yourself up about the past?' he asked. 'What you went through was terrible. Erin, your parents both abandoned you at a time when you needed a bit of support, you had to deal with your mum's new man behaving inappropriately towards you and then you were raped by the boyfriend you believed loved you. The fact you've managed to get through all that and you've become a doctor who makes a real difference to people's lives—you're amazing, Erin.'

'I don't feel amazing,' she said. 'And don't try to sugar-coat it. I didn't behave well when I was fifteen. I was rude, surly and uncooperative. I drank alcohol when I was under age, and I went to clubs with a fake ID. I skipped school and I failed every single one of my exams.' Between the shock of Mikey's accident and finding out that she was pregnant, and then losing the baby, she'd given up. She hadn't even seen any point in turning up to write her name on the exam paper. So she'd stayed at home, curled in a ball underneath her duvet and crying about the wreckage of her life.

'That was then. Half a lifetime ago,' he said. 'You're a different person now, and it's the you of today I want to get to know better.'

Nate really still wanted to know her? Even after what she'd done?

Hope bloomed in her heart.

She knew she ought to tell him the rest of it—about the baby and the miscarriage—but right now she was too raw.

'But.'

Ah. She'd known it was too good to be true. This was where he'd do the 'it's not you, it's me' speech. He'd take the blame, to make her feel better—but he'd still leave her. Just as she'd always thought: relationships didn't work for her.

'The thing is,' he said, 'Caitlin needs all my attention right now. I want to get to know you better, Erin, and to date you properly, but I don't see how that can happen for a while. Not until Caitlin's really settled. It's not fair of me to ask you to wait for me for an unspecified amount of time.'

He was right. She couldn't complain. Especially as she agreed with him. Completely. 'You're right about Caitlin. She needs you,' Erin said. 'And I—well, everything that happened means I don't tend to get too deeply involved with anyone.'

'Because you blame yourself and you don't think you're worth loving?'

She flinched. 'You don't pull your punches, Nate.'

'Neither do you. But you *are* worth loving, Erin. If things were different...'

'Yeah.' She knew that one well. It was a line she'd used herself, often enough, to get out of emotional involvement. To back away rather than being the one who was rejected.

'Or,' he said, 'we can try something.'

'Such as?' She couldn't quite let herself hope.

'Let's look at it logically. You don't want to date anyone, because you can't forgive yourself for a mistake you made when you were fifteen—half a lifetime ago. When you were still a *child*, Erin. I don't want to date anyone, because I've already made enough mistakes where my daughter's concerned and I need to put her first.'

'Uh-huh.' He'd summed it up pretty fairly.

'So maybe,' he said, 'we can date in secret.'

'Date in secret?' she asked. How on earth could he think that was a logical solution?

'Nobody else needs to know about this,' he explained. 'Just you and me. No pressure. We take it at our own pace and see where things go between us.'

'You really want to date me?'

'I really want to date you,' he confirmed, his blue eyes full of sincerity.

She blew out a breath. 'Even though you know the truth about me now?'

'Even more so,' he said. 'So, you and me. How about it?'

'I...' She stared at him. 'I don't know what to say.'

He pressed a kiss into her palm and folded her fingers over it. 'No strings attached, Erin. We simply go on dates and get to know each other better.'

'How are we going to find time to date, between work and Caitlin?'

'Maybe we can snatch a little time between work and home,' he said. 'I didn't say it was going to be conventional dating. It'll probably be breakfast out rather than dinner, or a snatched coffee here and there, or a walk in the park. But we can still make time for each other and get to know each other properly.' He paused. 'If you want to.'

Oh, she wanted to. So much. He was the first man in years to make her want to take a risk. And if he was prepared to take the risk, too... She smiled, then. 'OK. Let's give it a go.'

'Good.' He stroked her face. 'We'll take the pace at one you're comfortable with. And I hope you realise that I'll listen to you—if you say no, then as far as I'm concerned you mean it and I'm not going to push you.'

She knew he meant it, and tears pricked at the back of her eyes. 'Thank you.'

'Have you ever dated anyone since Andrew?' he asked.

She'd already told him that. And that she'd kept her

relationships very short. But she also knew that wasn't quite what he meant. 'You mean, have I had sex with anyone since I was raped?'

He raised an eyebrow. 'What was that you were saying about not pulling punches?'

'I guess,' she said wryly. 'To answer your question, yes, I have. I had counselling, thanks to my best friend's mum. I told Rachel in the end, but there was no point in going to the police because it was too late to have any evidence. But she got me to go to counselling to help me come to terms with it all. She even went with me to the first appointment. And I've had full relationships since. I just haven't wanted to get too deeply involved, that's all.'

'I'm sorry that you had to go through such a rough time,' he said gently.

She shrugged. 'Don't they say that whatever doesn't kill you makes you stronger?'

'You,' he said, 'are an incredibly strong woman, and I really admire your courage. And I'm glad you trusted me enough to tell me about your past.'

'I'm glad, too.' It felt as if the weight of the world had been lifted from her shoulders. And it was the first time in years that she'd actually felt hope about any kind of relationship.

He kissed her cheek, and her skin tingled at the touch of his lips. 'Given that you've just told me something so painful, I really don't want to leave you. I don't want you to think I'm just abandoning you. But—'

'—you need to collect Caitlin,' she finished. 'It's OK. I understand, Nate. You come as a package.'

'I don't want you thinking that I'm just grabbing the

first excuse to scarper and then you won't see me for dust. Because I *do* want to date you, Erin. I want to get to know you better. And I want you to get to know me. Not just as a surgeon or as Caitlin's clueless dad who really needs help to connect with his daughter, but the real me.'

'Yeah.' She kissed the corner of his mouth, then slid off his lap. 'Go and collect Caitlin. I'll see you at work tomorrow.'

He stood up. 'I'll wash up my mug before—'

'No, it's fine,' she cut in with a smile. 'I know you're house-trained. You don't have to prove anything to me.'

'I guess.' He tucked a strand of hair behind her ear. 'I was going to say, seeing you makes me feel like a teenager again. But I guess your memories of being a teen are pretty unhappy, so that isn't tactful.'

'Other people had nicer teenage years than I did,' she said. 'But I'm not angry about it. Envious sometimes, I admit. But life is what it is, and you just learn to make the best of it.'

'Maybe,' he said, 'I can make you feel like the way you make me feel. Like a teenager, but in a good way.'

'Start a brand new slate.' And oh, how she wished that could be possible.

'Something like that.' He kissed the tip of her nose. 'If anything I do makes you uncomfortable, tell me, because I'm not a mind-reader.'

'You're doing pretty well so far,' she said.

'Good. I'll see you tomorrow. Though I reserve the right to send you soppy texts in the meantime.'

She laughed, then. 'I can't imagine the formal, slightly snooty surgeon I first met sending soppy texts to anyone. Or even Caitlin's clueless dad, because he wouldn't even know where to start with textspeak and the kind of acronyms teenagers use.'

'That,' he said, 'was a definite gauntlet you've just thrown down. Keep your phone on. I'll respond to that challenge later tonight.'

And his smile made her feel warm all the way through.

He stole one last kiss. 'Later.'

It was a promise. And one she knew he'd keep.

CHAPTER SEVEN

Roses are red, violets are blue, I can't write rhymes but I really like you :)

IF ANYONE HAD told Erin that Nate could write the kind of verses beloved of teenage boys—and would send them to her in a text, complete with a smiley face—she would never have believed them.

But his text made her smile for the rest of the evening.

You, too, she texted back.

Am in late on Friday, he added. Can you make breakfast?

Well, that was direct.

Sure. Let me know what you want me to cook.

He called her immediately. 'Sorry, I didn't mean I was expecting you to cook breakfast for me. I meant, if you could make it, I'd like to take you out to breakfast. You know, dating stuff?'

'Out for breakfast? How very decadent of you,

Mr Townsend,' she teased. 'Thank you. That would be lovely.'

'Do you know anywhere nice that's not too far from the hospital?'

'But far enough away to keep us safe from the hospital grapevine?' she suggested.

'Got it in one.'

She could practically hear the smile in his voice. 'Yes. I'll text you the address and I'll meet you there. What time?'

'I'll drop Caitlin to school first. Give me time for traffic. Say, nine?' he suggested.

'Nine's perfect.'

'Good. See you tomorrow. Sweet dreams.'

'You, too.'

At work the next morning, they kept things completely normal between them. They did ward rounds together, then discussed a case where one of her patients needed to talk through the possible surgical options. As far as everyone else on the ward was concerned, Nate and Erin were simply colleagues. But she could see from the expression in his eyes that he didn't think of her as just a colleague any more. She didn't think of him that way, either.

And she couldn't wait for their breakfast date.

On Thursday afternoon, after her shift, Erin met Caitlin at the sensory garden as they'd arranged to do on alternate Thursdays; they worked together, then had a hot chocolate in the hospital canteen while they waited for Nate to finish his shift.

'School's asked me to do a photo diary for their website,' Caitlin told her proudly.

'Good idea. Maybe you could do an article for the hospital website, too,' Erin suggested. 'I could ask the PR team for you, if you like.'

'I know you're too young to be thinking about that sort of thing now, but it'll look great on your CV. Go for it,' Ed added with a smile. 'Right. Come and see these plants with me, and you can ask me whatever you like about why I've chosen those particular plants for those particular locations.'

Caitlin beamed at him and grabbed her notebook.

Nate sent Erin another text that evening.

Roses are red, violets are blue, my daughter's smiling, it's all down to you.

Not just me, she texted back. You have a lot to do with it. And Caitlin herself.

We'll agree to disagree, Nate said, though you'll admit I'm right eventually.

Yeah, yeah. See you for breakfast tomorrow.

He'd said that she made him feel like a teenager again—and she understood what he meant. That breathless excitement, that sense of wonder and expectation and hope. Her own teenage years had been much darker, but maybe he could bring that lightness back to her life.

Though doubts stomped through her all the way to the café, the following morning. What if he'd changed his mind and didn't turn up? Or, worse still, if he did turn up and then told her he didn't want to see her as more than a colleague in future? Or what if she really messed this up, the way she'd messed up all her past relationships?

But when Erin walked into the café Nate was already there, waiting for her in one of the booths and skimming through the menu. He looked up and smiled at her and her heart skipped a beat. If he could be brave enough to turn up simply because he wanted to date her, then she could be brave, too. So she walked up to him, kissed him lightly on the mouth and slid into the booth opposite him. 'Good morning, Mr Townsend.'

'Roses are red, violets are blue, you look beautiful... and you just kissed me, so I can't think of a rhyme,' he finished.

'That's incredibly feeble, Nate,' she said, laughing. 'I know you can do better than that.'

'All the words fell out of my head, the moment you walked into the room,' he said. 'I told you that you make me feel like a teenager.'

'Hmm.' She smiled, and he handed the menu to her.

'My treat. Whatever you want.'

'Thank you.' When the waitress came over, she ordered eggs Florentine, a skinny cappuccino and a glass of water.

'The hollandaise sauce cancels out the healthiness of the spinach, you know,' he teased.

She laughed. 'I don't care. It's my favourite breakfast ever.'

'Bacon sandwich with tomato ketchup all the way for me,' he said with a smile.

'Me, hunter,' she teased back.

And then, once their breakfast arrived, the conversation stalled.

'This is ridiculous,' Nate said. 'We've worked together for a couple of months. We've been out together with Caitlin a couple of times. We know we can talk for hours because we've already done that. So why do I not have a clue what to say to you right now? Why do I feel as if a toddler has better social skills than I do?'

'Because this is different,' she said. 'It's a proper date. We know the rules at work, and when we've gone out with Caitlin. Whereas dating...'

'It's all new stuff we have to negotiate,' he agreed. 'Risky.'

'Yeah. I haven't dated in a while. I can't quite remember how to behave,' she admitted.

'I made a real mess of my last relationship,' he said. 'So that makes two of us.' He reached across the table and squeezed her hand. 'Didn't we agree earlier that there weren't any rules? That we were just going to take it as it comes?'

'We're just not very good at actually doing that,' she said.

He laughed. 'I guess. Maybe we ought to pretend we're at work.'

'Just not discussing our patients,' she agreed.

Weirdly, admitting their doubts was the thing that made the atmosphere between them easy again, and she found herself relaxing with him until it was time for them to leave for the hospital.

He paid the bill, then walked outside the café hand in hand with her. 'I take it we're going to the ward separately?'

'Indeed we are.'

He kissed her lightly. 'I wish we weren't at work so

we could spend the day together and do something. I want to date you properly, Erin.'

'We agreed it'd be an unconventional courtship,' she reminded him, 'and that's fine. We'll cope.' She kissed him briefly. 'I'll see you at work.'

Again they managed to behave as if they were colleagues only, when they were at the hospital; though when they were in a meeting together Nate pressed his foot lightly against Erin's under the table. She glanced at him and the sheer desire in his eyes made her catch her breath.

Could this work out?

Could they really have it all?

Or was she setting herself up for the biggest fall ever?

'Oh, you are joking.' Nate groaned when he walked onto the ward on Monday morning and saw the newspaper article pinned up on the notice board. *'Local hero builds Barney's new back'*, said the headline. And there was a photograph of Nate, in a suit, looking serious. 'Where did this come from?' he asked.

'Local paper,' Ella, the receptionist, told him with a smile. 'You're famous.'

'But I didn't talk to anyone—or give anyone a photo.'

'Must've been the hospital PR team who gave everything to them,' she said. 'But it's a good photo. Of course, this means that you're now our official departmental pin-up.'

Nate groaned again. 'I am so not a pin-up. Or a hero. I'm just a surgeon—part of the team, like everybody else.'

He just about managed to live down all the ribbing at work; but when he went to pick up Caitlin from his mother's house, she waved the article at him. 'Gran found this today,' she said. 'You're in the paper, Dad!'

He sighed. 'Just ignore the headlines, Cait. I'm not a hero. I'm simply one part of a big team who fixed Barney's back. I just did my job. It's what I trained to do.'

'It's still impressive,' his mother said. 'That photograph of that poor man's X-ray—it looked more like a jigsaw puzzle than a spine. There aren't many people who can do what you do, Nathaniel.'

'Hmm,' he said, rolling his eyes. 'It's my job, that's all.'

He thought that was the end of it until Ella from their reception desk patched a phone call through to his office on Thursday afternoon.

'Dr Townsend? I'm sorry to bother you at work. It's Jenny Olland, Caitlin's form tutor.'

Nate went cold. 'Is she all right?'

'She's absolutely fine,' Jenny reassured him. 'She's settled in a lot better now. No, I'm calling you because I'm also her Personal Development teacher. I gave my students an essay to write, this week, on the subject of "my hero", and Caitlin wrote hers on you.'

'On me?' Nate was so shocked that if he hadn't already been sitting down he would've fallen over.

'Yes. She included the article about you from the local paper. And I was thinking—we like to have a range of people coming in to school to talk to our students. I think they'd find you inspiring. Would you be able to come in and give our students a talk about your job at one of the assemblies?'

Nate was still trying to get his head round the fact that Caitlin had written an essay about her hero—and it was about *him*. 'I, um—do you mind if I talk it over with Caitlin first?' He needed to be sure that she was comfortable with the idea before he agreed. The last thing he wanted to do was to ruin all the progress they'd made by embarrassing her and making her feel awkward in front of her new friends.

'Of course, Dr Townsend.'

'I'll call you tomorrow,' he promised.

When he replaced the receiver, he stared at his computer screen, not seeing the X-rays or his patient's notes. He couldn't quite believe that phone call had just happened.

Then he was aware that someone was knocking on his open door. He looked up to see Erin standing there.

'Are you OK, Nate?' she asked.

'I… No, not really,' he admitted. 'That was Caitlin's form tutor.'

Erin frowned and came over to his desk. 'Oh, dear. Is there a problem at school? Anything I can do to help?'

He explained what had just happened, and she reached over to squeeze his hand. 'That's *brilliant*. I'm so pleased.'

'I can't quite get my head round it,' he said.

'Be proud,' she advised.

'I am. And thrilled. And shocked. And I never thought…' His voice tailed off and he shook his head, all out of words to describe how he felt right then.

'I know,' she said softly. 'But you deserve it. You've put the effort in with her. What are you going to do?'

'Talk to her about it,' he said. 'If she wants me to do it, I will—if she doesn't, I'll make up an excuse.'

'Good plan,' she said.

'Sorry, did you want me for something?' he asked.

'No. I was just passing and saw that you looked a bit shocked,' she said. 'But, now you come to mention it…' She lowered her voice. 'How about breakfast, to-morrow? My treat?'

Odd how planning a secret date with her made his heart beat faster. And Nate was pretty sure it was the same for her, given that her eyes were almost black in-stead of grey right now. 'Same time, same place?' he suggested, keeping his voice equally low.

'Perfect,' she said. 'Catch you later. Let me know how it goes with Caitlin.'

He caught up with his daughter later that afternoon in the sensory garden, during her weekly roster session.

'You planted that whole section?' he asked.

She nodded. 'I think I did it right. Nola—she's the one in charge today—is going to come and have a look at it in a minute and let me know if it's OK.'

'It looks good to me,' he said. 'By the way, Miss Olland rang me today. She told me about your essay.'

Caitlin went pink and stared at the ground. 'Oh.'

'I can't believe you wrote that essay about me.'

She bit her lip, looking anxious. 'Did I do wrong?'

'No.' The lump in his throat was so big that it al-most blocked his words. 'I'm thrilled that you did that—though I did tell you I'm not a hero, Caitlin. I'm just doing my job here and I'm trying to be the best dad to you I can be, and we both know I'm still not very good at it.'

She shuffled her feet and looked awkward.

'Miss Olland asked me to come in and talk to the school about my job.'

Her eyes widened. 'What did you say?'

'That I'd check with you first,' he said. 'If you want me to come in and do the talk, I'll do it. But if it'll be embarrassing to have me at school, then I'll tell them I'm sorry, I can't make it due to pressure of work. I said I'd give her an answer tomorrow, so think about what you'd rather I do.'

'OK.'

'Would you, um, like to come in and see where I work?' he asked.

Her smile almost broke his heart. 'Yes—what, now?'

'When you've finished here.'

'I'm finished, if Nola says it's OK. I just need to check with her and wash my hands.'

They went in search of Nola, who inspected Caitlin's work and pronounced it first class. Nate showed his daughter to the nearest washroom and waited outside until she was ready. Then he took her up to see the theatre where he operated, and finally the ward, introducing her to his colleagues who were on duty.

'You've got a photo of me on your desk,' she said when he showed her his office.

'Well—yes. Do you mind?' he asked.

'No. I...' She swallowed and shook her head. 'It's nothing.'

'Tell me.'

She looked away. 'Mum said you never really wanted me,' she said. 'That's why I didn't want to come and live with you.'

He could've shaken Steph for that until her teeth rattled. How mean was it to use their child to score points off him? But Steph wasn't the important one here; Caitlin was. He wrapped his arms round her and hugged her fiercely. 'Of course I wanted you, Cait! I admit, we didn't plan to have you, but I was so thrilled when I found out I was going to be a dad. I went to every single scan and every single antenatal class with your mother—I changed my shifts at work to make sure I was there. I know your mum and I didn't manage to make it work, and I probably should have moved to Devon and changed my specialty so I could see more of you.'

'But then you wouldn't have been able to fix people like you do now.'

'True, but you're the one who paid the price of me putting my job first, and I regret that so much. I wanted to have a good job so I could support you and your mum—but really you needed me to be around more, not just a voice on the phone or a face on a video call, or someone you saw for just a couple of days at a time. I thought I was doing the right thing, though now I know I wasn't and I'm so sorry that I got it wrong. I've still got a lot to learn about being a dad but, Cait, I'm really glad you're living with me now and I'm so proud of you.'

She hugged him back. 'I'm glad I'm living with you, too.'

Nate felt as if his whole world had just turned full Technicolor™. And he knew it was all thanks to Erin that Caitlin finally seemed to have accepted him.

Erin.

His secret date.

Would Caitlin accept her as more than just a friend?

But it was way too soon to ask that kind of question. He'd promised that he wouldn't rush Erin and the same was true of his daughter, too. So he'd just have to take things slowly. Even though he was pretty sure where his feelings were going.

Erin was waiting for him in the café, the next morning.

'I think we should adopt this one as "our" booth,' he said, sliding in opposite her.

'Sounds good to me.' She smiled at him, and his heart felt as if it had just done a triple somersault.

'Hey. Good morning.' He leaned over the table to kiss her; and he kept his hand entwined with hers as they looked through the menu and argued over the merit of pancakes versus croissants.

'So what did Caitlin think about you doing a talk at school?' Erin asked when their breakfast arrived.

'She's thinking about it,' he said. 'I have a feeling she's probably going to talk to her friends about it today.'

'Good idea,' Erin said. 'And it's great that she's settling in better.'

'I know she really enjoys her alternate Thursdays when she works with you on the sensory garden,' he said.

'Me, too. She's a nice kid. And I'm not just saying it because she's yours.'

'She likes you,' Nate said.

Erin smiled. 'It's mutual. And it's important to have an adult friend who can listen to you.' She wrinkled her nose. 'Sorry. I'm overcompensating. I guess it comes of growing up with parents who didn't connect with me,' she said.

He shook his head. 'Don't ever change, Erin. I like you exactly as you are.'

'Same goes for you,' she said. 'Now you've got over being a grumpy old man about the garden.'

'Yeah, yeah.' He liked the way she teased him, too, and stopped him being over-serious.

And all too soon it was time for them to leave for work. He'd definitely have to figure out a way to snatch more time with her, he thought. He'd just need to be a little more creative.

Nate did the talk at Caitlin's school assembly the following Wednesday, having asked permission of some of his patients to use their X-rays as examples and taking along a model of a spine.

He was surprised by how much he enjoyed talking to Caitlin's year group—especially when he'd finished the talk and threw the floor open to questions.

'So people who've been paralysed—can you do all that robotic stuff to make them walk again?' one of the children asked.

Nate knew exactly what the boy was talking about; the case had hit the headlines in some of the national papers recently. 'We don't do that in our hospital at the moment, and I'm a spinal surgeon rather than a neurosurgeon,' he explained. 'But there's some research in America where they've been working on a kind of neural bypass, so the neurosurgeons can transmit signals from someone's brain to electrodes in their knees.'

'Making them into a human robot?' the boy asked. 'A cyborg?'

'Sort of,' Nate said with a smile. 'It's especially amazing because the nerves of the spinal cord can't regenerate. In the research report I read, the patient needed support from a harness and a walking frame to stop him falling, but he did actually manage to walk on his own—after years of being paralysed. It gives a lot of hope for people in the future.'

'The paper said you're a hero and you built that man a metal spine,' one of the girls said.

'I built him a kind of metal scaffold around his spine so it can heal without any pressure on it and so he doesn't have to stay lying down until the fractures heal,' Nate explained. 'And what the paper forgot to say was that I'm only one part of the team. Everyone's important in Theatre, from the anaesthetist to the nurses, and without them I couldn't do any operations. As far as I'm concerned, I'm not a hero. I'm part of a team.'

'So being a surgeon—does that take longer than being a normal doctor?' another asked.

Nate nodded. 'Once you've done your degree and your two foundation years, you need to keep studying for another set of exams. It takes a lot of dedication and sometimes you have to make sacrifices—and so does your family. But it means you can make a real difference to people's lives and I can't think of any other job I'd rather do.'

'Even though there's a lot of blood?' one of the children asked.

Nate grinned. 'Yeah. You get used to that bit fairly early on.'

At the end of the assembly, he said goodbye to the children and the teachers and headed back to the hospital. Erin was in clinic all morning so he didn't get to see her until lunchtime, when they grabbed some sandwiches from the kiosk outside the canteen and headed to the park.

'So how did your talk go?' she asked.

'It was good,' he said. 'Some of the boys were really interested in the robotics stuff.'

'The neural bypass and electrodes in the knees?' she asked, looking wistful. 'Yeah. If we ever get a chance to do a research project like that...'

'Mikey?' he asked softly.

'If I could help my brother walk again, and give him back everything I took away...' She swallowed. 'Yeah.'

'Everything the accident took away,' he corrected, and twined his fingers through hers. 'And, from what you told me, he already lives his life to the full. He just got that promotion, he's getting married and he and his fiancée have been accepted onto the IVF programme.'

'Which is all good stuff, I know.'

'He's forgiven you. Why can't you forgive yourself?' Nate asked.

'Habit, maybe. I'll try harder,' she said lightly. She looked at him. 'I hate to remind you, but we're in the park opposite the hospital. We could see someone we know, any second now.'

Regretfully, he disentangled his hand from hers. 'Yeah. Sorry. Right now I really, really want to kiss you. But you're right. This is too public.'

'Later,' she promised.

'I'll hold you to that, Dr Leyton,' he said.

And funny how even the idea of kissing her made the day feel that much brighter.

He's forgiven you. Why can't you forgive yourself?

Erin had brushed it aside when Nate had said it, but she thought about it all evening. Was she using her guilt as an excuse, so she didn't have to risk trusting someone—or letting someone trust her?

Yet she was letting Caitlin trust her.

And Nate trusted her with his daughter.

If they could trust her, then surely she could trust herself not to mess this up and let them both down?

But she wasn't the only one to think about in this relationship. There was Nate. And Caitlin. Both of them were vulnerable, in different ways. Caitlin saw her as a friend—but would she be able to accept Erin as Nate's girlfriend? Especially since her mother's new husband had rejected her; and Caitlin had told Erin privately that her dad's ex-girlfriend had made her feel as if she was a nuisance and in the way.

Then again, Caitlin knew that Erin had been in her shoes as a teen, and would never put anyone else in that position. And after those first couple of outings, Erin had encouraged Nate to take Caitlin out on his own, using work as an excuse not to join them—it was important that the father-daughter bond didn't rely on someone else being the glue.

Erin blew out a breath. There were no easy answers. For now, she'd take each day as it came and just enjoy her stolen moments with Nate.

CHAPTER EIGHT

On Wednesday, Joe Norton called up to Erin. 'We've got a patient coming in with a spinal cord injury, in about ten minutes. The paramedics say that she's bradycardic, but her blood pressure's through the roof. We could really do with an expert opinion.'

'Sure—I'll come down. Would the spinal injury be T6 or above?' Erin asked. 'And the injury was less than a year ago?'

'I'll check the file. Yes, T5 and six months ago,' Joe confirmed. 'How did you know?'

'Because it sounds to me like autonomic dysreflexia,' she explained. 'I'll come down.'

'Everything OK?' Nate asked as she put the phone down.

'Emergency department—sounds like a patient with AD,' she said.

He smiled at her. 'Your side of things, then, not mine—so you don't need me to join you.'

'Not this time,' she said with a smile. 'See you later.'

By the time she'd gone down to the emergency department and explained about the condition to Joe Norton, the patient had been brought in.

'Kiki Lomax, aged thirty-five,' Doug, the paramedic, explained. 'Her blood pressure's high, she's got a pounding headache on both sides, her chest feels tight and her heart rate's on the low side. I've given her medication for her blood pressure, loosened her clothing and kept her sitting up.'

'Exactly the right stuff,' Erin said with a smile. 'Thanks, Doug. Kiki, hello—I remember when you first came in to the spinal unit,' Erin added. 'I don't know if you remember me, but I'm Erin Leyton.'

'Yes, I remember you,' Kiki said.

'How are you feeling, apart from the headache and the tightness in your chest?' Erin asked.

'Sweaty and hot on my top half, but cold on my lower half,' Kiki said.

'I had a feeling you were going to say that. You have something called autonomic dysreflexia. It happens quite often to someone with your kind of injury, and we can fix it,' Erin reassured her.

'Autonomic dys…?' Kiki frowned.

'Dysreflexia,' Erin repeated. 'Or AD for short. Your autonomic system is part of your nervous system. It's the bit that regulates your blood pressure, breathing and digestion. What happens is that something below the level of your injury is irritating your system and sending messages through your nerves up to your spinal cord. The messages travel upwards until they reach the site of your injury, and that's where they get blocked. That starts off a reflex from your nervous system that narrows your blood vessels and makes your blood pressure rise. The receptors in your heart and blood vessels send a message to your brain to tell it what's going on, and your brain sends a message to make your heart beat slow down a bit—but it can't send messages below the site of your injury, so it can't regulate your blood pressure.'

'So what made it happen?' Kiki asked.

'Often it's a problem with your bladder that causes AD—you might have a urinary tract infection, which means your bladder's overfull,' Erin said. 'Would you mind if I examine you?'

'Sure,' Kiki said.

'Joe, I'd like you to keep monitoring Kiki's blood pressure, please, if that's OK,' Erin said.

'Yes, of course,' Joe said.

Erin examined her patient swiftly. As she'd expected, Kiki's skin was flushed and sweating above the level of her injury, but pale and with goose bumps below. But Kiki's bowel and bladder both appeared normal, with no distension.

'Your bowel and bladder both seem fine,' Erin said. 'I'd like to check out if you have any bruising or a pressure sore, because that might be a clue to what's irritating your system.'

'Sure,' Kiki said again.

There was no bruising evident—but as soon as Erin removed Kiki's socks she could see the problem. 'You've got an ingrown toenail,' she said.

'I have?' Kiki looked surprised.

'Whoever cuts your toenails for you has been cutting the nail on your big toe a little bit too short, so the skin's folded over your nail and your nail's grown into the skin. I can see that it's red, swollen and tender just here. We can sort that out for you—we'll give you a little bit of local anaesthetic to numb your toe and cut away the edges of the nail, then put a chemical on the edge to stop that bit of the nail from growing back, so you won't get the problem again in future.'

'And that's what's made me feel this terrible and given me that pounding headache? Just an ingrown toenail?' Kiki looked shocked.

'Basically the pain receptors in your toe tried to send a signal to your brain, but it didn't get through and your nervous system reacted badly,' Erin explained.

'Can I get this again?' Kiki asked.

'It's very likely—as I said, the most common cause is if you have a water infection. I've got an information leaflet upstairs that I can give you, and it's a really good idea to keep a record of your blood pressure at home so you can show any medics what your normal baseline is.' Erin smiled at her. 'Once we've sorted out your toe, you'll be feeling better pretty quickly, but we'll keep a check on your blood pressure for a couple of hours before we let you go home again.'

'I'll get the local anaesthetic and sort out Kiki's toe,' Joe said.

'And I'll get you the leaflet,' Erin promised.

'So how was your AD patient?' Nate asked when Erin met him for lunch. 'Was it caused by a water infection?'

'Nope. Ingrown toenail,' Erin said. 'She's doing fine now. I've given her a leaflet about AD, and suggested she keeps a record of her blood pressure so if it happens again she can show the emergency team what's normal for her and flag up what the problem is so they know how to deal with it.'

'You know, it might be worth us doing a training session for the Emergency Department, covering a few of the complications they're likely to come across after our patients leave us,' Nate suggested.

'That's a good idea. We could go and talk to Nick about it.'

'Let's grab him before he goes into an afternoon meeting,' Nate said.

Nick was in his office when they went back onto the unit, so Erin knocked on his open door. 'Can we have a quick word?' she asked.

'I have a meeting in about fifteen minutes,' Nick said, 'so either it has to be really quick, or put something in my diary if you need a bit more time.'

'It'll be quick,' Nate said. 'Basically we want to do a training session with the Emergency Department, to give them an idea of the sort of complications they can come across with spinal patients after they've left us.'

'They had one of our old patients in with AD this morning,' Erin said, 'and we'd like to start with a session on that.'

'Are you talking about joint training sessions?' Nick asked.

'Yes,' Nate confirmed.

'It's good to see both sides of the team working together,' Nick said with a smile. 'By the way, Nate, I've seen your daughter's pieces about the sensory garden on both her school website and the hospital website. They're very good, but I was a bit surprised, given that the last time you discussed the sensory garden with Erin you seemed quite anti the idea.'

Nate laughed and said, 'I backed down. Let's say

women can be persuasive—so, between Caitlin and Dr Leyton here, I didn't stand a chance.'

Erin punched his arm. 'Oh, come on, Nate. You admitted I was right. Or are you looking for another fight?'

'Yeah, yeah. Bring it on,' he teased. 'You missed me more times than you hit me in dodgeball.'

'Dodgeball?' Nick looked at them, his eyes narrowing. 'When did you play dodgeball together? Are you two—well, an item?'

'Absolutely not,' Erin said, at the same time as Nate said, 'You have to be kidding.'

Nick didn't look particularly convinced.

'My daughter came to live with me almost three months ago,' Nate said, 'and Erin here knows way more than I do about how a teenage girl's mind works. And she kindly offered to help when I was making a real mess of things—she took us to the trampoline park and ganged up on with me with Caitlin, playing dodgeball.'

'I was checking out the place to see if it would work as a venue for a team night out, at the same time,' Erin added. 'So everybody wins.'

'Hmm,' Nick said, but at least this time he sounded as if he believed them.

Erin and Nate exchanged a glance. Their first real slip-up. In future they'd need to be a lot more careful about how they acted towards each other on the ward, or the news of their relationship would leak out before they were ready.

'That was a near-miss in Nick's office,' Nate said when they met for breakfast on the Friday morning.

'We need to be careful,' Erin agreed. 'Maybe we should cool it a bit.'

'Too late,' he said, and reached across the table to hold her hand. 'You make me feel hot all over. Even just exchanging a glance with you makes my temperature spike.'

'You're thirty-five, not thirteen,' she reminded him with a grin.

He laughed. 'You missed your cue. You were meant to say that I make you feel hot all over, too.'

'You do,' she admitted.

Nate ate a forkful of his pancake and moaned.

'Was that me or the pancake?' she asked.

'Both.' He loaded his fork and leant across the table. This felt *intimate*. But Erin let him feed her the forkful of pancake, then moaned in bliss.

'Was that me or the pancake?' He echoed her question.

'What do you think?' she teased.

He groaned. 'Play nice.'

'Both,' she said softly. 'I'm having pancakes next time. Cinnamon ones.' She waited a beat. 'But I'd prefer to share them with you somewhere else.'

'There's somewhere that makes better pancakes than this place?'

'Probably not quite as good. But the setting's more… intimate.'

His eyes went very dark. 'Are you suggesting what I think you're suggesting?'

'It involves wrought iron. And interesting lighting.'

He dragged in a breath. 'When Cait decides to visit

Steph, we'll have a few days free.' He paused. 'We could have dinner. And breakfast.'

And in between, she thought; a shiver of pure desire slid down her spine. 'Half term?'

He shook his head. 'Cait already asked. Steph's too busy. Just as she's been too busy every weekend and school holiday since Cait came to live with me. I think she's scared that if Cait goes back to Devon, she'll refuse to come back to London.'

'Do you think that's likely?' Erin asked.

Nate thought about it. 'I hope not. I think she's settled with me. But I can't seem to make Steph see that every time she says she can't make a weekend or what have you, it makes Cait feel as if she's rejecting her.' He sighed. 'Given that I spent too many years putting my job before my daughter, I don't have room to criticise. And I don't want Cait feeling that I'm trying to get rid of her.'

'Then we'll take a rain check on the pancakes. Maybe I can swap a shift or two during the holidays and we can do something fun together instead, to take her mind off it,' Erin said. 'Maybe we could do that locked room thing, and she could bring a friend.'

'That'd be nice,' Nate said. 'Are you sure you don't mind using your annual leave like that?'

'Of course I'm sure.' She squeezed his hand. 'And I get to spend time with you, too.'

'Not like this. Not just the two of us,' he said. 'I won't even be able to hold your hand.'

'That's OK. I can imagine it.' She moistened her lower lip. 'I have a good imagination.'

He groaned. 'And you've just put all sorts of pictures

in my head. How am I supposed to spend the day being a sensible, level-headed surgeon when I want to pick you up and carry you off to some hidden corner and…'

'And?' she prompted. 'What happens next?'

He gave her a slow smile. 'Use your imagination.'

'And now you expect *me* to concentrate?'

'Sensible, level-headed neurologist. Yup.'

'We'll get our time together,' she said softly. 'We just have to be patient. And maybe waiting will be good for both of us.'

They managed to keep things professional at work, but snatched some time together whenever they could—meeting for breakfast on Fridays, and going to the park across the road from the hospital at lunchtime as many times as they thought they could get away with before anyone on the ward started commenting.

'I really want to dance with you,' Nate said one lunchtime. 'You and me in a little nightclub somewhere.'

'Which would mean asking your mum to babysit Caitlin—and what excuse are you going to give them for going out to some mysterious place with some mysterious person?' Erin asked. 'Because you can't say you've suddenly been called into Theatre, not if you're dressed up for a night out.'

'True,' Nate said with a sigh. 'And we're not ready to go public yet.'

They'd have to tell Caitlin, first; and this was still all so new. Plus part of Erin was scared that if they went public, it would be the first step to everything going wrong. 'Soon,' she said.

But Nate had a solution, the next time they walked in

the park. He took a set of earphones from his pocket and plugged it into his phone. 'I've been thinking about it, and this is a nightclub substitute,' he said with a smile. 'I'd much prefer this to be a dimly lit nightclub with a little jazz band playing at midnight, but the best I can do is midday, in the middle of these trees in the park, with music from my phone. One earphone each.'

Erin smiled. 'Very inventive, Mr Townsend.'

'Dance with me, Erin. I want to hold you,' he said softly, opening his arms.

She stepped forward, putting her arms round him, and let him put one of the earphones into her left ear. He put the other earphone into his right ear, then wrapped his arms round her.

'Close your eyes,' he said, 'and pretend we're on a real dance floor.'

She recognised the song as soon as the piano started playing; he'd picked one of the most romantic songs she knew. And the lyrics brought tears to her eyes. Had he chosen it because it was a nice tune, or because he meant the words and wasn't quite sure how to say them to her?

Did he want to make her happy, and make her dreams come true?

Because she was pretty sure that was how she felt about him, too.

Still with her eyes closed, and her cheek pressed against his, she swayed with him to the music. And when he moved to kiss the corner of her mouth, she moved too so that he could kiss her properly—warm and sweet and poignant.

But then a passing teenager catcalled them.

And Erin remembered where they were: in the park

opposite the hospital. Where anyone they knew could have gone for a lunchtime stroll and seen them.

She pulled away. 'I guess we'd better wait until it's a proper nightclub.'

'I guess,' Nate said, and his eyes were full of longing.

'Next time, the music ought to be "Somewhere" from *West Side Story*,' she said wryly.

He sang the first few bars of the song, and her eyes widened. 'I didn't know you could sing that well. I'm impressed.'

'Don't be. I only know it because it was on a TV talent show programme and Cait loved it.'

She stroked his face. 'You still have a lovely voice. Don't do yourself down.'

'We'll get our somewhere. Some day,' he said.

'But for now we need to go back to work,' she said.

'And I can't even hold your hand across the park, because we'll be spotted and the hospital rumour mill will start.' He sighed. 'I guess we were lucky that it was teenagers who saw us dancing together, and not somebody from work.'

'This is hard,' Erin said. 'Half of me wants to go public. And half of me is scared it's going to go wrong.'

'Me, too,' he admitted. 'But Caitlin likes you.'

'As a friend. Being your girlfriend is a different thing,' she said. 'Especially given the way things are with her mum, right now. We can't rock the boat yet. Give it a little more time.'

'I know you're right,' he said. 'But I'm looking forward to our someday.'

'We just have to be inventive,' she said. 'Like your impromptu nightclub.'

* * *

Later in the week, Erin texted Nate.

How do you feel about some late-night cinema?

Love to, but I can't leave Cait on her own, he replied.

You don't have to. Welcome to the twenty-first century.

He called her. 'Explain.'

'We use technology,' she said. 'We can watch a film together, but we'll be in different houses.'

'Ah—using laptops,' he said, catching on quickly, 'so we're watching the same films.'

'And we can use video calling at the same time, so we can talk to each other during the film.'

'It isn't quite the same as sitting in the back row, holding hands,' he pointed out.

'Cinema substitute. Like your nightclub,' she said.

'Got you.'

They arranged to watch a film together at eleven p.m. that Sunday night.

'So, just to get this straight,' Nate said on screen, 'we're both sitting on the sofa and we're going to watch the same film.'

'Snuggled up with a throw,' Erin said. 'Which is the nearest we get to snuggling up with each other.'

'No throw, here. Would a cushion be an acceptable substitute?'

She laughed. 'Squishy in the middle? Yeah.'

Being warm and snuggly under a throw wasn't really a good substitute for curling up on the sofa together, but until they were ready to go public it was the best they could do.

'This is a bit like *Pillow Talk*,' Nate said.

'Hardly,' she scoffed. 'Apart from the fact we're not using a shared phone line and I know who you are instead of thinking you're this lovely, charming stranger, I'm not a repressed interior decorator. Plus you don't have a string of floozies—or do you?'

'No.' He groaned. 'Never argue films with someone who clearly had a misspent yout—' He stopped abruptly, looking horrified. 'Sorry. I didn't mean that.'

'I know,' she said, equally softly. 'Actually, that's when I used to watch loads of films, day and night—and that was what got me through the worst bits. I wasn't picky about it; I just watched whatever was on satellite TV, so I saw everything from nineteen-thirties horror films through to musicals and action films.'

'I'm glad you had something to help.' He sighed. 'I wish I was with you right now, Erin. I really want to hold you.'

'Me, too—but at least we have video calling. If we'd been back in the fifties, with *Pillow Talk*, you're right—we would've been forced to use a party telephone line and all the neighbours would've been listening in to our conversation.'

'Yeah.'

'Now stop worrying about it and we'll watch the film together.'

It was an old one but it was one of Erin's favourite romcoms. She loved the scene where the hero declared himself at midnight on New Year's Eve, but it made her wonder: would she and Nate ever be able to declare how they felt to each other?

As if he'd picked up on her wistfulness, he said, 'Maybe we can snatch a day's annual leave and spend a day together—dating like normal people.'

'Sounds good,' she said.

'How does next Friday sound? So, instead of having breakfast before work, we actually get to go somewhere together?'

'Sounds perfect,' she said. 'Provided we can arrange the off-duty, it's a date.'

'Our first. Well, first proper date,' he amended.

And maybe one day they'd have a proper cinema date, holding hands in the back row. 'I'm looking forward to it,' she said. 'Night, Nate. Sweet dreams.'

'You, too,' he said, and blew her a kiss.

CHAPTER NINE

THE OFF-DUTY WORKED out just fine; so Nate and Erin had Friday off.

A whole day to spend together. Doing whatever they wanted. Far enough away from the hospital or anyone who knew them so they could hold hands and kiss in public without being spotted.

A normal date.

But, even though Nate had been longing for this, guilt nagged at him. He was supposed to be spending his time off with his daughter—and yet here he was, putting himself first.

Clearly the guilt showed in his face, because Erin raised an eyebrow when she saw him at the Tube™ station. 'Problem?'

'Not exactly,' he hedged.

'Spill,' she said.

The woman who didn't pull her punches. Who told things exactly like they were. Who expected the same from him. 'I feel pretty guilty about this,' he admitted.

'Because you ought to be saving your days off to spend with Caitlin?' she asked.

Typical Erin to get straight to the root of the problem. 'Yes.'

'Single parents are allowed to have a life of their own, too, you know. It's fine,' she said softly, and brushed her mouth against his.

Desire spun through him. Everything about this woman attracted him. Not just the way she looked: he liked her intelligence, her kindness, her calmness. And he was more than halfway to being head over heels in love with her. Not that he was going to tell her. It was still relatively early days, and he knew she had just as much emotional baggage to deal with as he did. The last thing he wanted to do was to scare her away by being too intense.

'I guess you're right,' he said instead.

She gave him a clenched-fist salute and a seriously sassy grin. 'Yes. The man admits it.'

He laughed, then, and tangled his fingers through hers. 'Maybe we should think about telling Caitlin about us.'

'Do you think she'll be OK about it?'

'I don't know how she'll react,' he admitted. 'Though I do know she likes you. A lot,' he added. 'She's always talking about you. In a nice way.'

'I like her, too. A lot.'

He coughed.

She grinned. 'Are you fishing for compliments, Mr Townsend?'

'Yup. Shamelessly.'

She kissed him again. 'I like you, too. A lot.'

'Ditto.'

She narrowed her eyes at him. 'Not good enough.'

'I like you a lot,' he said. 'More than I've liked any-one for a very long time.'

'Ditto,' she said.

'If I said to you that that wasn't good enough, you'd just laugh at me.'

'Yup.' She smiled. 'Stop worrying, Nate. And let's wait a little longer before we tell Caitlin. Let's think about the best way to tell her so she knows that, whatever happens between you and me, you'll always love her and she'll always be friends with me.'

'Yes. It's finding the right words that's the problem.'

'They'll be there when the time's right,' she said. 'That's one of Rachel's sayings.'

'Along with "Never trouble trouble, till trouble troubles you",' he said. 'I remember you telling me once.' He drew her closer to him. 'I can't believe we're actually going on a proper date.'

'Are you saying our breakfasts and our sneaky walks in the park at lunchtime and our cinema session using video calling weren't proper dates?' she teased.

He laughed. 'You know what I mean. We're actually doing something that normal couples do.'

'We're doing OK,' she said. 'Unconventional's working for us.'

'True.'

They headed for the British Museum where he'd booked tickets for the exhibition they both wanted to see, and wandered hand in hand round the displays.

'Oh, I love this. It's like a boar's head,' Erin said, stopping by one case. She read the display notes quickly. 'It's a carnyx—an ancient war-horn from Scotland, used to terrify their enemies. And look—you can listen to someone playing a replica.' She picked up the headphones and pressed the buttons. 'Yep. I think this would scare me, hearing this booming across the glens.'

Nate didn't think that anything would scare Erin. She faced things head-on. But he dutifully listened to the recording of the carnyx.

Erin was delighted by the intricate patterns in the shields and the stonework. When they wandered over to the display of golden torcs, he looked at her. 'I can imagine you wearing one of those. A Celtic warrior queen.'

'Shouldn't a Celtic warrior queen have red hair?'

'Yours is the colour of ripe corn—and I love these wild curls.' He twined the end of one soft curl round his finger. 'I understand why you have to wear it tied back at work, but I'd love to see your hair loose some time.'

She wrinkled her nose. 'It's not great, you know. It just goes mad and frizzy.'

He wanted to make the rest of her feel mad and frizzy, too—but he knew he needed to take things at her pace. 'You'd still look beautiful wearing one of these torcs. Wise and regal, then.'

She bowed her head in acknowledgement. 'Why, thank you.'

When they reached the end of the exhibition, she took him in search of the Lewis Chessmen. 'I've always loved these. Mikey bought me a full-sized replica set for my twenty-first birthday.'

'I didn't know you played chess.'

'I learned after Mikey's accident. It helped both of us, I think.'

'Your brother sounds like an amazing guy.'

'He is.' She paused. 'Maybe you could meet him some time.'

'Have you told him about me?'

She nodded.

'And?'

'He likes the sound of you—but he also knows you're not going to meet him and Louisa, his fiancée, until I'm ready.'

Was she ready to introduce him to her closest family? Nate wondered. And he hadn't asked Erin to meet anyone in his family other than Caitlin. Maybe it was time to introduce her to his mother—though he was pretty sure that Sara had worked out the situation for herself already.

As if Erin guessed what he was thinking, she said softly, 'I don't think we're quite ready to go public yet.'

Maybe she was right. They still didn't have the right words.

'Let's go and have lunch,' she suggested.

'Good idea.' He let her switch the subject and chatter about museums while they ate, and he was about to order coffee when she said, 'How about coffee at my place?'

'I'd like that. Thanks.'

They walked hand in hand from the Tube™ station back to Erin's flat. When she'd made coffee, she sat down next to him on the sofa and Nate scooped her onto his lap. 'Is this OK?' he checked, wanting to be close to her but wanting to keep things at a pace where she was comfortable.

'Very OK.' She smiled and kissed him.

The touch of her mouth against his made him feel as if all his senses had gone into overdrive. He wrapped his arms round her and kissed her back; but when he broke the kiss, he realised that his hands had slid underneath the hem of her top. Too much, too soon.

'Sorry.' He moved his hands away, even though he missed the warmth and smoothness of her skin against his palms.

She stroked his face. 'I wasn't saying no, Nate.'

He went very still. Was she suggesting…?

'But you're right about something,' she continued. 'My sofa isn't a good place to do this.'

No, he was definitely jumping the gun. Clearly she wanted him to stop.

He was about to scoop her back off his lap when she said quietly, 'Maybe we need to move to my bedroom.'

He stared at her, his heart pounding. 'Are you saying…?'

She nodded.

'Are you sure about this?' he checked.

'I'm sure.' Her eyes looked huge and full of sincerity. 'Completely sure.'

'But—' His throat dried. 'I don't have any protection with me.'

'I do.'

His surprise must have shown on his face because she said, 'I bought condoms last night.'

So she'd planned this? For a moment, he couldn't breathe. Couldn't think straight. Then he kissed her, very gently. 'Just so you know,' he said, 'if you change your mind at any point, that's totally fine. If you need me to stop at any point, even if you think it's too late, just tell me and I'll stop immediately.'

Her eyes filmed with tears. 'Thank you. I know you're not Andrew and I trust you. But it's nice that you…' Her breath caught. 'That you understand.'

'I do. And you have no idea how good it makes me

feel that you trust me. Just as I trust you.' He wanted to say a different word there, but he didn't want to push her. To rush her. To scare her away. 'Make love with me, Erin.'

'What a very good idea, Mr Townsend.' She slid off his lap and he stood up, letting her lead him to her room.

The walls were cream, the curtains were burgundy— but best of all was the wide double bed with fairy lights wound round the wrought-iron frame.

'Now I know what you meant about interesting lighting. That's *so* girly,' he said with a grin.

'Funny you should say that, with me being a girl.'

'You're not a girl,' he corrected. 'You're all woman. And you're gorgeous, inside and out.'

She blushed. 'Nice line.'

'No line. It's how I feel.' His gaze held hers. 'I already told you, I like you a lot.'

'Ditto.'

'And any time you need me to stop,' he repeated, 'we stop.'

'No stopping,' she said, went over to the window and closed the curtains. Then she switched on the fairy lights. 'Still think they're girly?'

'Yup. But they're sexy, too.' He waited a beat. 'Like you.'

'Well, hey.' She brushed her mouth against his, then undid the top button of his shirt.

Then he realised that her fingers were actually shaking.

He drew her hands to his mouth and kissed her fingers. 'You OK?'

'Nervous,' she admitted.

'Me, too.' He kissed the tip of her nose. 'But this is you and me. It's going to be just fine.'

For a moment, she looked unsure. But then she lifted her chin and finished unbuttoning his shirt. She tugged the soft cotton free from the waistband of his trousers, then slid the garment from his shoulders. 'Nice pecs, Mr Townsend.'

'Why, thank you, Dr Leyton. I value your personal opinion as much as your professional opinion.' He held her gaze. 'My turn?'

'I think so.' She lifted her arms to make it easier for him to remove her top.

He drew the tip of his forefinger around the lacy outline of her bra. 'Your skin's so soft, Erin.' And touching wasn't enough. He dipped his head and kissed all along the line of her collarbone. When she caught her breath, he held back again. 'OK?' he checked.

'Very OK,' she said. Her voice was shaky, and he really wasn't sure about this until she added, 'I'm kind of looking forward to those clever surgeon's hands touching me.'

'Oh, are you, now?' He stole another kiss, and removed her bra one-handedly. 'Clever enough for you?'

'Showing off, a tad,' she said, and removed his trousers.

The touch of her fingers against his skin sent desire lancing through him. 'How about this?' he asked, and removed her jeans, stroking every centimetre of skin he uncovered.

'Better,' she said, and he was gratified to hear the huskiness in her voice.

He kissed her lightly. 'Protection,' he said. 'And then I'm all yours. Do what you will with me.'

She took a packet of condoms from her bedside drawer and handed it to him.

'I think,' he said, 'I'd like to see how clever those neurologist's hands of yours are.'

'Hmm,' she said. 'That sounds like a challenge.'

'It is.'

He wasn't sure which of them removed the last bits of each other's clothing, but then he'd pushed her duvet aside and was lying against her pillows, and she was kneeling beside him.

He took a condom from the packet and handed it to her. 'You're in control,' he said, and grasped the wrought-iron headboard between the fairy lights.

She brushed her mouth against his. 'Thank you. For understanding.'

'Any time.' And how he loved her for being brave enough to get past the vulnerability. For being brave enough to trust him.

She ripped open the foil packet and eased the condom over his penis. And then she straddled him. When she slid her hand round his shaft and positioned him against her entrance, he had to grip the headboard that little bit more tightly. And then slowly, gently, she lowered herself onto him.

He desperately wanted to wrap his arms round her and hold her close, but he needed her to trust him completely. So he lay still, letting her set the pace. And he was rewarded by seeing the confidence grow in her face as she moved over him.

Just as he felt his climax starting to bubble through

him, she peeled his fingers off the headboard; in response, he sat up and wrapped his arms round her, pushing deep into her at the same time.

She jammed her mouth over his, and he felt her body surge against his, pushing him into his own climax.

And he'd never, ever had such a feeling of sweetness before.

After he'd dealt with the condom, he climbed back into bed beside her, wrapped her in his arms and pulled the duvet over them.

'Erin. I lo—'

Before he could finish the sentence, she pressed her forefinger against his lips. 'Don't say it, Nate.'

Because she didn't feel the same, and she didn't want to let him down by admitting it?

As if she guessed what he was thinking, she said, 'Because it's too soon, not because I don't feel the same way about you. Those particular words... I don't really trust them.'

The shadow of her ex. Again.

And it would take time before he could melt that particular shadow away. He needed to take it slowly. 'OK. I understand,' he said.

'For now, let's just be,' she said.

It felt good, lying there with her in his arms. Nothing to think about or worry about except each other.

Though he couldn't help noticing the time.

'Erin. I really don't want to go, but I need to pick Caitlin up—'

'I know. It's OK.'

'One day,' he said softly, 'we'll get to spend the night together.'

She chuckled. 'I'm glad you're a better surgeon than you are when it comes to words. Day and night are two separate things, you know.'

'They won't be,' he said. 'Because I intend to make you lose track of time.'

'I'll take that as a promise,' she said, and kissed him lightly. 'You'd better go, or you'll get stuck in traffic. But thank you for today. For—well, being understanding.'

Which told him that either the men she'd dated since her ex hadn't been understanding, or she hadn't trusted them enough to get as far as telling them what had happened to her. 'Thank *you*,' he said. 'For trusting me.'

'I'm older and wiser and a better judge of character, now,' she said. 'And I like you, Nate Townsend. I like you a whole lot.'

And one day, he hoped, she'd let herself love him.

He climbed out of bed and started to get dressed. When she sat up, he shook his head. 'Stay there. You look comfortable. And cute.'

'But—'

'I can see myself out,' he said. 'And I guess I'll see you tomorrow.'

'You can count on that.'

He finished dressing, then gave her a lingering kiss goodbye. 'One day,' he said softly. 'Keep that in mind.'

'I will,' she promised.

CHAPTER TEN

ERIN LAY CURLED in her bed, all warm and cosy and totally replete.

Nate had been a considerate lover, and she really appreciated the fact that he'd been so careful with her. She had a pretty good idea how he felt about her, now—though she'd stopped him saying it out loud, because the words scared her stupid. In her experience, love didn't work out, and she really wanted this to work out. Nate was important to her and so was Caitlin.

But what if it all went wrong, the way it usually did for her relationships? It wasn't just her feelings at stake any more. Maybe she should back off before everyone ended up hurt…

On Monday morning, Erin was busy in clinic. 'So tell me about your symptoms,' she said to the worried-looking woman in front of her.

'I've been getting these weird feelings in my neck for the last couple of weeks,' Harriet said. 'It's kind of like jerking—I can't stop it happening. I saw my doctor and he said I'd probably just slept awkwardly and it would go away, but it's got worse over the last two weeks so he sent me here.'

Erin had already seen from the notes that Harriet had no previous significant medical history and wasn't on any medication. 'Does anyone in your family have a history of neurological illness?' she asked. 'Anything like epilepsy?'

'Not that I know of,' Harriet said. 'Is that what I've got?'

'I'll need to examine you properly before I can give you a diagnosis,' Erin said, 'so I'm afraid I have a few more questions. Is there any pattern to the movements? Do they stop or get better when you're relaxed? And do you know if you get them in your sleep?'

'There's no real pattern—they just start and I have no idea when it's going to happen or how long it'll go on. Though they seem a bit worse when I'm stressed,' Harriet said, 'which is probably why they're getting more frequent. I get them in my sleep, too. My boyfriend's the one who noticed it first. It woke him up.'

Erin had to damp down the little flare of envy. What would it be like, to wake up in your boyfriend's arms? It was something she'd never done, something she'd never allowed herself to do, because she'd always compartmentalised her relationships.

Would Nate be the one she finally woke up to?

'I'm really scared that there's something really wrong with me,' Harriet said. Then she grimaced. 'Oh, no. It's starting again.'

Erin could see immediately that the muscles in the nape of Harriet's neck were jerking rhythmically, on both sides.

'I'm going to do a full neurological examination,' Erin said, 'and then I'm going to run some tests to find out what's causing the twitching—it's something called myoclonus, which basically means that your muscles contract and relax. It's the same sort of thing as hiccups or if you're dropping off to sleep and suddenly feel a "start", though it's rarer for the muscles in your neck to be affected.'

'Is it serious? Am I going to die?' Harriet asked. 'Is it catching?'

'It's not catching and it's not fatal,' Erin reassured her, 'and actually your doctor was right because with some people it does just disappear.'

'So what causes it?'

'Epilepsy, which is why I asked you if anyone in your family had it,' Erin explained, 'or an infection. Sometimes it happens if someone has a spinal injury or a brain injury—and sometimes it just happens and we don't know why.'

'I haven't had any accidents or banged into anything,' Harriet said. 'So it can't be a brain injury, and my back's fine. And I haven't had any kind of bug.'

'OK. Let me examine you and we'll take it from there,' Erin said. 'I might need to run quite a few tests, and there will be a bit of waiting around, so are you OK to be here all day? Do you want me to call anyone to come and keep you company? Your boyfriend?'

'No. I'll be OK,' Harriet said.

There was nothing unusual in the neurological exam; a routine electroencephalograph, blood tests and an MRI scan all came back clear, too.

'So far, I can't find a physical cause, so I'm going to

give you a needle EMG,' Erin said. 'That stands for an electromyograph. What it means is that I put a needle into your muscles—it sounds much scarier than it is, and it doesn't hurt—and it records the electrical activity of your muscles and plots everything for me on a graph so I can analyse it. I normally use an EMG to help me diagnose the cause of pain in the back or the neck, or to show if there's a nerve compression injury, such as carpal tunnel syndrome.'

But the EMG was clear, too.

'So the good thing is that there isn't a physical injury,' Erin said. 'What I'm going to do is give you some anti-epilepsy medication, and ask you to come back and see me in a fortnight to see how you're getting on. I'm pretty sure the medication will stop the muscle contractions, but if it doesn't then I can try a couple of other treatments. The most important thing is that you don't worry.' She smiled at Harriet. 'Which I know is easier said than done. But you can call me here at any time, and if it gets worse instead of better then come back before your appointment and we'll try something else.'

Over the next couple of weeks, Nate and Erin managed to snatch time together around their shifts, and sneaked in a half day where Nate whisked her back to his house for lunch in bed.

'I'm sure people are going to start to guess about us at work,' he said. 'I have a goofy smile on my face every time I look at you.'

'Me, too,' she said. 'You know you said you wanted to make me feel like a teenager? Mission accomplished.'

'The way I feel about you—I know, I know, you

don't want me to say the words. But I never expected to feel like this about anyone again.' He stroked her face. 'Maybe it's time we went public.'

'We need to tell Caitlin, first,' Erin said. 'If she's OK with it, then we'll go public.'

'So when are we going to tell her?'

'Saturday?' Erin suggested.

'Saturday,' he agreed. 'And we'll plan our strategy over breakfast on Friday.'

'Sounds perfect,' she said.

On Thursday evening, Nate's phone pinged with a text.

'I'll get that for you, Dad,' Caitlin said, before he could tell her that it was fine and to leave it.

She picked up the phone, and because the message was short it was fully visible on the front of his lock screen. 'It's from Erin—she says see you at breakfast.' She paused. 'And there's a kiss.' She stared at him, and was it his own guilty conscience or was there a note of accusation in her voice when she asked, 'Why are you seeing Erin for breakfast?'

'To discuss a patient,' he said swiftly.

'But you'd do that at work, not at home.' She frowned. 'I was talking to Shelby at school about you and she thought Erin was your girlfriend. I said she wasn't, but *are* you dating Erin?'

Stalling for time, he asked, 'Why would I be dating her?'

'Are you seeing her secretly?' Caitlin demanded. 'Because otherwise why would she text you with a kiss on the end?'

Oh, hell. Clearly his expression had confirmed her

worst fears because then Caitlin shook her head, looking hurt and miserable. 'When you and Erin took me to Kew and that locked room place, it wasn't because you wanted to be with me, was it? You just used me as an excuse to date Erin in secret.'

He could definitely tell her that wasn't true. Of course he'd wanted to spend time with his daughter. 'That's not true, Cait, I—'

But it was too late. She was already running upstairs and he heard her bedroom door slam. His heart sinking, he realised that they'd gone right back to how things had been when Caitlin had first come to live with him. He'd just managed to ruin all the progress they'd made.

This was a row he couldn't handle on his own. Caitlin wouldn't believe anything he said. It was way past the time of telling her the truth—and he needed to do that with Erin at his side. Just as they'd originally planned to do.

He grabbed his phone and called her. 'Erin, we've got a problem. Caitlin picked up your text and she's worked everything out for herself. Except she thinks I used her to date you in secret—and she didn't believe me when I said that's not true. I know it's a lot to ask, but could you maybe come over and help me talk to her?'

'Of course I will.' Erin's voice was calm and reassuring, and Nate realised then how much he was panicking. Which was ridiculous. At work, he performed operations that carried a high risk of paralysis for his patients and he was cool, calm and in absolute control. Why couldn't he be like that at home with his daughter?

'Even if she's upset and angry, she might listen to me because she knows I've been in her shoes,' Erin continued. 'I'm on my way now. Go and talk to her—even if it's through a closed door and she doesn't answer you. It'll reassure her that you care.'

He didn't have a clue what to say but he'd wing it. There was no other choice. 'Thanks.'

When he ended the call, he went upstairs and knocked on Caitlin's door. There was no answer, as he'd half expected. But at least she wasn't blasting out music, so she'd be able to hear whatever he said. He took a deep breath. All he could tell her was the truth and open his heart to her.

'Cait, I admit, I am dating Erin, but it's not why I asked her to come out with us. We really were just friends at the beginning, but I've come to see her as more than a friend over the last few weeks. And when I've taken her out with you it's because I want to do things with *you*, Cait—to do things with you as a family.'

She didn't answer.

He tried again. 'I love you. Yes, I know it was tough when you first came to live with me, and we've both had to make a few adjustments, but I thought we were getting along pretty well.'

There was still no answer.

He battled on grimly, telling her how important she was to him. Even though he didn't think the message was getting through, he had to try.

Finally, to his relief, the doorbell went. It had to be Erin. He went downstairs to let her in, and then she followed him up to Caitlin's room.

When Erin knocked on the door, there was still no answer.

'Caitlin, it's Erin. I'm coming in because we need to talk and sort this out, OK?' Erin said.

When Caitlin still said nothing, Erin opened the door. But, to Nate's shock, his daughter's room was empty.

'Oh, my God—no wonder she didn't answer us. She's not here.' He dragged in a breath. 'She can't have run away. She *can't*. And when could she have left the house? I was right here outside her door all the time…' He closed his eyes. 'Except when I rang you. She must have gone out then, and I didn't hear the front door.'

He dragged his phone from his pocket and called Caitlin's mobile. 'Switched off,' he reported grimly.

'OK. Let's think logically. Where's she likely to have gone?' Erin asked. 'The back garden? Didn't you say you were giving her a patch of her own there?'

But the back garden was empty, too.

'She might have gone to my mum's. Or maybe her friend Shelby's.' He called both homes, with the same result: Caitlin wasn't there, but if they heard anything from her they'd call Nate immediately.

'She wouldn't have gone back to Devon,' Nate said, 'because she doesn't have the money for a train ticket.'

'Maybe she called her mum,' Erin suggested. 'Steph could've bought her a ticket to pick up at the station.'

It wasn't a call he relished, but if it meant his daughter would be safe he would've walked a mile across burning coals. He rang Stephanie. 'It's Nate. Just a quick question—has Caitlin called you at all this evening?'

'No. Why—what's happened?' she asked.

'We had a bit of a fight,' Nate admitted.

He could almost see her shrug when she said, 'She'll get over it.'

How could Steph be so matter-of-fact about it? Didn't it tie her up in knots when she fell out with their daughter? 'Uh-huh,' he said, trying to sound noncommittal.

Her voice sharpened with suspicion. 'What aren't you telling me, Nate?'

He owed it to her to tell her the truth. Plus if Caitlin did ring, Stephanie could maybe find out where she was and call him to let him know so he could go and fetch her. 'Don't panic, but she's not actually here at the moment. I'm trying to work out where she's gone. I wondered if she'd called you and asked you to buy her a train ticket to Devon.'

'Oh, my God—you're telling me you've lost my daughter?' Stephanie's voice rose to a shriek.

'She's my daughter, too,' Nate pointed out, 'and right now I'm trying to find her. Look, if she calls you, please just keep her talking and let me know where she is so I can go and get her. Meanwhile I'll keep looking for her—and I promise I'll call you the second I've found her.'

'Maybe she's gone to the sensory garden,' Erin suggested when he ended the call. 'It's somewhere she loves and she can be on her own to think things through. That's what I'd do in her shoes.'

'OK. Let's go.'

'Wait—we can check from here.' She called Ayesha, the chair of the Friends of the London Victoria, who organised the rota. 'Hi, Ayesha, it's Erin from the spinal unit. I was just wondering—who's working at the sensory garden this evening?' She explained the situation swiftly. 'Can you do me a huge favour and contact Nola for me and ask her if she can check if Caitlin's there, then call me to let me know either way? Thanks so much. I really appreciate it.'

To Nate's mounting dismay, when Ayesha called Erin back it was to report that there was no sign of Caitlin at the sensory garden.

'Ayesha gave my number to Nola, and Nola's going to call me straight away if Caitlin turns up there,' Erin told him. 'OK. Green spaces. Where's the nearest garden to here?'

'There's a park on the corner,' Nate said.

'Let's try there.'

There were little groups of teenagers scattered about the park, but Caitlin wasn't among them.

'OK. I'm out of places where she could've gone. Time to call the police,' Nate said. He'd just found the number of the local station when Erin's phone shrilled.

'Hello? Yes, Nola? She's—oh, thank God.'

Nate closed his eyes for a moment, grateful beyond belief that his silent prayers had been answered.

'Thank you. Yes, we will.' Erin ended the call. 'She's at the sensory garden,' she said. 'Nola's giving her a mug of hot chocolate and keeping her there until we get there. I said we'd go and fetch her now.'

Nate drove as fast as he could to the hospital, inwardly cursing the heavy traffic. But at least he knew his daughter was safe. That was the main thing. Once he'd got her back, he was never letting her go again.

Nate was silent on the drive to the hospital, and Erin noticed that his fingers were white where he was gripping the steering wheel so hard.

He'd obviously just had one of the worst scares of his life, thinking that his daughter had gone missing.

And it was all her fault.

If she hadn't sent that stupid text, Caitlin wouldn't have picked it up and gone into a meltdown.

And the fact that Caitlin's reaction to the idea of them dating was to run away told her that the girl was really panicking about it. Given that Caitlin had been sent to live with her dad after her mum remarried, the girl was clearly worrying that Nate was going to abandon her, too, and she'd have to start all over again somewhere else.

What Erin had kept from Nate was that Nola had said that Caitlin had started uprooting plants in the sensory garden. To Erin, it was a clear signal that Caitlin wasn't ready to consider even the idea of Nate and Erin dating, because she'd gone straight to the place that had brought them together in the first place and started destroying it.

And it was a sharp reminder of what she'd believed for years—that love didn't work out. Her own relationships had always gone wrong. It hadn't worked out for Nate and Steph, either, and the situation with Caitlin now was the fallout from that.

Nate was a good man. He was doing his best for his daughter. But he hadn't been able to make it work with Caitlin's mother. With Erin's track record, what chance did they stand? And if she let him get any closer—or let Caitlin get any closer—when it went wrong that would be three lives shattered.

So there was only one thing Erin could do, even though this was going to break her heart, and that was to call things off between her and Nate. Walk away.

When he parked the car, she touched his hand.

'Nate, I think you need to talk to her on your own and reassure her that she comes first.'

He frowned. 'It'd be better if she hears it from both of us.'

'There can't be an us,' she said softly. 'Not any more. It's over.'

He stared at her, looking totally shocked. 'Erin, no.'

'There is no other way,' she said. 'You're important to me, Nate, and in another life I really would've wanted to make a life with you, but it's not going to work out between us. I've already made someone pay a high price for my selfishness and I'm not going to do that again. Remember, I've been where Caitlin is. I understand how she feels. And right now she needs you to put her first. So go and see your daughter, show her how much you love her and it'll be OK. But from now on you and I can only be colleagues.'

Saying the words was easy. The hard bit was trying not to let it show that it was ripping her heart out. 'Good luck. I hope it all goes OK.' And she got out of Nate's car and walked away before she started crying and gave herself away.

CHAPTER ELEVEN

ERIN WAS ENDING it between them?

But—but…

Feeling more helpless than he'd ever done in his life, Nate watched her walk away, her steps sure and swift. His first instinct was to go after her; and yet they were here because Caitlin had run away. Right now, his daughter needed his full attention. And, no matter how much he wanted to be, he couldn't physically be in two places at the same time.

The realisation sickened him: he'd been deluding himself all along in thinking that he could have it all. He had to choose between his daughter and the woman he loved, after all. Steph had chosen her relationship over their daughter, and if he did the same then Caitlin would be completely alone. Nate also knew that Erin had been in Caitlin's shoes, so she understood exactly how the teenager felt and had done the right thing. He needed to follow Erin's example and do the same. Even though it was ripping him in two.

Grimly, he walked into the sensory garden area. Several people he recognised were working on the raised beds; they looked up as he came over.

'Caitlin's with Nola in the potting shed,' one of them said.

'Thanks—Mindy, isn't it?'

She nodded. 'I'm afraid Caitlin's been uprooting most of the plants in the bed she's been working on.'

The area she'd spent hours working on over the last few weeks? And she'd just trashed it? Nate stared at Mindy in disbelief. 'But she loves the garden! Oh, no. I'm so sorry.' He rubbed a hand across his face. 'Look, I'll pay for the replacement plants and what have you.'

'She was pretty upset. And she could've done a lot worse,' Mindy said sympathetically.

'Even so, this isn't like her. And I'm really sorry.'

'I know this isn't like her. She's a good kid,' Mindy said. 'We all think a lot of her. It'll sort itself out.' She patted his arm. 'I think right now she needs her dad.'

And her dad needed to put her first instead of focusing on his own selfish feelings. Yeah. He got that. 'The potting shed, you said? Thanks.'

Caitlin was silent and white-faced when he knocked on the door of the potting shed.

'She's quite safe,' Nola said.

'Thank you for looking after her,' Nate said. Though he knew there was an awful lot of damage to repair—and not just to the garden. 'I talked to Mindy. We'll sort everything out.'

'Absolutely,' Nola said, and to his relief she was tactful enough to leave them alone.

'Ready to go?' he asked Caitlin.

She refused to talk to him.

'OK. Let me give this to you straight,' he said. 'Ready or not, we're going home. It's up to you if you want to finish your hot chocolate first, but we're going home. Together. End of discussion.'

Again, Caitlin said nothing, but she put her mug down. Then she walked to the car with him in silence. He sent a quick text to all the people he'd called about Caitlin, saying that he'd found her and she was fine; he'd be in touch later but needed a serious talk with her first. Then he drove them home. Caitlin kept her face turned away throughout the whole journey, and as soon as they were inside the house she ran upstairs and slammed her door.

Last time he'd made the mistake of leaving her be. He'd learned from that, so this time he went straight after her, opened the door and went to sit on her bed.

'Go away,' she said through clenched teeth.

He could see that she was close to tears. 'I'm not going anywhere. I'm your dad, I love you and we need to talk,' he said.

She stared at him. 'But you hate me, and I've messed everything up.'

'I don't hate you. Far from it. I was worried sick when I realised you'd gone. And you haven't messed everything up. You made a mistake, yes, but that's what life's about,' Nate said. 'Nobody's perfect and nobody gets everything right all the time. The important thing is to admit that you're wrong, apologise, learn from your mistake and then do what you can to put it right.'

'But I ruined the garden—they'll never let me back there now,' she said miserably.

'Caitlin, you uprooted a few plants and it was only in the patch you'd worked on. You damaged your own work, yes, but nobody else's. You can explain that you were upset and you're sorry and you'd like to make amends. Tell them you'll pay for the damaged plants from your pocket money and you'll go on the rota to do your least favourite job for the next month.'

'They won't have me back,' Caitlin repeated.

'Yes, they will. They like you and they know this kind of behaviour isn't normal for you.'

She stared at him. 'And you don't hate me?'

'Not even slightly. I love you,' he repeated.

Her eyes narrowed. 'But you left me when I was little, so how do I know you really mean it now?'

He sighed. 'Your mum and I were very young when we had you. I'm not making excuses or blaming anyone, because your mum and I both made mistakes and we should both have done things differently. When you were born, I was still a student and then a junior doctor, so I worked really long hours and I was too tired to help your mum as much as she needed. Maybe I should've given up my dream of being a spinal surgeon and worked in a different area of the hospital instead, but I didn't—and that was my fault.'

'But if you hadn't trained as a spinal surgeon then you wouldn't have been able to fix that man's back.'

'No,' he admitted. 'Though someone else would've done it.'

'So you're saying you chose your job over me.'

'I wanted everything,' Nate said. Just as he did now. 'But it didn't work out that way.' Just as it wasn't going to work out now. But this time Caitlin wasn't going to be the one who paid the price. 'I can't change the past, but I have learned from it—and that's why I'm here for you now and I always will be.' He took her hand. 'I'm not going to abandon you, Caitlin. You're my daughter and you live with me now, and nothing's going to change that—least of all a few uprooted plants.'

'But how do I know?'

'That I'm telling you the truth?' He took his wallet from his pocket and handed it to her. 'Look in the flap.'

She did, and saw the photograph of herself as a toddler sitting on his shoulders. 'That's you? But you're so young! And the photograph…it's a bit creased.'

'It's a very old photo,' he agreed. 'And it's creased because it's had to fit in every wallet I've owned over the last eleven years. It's my favourite photograph of you. I've got others—lots of others—but this one's special. Now look on the other side.'

It was a much more recent photo of them together in the Sky Garden. They were smiling, with their arms wrapped round each other.

'Erin took that.'

'Yeah.' Erin. He still couldn't believe she'd gone.

Caitlin bit her lip. 'She's going to hate me for this.'

'Erin's been in your shoes, remember. She's going to understand.'

'But it's her garden and I wrecked it.'

'You uprooted a few plants and that can be fixed,' he repeated. 'You and Erin get on well and what you did tonight isn't going to change that.' Though it had changed something else: Erin had ended their romance. She'd walked away to let him salvage his relationship with his daughter.

'Does she know I—well…?' Caitlin bit her lip again.

'Ran away? Yes. And she knows about the garden.'

Caitlin looked worried. 'And she's not here now.'

'She's busy,' Nate fibbed. 'I'm sure she'll speak to you later. But whatever happens you're my daughter, I love you and nothing will ever change that.'

'You were dating Georgina when I came to live with you, and you broke up with her because of me,' Caitlin pointed out.

'Georgina and I weren't getting on that well before you came to London, believe me. We would've split up anyway, so that wasn't because of you,' he reassured her.

'Are you and Erin going to split up because of me?'

They already had, but he wasn't going to make Caitlin feel guilty. 'I thought you weren't happy about me seeing Erin?'

'I wasn't. Because when I found out you were seeing her, I thought you'd choose her over me, the way Mum chose Craig over me, and I was scared about where I'd have to go next.'

'You're not going anywhere. You live with me. And the only reason we didn't tell you we were dating was because we didn't want to worry you—we were trying to protect you in case things didn't work out between us and we didn't want you getting hurt, but we got it very wrong and I'm sorry for that. I can't answer for your mum,' Nate said gently, 'but sometimes we get into a complicated situation and can't see an easy way out. Your mum loves you, too.'

'It doesn't feel like it.'

'Relationships aren't always easy,' Nate said. He made a mental note to ring Stephanie and get her to tell their daughter that she loved her. 'And love stretches. Just because you love one person, it doesn't mean you can't love anyone else. Otherwise people wouldn't have more than one child, would they?'

'You and Mum only had me.'

'Circumstances,' he said. 'If we'd stayed together—and maybe if I'd had a different job—you might've had a brother or a sister. Maybe one of each.'

'So you and Erin—you're not going to split up because of what I did?'

'Erin's been where you are,' he said. 'She'd never put you through that by making me choose between you.'

A tear trickled down her face as she worked it out for herself. 'You mean she walked away instead, so you didn't have to choose?'

'It's OK,' Nate said. Even though it wasn't and there was a massive Erin-shaped hole where his heart should've been.

'No, it's *not* OK. You have to talk to her. Make her change her mind,' Caitlin said, her face desperate. 'Make her come back. Fix this, the way you fix people's backs.'

Spinal surgery was an awful lot less complicated than fixing relationships, he thought. And Erin came with complications that Caitlin didn't know about; she'd admitted that she never usually let people get close, so had she seized on Caitlin's reaction as an excuse not to let him and Caitlin close?

'Sometimes life doesn't work out the way you want it to,' he said gently.

'But if you talk to her…' Caitlin pleaded.

He could talk to Erin until he was blue in the face, but he still wasn't sure if he could change her mind.

'I wouldn't mind if you did end up getting married to Erin—she's a lot nicer than Craig.'

He smiled and ruffled her hair. 'Right.'

'Talk to her, Dad. Fix it. I'll do—I'll clean the bathroom for the next month.'

Nate had to hide a smile. She'd been listening, then, when he'd suggested that she put her name down at the sensory garden for the chore she hated most, and she was offering to do the same at home.

'OK. I'll talk to her. Tomorrow.'

'Talk to her *now*,' Caitlin said.

He shook his head. 'I'm not leaving you on your own.'

'I'm not going to run away again, Dad. I know that was stupid.'

He hugged her. 'I know you won't run away again, but you're upset and I don't want to leave you on your own.'

'Can I go and stay with Gran, then?' She bit her lip. 'Does Gran know I ran away?'

He nodded. 'So does your mother. And Shelby's mum.'

'Everyone knows?' she whispered, looking miserable and embarrassed.

'And everyone understands,' he said. 'Everyone will have forgotten about it by Monday.'

'Does Gran hate me?'

'Nobody hates you,' he reassured her. 'Here. Let her tell you herself. Call her.' He took his phone from his pocket and handed it over. And he sat with his arms round his daughter while she talked to her grandmother.

'Gran says she'll come over,' Caitlin informed him when she'd ended the call. 'So now you can ring Erin.'

'She might be out.'

She gave him a speaking look, then took her own phone from her pocket and called a number.

'Erin? It's Caitlin. I want to say sorry. I messed things up and I got everything wrong. I don't really know what to say to make things right, but I know you're important to Dad—and you're important to me, too,' she said.

There was a pause; Erin was clearly speaking, but Nate couldn't hear any of the words.

'Uh-huh,' Caitlin said.

Another pause, with more he couldn't hear from Erin.

'I don't want you and Dad to split up because of me. You make him happy,' Caitlin declared.

Another pause. And then Caitlin really shocked him by saying, 'Erin, you need to talk to Dad and make it up.' She handed the phone to Nate, and walked out of the room. 'Talk to her. I'm going to put the kettle on for Gran.'

Which left him no choice but to talk to her, though this was a conversation that Nate would much rather have face to face. 'Hi,' he said carefully.

'Is Caitlin OK?'

Typical Erin, thinking of someone else first. 'She is now. We've talked. We understand each other better.' He took a deep breath. 'Erin, you and I need to talk, too. But I don't want to have this conversation on the phone. My mum's coming over to sit with Cait—not because I don't trust her, but because I don't want her to be on her own.'

There was a long, long pause. And then Erin said, 'You're right. We need to have this conversation face to face.'

'Can I come over when Mum gets here?'

'OK.'

Though she sounded unsure, he thought. 'I'll see you soon.'

Once his mother and Caitlin were settled, he drove over to Erin's flat. She answered the door immediately, and he could see the strain on her face. He wanted to wrap her in his arms and keep her close, but he knew he didn't have the right to do that. Not yet. So he simply said, 'Hi. Thanks for letting me come over.'

'Coffee?'

He shook his head. 'I just need to talk to you.'

She ushered him into the living room, and to his relief she sat next to him on the sofa.

'I think maybe we need to revisit the situation,' he said, 'now I've talked to Caitlin and we understand each other. I was there when she called you, so I heard her end of the conversation—she told you you're important to both of us, and that's true.' He looked her straight in the eye. 'She's given us her blessing. You know how I feel about you, Erin, and I think you feel the same about me—even if you're too scared to say the words.'

'So you're not pulling your punches tonight, either, then?' she asked wryly.

'Erin, it's obvious you're scared. And I think you ran away tonight, just like Cait did—because you're scared to take a risk.'

'You think I'm a coward?'

'I think you're the strongest woman I know,' he said. 'But I also think you don't want to risk letting people close. It scares you. You're one of life's fixers—but you keep yourself busy and that helps you hide how vulnerable you are. From yourself, as well as from others.'

His words hit home, particularly as her brother had said the same thing. And Erin knew they were both right. She *was* scared of letting people close—scared that when they saw who she really was, she'd lose them. And she buried her fears and vulnerability beneath hard work, hiding from herself as well as others.

Could she take the risk with Nate?

As if he guessed what she was thinking, he said softly, 'Don't use Caitlin as an excuse. You know how she feels about you. You know how I feel about you. And, just so we're clear on this, I'm not looking for a mother for my daughter—I'm looking for someone for *me*. There's only one woman who's everything I'm looking for, and that's you. I know you've made mistakes in your past. They're understandable and you've more than paid for them, over the years. So when are you going to trust yourself enough to move on and have a really serious relationship—a for ever relationship?'

'But you can't want me. You don't know the full story,' she said.

'Is that another excuse to keep your protective barriers round yourself?' he asked.

It stung. Partly because she knew he was right. 'OK. You asked for this. What happened with Andrew...there were consequences.' She took a deep breath. 'He didn't use contraception and I wasn't on the Pill.'

He stared at her as if he was doing the maths in his head. 'So you have a child the same age as Caitlin?'

'No. I would've done, except I had a miscarriage,' she said. 'I'm sad that I never got to know my baby. But I'm also relieved that I didn't end up being a mum when I was too young to cope with it—and I still feel guilty about being relieved.'

'Hey. First of all, Andrew raped you. He didn't even give you a chance to say no, let alone use protection.' He wrapped his arms round her. 'Secondly, you were fifteen, so you would've been still only sixteen when the baby was born. Actually, you probably would've made a good job of being a mum, but your life would've been very different. You wouldn't have been able to train as a doctor, and I can say on your patients' behalf that that would've been a massive loss to medicine. And thirdly, it wasn't your fault that you had a miscarriage. It's one of those things that just happen. You don't have anything to feel guilty about. Anything at all.'

Could she let the guilt go, after all those years?

'Did you have anyone to support you through it?' he asked. 'You said your dad wasn't very good with emotional stuff and your mum's…well…'

'Difficult.' She nodded. 'I was in denial about being pregnant. And then, when I did face up to it, I didn't know what to do. Gill found me crying in the toilets at school and she made me talk to her mum. That's when I told Rachel about what Andrew did—and the consequences I wasn't expecting. She helped me come to terms with everything. And then, after the miscarriage, she pushed me into going back to school—a different school, one where people didn't know me and couldn't judge me, so I could re-sit my exams and get my life back together.'

'I'm sorry you had to go through such a rough time,' he said. 'I thought I had it hard but my family was always there for me.'

'Mikey was there for me. As much as he could be.' She paused. 'So now you know the rest of it.'

'And it doesn't change my feelings for you in the slightest. Except that maybe I admire you even more. Your strength is amazing, Erin.'

'It doesn't feel that way,' she said tiredly.

He kept his arms round her. 'You're vulnerable but you've always had to be the strong one, the one who does the rescuing and sorts things out for other people.'

'And you're right when you said I used that to hide things from myself,' she said.

'Maybe,' he said, 'it's time you were the rescuee instead of the rescuer.'

'The rescuee?'

'Because what I'm going to ask you now needs a lot of strength,' he said. 'A lot of trust. You saw your parents' marriage break down—and the little you've told me makes me think that some other relationships didn't work out for them. You saw your brother's girlfriend walk away when she found out he'd be in a wheelchair. You were let down in the worst possible way by the boyfriend you thought loved you. It's understandable that you don't have a lot of trust in relationships.'

'I don't,' she admitted.

'And not being able to trust is why you've dated but it's never been really serious since,' Nate said.

She frowned. 'I thought you were a spinal surgeon, not a psychologist?'

'I am. And I'm not going to let you push me away, Erin—whether it's with a sharp remark like that or whether you walk out on me. I'm not leaving. I love you for who you are. You make my world a better place, and I want you there in the centre of my world, where you belong.'

'What does that have to do with being a rescuee?' she asked.

'What I'm asking you is hard. I'm asking you to trust that our relationship is going to make it—that it's going to be different from everything you were used to in the past. Having that kind of trust is hard to do on your own; but you don't have to be on your own any more. You've got me. And Cait. And—even though you haven't met her yet—my mum's lovely and she'll adore you.'

The way Erin's own mother didn't.

'I want to rescue you from all that loneliness and doubt, Erin. I want you to marry me. And I'm asking you to marry me because I love you and I want you to be my wife. I want you to be the centre of my family—but most of all I want you for *you*.' He took her left hand and kissed her ring finger. 'Sorry. I've timed this all wrong. I haven't got a ring to offer you, or…'

'You don't need a ring,' she said. 'Because what you're offering me is more precious than any jewellery can ever be. I love you, too, Nate. It scares me because I've never got it right in the past, and I don't want it to go wrong this time. With Caitlin, too, there's more at stake and it won't just be me who gets hurt if it goes wrong.'

'It's not going to go wrong,' Nate said. 'I believe in you. I believe in us.'

She swallowed hard. 'I do, too. And you're right—I was running away from you because I was scared I'd mess this up, the way I've messed everything up in the past. But now you've made me think about it, I realise that this time it's different. I'm not the only one trying to make things work; you're right there by my side, working with me. So I don't need excuses or barriers any more. Because I'm not alone.'

'So will you marry me, Erin?'

She leaned forward and kissed him. 'Yes.'

EPILOGUE

Six months later

'OK?' MIKEY ASKED, looking up at Erin and clearly seeing the nervousness in her eyes.

She took a deep breath. 'Yes.' And then she smiled. 'Yes. I really *am* OK, Mikey.'

'It doesn't matter that Mum decided not to come. It's probably better, actually, because you can enjoy your wedding without worrying what she's going to say to you,' Mikey said. 'And it's her problem, not yours.'

She nodded. 'Nate's mum kind of showed me that.' Sara was warm and loving, and had immediately made Erin feel as if she was part of the Townsend family. It was the first time in so many years that Erin had felt that she really belonged in a family, and the memory still brought tears to her eyes.

'Don't cry,' Mikey said hastily. 'Your make-up will run, and then Lou will kill me.'

Erin smiled. 'No, she won't. My sister-in-law loves you to bits. And so do I. That's why I asked you to walk me down the aisle.'

Mikey squeezed her hand. 'And I'm so glad that you did. I'm really proud of you, you know.'

'Thank you.' Being with Nate and Caitlin had taught her finally to accept praise gracefully. 'I'm proud of you, too.' She took a deep breath. 'Right. I'm ready to walk down that aisle and plight my troth.'

'That's my sister. Awesome as always.' He smiled back at her. 'You look beautiful.'

'Thank you.'

'And Nate's one of the good guys. Better still, he's good enough for you and he really makes you happy.'

She grinned. 'Yeah. He is and he does.'

'Then let's go get 'em, kiddo.'

The usher opened the door to the Victorian glasshouse. They'd deliberately widened the aisle to give enough room for Mikey's wheelchair, and in front of them were rows of white wooden chairs with padded seats, with posies tied to the end chair in alternate rows and tubs of standard cream roses trained into a ball at the top of their perfectly straight stems. Light streamed through the three glass sides of the building, and the whole place felt filled with happiness.

Everyone turned round to look at Erin and Mikey as they made their way down the aisle.

At the end, Nate was waiting for her, along with Caitlin. They'd given her the choice of being Erin's bridesmaid or Nate's 'best daughter' instead of a best man, and Caitlin had loved the unconventionality of the idea. Especially as Erin had told her that she still got to have the pretty dress and could choose the colour.

And where else could they have got married but at

Kew, where they'd first started to fall in love with each other and to make a family with Caitlin?

When Caitlin nudged him, Nate turned round. Erin looked amazing, wearing a simple cream knee-length shift dress; but she'd teamed it with high-heeled turquoise shoes, which matched Caitlin's dress and Nate's tie. She carried a simple bouquet of cream roses in one hand and held Mikey's hand tightly with the other. She wasn't wearing a veil, but she'd left her hair loose, just held back from her face by a silver wire headband decorated with tiny roses, very similar to the one his daughter was wearing, too.

When she caught his eye, her face lit up with a smile that made his heart do a somersault.

And then she was standing beside him, ready to make a promise to him in front of their family and friends.

'I love you,' he mouthed.

'I love you, too,' she mouthed back.

Once the vows were made and Nate had got to do his favourite bit of the ceremony—kissing the new bride—they signed the register, posed for photographs and headed to the Orangery for the wedding breakfast. The eighteenth-century building was incredibly pretty, with its high ceilings, tall arched windows, and black-and-white-tiled floor. One end was set up for the formal wedding breakfast, with circular tables covered in white cloths and with cream rose centrepieces; the other end was ready for the evening reception, with a small stage for the jazz trio Nate had booked flanked by massive ferns.

'I can't wait to dance with my bride,' Nate said with a grin. 'No more sneaking about in the trees in the park, with one earphone each, pretending that we're in a nightclub or what have you—tonight it's real music and a real dance-floor.'

'With trees,' she pointed out, laughing. 'We can't escape the trees. But I can't wait to dance with my new husband, either.'

After the meal, the speeches started.

Mikey tapped his glass with a knife. 'For obvious reasons, I won't be standing,' he said, 'but I'm very proud to make the speech at my sister's wedding. Thank you, everyone, for coming. My sister's a gorgeous bride, and I'm delighted to welcome Nate and Caitlin into our family. I'd like you all to raise your glasses to the bride and groom—to Erin and Nate.'

Everyone echoed the toast, and then Nate stood up. 'I'd like to thank Mikey and Lou for helping us so much with the wedding, my mum, Sara, for being generally wonderful, and Rachel and her family for coming all the way from Dundee to be with us today. Thank you all for coming to share our special day. But then, I knew we'd have a lot of people wanting to share it with us, because Erin's a very special woman and she's made a real difference to so many lives. And I'm really, really proud to call her my wife. I'd like you to raise your glasses to Erin—to my wonderful bride.'

'To Erin,' everyone chorused.

'And finally I'd like to thank my best daughter, Caitlin,' Nate said with a smile. 'Who I believe might have something to say.'

Caitlin stood up. 'Dad and Erin decided to have a best daughter instead of a best man. Long speeches can be a bit boring and my jokes are terrible, so I'm going to keep this short. All you need to know is that my dad and Erin love each other to bits, and I'm really glad they're married because they make each other really happy. And they make me happy, too,' she added. 'So please raise your glasses to my new stepmum and my dad, Erin and Nate.'

And finally it was Erin's turn to make a speech. 'I never thought I'd find the love of my life, and I definitely didn't think it would be Nate—especially when we started by having a fight over a garden,' she said with a grin. 'But we kind of worked it out—and a garden's what brought us together as a couple and as a family with Cait, so we just had to get married here. Thank you everyone for coming and sharing our special day, and I'd like you to raise a toast to my new husband and my new daughter, Nate and Caitlin.'

After the speeches, they cut the cake. And then, at last, there was the bit Nate had been waiting for.

When the jazz trio started playing a soft instrumental piece, he said to Erin, 'This is our cue,' and drew her to her feet. 'Finally I get to dance with my bride.'

As they walked into the middle of the dance floor, the pianist started to play 'Make You Feel My Love'.

'Our song,' he said softly. 'And I mean every word of it and more. I'd go to the stars, and back, for you.'

'Just as I would for you,' she said. 'I love you, Mr Townsend.'

'I love you, too, Dr Townsend,' he said.

And then, as they swayed together to the music, he kissed her.

* * * * *

*If you enjoyed this story, check out
these other great reads from Kate Hardy*

*HER PLAYBOY'S PROPOSAL
A PROMISE...TO A PROPOSAL?*

*BILLIONAIRE, BOSS... BRIDEGROOM?
HOLIDAY WITH THE BEST MAN*
(Both in BILLIONAIRES OF LONDON *duet)*

All available now!

DOCTOR, MUMMY...
WIFE?

BY

DIANNE DRAKE

Published in Great Britain 2016
By Mills & Boon, an imprint of HarperCollins*Publishers*
1 London Bridge Street, London, SE1 9GF

© 2016 Dianne Despain

ISBN: 978-0-263-91501-3

Printed and bound in Spain
by CPI, Barcelona

Dear Reader,

Years ago a friend of mine decided to have a baby on her own. Her biological clock was winding down and her doctor said her baby-making days were limited. So she went through all the testing and finally had the baby she wanted—a fine, healthy baby girl. The joy of my friend's life. Back then it was scandalous, making that kind of decision. People talked about her, raised their eyebrows in speculation, but my friend withstood it all because she knew exactly what she was doing. And she never regretted a second of it, or the years since then. Today her daughter is on the verge of graduating at the top of her class from nursing school and she'll be an asset to her profession.

In my story Del finds herself in much the same spot. She wants the baby but doesn't want the man. Until she meets my hero she pictures herself in a life without a man, and she's quite happy there. Of course she meets the right man, and life changes for her. But in the meantime she proves that a woman *can* do it all and have it all these days. The old conventions no longer stand.

My friend never met the man of her dreams, but she was a strong, fantastic mother and one of the best nurses I'll ever know. All because that was what she chose for herself. So, whether or not it's a traditional life doesn't matter. We can do it all if we have a mind to. My heroine does, and she finds just what she wants in her life. So did my friend.

Until next time, wishing you health and happiness,

DD

Books by Dianne Drake

Mills & Boon Medical Romance

Deep South Docs

A Home for the Hot-Shot Doc
A Doctor's Confession

Firefighter With A Frozen Heart
The Runaway Nurse
No.1 Dad in Texas
The Doctor's Lost-and-Found Heart
Revealing the Real Dr Robinson
P.S. You're a Daddy!
A Child to Heal Their Hearts
Tortured by Her Touch

Visit the Author Profile page
at millsandboon.co.uk for more titles.

Praise for
Dianne Drake

'A very emotional, heart-tugging story. A beautifully
written book. This story brought tears to my eyes in
several parts.'

—*Goodreads* on
P.S. You're a Daddy!

CHAPTER ONE

Dr. Del Carson stumbled out of bed and groggily dragged herself into the nursery. A blue ceiling with white clouds, yellow walls with blue and white ducks and puppies greeted her as she turned on the overhead light and sighed.

"What now, sweetie?" she asked in a typically sleep-deprived thick voice as she trudged over to the crib and looked in at the six-month-old, who looked up at her and laughed at her with glee, as if he was eager to get his day started in the middle of the night. "Is it a diaper, or is this just your way of making sure your mommy doesn't get to sleep more than an hour at a time?"

Or maybe he just had her wrapped around his little finger; since it was just the two of them, she'd spent the first six months of his life catering to his every need.

It didn't matter, really. This was what she'd signed on for when she'd decided to become a mom, and any chance to make her baby's life better was welcome.

Tonight Charlie was particularly restless, all bright-eyed and ready to play, but, personally, she was played out. Even though the diaper seemed clean and dry, she changed it anyway out of habit, then sat down in the

Victorian rocker, the one her mother had rocked her in, rocked little Charles Edward Carson until he was ready to go back to sleep for another hour. Two if Del was lucky.

Single motherhood was difficult, and she got all the support she could want from her family and friends. Being an only child, though, she missed the camaraderie of a sister or brother to take part in Charlie's life. He had no aunts or uncles, no cousins. Not on her side, and the father's side didn't matter since he was just a matchup on paper. A statistic that had struck her fancy.

It made her wonder sometimes if she should have another baby so Charlie wouldn't be raised in an isolated situation the way he was now. Del was a firm believer that children did better with siblings, and that was a thought she had tucked away in the back of her mind to visit in another year or two. "We'll get it worked out, Charlie," she said to the baby in her arms. "One way or another this will all have a happy ending."

The issue of single motherhood to deal with took an awful lot of hours when it was just the two of them—her and Charlie. She was continually amazed how much time someone so young could take up in the span of a single day. It was as if he'd hatched a plan to run away with every free second she had. But she loved it, loved her choice to become a mother on her own. No father involved, except Donor 3045, and she was grateful for his good genes because he'd given her such a healthy, beautiful child. The perfect child, as far as she was concerned.

She loved being a mother, even with the inconveniences. Loved spending time with her son. "My one and only true love," she would tell him. "For now it's just the two of us against the world."

Her parents lived in Costa Rica. They were supportive but not close by, which was one of the reasons she'd chosen to do this now. Her parents would have spoiled little Charlie rotten, and that was fine up to a point, but not to the extent she feared they might have gone. After all, five years in a horrible relationship had made them spoil her rotten when she'd finally found the courage to end it. That was just who they were, but she didn't want to raise a spoiled-rotten or privileged child. So they'd made their plans and, accordingly, she'd made hers. And she didn't regret it one little bit.

"Well, Charlie," she said as she put the baby back into his crib. "Are you going to let your momma sleep the rest of the night?" She was so tired she gave some thought to simply curling up in the rocker and pulling up a comforter. But little Charlie was fast asleep, so she held out some hope for three hours of sleep before he woke up and wanted to be fed, changed or just cuddled some more.

The life of a single mom. It wasn't easy, but she was taking advantage of it because in another two weeks' time she was trading in her maternity leave and returning to her medical practice with some on call and nighttime exclusions. Charlie was going to the hospital day care so she'd have easy access to him whenever she needed her baby fix. Sure, she was going to miss him. But she missed her old life, too, and she happened to be a staunch advocate of women who wanted it all. She certainly did. Every last speck of it except the part where there was a man included, and she wasn't ready to go there again. Not for a very long time to come. If ever again. And if she ever did that again he was going to have to be awfully special. Someone who'd love Charlie as much as she did.

Del, short for Delphine, sighed. She loved her work as a pediatrician in a private practice attached to Chicago Lakeside Hospital. In fact she had a passion for her work that couldn't be quelled by anything but work. Yet somehow, now that she was a mom, she knew her sensibilities had changed. To a doctor who now had a child, those little coughs and colds meant so much more. And when a mother's instinct dictated something wasn't right, the mother's instinct won. Being a mother-pediatrician rather than a plain old pediatrician was going to be a big advantage and, as much as she hated thinking about leaving Charlie behind for her work hours, she was looking forward to getting back to her normal life and trying to make all things fit together. It wasn't going to be easy, but if there was one thing Del was, it was determined, and she was determined to make sure all things worked together in her life.

"Good night again, love," she said quietly as she tiptoed from the room, turned on the night-light and lumbered down the hall back into her own bed. Unfortunately, sleep didn't happen as quickly as she'd hoped, and she lay awake staring off into the dark for about half an hour before her eyelids finally drooped. "I'm a lucky woman," she whispered into the dark as she was drifting. "I have everything." A beautiful child, a strong, supportive family, a good job. Best of all, no man to interfere.

She'd given away five *long* years to a man, always

holding out the hope that he was the one who would complete her life. Problem was, he was completing the lives of several other women while she and Eric were going nowhere. So when she finally opened her eyes at the five-year point and took a good, hard look at the situation, she kicked him to the curb and decided she was in charge of creating and fulfilling her own dreams. No one else except one anonymous sperm donor needed.

It was a good choice, and as she drifted off to sleep, she did so with a smile on her lips.

Dr. Simon Michaels took a look out over the receptionist's shoulder at all the mothers and fathers waiting with sick children. It was cold and flu season, and if he didn't pick up the bug from one of these kids it would be a miracle. "How many more do I have to see?" he asked Rochelle, the girl at the desk. Rochelle was a tiny little thing who looked like one of the patients, and by comparison Simon felt he overshadowed her by a good foot. He, with his broad shoulders and longish brown hair, had to make sure he didn't treat Rochelle as a kid because, after all, she was well over twenty-one, and very efficient in her job.

She looked over the top of her glasses then laughed. "That's just what's left of the morning appointment block. You're going to have at least that many this afternoon, and tonight's your night for on call, so look out. Around here we look at Halloween as scary but not for the same reason most people do. We'd much rather see a goblin than a flu bug."

"Any word on when the mysterious Del Carson will be back?" He'd been hired to replace Del during her leave, then asked to stay on as a permanent member of the pediatrics clinic team. He'd heard of Del, but never met her. In fact, what he'd been told was that she was an excellent doctor, if not an overprotective mother who didn't want to come in for fear that she might contract some disease and take it home to her baby. He didn't know if that was true or not, but the only truth he knew was that she was merely a name in passing. Someone who would be his boss when she returned.

"Be patient," Rochelle warned. "She'll get here when she's ready. That new baby of hers is taking up a fierce amount of her time right now, but I expect she'll be back in a couple weeks or so, if she doesn't change her mind and stay home another half year." Rochelle smiled. "She loves being a mother."

"And there's no father?"

Rochelle shook her head. "Her choice. And she's proud of it, not shy in the least to talk about it."

"Well, that's something you've got to admire—a woman who knows what she wants and goes out and gets it." It couldn't be easy, and it would get a whole lot more difficult once she was back at work. He wondered if she fully realized what she was letting herself in for. "Can't wait to meet her. It will be nice having more help," he said, even though it wasn't his intention to complain. And he wouldn't. After all, he had a job in the location of his dreams. He was finally back home in Chicago after all those years in Boston and, as they said, "There's no place like home."

In fact, he lived only a few blocks from where he was raised. All within sight of the Navy Pier and the lakeshore. It was good. Pediatrics was such a full field here, though, that when he'd got the call to come and interview, he couldn't believe his good luck. No place at County Hospital, no place at Lakeside. Just no place. Then this spot came open—the pediatric clinic attached to Lakeside—and it was a godsend at a time that couldn't have suited him any better. Divorced from Yvette, who hadn't turned out to be the woman he'd thought she was, working in a practice where he was clearly never going to advance, cynical about life in general, feeling as if the whole world were closing in around his bad choices… Coming home was better, even if his workload was crazy big right now.

What the hell did that matter, though? It wasn't as if he had anything else going on in his life other than his work—a situation that suited him just fine. In fact, to avoid some of the long lonely nights he even took call for his colleagues just to give him something to do. Some might call it crazy, but he called it picking up the pieces of his broken life.

"So the plan is for her to be back in two weeks?" He grimaced. There were two weeks of work waiting to see him right now, and he was the only general pediatrician in the house today. The other two had succumbed to the virus that was being spread like wildfire. Leaving him to roll up his sleeves and just pitch in, keeping his fingers crossed that he stayed healthy so he could handle the workload.

Pulling up his surgical mask and snapping on a fresh pair of gloves, he sighed. "Send in the next one."

Rochelle chuckled. "Wouldn't it just be quicker to go out there, sit them in a circle and look at them as a group?"

"What would be easier would be flu shots. But people don't think about getting vaccinated until they're already sick with the flu."

She pointed to her upper arm. "Got mine. Hope you got yours."

"I've been a pediatrician too long not to." But that didn't mean he wasn't susceptible. Because vaccinations weren't foolproof, as his colleagues had discovered.

Two more weeks and Del Carson might reappear. Admittedly, after six months of hearing glowing reports about her, he was anxious to meet her. "You don't suppose we could convince Dr. Carson to come back early, do you?" he asked as he grabbed up the next patient chart. Five years old, fever, runny nose, cough, generally out of sorts.

"She values her baby time. She'll be back when she's back."

Of all the bad timing to be on leave... He signaled for his nurse, Ellie Blanchard, and off they went, back to work. Vaccinating children and parents alike, dispensing antinausea medicine, and generally just trying to make it through the day. "Next," he said as he stepped into Exam Four. "And get me two more ready to go. We've got a lot of patients to see in the next hour." Glancing up at the clock on the wall, he shook his head. Not enough time. Not nearly enough time even if he worked through his lunch hour.

No trying to hide it, she had tears streaming down her cheeks as she handed Charlie to the day-care director then headed down the winding walkway to the clinic. It wasn't as if she didn't trust the center to take good care of him. They had an excellent reputation and the staff in general spoke very highly of them—but this was her baby she was handing over and being only a building away didn't make any difference. She hated doing it. Considered at the very last minute whether or not she was ready to go back to work or if another six months' maternity leave might be called for.

But one look at the swamped clinic told her she was doing the right thing. Other children needed her, too. And admittedly, she did feel that tingle of excitement the moment she stepped through the front door—a tingle that told her she was back where she belonged.

There were lots of single moms just like her who left their children and went to work every day. She didn't have someone to support the two of them. It was up to her. Besides, she loved her work. Still, she was sniffling as she approached her office door and went inside. Leaving Charlie behind made her feel so empty, so alone. "Suck it up," she told herself as she pulled on her lab coat, the one with her name embroidered onto the pocket. "You knew this was how it was going to be when you did this."

Still, she hadn't counted on it being so difficult. "But you're lucky," she said as she looked in the bathroom mirror and touched up her streaky eyes. "You've got excellent day care and you're only a few steps away." A few steps that seemed like miles. Damn it! She wanted to be home with her baby even though she knew she was needed here. Torn in half—that was how she felt. Completely ripped down the center.

Taking in a deep breath, she exited her office and stepped almost directly into the path of a doctor she didn't recognize. The new hire? "Sorry," she said, trying to find a smile for him even though it simply wasn't in her to be found.

"You must be Dr. Carson," he said, extending his hand to her.

She gripped it weakly. "And you are... Was that Dr. Michaels?"

"Call me Simon."

"And I'm Del," she said, appraising the hunk of man standing right in front of her. OK, so she'd vowed off involvement, but she could still look, and what caught her attention first, outside his very soft hands, were his stunning green eyes. They were serious, but she could almost picture them smiling and sexy.

"Well, Del, I'm glad you're finally back. We've been too busy to make much sense of our patient load for a while, and we've needed you."

"My baby needed me more than the clinic did."

"I imagine he did," Simon said, "but you haven't been here and the pace has been crazy."

She looked over his shoulder to a normal waiting room. "Looks like things are under control to me."

"Want to know how long it's been since I've been able to take a lunch break?"

She laughed. "No guesses from me. We all have to make sacrifices, Dr. Michaels. Some bigger than others."

"You're referring to leaving your baby in day care?"

"That, and other things." But mostly that.

"Well, at least it's a good day care and nearby. That's an advantage for you."

"But I don't have to like it."

"All I said was I'm glad you're finally back. You were needed."

"And I appreciate that, but I was also needed at home." Where she wished she could have stayed. "But it's nice to be missed. I take it you don't have any children?"

He paused for a moment, then winced. "No children. Divorced. No future plans for anything except working."

"And yet you complain about too much work."

"Not complain so much as remark. We're busy here. We needed you. Simple as that." He chuckled. "Almost as much as you need me."

"Well, you've got me there. We do need you, especially right now."

Simon nodded. "During the flu outbreak the average wait time was an hour per patient. Which is too long for a sick kid to have to sit there and wait."

"See, you could have told me that right off."

"Pent-up frustrations," he said. "I've been working hard."

"I can see that." She smiled at him. "Well, you're right. An hour is too long. We like to guarantee no more than twenty minutes. Shorter if we can get away with it."

"Sorry about my attitude, but all I could picture in my mind was you sitting at home playing with your baby when we had patients lined up in the hallways."

"Trust me, it wasn't all play. Babies require a lot of work."

"I know, I know. I'm think I'm just tired... I know

it must have been hard work, especially on your own," he said.

"So how about we get off to a fresh start? Hello, I'm Del Carson and you're…"

"Simon Michaels." He held out his hand to shake hers and they both smiled. "So how was your maternity leave?"

"Great. I hated for it to be over with but all good things must end. So, how many patients do we have to see this morning?"

"About twenty, barring emergencies."

She nodded. "I'll grab some charts and get started."

"And after I get my foot out of my mouth, I'll do the same."

Del laughed. "You were right up to a point. I was entitled to my maternity leave and I don't regret taking it. But things shouldn't have gotten so out of control here at the clinic. Someone should have called me and I might have been able to get a couple of our specialists out here to help with the overflow."

"I tried," Simon confessed, "but I'll admit my attitude might have been better."

"I didn't read anything about a bad attitude in your application or your letters of recommendation. And even though I never met you until just a few minutes ago, I called your superiors in Boston and they gave you glowing reviews."

"Probably anxious to get me out of there. I'm a pretty fair doctor but I do let things get to me too easily, I suppose. You know, take it all too personally."

"We all do at times. And I suppose especially the

newcomer who's being the logical target." For a moment, a softness flashed through his eyes.

"Six months *is* a long time to be away."

"Not long enough," she replied. "I was actually thinking about another six, but I love my work as much as you seem to love yours. So I came back."

"Straight into the arms of a disgruntled employee."

"Nice, sturdy arms, though. And I'm willing to bet they hold no grudges."

"Me? Hold a grudge?" He laughed outright. "Grudge is my middle name. Ask my ex-wife."

"Think I'll stay out of the family problems."

"So, I understand you're raising your baby all on your own."

"Yes, it's just Charlie and me but that's the way I planned it."

"Well, I suppose that's the way to do it if you want to keep your autonomy."

"More like my sanity." They meandered down the hall to the clinic's nursing hub and she picked up the first chart off the stack. "And contrary to popular belief, I *am* sane."

"Reasonable, too, dealing with me as diplomatically as you have this morning. I must confess that when I heard you were coming back I put together some mighty well-chosen words for you."

"So I noticed," she said as she opened the chart and looked at the info contained inside. "But they could have been worse." The first patient was a child named Sam with some sort of rash. Her first fear was a communicable rash and her next fear was that she might transfer something to Charlie. Truth was, if she didn't get over her irrational fears, she wasn't going to be any good as a pediatrician anymore. Most kids that came in were communicable and if she worried about carrying something home to her baby every time she came into contact with a sick kid, she'd drive herself crazy. Plus there was also the possibility that she might be too cautious to make a proper diagnosis. Obsession. That was what it was called. She had an obsession, and she wondered for a moment if she should seek professional help for it. But the instant she stepped in Sam's exam room and saw the rash she knew the poor kid was miserable. He was obviously allergic to something with which he was coming into contact.

"Does it hurt or itch?" she asked him.

"He scratches it like crazy," Sam's mother answered as Sam's eyes filled with big, fat tears.

"When did it start?"

"Three days ago?"

"What happened three days ago that changed his routine?"

"Nothing except...we went picking pumpkins in the pumpkin patch for Halloween. He's not allergic to pumpkins, is he?"

"You've had pumpkins in your house before?"

"Every year," the mother replied.

"And what about the pumpkin patch?"

"This was our first year to go."

"I'm betting the rash is connected to the pumpkin plant."

"He's allergic to the plant?"

"Has there been anything else new introduced in his life since the rash popped up?"

"Not that I can think of," the mother answered, a frown on her face indicating she was thinking. "No new food, no new clothes, my laundry detergent hasn't changed."

"Then for now, let's go on the assumption that he has an allergy to the actual pumpkin plant and if the rash doesn't clear up in a few days or it comes back we'll investigate other possibilities and take some tests. For now, I'd rather save him the trouble, though. So, any of the over-the-counter hydrocortisone creams will help with the rash, and I'm going to give him a shot today that should speed things along."

She looked down at Sam, who looked back at her with big, sad eyes. "Will it hurt?" he asked.

"A little bit, but you're a big boy and you can take it." In reality Sam was only five and at an age where needles really scared kids. Some people never outgrew the phobia and she didn't want to make this too traumatic on this poor child. "Anyway, let me go get you some ointment samples, and have the shot prepared, and I'll be back in a couple of minutes."

True to her word, Del appeared back in Sam's room a few minutes later with a syringe full of antihistamine and a bag full of samples. Once she'd convinced Sam the needle wouldn't hurt that much, she gave him the injection, and wrote down instructions for his mother to follow, including the antihistamine to be taken three times a day in small doses. "This should clear up in about three days," she told Sam's mother on the way out. "If it doesn't, call me. In fact, call me either way because I'm curious if he is allergic to pumpkin vines. That's kind of an odd allergy…"

Actually, nothing in the allergy world was odd. People had reactions to everything—to the expected as well as the unexpected, as in Sam's case.

Her first day back dragged. She couldn't get herself into the rhythm to save her soul. And between her hourly calls to check on Charlie and her work she was ready to go home by noon. But she'd just have to understand that this was the way it was. She loved her baby and she worried. Although, by the time her fourth call rolled around, she was sure the child center over at Lakeside was probably sick of her calling. So she vowed to not call after she took her lunch hour with Charlie. Which turned out to be around one o'clock.

"Momma missed you," she said, picking him up and kissing him, then walking around the room with him.

"Am I being a nuisance?" she asked Mrs. Rogers, the director.

"Pretty much, yes," she answered, smiling. "But the first few weeks aren't easy. So we're pretty forgiving."

"I miss him, and it's all I can do to keep from coming over here, getting him and taking him home."

"You're not the first, and you won't be the last," Mrs. Rogers replied. She was an older woman, short gray hair, and a registered nurse, retired.

No one could have better credentials or more experience with children, and Del considered herself lucky that they'd had an opening for Charlie, as the child center was usually booked months in advance. As it turned out, she'd reserved a spot even before he was born in the anticipation of returning to work and the timeline had worked out perfectly.

Del sighed heavily as Charlie snuggled into her and dozed off. "It's amazing the way they can change a life so drastically, isn't it?"

Mrs. Rogers laughed. "Too bad we can't keep them all young and innocent, the way he is now. But if we did we wouldn't get grandbabies, and I've got to tell you there's a certain sense of satisfaction in being a grandmother."

"How many grandkids do you have?" Del asked her as she laid Charlie back down in the crib.

"Five, so far. One on the way."

"That's awesome," Del replied.

"What about your parents?"

"Grandparents in absentia. They live in Costa Rica and travel back every couple of months to spoil Charlie."

"No husband?"

Del shook her head. "By design it's just the two of us."

"I admire a woman who knows what she wants and goes out and gets it."

"And I admire you for taking such good care of all these children."

"My assistants and I love children, and, since we're all retired pediatric nurses, it's a good way to still stay involved."

Del smiled as she kissed her sleeping Prince Charming goodbye and returned to her clinic, feeling much more relieved than she had only an hour ago. In fact, this was the first time she thought it might actually work out, working full-time instead of part-time as well as being a full-time mom. At least, there was room for optimism in the scenario now. For which she was glad because she loved her work with a passion.

"Little Tommy Whitsett is here," Rochelle said to Simon as he left an exam room where the child had a blueberry stuck up his nose. "I think it's another case of nurse-maid's elbow." Where a quick tug of a toddler's arm oftentimes resulted in partial dislocation of an elbow ligament. In Tommy's case it was a chronic condition, one caused when his older brother tugged a little too hard on Tommy's arm, causing the ligament to snap out like a rubber band and not reset properly. It was typical of toddlers and Tommy would most likely outgrow the tendency in another year or two, but until then there was nothing really fixable as it wasn't a serious injury. And the fix was easy. One gentle pop usually set the ligament right back where it belonged. Tommy got his lollipop and went home to have other wrestling matches with his brother.

"Have him shown to Room Three," Simon said, and joined Tommy there a moment later. This was the third time he'd seen the child for the same injury in the past couple of months.

"I'm sorry this keeps happening, Doctor," his poor, red-faced mother said. "But when they get to playing..." She shrugged.

"No big deal. He'll outgrow this eventually, and that will be that."

"But I feel so foolish coming in here so often. I'm afraid it might look to some like I'm an abusive parent."

Admittedly, at one time Simon had wondered if Tommy's handling at home was too rough, but he had a different attitude now that he'd met the cause face-to-face—a much bigger, sturdier brother—and witnessed the worry in Tommy's mother's face. "Boys will be boys. You just happen to have one who's a little more elastic than the other one ever was. No big deal. Maybe have a word with his big brother to try and persuade him pulling his brother's arm isn't such a great idea."

"I have tried, Doctor. It always scares me."

"A lot of mothers get petrified if their child coughs or sneezes. That's the proof of parenthood, I guess."

"You're not a parent, are you, Doctor?" she asked him.

He hesitated for a minute, then shook his head. "Haven't had that opportunity yet." If ever again.

"Well, it's not easy."

He thought back to Del and recalled the strain on her face at simply leaving her baby behind in a safe environment. Maybe he should have more empathy for her, going through separation anxiety as she was. But he found that difficult as he didn't know how to show it for someone who'd made deliberate choices. Like Yvette, who'd pulled Amy out of his life altogether. He'd been the only father the child had known, albeit he was the stepfather. Then when his ex-wife met someone else, his feelings for Amy didn't matter. So he was understandably still bitter and some of his personal reactions still reflected that. "You're right. It's not easy," he said to Tommy's mother.

"I guess," Tommy's mother said. "But I wish it was sometimes."

"Parenting is never easy. It makes us realize just how powerless we are in so many situations. And I know you hate that vulnerability, but in your case you've got two fine, healthy sons and at the end of the day that's quite an accomplishment."

"Let me tell you a secret, Doctor. There's never an end to the day. Parenting is so hard, and it never stops."

"And you love it, don't you?"

"Except for when I have to bring Tommy in for another case of nursemaid's elbow." She smiled. "But I wouldn't change a thing."

"Challenging case, Dr. Carson?" Simon asked after he walked Tommy and his mother back to the waiting room.

"If I thought you were interested because you were really interested, I might answer that question, but somehow I think you'll snipe at me for taking the easy cases today since you're so distracted, so all I'll tell you is that we divide them as they come in and leave it at that."

"That's right. I'm not a partner. Just a lowly employee. I'm not privy to the inner workings of what goes on around here."

"You're causing a scene over a case of pinkeye?"

"You're treating pinkeye, I'm treating a kid with possible asthma. Are you going to tell me it all evens out?"

"I'm sorry for your diagnosis," she said sympathetically. "And if you'd rather not..."

"It's not that I'd rather not. But what I was wondering is if we get to pick and choose our cases or if we just get them according to what's up next, and who our established patients are."

"If you're trying to insult me, I have thick skin, Doctor."

"Not trying to insult you, Doctor. Just trying to figure things out now that you're back."

"Well, figure this out. It's a fair system. I don't take
all the easy cases and assign the tougher cases to my
colleagues. You were treating an easy case of nurse-
maid's elbow when I was treating a little girl with Erb's
palsy. Unless a patient requests a specific doctor we
take whoever's up next, regardless of the easiness or
severity of their condition." She bit her tongue to hold
the rest in but didn't do a very good job of it because
the rest slipped out. She knew this had to be tough on
Simon, working in basically a new situation, especially
with his credentials. "Trust me—it's fair."

"It's always good to know my standing."

"Sure it is. You got stuck in a jammed-up clinic when
I was gone and you're blaming me for it. So now you
want some answers. Can't say that I blame you. Reverse
the situation and I'd be asking the same questions."

Simon kicked off his shoes and set his mug of coffee next to the sofa. Sighing, he popped an old classic
movie into his DVD player then dropped down on the
couch with his bowl of cold cereal, contented to spend
the evening vegetating.

He'd gotten off to a rough start with Del and, to be
honest, was surprised she hadn't fired him on the spot.
There really was no excuse for his questions, especially
when he knew the answers. But he'd been in the mood
to antagonize someone and Del had seemed to be it.

The thing was, he'd called to talk to Amy this morning and was told by her latest stepfather that he had
no rights to the girl any longer, to please not call back

or he'd be served with a restraining order. Damn! He missed her. Red hair and freckles, with a little gap between her front teeth—sometimes he swore he'd stayed married to her mother just because Amy was so endearing. But that was obviously over and now he wasn't even allowed to talk to her any more. It hurt. It stung to the bone because he missed Amy with all his heart. Didn't know how he was going to get along without her. And Del, well...she'd just caught some of his fallout. Wrong place, wrong time and with a child who was making her so happy—happy the way he'd used to be.

Well, one thing was for sure. He'd never, ever get involved with a woman who already had a child. It just opened him up to getting hurt again.

In the meantime, he owed Del a big apology for being so confrontational over everything today. She didn't deserve it just because she'd had a child.

He owed her an apology and it wouldn't keep until tomorrow. He opened his clinic information packet and found her cell-phone number. On impulse, he dialed.

"Hello," she answered, almost in a whisper.

"Del, this is Simon Michaels."

"And?"

"I may have been a little harsh with you today."

"Not so I noticed," she lied. "It was a tough day for everybody."

"Still, I wasn't myself and I'm calling to apologize."

"No need. I wasn't at my best, either, this being my first day back and all. Look, you woke up my baby. I've got to go. Can I call you back?"

"No need for that. I just wanted to apologize."

"Thanks, Simon," she said, and with that she hung

up on him. And he actually chuckled. She was interesting, to say the least. Definitely her own woman marching to her own beat.

CHAPTER TWO

"HE'S NOT VERY pleasant at times," Del said to Charlie as she gave him his nightly bath. "On the verge of rude and insulting. Then he calls and apologizes. Like what's that all about?" Although he did exude a general sexiness about him, which was nothing she was going to admit out loud. Even when brooding he was sexy and she wondered, for a moment, what kind of social life he had going for himself. "It's none of my business," she told Charlie. "And I want you to point that out to me every time I have a straying thought about the man. OK? He's handsome and has the ability to be charming, but that's as much as I want to notice."

The baby's response was to splash around in the water and giggle.

"I'm not sure why my partners would have chosen him, except for the fact that he's a good doctor, but that was their decision, not mine. And his credentials are good. At least he's licensed here in Chicago, which saved a little bit of hassle. But that attitude… I've got to tell you, Charlie, you're not going to grow up to be a man like he is, who goes back and forth. I'll swear by all that I know as a doctor and what I'm learning as a

mother that you're going to have manners and respect."
Yeah, until he was an adult; then he could do anything
he wanted, which scared her because somewhere there
was probably a mother who'd said the same thing to her
baby Simon. And look at the way he'd turned out. "I
suppose a mother can only do so much," she said as she
pulled Charlie out of the baby bath and wrapped him in
a towel. "But I'm going to teach you anyway and keep
my fingers crossed I don't go wrong somewhere." Not
to imply that Simon's mother had gone wrong. Because
Simon did have manners and just a touch of arrogance
to offset them.

"Now, let's get you dressed and I'll read you a story.
How about the one with the giraffe, tonight?" Sure, it
was all in her mind but she thought that was Charlie's
favorite story. Of course, any story might have been
his favorite, as he seemed delighted by everything she
read him, including pages from a medical journal she'd
read aloud to him one evening when she was trying to
catch up on her own reading. It was the mother-child
bond that mattered, the one she'd missed all day today
while she'd been at work.

But on the other hand, work had had its number of
fulfilling moments, too, and it was good getting back.
She was still plagued with guilty feelings, though.
Those weren't going to go away, and she could foresee
the time when the conflicts would become even greater,
such as when Charlie learned to walk, or started talking.
She didn't want to miss those things, but it was conceiv-
able he might say his first word to Mrs. Rogers or take
his first step when she wasn't around to see it. Sacrifices. Yes, there were definite sacrifices to be made,

and she could feel them tugging at her heart. But she was still drawn to being a pediatrician, and while she felt guilty about working she felt no guilt at all about the work she did. It would have been nice, though, to have that proverbial cake and eat it, too.

Well, that wasn't going to happen. She had a child to support now and her savings, while sufficient, weren't enough to carry her through until he went to college. So off to work, get over the guilt. She supposed in time it would lessen, but her preference would always be to be there for her son.

"Once upon a time, there was a giraffe named George, who was shorter than all the other giraffes in the jungle. 'Why can't I be tall like my mother?' he asked." This is where Del tickled Charlie's tummy with a stuffed giraffe. "'Why can't I be tall like my daddy?'" She tickled Charlie's tummy again and took such delight in watching him laugh and reach out to hold his giraffe. "'Why can't I be tall like my brother...?'" And so the story went, until Charlie usually wore himself out and went to sleep. Which was the case tonight. He dozed off before the end of the story, clinging to his stuffed giraffe, and she tucked him into his crib, crept out and made sure the night-light was on for when he woke up later as she hated the idea of her child waking up in total darkness and being afraid.

Afterward, Del fixed herself a cup of hot tea and settled down on the couch to catch up on some reading, but she was distracted by her cellphone, which she'd set to vibrate now that Charlie was down. She'd been awfully rude to Simon and for no reason other than Charlie couldn't wait a minute or two—which he could have since he hadn't been crying for her. She'd set a bad example for Charlie even if he was too young to understand that. But there would come a time when he would and she dreaded that day. So in the end, she picked up her phone and made that call.

"Simon," she said when he answered. "This is Del."

"Let me guess. You want me to go in tonight."

"You caught me at a bad time earlier," she said.

"Apparently."

"Look, I had just got my baby to calm down and go to sleep after his first day away from me, and you disturbed him. You're not a parent, so you wouldn't understand," she said.

"No, I'm not a parent," he answered, then sighed so loud into the phone she heard it.

"Well, you couldn't understand what I'm talking about, but I like my evenings undisturbed."

"Which is why you've begged off call for the next six months."

"It was a compromise. Originally I was going to take off a whole year to stay home with Charlie, but that didn't work out so I decided to come back during the days so long as I have my evenings and nights to myself."

"Not that it's any of my business."

"Look, Simon. I called to apologize for being so rude. We got off to a bad start and when you called to apologize I wasn't in the frame of mind to deal with it."

"Guilty-mother syndrome?"

"Something like that."

"I understand children, Del, but I don't even pretend to understand their parents."

"You would if you were a parent."

"Well, thank God I'm not. My marriage was hell and it makes me queasy thinking we could have easily brought a child into it."

"So you're divorced."

"Blessedly so."

"Sorry it didn't work out. Is that why you hate women?"

"Who says I hate women?"

"Your scowl, every time I looked at you today."

"Well, I don't hate women. I'm just...wary."

"Sorry you feel that way. Anyway, I just wanted to let you know I'm sorry I was abrupt with you on the phone earlier. Normally I silence my phone so I won't be disturbed, and people who know me know when to call and when not to call."

"I didn't get the memo," he said.

"Then I'll make it simple. Evenings are my time unless it's an emergency. That's the memo." He was impossible and she was already dreading working with him. But what was done was done. He was hired, the partners were happy with him and he was a hard worker. Everyone in the office shouted his praises, so it had to be her. He rubbed her the wrong way, or the other way around. Anyway, her feelings for the man were no reason to give him grief, so before she hung up the phone she made a silent vow to tolerate him in the office. If he did his job and she did hers there'd hardly be any time to socialize anyway.

"So, as I was saying, I'm sorry for being so abrupt and it won't happen again."

"Let's call it a professional standoff and leave it at that."

"Professional, yes, of course. But that's all. And just so you'll know, you don't even have to acknowledge me in passing if you don't want to."

"Wouldn't that look unfriendly?" he asked.

"Maybe. But who's going to notice."

"Everybody." He laughed. "Are you afraid of me?"

"No, not really. I'm just not in the mood to have a man in my life—especially one I'll be working closely with."

"You formed that opinion of me after one day?"

"I form fast opinions."

"You must. But just so you know, I don't hate you and I don't even dislike you. I got off to a bad start this morning because of some personal matters and it carried over. But it has nothing to do with you." He smiled gently. "In fact, I've felt bad all day for the way we got started."

"You did?" she asked.

"I'm not usually quite so abrupt."

"Neither am I."

They both laughed.

"So tomorrow maybe we get off on a better foot?" she asked.

"Well, now that that's settled, let me be the one to hang up this time." With that he clicked off.

Her second and third days at work went a little better than her first, but she still missed Charlie so badly. Her situation with Simon didn't improve, though. She tried being friendlier, and he reciprocated, not in an out-and-out way but at least in a friendlier manner. Still, to Del their relationship felt distanced. Cordial but not particularly friendly. And somehow she had the impression it didn't have anything to do with her. At least she hoped it didn't because she wanted them to be just a touch more than cordial.

It was the fifth day when he actually greeted her with some hospitality. "Would you mind taking over a case for me?"

"Symptoms?"

"First, he's four years and his mother admitted to some pretty heavy drinking during pregnancy."

"So let me list some symptoms for you. Poor impulse control, poor personal boundaries, poor anger management, stubbornness, intrusive behavior, too friendly with strangers, poor daily living skills, developmental delays—attention deficit/hyperactivity disorder, confusion under pressure, poor abstract skills, difficulty distinguishing between fantasy and reality, slower cognitive processing. Stop me when I hit five of these."

"You hit five of the symptoms a long time ago."

"So you know what it is?"

He nodded. "But you're the expert in treatment for FAS."

"I'll be glad to take a look and get started with a plan, but you do realize that most treatments respond best to behavioral therapy. Poor thing's going to be saddled with a disability for his entire life."

"Well, you're the best one for the job," he admitted.

That took her by surprise. "Thank you. I appreciate the compliment," she said, almost stumbling over her words.

"Look, is there any chance we could start over... again?"

"Maybe," she said, hiding a smile. She liked this side of him and she was glad she was finally going to coax it out of him, if for no other reason than a better working relationship. "Is the mother or father more responsive now?"

"Child's under protective service. He has a foster family who really cares."

"That's a step in the right direction."

"Anyway, I told them we have an expert on staff so I'm leaving it up to you to schedule them in. I slid the note with his file reference under your office door."

"I appreciate the vote of confidence," she said.

"When you've got the best on staff you'd be crazy not to."

She didn't know whether to take that as a compliment or a disparaging remark in disguise. For a moment or two she'd been flattered, but now...she didn't know. It seemed more like a professional request and not something that spoke to his opinion of her abilities. Oh, well, she decided. It was what it was, whatever that might be. "I'll read the file and call the foster parents to see what we'll be addressing."

"I appreciate it," he said as he walked away.

"Do you really?" she whispered. "I wonder."

It was hard getting a beat on the good Dr. Del. One minute she seemed friendly enough and the next she was glacial. So, what was her game? Simon wondered as he watched her stride through the hall without so much as a glance in his direction. Did she hate men? Or did she

feel that he jeopardized her position at the clinic? Whatever the case, they were barely any further along than
they'd been two weeks ago when she'd first come back
to work, and now it was becoming frustrating. While
he didn't expect a friendship out of the deal, he did expect a civil work environment, which she barely gave
him but only because it was required. And, it was getting to him. Maybe it was the whole social conquest of
the deal but he did have to admit the more she stayed
away, the more he wanted to get close. With her long,
nearly black hair and her dark brown eyes, she had a
drop-dead-gorgeous body that begged to be looked at
and he enjoyed the looking.

Was she becoming a habit or an obsession? Maybe
a little of both. But he wasn't the only man doing the
looking. He was, though, the only one she treated with
woeful disregard. Except in the professional capacity
and there she was cordial.

Well, never let it be said he was the one who gave up
the fight. "How's little Curtis doing?" he asked.

"It's like you thought. Fetal alcohol syndrome. He's
got a tough life ahead of him but I got him in a program that has some luck treating kids with his disorder.
I'll be following him medically. He's a cute little boy."

"I'd be interested in learning more," he said, out of
the blue. "Maybe we could get together sometime and
you could give me some pointers."

She looked almost taken aback. "Um…sure. Why
not?"

"You name the time and place," he said, "and I'll
be there."

"Friday night, if I can get a sitter? Or do you have plans?"

He chuckled. "Plans? Me have plans? Not for a long, long time."

"Good, then, Friday it is…" She paused. Frowned.

"Anxiety over leaving the baby behind?"

"Other than my work days it's the first time I'll have left him."

"Well, you need a night away from the kiddies—all of them. Some good old-fashioned adult company. So how about we grab a pizza and you can give me the basic crash course on FAS? I understand you've done some writing on it and presented some lectures."

She shrugged. "I used to, but I'm not inclined to take up my time that way, now. Oh, and we'll have to make it an early evening because I don't want to disrupt Charlie's schedule. In fact, instead of going out for pizza, how about we order in? Then I won't have to get a sitter or disrupt anything."

"A night in with you and…?"

"Charlie. Named after my dad."

"A night in with you and Charlie. Sounds doable."

"Great, come over early, around six. He's usually tired out from day care and ready to go down for a nap for an hour or so. We can have the pizza then. Then after bedtime we'll talk about FAS, if that's OK with your schedule."

She almost sounded excited. It was as if she was starved of adult interaction. She must have been to invite *him* over. Of course, she still wasn't going to get too far away from her baby. There'd been a time when he was like that with Amy. He'd been married to Yvette for six months before knowing of her existence. When Amy's dad had dropped a small child at their door, Simon had immediately stepped into the role of protective father. He'd been the one to feed her, and put her to bed and spend evenings at home with her while Yvette was out running around. He'd been the one to take care of her when she was sick, and take her off to her first day of school. He'd gone to "meet the teachers" night and to the play her first-grade class had put on. Never Yvette. And with that kind of relationship he'd never expected Yvette to simply yank Amy out of his life the way she had. But it was done now, and there was nothing he could say or do to change that. His parenting days were over and, yes, he could understand Del's overprotectiveness because he'd been much the same way.

She reminded him of him, back in happier days. Which was why he resented her. She had what he wanted. But he didn't want it from another one like Yvette, who came equipped with a child already. He wanted his own child next time, one that couldn't be ripped away from him the way Amy had been. "It sounds fine since I don't have anything else to do."

She jotted down her address and gave it to him. "Good. I'll see you then."

"Do you drink wine, or are you…?"

"Nursing? No, I'm not. You can't put your child in the day-care center if he or she's still nursing. So it's strictly the bottle and baby food all the way. And yes, I drink wine. Not much, though, since I work with FAS and I've seen what alcohol can do to a child."

"Then you wouldn't be offended if I bring over a bottle?"

"If you're not offended that I'll have only one glass."

He nodded. "One glass it is." It sounded more like a business transaction than arranging a date, even if it was a working date. So maybe in Del's mind it was a business transaction. Who knew? Admittedly, he was a little disappointed by her attitude, but what had he expected? A real date? They were hardly friends, barely cordial colleagues, and all of a sudden he'd asked her out. Of course, she had a child, which made her safe and he supposed that was part of it. He felt safe with Del because of his personal resolution. So, it wasn't such a bad situation at all. And it would save him from spending another long, dreary night at home alone, looking at pictures of Amy or mulling over how much he missed her.

"Well, he's down for a nap, and the pizza's hot so what say we dig in?" Simon said, pouring himself a glass of wine and leaving the bottle on the table so Del wouldn't feel pressured into drinking if she didn't want to. As it turned out, she poured half a glass and sipped it almost cautiously as they ate their pizza and talked about the clinic. "He's a cute kid," Simon said. "Your Charlie."

"Thank you. I think so, but then I'm a little partial."

"Better that than some of what we see come into the clinic."

"Why did you choose pediatrics?" she asked.

"Liked it when I rotated through when I was an intern. Liked the kids, like the way they're braver than many adults. And they show so much heart and trust. I think it's the vulnerability and trust that got to me. Most adults don't have that. They're cynical, or mistrustful. I remember one patient who told me right off the bat he had the right to sue me if he didn't like the way I treated him and the hell of it was, he had his choices but as an intern I didn't have those same choices, as in not treating him. Luckily his diagnosis turned out to be something simple, but you know the guy never even said thank you. He simply accused me of overcharging his insurance company. Which is one of the reasons I went with children. They're not so vindictive."

"Most adults aren't, either. You just happened to have a bad one at a time in your early career where you were open to influence."

"I gave some thought to going into a straight family practice but I just didn't like treating adults the way I enjoyed taking care of the kids."

"Which is a good reason to go into pediatrics. Family practice's loss."

"Not really a loss so much as I never gave it a fair trial. I'd already decided I wanted to treat children."

"Because you like kids that well?"

"Generally, yes. Says the man who isn't a father."

"You don't have to be a father to be a good pediatrician. All it takes is a passion for what you're doing."

He looked away for a minute, turned deadly serious. "I had this one little guy who was born with cerebral palsy. He wasn't too severe but he had some limitations in walking and coordination, and the way he took to his physical therapy just made me so proud of him. He worked hard, never complained, never questioned. Just did what he was supposed to do when he was supposed to do it and I suppose he was my turning point. I'd always thought I'd be a surgeon, or something a little more showy, but with the kids I found that I liked the courage I saw every day. So I stuck with children and I have no regrets. Now you tell me yours."

"There was never a choice for me. I never had any grand delusions of going into one of the higher profile types of medicine. I liked children, liked working with them, and I think a lot of that stems from my childhood pediatrician, Dr. Dassett. He was a kind man and I was never afraid of going to see him. So even when I was a kid myself I always told my parents I was going to grow up and be just like Dr. Dassett. And here I am."

"But FAS? How did you get interested in that?"

She shrugged. "One of my earliest patients was born with FAS and it interested me that a mother could do that to her child. So, I studied it, and eventually specialized in it." She took a bite of pizza and washed it down with a sip of wine. "I still can't explain the mind that thinks it's OK to do that to your child, but my job is to coordinate care when I get the opportunity. Admittedly, we don't see a lot of that at Lakeside, but I do get called out on referrals to other local hospitals from time to time."

"Isn't it discouraging?" he asked her as he grabbed up his second piece of pizza.

"Very. But somebody has to do it, so why not me? I see all the expectant mothers who drink—it's all just selfishness, or that 'bury your head in the sand' attitude where you think it can't happen to you. And odds are it won't. But occasionally…" She shrugged. "It's one of the ugly sides of medicine, but I can do it and make a difference, which makes me glad I've chosen FAS as my specialty because when you see one of these kids succeed…" She smiled. "If you want pretty you become a beautician. If you want to make a difference you become a doctor. And personally, I've always wondered what's up with someone who wants to practice proctology. Now to me, that's a field of medicine I'd rather not think about."

Simon laughed. "When you put it in those terms, I can kind of agree with you. But for me it's radiology where you don't get much patient contact. I like patients. Like working with them, like curing them or making them feel better, and viewing film and images just isn't what I care to do. Although the world certainly does have need of great radiologists, especially in so many of the specific treatments and tests that get referred to them. Most everything starts with an X-ray of some sort, I suppose, but I can't see myself in that role."

"So do you like Chicago?" she asked. "Is that why you applied here? Or were you just looking to get away from Boston and Chicago is where you were accepted?"

"I'm from Chicago originally and I wanted to get back here. Had that little hiccup called marriage back in Boston when I was finishing my residency, which didn't make moving home too practical since my wife was born and raised in Boston and wouldn't leave there for me, even though I begged her. So I had to be the flexible one. And then she moved to Chicago anyway, so I did, too. It's nice to come home to the big city. Not that Boston is small, but I love the lakeshore here, which is where I grew up, love the Navy Pier and all the park along the river." He smiled. "It's nice to be back where I belong. So are you from here?"

"South side. Some people call it Indiana, but once you get past Merrillville, which is where I'm from, it all turns into Chicago whether or not it really is. I love a happening city. Love the restaurants, the theater, the museums. And like you I'm hooked on the lakeshore. I can't wait until Charlie's old enough to go to the Museum of Science and Industry, or take a ride on the Navy Pier Ferris wheel. I've got big plans for him. Already have him enrolled in a private school for when he's old enough."

"Well, the coincidence is, we live only a block apart. And I was raised three blocks from here. So who says you can never go home? Because I have and I'm glad to be here."

"Are your parents here?"

"Same condo building I was raised in. They love it, too, although now that they're older they winter in Florida."

"My parents vacationed in Costa Rica and loved it so much they stayed. Now with Charlie, though, they come back every couple of months, which is good because he's really the only family they have."

"No brothers or sisters?"

She shook her head. "Just me. And you?"

"One brother, who's also a doctor, and a sister, who's a military surgeon."

"Your parents wouldn't happen to be doctors, would they?"

"My dad was a surgeon, my mom was a teacher."

"And they both worked and raised you kids at the same time?"

He nodded. "It worked out."

"My parents were both practicing physicians. My mother has had fits with me now that I've chosen to have a baby and work at the same time, which is what she did. She wants me to stay home with Charlie, and they'll help me out financially if I need it. First grandchild and all."

"Doesn't sound like a bad deal," he said, taking his third slice of pizza.

"But it's not my deal. I want it all, and that includes my job. Speaking of wanting it all, I hear someone stirring in his crib. Sounds like it's bath and snack time for Charlie."

"Does he like it?" Simon teased.

"Give him time." She hopped up and went to get Charlie, then brought him out to see Simon. "Want to hold him while I get his snack ready?" she asked.

"Sure," he said, but reluctantly. He stretched out his arms to take the bundle from Del as she got a jar of smooshed bananas ready for Charlie. Then when she took him back the baby giggled in anticipation of what he knew was coming.

"He loves his bananas," she said, putting him in his high chair. "Everything but vegetables. He spits out anything that's green."

"Smart kid. Vegetables..." He turned up his nose. "Not a big fan myself unless they're on my pizza."

Snack time was finished, then came bath time, play time and bedtime story, and Charlie was ready to crash for the night. Or at least part of the night. So she put him down and came back out to the living room only to find that Simon was cleaning up the kitchen mess Charlie had made. "You don't have to do that. He hasn't got the finesse of fine dining down yet so half of everything goes on the floor."

"What's a few spilt bananas among the boys?" he asked, laughing. "Besides you look tired and I thought some help might be welcomed."

"Help is always welcomed, but I thought you wanted to talk FAS."

"Not tonight, Del. I've had a nice evening so why ruin it with something so serious?"

"In that case I might be up to another half glass of wine before you leave, if you don't mind."

"Want to keep the bottle?"

She shook her head. "Drinking alone is sad. Even if it is wine."

"Which is why I never drink alone," he replied. "It doesn't go with cold cereal anyway."

"Cold cereal?" she asked as he wrung out the washrag and placed it on a drying rack inside the sink cabinet door.

"My usual evening fare. Unless I stop and take something home with me like Chinese or Thai. Trust me, eating is not high on my priority list."

"But you don't look emaciated."

He laughed. "I'm not emaciated. I just have bad eating habits. Besides, I usually have a pretty good lunch at the hospital. The doctors' cafeteria is fairly respectable."

"What about a home-cooked meal?"

"What's that?" he asked.

"What I'm going to cook for you Sunday night if you don't have other plans. I'm not a gourmet chef by a long shot but I do love to cook, and I've been practicing for the time when Charlie starts to eat real food. So, dinner?"

"You sure you want to do this?"

She nodded. "I'm working tomorrow, but I'm off Sunday, so I think I can whip up something you'll like and maybe we can talk FAS then."

"What time?"

"How about eight o'clock, after Charlie's down for the first part of the night?"

"He doesn't sleep through the night yet?"

"He's rambunctious. And eager to get up and play. What can I say? He's all boy."

"And you indulge that?"

"I embrace it." She smiled. "Love it, too, even if the clinic staff has to suffer my grumpiness the next day."

"So now I'll know why to stay away from you on the days you look frazzled."

She shrugged. "I've enjoyed our evening, Simon. You're very considerate, actually. Better than what I expected."

"You were expecting an ogre?"

"Not so much as a grouch."

"Well deserved."

"But you're not really a grouch, either. Just someone who's preoccupied."

"Not so preoccupied as grumpy."

"Why?"

"I had a daughter, Amy. Stepdaughter, actually. Raised her from being tiny and when her mother and I divorced, I lost the battle. She had a restraining order taken out on me. I can't see her, or talk to her. When I'm grumpy that's usually what it's about."

"Simon, I'm so sorry. I didn't... Can't even imagine..."

"Most of the time I still can't imagine it, either. But

it is what it is and so far there's been nothing I can do about it."

"You've gone to court?"

"Several times without any luck. Yvette says no, that my presence wrecks her little family and she doesn't want me around. So I'm excluded."

"I wish I knew what to say or do."

"So do I, but the battle is over and I lost." He shrugged. "And Amy's the one left to suffer."

"I can't even imagine what I'd do if someone took Charlie from me."

"You'd let it tear you up. You wouldn't sleep, or eat. You'd walk around in a blur."

She corked the wine bottle and handed it to him. "So you would consider coming over Sunday night for dinner?"

"Looking forward to it," he said, taking the bottle of wine from her. "My days off get lonely."

The brush of his smooth hand across hers gave her goose bumps. Luckily, she was in long sleeves and he couldn't see them, but she could surely feel them skipping up and down her arms. "Good night, Simon."

"Good night, Del," he replied, then headed to the front door of her condo. It was on the twenty-first floor overlooking the lake, and she wondered since he lived only a block away if it also overlooked his condo. But she didn't ask. Didn't want to be tempted. Didn't want to catch herself going to the window and gazing out wondering if he was gazing back.

It was physical attraction, that was all. But she did like him better than she had before this evening. In fact, she liked him a lot. If only Eric had been this nice to be with she might not have left him, but he'd been a bully. Never lifted a finger to help, always criticized, and most of all he always cheated and lied afterward. Somehow, she didn't see those ugly traits in Simon. In fact, now that she knew him a little better personally, she had an idea he was full of good traits. Except for his grumpy days, but now she knew what that was about and felt bad for him.

Del frowned as she put Charlie to bed. Life was good to her. Very good. She was glad for what she had.

CHAPTER THREE

SATURDAY WAS BUSY and complicated after her first non-date date with Simon. They had time to catch a quick lunch in the doctors' cafeteria but she missed out on Charlie's lunch altogether. She felt guilty about that but there was nothing she could do because work came first.

"You OK?" Simon asked her that afternoon.

"I miss Charlie. I hate not being there for his lunch."

"I'm sure he won't notice."

"I think he will. It's part of his routine now. And I'm sure he misses it."

"Babies are forgiving at that age. Take him to the park or something on his way home. I know it's getting chilly out so his outside days to play are numbered until spring. In fact, take off work now and I'll cover for you."

"Do you mean that?" she asked excitedly.

"Of course I mean it. Take Charlie out and go have some fun."

She was taken aback by Simon's generosity. And to think her first impressions were that he was grumpy. Yet he was the furthest thing from ill-tempered she could think of. "You're sure?"

"It's a beautiful day. We're not busy for once. Go take advantage."

Stirred by the moment, Del reached up and kissed him on the cheek. "Thank you. You don't know how much this means to me."

"Yes, I do," he whispered in return as she sped to her office to grab her jacket. "I really do."

The afternoon couldn't have gone more perfectly. They played in the park, stopped at the pier for dinner and ice cream and went home exhausted. By the time the doorman buzzed them in, Charlie was sound asleep, his face covered with chocolate.

"Looks like you two had a big afternoon," he said. Del smiled.

"We did. Sort of a gift from a friend."

"He must be a good friend."

"Getting to be." More than she'd ever anticipated.

"Well, have a pleasant evening. And tell Charlie he looks good in a chocolate moustache."

Laughing, she caught the elevator and rode all the way up thinking of Simon for most of the ride. She was looking forward to fixing dinner for him tomorrow night, which made her wonder what these growing feelings for him were all about...

CHAPTER FOUR

"I WASN'T SURE what the proper etiquette was so I brought flowers." Simon handed Del a spray of white and red carnations at the door before he entered her condo. "Hope nobody here's allergic to them." Truth was, they were a last-minute detail. He knew it was appropriate to bring a hostess gift like a bottle of wine, but she'd take months to drink the whole thing and it would turn to vinegar in the meantime, so flowers were second on his go-to list, not that he'd ever bought flowers for anyone before. But for Del, and all her feminine ways, they seemed appropriate.

"They're lovely," she said, taking the flowers from him and stepping back to let him in. "You really didn't have to, Simon, but I'm glad you did."

He wondered for a moment if the gesture was too romantic, as he clearly didn't want to shoot that intention out there. Sure, Del was drop-dead gorgeous, and she was actually very nice when they were getting along. But now he worried if the flowers signaled something more than a thank-you for the dinner tonight. "Well, my mother taught me it was customary to take a hostess gift and…"

"And you had a very conscientious mother."

"She insisted on all things done properly and I can almost hear her berating me for skipping a hostess gift."

"Well, flowers are perfect. They brighten up the place." She dug out a vase from under the sink, filled it with water and put the flowers in it, then set the flowers on the kitchen table. "Sorry, but I don't have a formal dining room here. When I bought the place I never anticipated having someone else living here with me, so I sort of low-balled my expectations of what I wanted in my living space. But I'm going to have to upgrade to something larger pretty soon to make room for the both of us, especially when Charlie gets a little older."

"I have too much space. Don't know what I was thinking when I bought it but I've got enough space to host an army. Bought the condo back in the days when I'd anticipated having some visitation privileges with Amy. Unfortunately, that never happened. So I've thought about downsizing but what's the point? I'm settled here and it's as good a place to stay as any."

"Well, if you ever decide to sell, keep me in mind. I figure I've got about two more years here, if that long. Oh, and I want to stay in the neighborhood. I love the lakeshore." She showed him to the kitchen table, where he took a seat and she poured him a glass of wine.

"You bought that for me?"

"It goes with dinner...lasagna and salad."

He smelled the delicious meal cooking. "How did you know Italian is my favorite?"

"Because Italian's everybody's favorite, isn't it?" she said, laughing as she pulled lasagna from the oven and popped in a loaf of garlic bread.

"Did you ever think about moving away from here…
from Chicago?" he asked as he poured a glass of wine
about one-third full.

"I had offers. Still get them because of my specialty.
But I like it fine just where I am and don't feel inclined
to uproot myself and Charlie just to take another job.
And you? Now that you're back home, is it for good, or
can other bright lights tempt you away?"

"You know what they say about Chicago. Once you
were born and raised there it will eventually call you
back home. I'm home this time. Nowhere to go. And
nothing else particularly interests me. Came back when
Yvette moved Amy here and I don't feel inclined to
move away."

"We're just a couple of old fuddy-duddies stuck in
our ways, aren't we?" she asked.

If only she knew how stuck he was. Simon raised
his glass and clinked it to hers. "Here's to a couple of
old fuddy-duddies."

"Fuddy-duddies," she repeated, then laughed. "Although I wouldn't say thirty-five is old."

"Your wisdom is, though."

"Why, Doctor, I think you just paid me a compliment
whether or not you intended to."

Oh, he'd intended to. Del was wise beyond her years.
And so settled into her life. He envied her that, in a way.
Of course, there'd been a time when he'd thought he'd
been settled into his own ways and look how that had
turned out! Disastrous, pure and simple. That was his
one and only mistake, though. Next time he'd know
better.

"I meant to," he said. "You've accomplished so much

in so few years, and now you're a successful mom. That's an amazing life no matter how you look at it, Del."

"Well, you're not so shabby yourself. I read where you were the head of your clinic and you gave it all up to come back home and take a lesser position just so you could be back in Chicago."

"I'll advance again. I'm not worried about that. And even if I don't, I like where I am."

"Are you sure, Simon? It seems to me that you prefer bigger challenges than we can give you."

"I'll admit I miss the challenge, but this is fine. It gets me exactly where I want to be." Closer to Amy.

"But you're not committed to staying with us if something better comes along?"

"We'll talk about that if and when we need to. Until then, how about we eat? I'm starved for that lasagna."

Dinner turned out to be a pleasant affair, from the salad course right down to the tiramisu she'd fixed for dessert. They talked about their childhoods and compared neighborhoods and schools, discussed families and friends. Avoided work and life goals pretty much altogether. And before he knew it dinner was over and he was stuck in the odd place on whether to extend the evening by staying on a little longer or going right home. Charlie took care of that problem, though, as he awoke and started crying.

"Look, you take care of the baby and I'll see myself out," he said.

"You don't have to leave," Del replied. "It'll only take me half an hour or so to get him to go back to sleep."

"He's the priority, Del, and I don't want you rushing

him through a routine he needs just because you feel guilty neglecting me. So, I'll go, and see you at work tomorrow."

"I'll bring leftovers for lunch," she said.

Was that an invitation to lunch? "Sounds good to me," he said, not at all sure what her intention was. Maybe she'd just hand him a bowl of lasagna and go on her merry way, or there was the possibility they'd sit together and enjoy a leisurely lunch. Whatever the case, he wasn't comfortable asking, so instead he walked over to Del, gave her a tender kiss on the cheek and thanked her for the evening. "It's nice to get out for a change."

"You don't date?" Del asked Simon as he headed toward the front door.

"Nope. Too soon. The wound hasn't healed enough and I'm generally not that trusting of relationships right now." If ever again.

"Too bad because I think you'd make a terrific date for someone. Maybe you'll meet someone in the clinic or the hospital."

Except he wasn't looking, as most of the women who fell into his age category had children and he wasn't going to do that to himself again. He'd been hurt badly the first time and he wasn't going to do that again. "Thanks again for the evening," he said, then disappeared out the front door.

"He's different, Charlie," she said as she laid her baby back down in his crib. "He seems like he'd be a great candidate for someone to date, yet he won't date. Maybe his divorce hit him harder than I assumed it did. But the thing is, I don't think he's even looking for companionship. He seems happy being single."

Charlie looked up at her and giggled.

"Well, I'm glad you think it's funny. But mark my words, one of these days you're going to be out there looking and it's not going to be easy finding the right one. Just look at the mess your mommy made of her life for five years. That should teach you something."

Five years of bullying and verbal abuse and she hadn't gotten out of it quickly enough. But she'd lived in the hope that Eric would change at some point, not that he ever had. It had forced her to change, though. Forced her out on her own into the world, where she'd had no choice but to make it all by herself. Surprisingly, she'd discovered she liked it that way. Liked everything about it including her notion to get inseminated and have a baby on her own, owing to her biological clock ticking and all that. Her doctor had told her time was running out for her. Her ovaries were beginning to fizzle out. No, she wasn't too old to have a baby yet, and that was still a ways off, but she hadn't wanted to put it off any longer since she really intended on having a brother or sister for Charlie somewhere down the road.

So one year from her breakup date she'd embarked on a new adventure and she'd loved every minute of it from the pregnancy to the birth. Having Charlie was the single best thing she'd ever done and she didn't regret even a moment of it.

Charlie reached his hands up for her to hold him and, while she normally didn't give in to his little stall tactics, tonight she wanted to feel him in her arms.

"OK, so you win just this once but don't think your mommy's going to be a pushover all the time, because it's not going to happen." Although it was happening more and more now that she was working and leaving him behind. "He's a nice man, though, Charlie. Just like yesterday when he covered so we could have time in the park together. I'll admit that Simon and I got off on the wrong foot but that seems to be behind us now."

She hoped so, anyway. Because she really liked him and could even fancy herself dating him sometime. Not that she intended for *that* to happen. But it was caught up in her daydreams. So she pushed it aside and sang Charlie one of his favorite little songs. *Down in the meadow by the itty, bitty pool…*as she glanced at the bouquet of flowers and smiled. Honest to goodness, this was the first time anybody had ever given her flowers and it made her feel special.

"Room Three has an advanced case of bronchitis," she said in greeting to Simon the next morning. "Room Two has a broken arm—just a greenstick fracture, I think. We're waiting for X-rays. And Room One has a little girl who's just started having periods and she has the cramps. So take your pick."

"Good morning to you," he said, looking up on the sign-in board. There were six other cases signed in to various other doctors. "Looks like today's going to be a busy one."

"It happens," she said, giving him a big smile.

"Then I'll start with the bronchitis and work my way down. How's that sound?"

"I'll take the cramps," Del volunteered. "At age eleven I think she'll be more at ease with a female doctor."

They parted ways and Simon went to have a look at his bronchitis patient, a little boy named Bart. He was eight. "How long have you been sick?" he asked Bart.

"Three days," his mother answered. "At first we thought it was a cold."

"Well, we'll get that fixed right up for you. Give you some medicine and send you home to rest. And you'll be up and around inside five or six days."

"Thank you," his mother said. "I was so afraid it would be something worse." She brushed a tear off her cheek. "I don't know what I'd do if he got really sick."

"You'd bring him here and we fix him up."

"It not easy being a single mother…no one there to help me through it."

"I can imagine how hard that is." Simon gave Bart a shot and a prescription and sent them on their way. Thinking about Amy in the intermittent seconds.

"Cute kid," Del said in passing.

"Mom's single. Having a rough time of it. No support." He sighed. "I told her I knew how hard that could be."

"You've got great empathy, Simon. Being a single mom without having support's got to be the hardest thing in the world. I'm lucky I've got all kinds of support."

"I learned to be empathetic and not to judge after I became a pediatrician."

"It's good that you care so deeply. I mean, word eventually got around when I was pregnant and I lived some pretty rocky months where I heard things like, *'She's a doctor, she should have known better.'* And, *'She's a doctor, how could she be a good example to our older patients?'*

"It hurt, Simon, and I'd be lying if I said it didn't. But it was my choice not to tell anybody the circumstances at the time because that would have only brought on more speculation and rumors. So I gritted my teeth and worked through it."

He admired her for her convictions and knew she was right. But he still thought of Amy and Yvette and wondered what kind of support Amy got from her mother.

He'd always been the better parent to that child, and it hurt him thinking what situation Amy might be living in now. But there was nothing he could do about it, just as there was nothing he could do to convince Yvette to allow him to have more time with Amy.

Yvette certainly wasn't abusive, more like negligent, but she'd be the type who put off an illness for too long, or sign away permission to a virtual stranger. She certainly wouldn't have been worried the way Del would be, or Bart's mother. Maybe those thoughts were where all his angst was coming from. Then to look at Del and see what kind of a super mother she was…that just made him angrier thinking how Amy deserved something like that.

"You're one in a million, Del," he said. "A lady with strong convictions who puts up with the ridicule simply to get what she wants. I admire that in you."

"Thanks," she said.

"Anyway, I'm going to run over to the hospital to

check on some patients. Got a couple I'm worried about." And getting his mind back on work would take it off Yvette.

"That's nice of you, Simon. I like it when a doctor goes above and beyond the call of duty."

The more she got to know him, the more she liked him. He was certainly unique to their staff in the way he cared. And she didn't even mind that gruffness in him. Most of it was justified considering the situation with his stepdaughter.

She wondered how long someone with his talent would stay around, though. Amy might move somewhere else. Or he'd have other offers. Offers better than any they could do for him. In fact, she could see him in charge of a hospital pediatrics department, he was so authoritative. That was what worried her. She liked having him here, liked his skill, and as far as she was concerned he was on the open market for something better. Well, it was one of those bridges she'd have to cross when she got to it, she supposed.

"Well, all my patients are doing fine," Simon said, strolling down the hall. "And everyone is happy. So what's next on the board?"

"Twins. Both with runny noses and fevers. Aged two. And a mother who definitely frets to the point of obsession."

"Good," he said, grabbing the chart off the stack, then heading down to Exam Five, where he found two-year-old twins, both with simple colds, and a mother who was worried to death. With all the worrying he'd been doing over Amy lately, it was nice seeing a good mother. It restored his faith in humanity.

"The lasagna is in the fridge with your name on it. Eat as much as you'd like. In the meantime I'm going to run next door and see Charlie. He's expecting me."

Admittedly, Simon was a little disappointed, but not surprised that she preferred to spend her lunch hour with her son. In fact, he would have been surprised if she hadn't. "Have a nice lunch hour," he said.

"Any time I'm with Charlie is nice," she replied as she trotted toward the front door of the clinic. Unfortunately, one of her patients walked in at the same time she was leaving and she had no recourse but to see the child. So she had the girl checked in and spent the next thirty minutes with her, only to send her over to the hospital for an appendectomy. By then it was too late to go see her son but Simon was on his way over there to check on a couple of patients so she stepped into the men's locker room to ask him to check on Charlie for her.

"Simon," she called out to him, admiring the lines of his body in the transparent curtain.

"Care to join me?" he teased.

She liked the contours of his lean body. And yes, even doctors could admire. Which she did. Immensely.

"Since I didn't go over there at lunch and he'll be going down for his afternoon nap any time, I was wondering if you might check in on Charlie for a minute to make sure he's OK."

"Sure," he called, then stepped out of the shower with nothing but a towel wrapped around him. "Now, you can either stay and watch me dress, which I wouldn't mind because I'm not really shy, or you can leave. Your choice." He grinned. "Want to think about it for a couple minutes? I'll be glad to wait." He adjusted his towel a little tighter around his mid-section so it wouldn't accidentally fall.

"Sorry," she mumbled, then backed out the door, leaving him laughing as she exited.

"I am a doctor," she said, as he left the locker room a few minutes later all scrubbed and fresh and ready to go. "It's not like I haven't seen a naked man before."

"But you haven't seen *this* naked man, not that he cares. But people might talk, especially if someone walked in on us while I was still naked," Simon said, coming up behind her.

Del blushed. "I wasn't thinking."

"I was," he said, grinning. "And it's been a while since I caused a lady to blush the way you are right now."

"But I didn't mean to…well, you know. Come gawking. All I wanted to do was ask you to look in on Charlie for me."

"Which I'll be glad to do." These were the words to which he departed and surprisingly, ten minutes later, Del got a short movie texted to her phone. It was Charlie, who was fast asleep, looking all innocent only the way a baby could. She texted Simon back to thank him, and saved the movie in case, well, she wasn't sure why since she'd see her baby in another few hours. But she was so touched by the gesture she didn't have the heart to get rid of it. And over the next hour, while Simon was at Lakeside checking in on various kids, she couldn't count the number of times she replayed that ten seconds' worth of video, thinking not only of Charlie but of Simon when she did.

"I've almost worn out the video," Del said as Simon walked through the clinic's front door. "Thank you so much for doing that for me."

"No big deal," he said. "I was there and it didn't disturb Charlie, so what the hell? I decided one video was worth a thousand words."

"Or more," she said, standing up on her tiptoes and giving him a kiss on the cheek.

He blushed and backed away. No way was he going to become that involved with Del, so he wasn't going to let it start even in the simple gestures. "What's up next?" he asked uncomfortably.

"A couple cases of the croup, an advanced case of diaper rash and a general physical. Take your pick."

"I'll start with the diaper rash," he said and grabbed up the chart and headed down to Exam Four. "Good afternoon," he said on his way in the door. "I'm Dr. Michaels, and I understand someone here has a persistent case of diaper rash."

"I've tried everything," the mother said. She looked worn out. "And nothing works."

"Well, take off Angela's diaper and I'll have a look."

Outside in the hall, Del stood and watched the door behind which Simon was treating a baby. She sighed. No, she wasn't in the mood to get involved with anyone, but another time, another place, and it might have been him. Except he seemed as uninterested as she did. So it was a no go all the way around. But he surely would have been a great dad for Charlie, if she'd been in the daddy-hunting business.

Except she wasn't.

"Too bad," she whispered as she walked away. Yep, too, too bad.

CHAPTER FIVE

IT WASN'T THAT she needed the company; wasn't even so much that she wanted it. But when Simon asked her and Charlie out for dinner she found it hard to turn him down. He understood the restrictions, too. Home by seven thirty so she could go through her evening routine with her son. Bath time, bedtime story, a little song, then sit with him until he was fast asleep. It was a routine that really didn't give her much time for a normal social life for herself, but that was fine and dandy with her. This was all she needed in her after-work hours. "I need to stop and pick up some diapers," she told Simon, before he followed her home in his car so he could drive them on their date for three. "And some baby food, if you don't mind waiting."

"I'll be glad to go with you—that way you won't have so much to carry."

"Would you?" she asked. "I'd appreciate that." Suddenly, she found herself looking forward to their abbreviated evening together. It had been a long time since she'd had a real date and while this was not so traditional, it was real enough that she was excited to get out for a little while. Life with Charlie was fulfilling, but she did miss adult companionship outside of work sometimes. So they made a quick stop at the grocery store, then she took her car home and changed clothes, changed Charlie and was back out and ready to go in a matter of minutes. In the meantime, Simon had fixed the baby's car seat in the backseat of his car just as if he knew what he was doing.

"Tell me about Boston," she said as they entered the restaurant. "Did you like it?"

"I loved it. It's such a historic town, so picturesque. And so expensive. I had to rent a parking space outside my town house that cost me fifty thousand a year. And I had to walk a block to get to it. By most standards that's obscene but that was part of the charm living in a Boston town house."

"That's why I like Chicago. It may be large but it's not inconvenient. And I love all the services and sights here. And the fact that in most areas you get parking to go along with your condo. It's all included in the price of the unit."

"I like that, too, and that's one of the reasons why I came back. Home is where the heart is, and this is home to me." The heart, and Amy.

"Do you ever miss Boston?"

"Some, but I miss Amy more." He sighed. "And you?"

"I was in Indianapolis with Eric for a while before he was in medical school. During our last year of medical school I'd already decided I wanted my own life, no outside interference from anybody. Eric and I were actually estranged the last year we were together, only it was just easier to ignore it. But I'd started making plans for when he was gone, and having a baby was part of it. Charlie wasn't an afterthought, but more like a sign of my independence." She smiled wistfully as she gave him a bite of food. "He's part of my liberation...the best part because I really did want him so badly, and my lack of relationship had nothing to do with it. And of course, the clock was also ticking.

"You're not that old."

"I didn't want to be that old when I had him, either. So I made the decision and stuck by it.

"Good for you," he said, picking up the baby spoon and giving Charlie another bite to eat.

It came so naturally to him, she thought. Just like the baby seat. It must have been looking after Amy. It was as if he was meant to have a child of his own. Of course maybe it was the pediatrician coming out in him, too.

"Well, it's nice being on my own. I was a mess at first, right after the breakup, and I almost gave in a couple times when he begged me to take him back. He promised to change. But he had habits that don't change so easily, like those other women in his life. And after all those years I found out he didn't even want children. He knew I did. I'd talked about it, told him I couldn't wait until we started to have our family, and he always said one day we would. Then I caught him cheating, and who wants to bring a child into that situation?"

"You knew he was cheating?"

"I suspected for a while, but I was afraid to confront him because I didn't want to know. That was me with my 'head buried in the sand' phase. Once I pulled it out, though, I discovered just how much was out there that I'd missed, and how much I was going to miss if I continued to hold on to him. My baby being the biggest thing. I wanted one so badly…" She brushed a tear from her eye. "So, did your ex cheat on you?" she asked him.

He shook his head. "She was faithful as far as I know. Just bored because she didn't bargain on a doctor keeping a doctor's hours. And back in Boston I worked pediatrics in the ER, which kept me pretty busy most of the time. So when she started complaining, I took a job in a clinic, but I still had long hours as I was the director and I didn't get the eight-to-five job she thought I'd get. Then there were my on call hours, hospital rounds…it was a busy job and she simply got tired of sitting around waiting for me to come home. So one day I came home to divorce papers and that's all there was."

"Did you love her?"

"I loved the idea of her, but I fell out of love with her because of all her nagging. I had a job to do and she never could understand that I was busy. So, after the divorce, she remarried someone who could give her all the attention she needed."

"You sound bitter."

"Maybe I am. She certainly surprised me without any kind of warning. Married one day and on my way to a divorce the next. It was a shock, to say the least."

"I'll bet it was," Del said, noticing that Charlie was nodding off. "And on that note, I think we need to call it a night." Too bad, too, as she was enjoying herself with Simon. It was good getting to know a little more about him, and telling him about her. Although there was still something she couldn't put her finger on. Something deeper in Simon that he wasn't talking about. About Amy? About the deep pain he went through when he lost her? She could see it in his eyes, hear it in his voice. Sense it in the way he wrung his hands as he looked as if he were a million miles away.

Still, in spite of it all, she liked him. He was a good doctor, which was where it started, and good with Charlie, too, which, for her, was where it all ended. Right now she was simply too frightened to get involved again. It didn't mean she never would, but not now. Not until she worked it around her head that she had it in her to trust completely another man. Not just for her sake now, but for Charlie's, too. He counted in all this. In fact, he counted in a big way.

"Why don't you bring Charlie and come to my place tonight?" he asked on their next day off together. "I'm a fair to good cook and I can make something Charlie will like."

"You really don't mind me bringing Charlie?" She wasn't sure why she was on the verge of accepting, but she was. Maybe it was because she enjoyed his company, or just needed an adult social situation. But she was tipped toward accepting.

"Not at all. He's a cute kid. Good manners for six months."

"We'd love to come." Well, there she'd done it. Gone and accepted.

Which left her in the same spot as she'd been in before. Getting involved where she didn't belong.

Simon smiled, but he also sighed. Maybe it wasn't what he really needed, either, wasn't where he needed to be. But they were growing closer and she liked him. So what did a little dinner again among friends matter anyway? It wasn't as if this were a date, and she wasn't going to let this turn into anything but two friends having dinner together. That much was for sure. Nothing but dinner. End of story. Yet she worried about that, too. So why did she worry so much?

"Why did I do this, Charlie?" she asked as she got the infant ready for his night out. "I invited him, which is bad enough, but then I accepted his invitation, which was even worse. I like the man, but not in the way I should be dating him. Or doing something that could vaguely be construed as a date."

One bad long-term relationship was enough to make her swear off all relationships for quite some time and concentrate on the only man in her life she truly loved—Charlie.

"Momma's going to get this right," she told her son, who was busy playing with a stuffed teddy bear as she tried to dress him. "I promise you, I'm not going to do anything stupid like get involved with Simon. You'd like him and, as a matter of fact, I like him, too, but now's not the right time for that. And I'm not sure if or when there's going to be a right time."

However, who said they couldn't be friends? She'd settle for that and be very happy with the outcome, as she didn't have that many friends on which to count— thanks to Eric, who had been so controlling she'd lost contact with most of her friends from medical school— and she felt as if she could count on Simon. But men always wanted to take it to the next level, and she surely wasn't ready for that. No way, no how.

"Your momma just wants an adult friendship," she

said to Charlie, who'd tossed his teddy to the end of his crib and started squiggling around trying to get it. "Which you'll probably never understand since you're going to grow up to be a man. But the truth is, it's not always about sex. Sometimes it's about a close relationship that can include everything that goes along with a good friendship and nothing more. I like Simon that way."

Although, who was she kidding? He was her type, at least physically. In fact, she'd picked out a man with Simon's features to father her child… She liked her men dark, with broad shoulders and green eyes, which fit Simon to a T. A trait she noticed over and over throughout the evening.

"Your cooking's very good," she said as she ate her Chinese stir-fry. "I hope I can teach Charlie to cook when he's older. There's always something appealing about a man who can cook."

"I'm not that good, but I do have a few specialties, so after you've been here four or five times you're going to have to settle for reruns or eat some of my more dubious dishes."

Was he implying four or five more invitations? Suddenly, that gave her very cold feet as it sounded like a dating relationship to her. And just after she'd convinced herself she could be friends with him. Del sighed. What was she getting herself into? "You do realize I don't date, don't you?" she said, being brutally honest with him lest he got ideas about the two of them.

"Neither do I, so that makes us even," Simon replied, then took a bite of the chicken in the stir-fry. "Haven't since my divorce and I don't intend to for a good long time, at least not in the dating sense. It's too rough getting involved then uninvolved."

"So we're OK with this, whatever it is?"

He chewed, then swallowed. "A few meals here and there, maybe a walk in the park... I am if you are. I'm thirty-six and one marriage at my age is enough. I've still got the battle scars to prove it."

"I have some of those myself." She laughed. "So we're both at the same points in our lives, it seems."

"Friendship. No dating. That sounds about right to me."

"But can that work?" she asked. "Because I honestly don't know. I've never been in this position before."

"There's only one way to find out," he answered. "We'll try it until we know one way or another."

"And no one gets hurt?"

"No one gets hurt."

In an ideal world that could work, but she knew they weren't living in an ideal world. They'd both had bad breakups and were gun-shy. Neither one wanted permanence. Well, she'd see. She'd just see what happened. Nothing ventured...

The evening hung on nicely. They ate, Charlie dozed off, and Del and Simon talked about various medical issues, including FAS. Then all too soon it was over and it was time to take Charlie home and put him to bed.

"Let me walk you," Simon offered. "It's not that far and it is dark outside now."

"I'd appreciate that," she said as she slipped Charlie into his coat and hat.

"It's hard to imagine how close we live and yet we've never bumped into each other on the street."

"I haven't gone out much," she said. "My whole life's been tied up with taking care of Charlie. It hasn't been easy doing it alone so I don't get out too much." She shrugged. "I'm not complaining. Just telling you the facts. Single parenting is difficult and I wouldn't trade it for anything in the world. So if I passed you on the street, nine times out of ten I'd be preoccupied with Charlie and wouldn't even see you." She smiled. "That's just the way it goes."

"I suppose it is. But since I'm not a parent…"

"You'd make a great father," she said, slipping her hand into his. "To any child." As they walked in sync, she could hear him sigh.

"The problem is the one I *want* to be a parent to isn't available to me."

She stopped and held onto him. "You'll work it out. One way or another you'll work it out. I have all the confidence in the world in you, Simon. You're meant to be that little girl's daddy and it will happen."

"All the confidence in the world?"

"Since I've gotten to know you better I do. You're a strong man and a caring one and it will happen for you one of these days. I'm sure of it."

"I'm glad we get along now. You're the strong one, Del. And you say the right words—the words I need to hear to give me hope."

She started to walk again, her hand still in his. "We can be strong in this together for each other. I need someone there to be strong for Charlie and me, and you need someone there strong for you and Amy."

"Equal in strength," he said.

"And needy in a way. It's nice to have someone to rely on."

"You'll make a great parent to your own child one day," she said as she put Charlie in the baby carriage. "When the right woman comes along…"

"You didn't wait," he said to her.

"Biologically, men can produce children much longer than women can. And my time was running out. Besides, I always wanted a child. Eric promised me we'd have one when the time was right, but there was never a right time for him because then he backed out on his promise when he found someone else. So I just decided to do it on my own. No fuss, no muss, no bother. Have my baby by myself and skip all that came in between like the role of the father. Made it easy that way. At least for me."

"But what will you tell Charlie someday?"

"The truth. When he's old enough to understand it."

"Don't you think that will hurt him?" he asked as they strolled down the street in the direction of Del's condo.

"Not if I do it the right way. He'll understand that he was my choice and not my obligation."

"You're sure of that?"

"If I raise my child the right way, I am. I'll just let him know he was a wanted child and not an accident."

"I hope that works out for you," he said as they stopped in front of her condo. "But you're a great mom, so I suppose it will."

"Thanks for the compliment. But I'll admit, I've

thought about that more than once. It's not going to be easy telling him."

"You'll do the right thing when the time comes, Del. Anyone who loves her child as much as you do is bound to."

"Thanks again." She reached up and placed a tender kiss on his cheek. "Maybe you'll find the right woman soon and we can raise our kids together."

"I'm not looking for the right woman right now. Did that once and that was enough for this part of my life."

Del laughed. "Never say never."

"Well, I'm about as close to never as you can get."

"Don't be so pessimistic. You never know what's going to happen in your life."

"True. But I've pretty well put myself into the no-relationship category for now. And what about you?"

"I think I'm sitting right there next to you. I'm not really interested in finding someone right now. Charlie's enough for me."

"You're lucky to have him."

"I know I am. Which is why I don't want to mess things up and bring in someone else. We're good the way we are."

"But what if you met the *one*?"

"What if *you* met the one?"

He thought about it for a minute. "I suppose that's one of those bridges you cross when you get there."

"And keep your fingers crossed you don't get there."

"Come on now, it's not that bad."

"Oh, it was that bad. And toward the end it got worse when he was cheating on me. It caught me off guard."

"You never expected it?"

"At the time I didn't. But later, when I thought about it, I realized he'd been playing me for a fool for quite a while. Then talk about feeling stupid."

"I guess that's the way I felt, too. Pretty damned dumb. She didn't cheat on me but she sure had another life going. Lied about it, and went through my bank account to do it. But in her defense I was busy looking the other way so I can't blame her for that."

"You'd think they'd be honest about it, though. If you don't want to be in the marriage get out, don't bully your way through it like Eric did our relationship. He could have simply left."

Simon shrugged. "Who knows what goes on with people and why they do what they do?"

"One thing's for sure. I'm going to teach Charlie to be better."

"With you as his mother, Charlie's going to turn out fine."

Del blushed. "I appreciate the compliment. I hope I do well with him." She hoped to heaven she did well. Charlie deserved that from her.

CHAPTER SIX

"I'M GOING TO see Charlie in a couple hours or so. Care to tag along and have lunch with us?" she asked the next day. "He sure does like you."

"Can't," Simon practically snarled. "Too busy."

Where did that come from? "Fine. But if you change your mind…good. I'll call you when I'm ready to go over." She glanced at the clock on the wall. "Charlie eats between eleven and twelve."

"And when do you eat?" he asked.

"Hardly ever when I'm on duty. Don't have enough time."

"Don't wait on my account. I have a lot to do." The sacrifices you make for your kids, he thought to himself. He remembered all the sacrifices he'd made for Amy—the missed meals, the days off work, adjusting his schedule to fit to hers as she got older—none of which had been appreciated by Yvette, yet he hadn't begrudged the child anything.

Charlie held his arms up to his momma and she picked him up and cradled him. As it turned out Simon wasn't able to make it, he was so busy. "He's fixed on something and I don't know what it is, but it's work, and you know that work comes first." Charlie giggled then burped. "And you, of course. You're always first."

She did wish there were something…anything she could do to help Simon, though. She felt so bad for him and she could understand what it would be like ripping your child from your arms because she had Charlie.

Charlie snuggled his head against his mother's shoulder, which indicated to Del that it was time for a nap. "I'll see you after work," she promised him, "or before if I can catch a break for fifteen or twenty minutes."

"He's doing splendidly," Mrs. Rogers said as she watched Del put Charlie down in his designated crib. "Plays with the other babies his age as much as a six-month-old can play, and he's caught on to his routine easily. No separation anxiety. He's really a good little boy, so there's really nothing to worry about."

Del breathed a sigh of relief. "I'm the one who has separation anxiety," she said. "And while you say there's nothing to worry about, I still worry."

"Because you're a good mother."

Maybe she was, but that didn't stop the pit in her stomach from growing every time she saw Charlie in day care. She wanted so badly to stay home with him it hurt. But there was nothing she could do. This was her life and she had to make all the pieces fit together. "Thank you," she said humbly. "But that doesn't make it any easier."

"Well, for what it's worth, it will get easier over time, once you've adjusted to *your* new routine. I've seen too many parents come in here and drop off their kids and be glad to get rid of them. It's refreshing to see a parent who frets so much. But I promise you, he's getting good care, as good as we can give him without being his mother."

"I appreciate that," Del said, bending over the crib to give Charlie a kiss on his chubby cheek even though he was already fast asleep. "And if I get in your way or start making a nuisance of myself, please let me know. I don't want to disrupt things here."

"We have fifty children, half that many workers and volunteer grandmas, and the presence of one more person here isn't going to disrupt a thing. In fact, it's good seeing a parent who wants to be so involved. Currently, we have only about a dozen or so parents who make an effort to have lunch with their children."

"That's surprising," Del said, quite stunned at the low percentage. How could a parent not want to spend as much time with his or her child as possible? "Look, I've got to be going," Del said, giving Charlie one last kiss. "I'll see you later, big boy," she whispered in his ear, then went off to find Simon, who was simply standing in the clinic hall, looking at the patient board.

"So many children, so little time." He gave her a sideways glance. "So how was your lunch with Charlie?"

"He slept through most of it. Seems he had a big morning."

"I'm glad someone did. I spent my lunch hour on the phone with the lawyer fighting for Amy. It seems like that's all I do lately."

"Any progress?"

"He said we can start from the beginning again but he wasn't very optimistic that anything would change. He said I'd need more evidence that Amy's being ne-

glected or mistreated—something new that they haven't
seen before."

"Is there anything new?"

"Not that I'm aware of. And since I never get to see
her…" He shrugged. "It's hard to tell."

"Would Amy ever call you?"

"If she had access to a phone she might, but they
make sure she doesn't have access."

"So you can't just call her?"

He shook his head. "That would only make it worse
on her and I don't want to do that."

"Do you want to chat about it?" she said. "I've got
fifteen minutes."

They went to the doctors' cafeteria, where they found
a secluded corner and sat down, he with his coffee, she
with her tea. "Let me make this long story short. Yvette
took everything I had—my car, my money, my house.
Everything. It was for Amy, she told me. She needed a
way to support her, and I let her do it. But like an idiot
I discovered she took it all for her new boyfriend. He
was a gambler and he was tapped out at the time. I felt
so stupid giving up everything, but that's what I did and
when I came here I barely had enough money to start
over. The condo isn't even mine—it's a rental. My life
is practically a rental because I wanted to take care of
Amy and as it turned out I was left with nothing. Talk
about being stupid."

"That's not being stupid. That's loving someone
more than you love yourself and you can't fault a person for that." She took hold of his hand. "If you need
more hours…"

"More hours aren't going to fix what ails me, I'm afraid. And it's not the money. It's being gullible to my ex. I didn't expect her to do what she did, especially since it involved Amy. If anything happens to her I don't have the means to take care of her properly."

"I'm so sorry, Simon. I can't even imagine what you're going through."

"I moved back to Chicago, because I love it here, but I was perfectly happy in Boston and would be happy anywhere Amy was. But Yvette and Amy are here now, and I'd hoped…well, let's just say I'd hoped she'd come to her senses one of these days and give me visitation rights."

"And there's nothing else you can do?"

He shook his head. "Not a damned thing. The court has spoken and I suppose I could appeal again but I really don't have a legal leg to stand on since she's not my daughter and Yvette would never allow me to adopt her for fear she'd lose child support from Amy's real father."

"Does he have visitation rights?"

Simon shrugged. "I suppose he does, but all he is to Amy is a name attached to a bad connotation. To Yvette he's a monthly check in the mail, and that's it."

"Maybe her new stepfather is good? Although the fact he's a heavy gambler doesn't really put him in a very good light."

"I'm not judging him, because I haven't met the man, but it's hard for me to picture."

"Maybe if you talked to him he might come around."

"Like he did when he took everything I owned before."

Del sighed heavily. "Would either one of them listen to me?"

"I doubt it. Unless you ante up and pay them. Nothing comes cheap or free wherever they're concerned."

"So they wouldn't be amenable to a civil chat from one of your friends?"

"Nope. It's all about what they can get out of any deal and they know they can't get any more out of me...and there's no reason for you to be involved in this mess."

"And in the meantime?"

"I get by."

"Does this explain your mood?"

"I hope so. Because nothing else does. I was on the phone with my lawyer earlier looking for another way in and he wasn't encouraging. Told me straight up that he'd send me a bill first of the month so we could settle up and call it quits."

Del couldn't even imagine what she'd do if someone usurped her rights with Charlie and took him from her. Someone such as the sperm donor who had changed his mind and wanted visitation or, worse yet, custody. The thought of that made her queasy and she pushed her cup of tea away. "You've got to be kidding!"

"I'm afraid I'm not. He fired me."

"Can he do that?"

"Apparently he can."

"Is there anything I can do?" she asked. "Give you a letter of recommendation or appear somewhere on your behalf?"

"I'm afraid the fight is fought. As the judge so eloquently pointed out, I have no rights whatsoever when it comes to Amy. She's not my child, I didn't adopt her, and all I did was what any for-hire child-care worker would do for her."

"Seriously?" She was shocked by the judge's lack of sympathy for a man who loved a child as if she were his own.

"The hearing lasted ten minutes, the verdict came in instantly. Amy is lost to me forever."

"How old is she?"

"Seven."

"Then she'll have memories of you, so maybe someday…"

"After Yvette does a number on me the way she did on Amy's father, there's not going to be any someday. She trashed Amy's father every chance she could and Amy heard it. Yvette never took care to mind her words around her child and that has to have an effect. And I expect if I keep trying to get back into her life she'll do the same to me. Kids that age are so impressionable, too." He shrugged. "I've exhausted everything I know how to do without hurting Amy, or without involving her. Even my own attorney told me it was time to give up for the sake of the child."

"Why did you marry her if she's so vindictive?"

"I never saw that side of her until we'd been married awhile. Then when it came out, it came out ugly. She looked like a good mother. Amy had everything she needed, mostly thanks to me. But I wasn't enough and she reminded me of that every day. I couldn't provide the life she thought she deserved. And to be honest, I think she'd already set her sights on finding her next victim by the time we'd split, because she went directly into his arms three months later."

"With the man she married?"

Simon nodded. "One and the same."

"Oh, I am sorry."

"So am I. Which is why I thought I'd better tell you the rest of the reason why I get so grumpy sometimes. I miss my daughter and there's nothing I can do about it. I owed you that much. And I know all the psychology behind it, went to a shrink for a little while and got my head straightened around. But it still doesn't take away the sting." He shrugged. "Mixed moods is my diagnosis. The doctor said I'll just have to put up with it because there's nothing I can do to fight against it."

"And Yvette won't even let Amy talk to you on the phone? I can't believe that!"

Simon shook his head. "No. It's totally no contact."

"That's cruel for both you and Amy."

"I can't even imagine what Amy's going through right now."

She let go of his hand. Let go of the smooth feel of his skin and hated to do so, but anyone looking on might misconstrue their hand-holding as something more than lending comfort in a bad situation. "Maybe things will change for you. Be patient. Something will work out. It just has to."

"That's what I keep telling myself. But I'm not counting on it."

"Well, like I said, if there's anything I can do..."

"I appreciate that. But I'm afraid I've run out of options."

"You say they're here in Chicago, though."

He nodded. "Which is one of the reasons I was desperate to come back home. First, because I love it here, but also because I felt more steady fighting for Amy here. And I'm closer in case...well, just in case."

Del glanced at her watch and stood. "I think it's time we'd better be getting back. We're already twenty minutes late. Oh, and, Simon—thanks for telling me. I know it can't have been an easy thing to talk about." Not easy at all, and her heart did go out to him. No wonder he didn't want to get involved in a relationship. It was obvious his first marriage was horrible and he was now taking time out to sort things. That was something she understood well.

The afternoon was uneventful, with a waiting room full of sick kids, none of them serious. Some were the products of over-zealous mothers who thought sniffles equated to something bad, while others were sick with various colds, flu bugs and cuts and sprains. By all counts it was a nice afternoon—nice to not see any-body who was seriously ill, and Del was grateful for it as her mind was fixed on Simon and his mess of a life. Even after he'd told her, she still couldn't believe that a caring mother would completely turn him away from her child. Which meant only one thing. Yvette wasn't a very caring mother. She did everything out of her own selfish gain and didn't care about her daughter enough to reunite her with someone who truly loved her.

It was a very self-serving motive, especially since Simon had no financial obligation to the child. Yet Del bet that Simon had supported her for five years, glad to do so, and if he offered to continue that support now, even though his circumstances were dire, she'd prob-ably let him back in. So devious. "What a rotten thing to do," she said to Charlie as she changed him out of his day-care clothes, gave him a bath and put him in his pajamas. "And there's nothing I can do to help him."

She gave Charlie his dinner and spread his play blanket on the floor, but tonight he was being fussy. Wouldn't eat, didn't want to play. Only wanted to sleep. So she took his temperature to make sure he wasn't coming down with anything, found it to be normal and simply sat in her antique Victorian rocker and rocked him to sleep. Just one of those fussy baby days and they did have them, as everybody did. So she didn't worry as he pulled up his knees, stuck his thumb in his mouth and drifted off into a fitful sleep.

After about fifteen minutes she put him down into his crib and leaned over to kiss him, but he shrugged away from her. "Tired from day care?" she asked. "Did you have a big day?"

He didn't respond to her voice, though. Instead, he simply shut his eyes and ignored her. So she checked him once again to make sure he wasn't sick, but he showed no symptoms of anything serious except being extremely tired, so she turned on the night-light and turned off the overhead light and left the room, leaving his door open a crack lest he should start to cry.

Her mother's intuition was instantly on alert, as was her doctor's intuition since Charlie wasn't acting normal, but so far there was nothing to go on that pointed to him being sick. So she settled down on the living-room couch and picked up a medical journal to read. But for some reason, she was too antsy to stay down so she got back up to do some household chores like laundry and dusting—things she barely had time for these days.

In fact, her time was so limited she was giving some thought to hiring a housekeeper to come in a couple days a week. She hadn't decided one way or another, though, as she was still pretty adamant she could do it all. Even though all of it was not getting done as much as it had before she'd gone back to work.

On impulse, she called Simon's number and felt silly when he picked up on the second ring. "You OK?" she asked. "After our talk this afternoon I just thought you might be down in the dumps."

"I am, but I'll get over it. I always do."

"Want to come over for a glass of wine or some coffee or something? Charlie went down early so I've got some time to myself this evening."

"That's nice of you but you don't need to feel sorry for me. I told you because you needed to know, not because I was looking for some sympathy."

"How could I not sympathize, though? That's my nature, why I became a pediatrician. I have great sympathy for children. Kids are great. They don't complain, they're brave, they do what they need to do without making a fuss over it. I fell in love with the field my first day in and that was that."

"Pretty much the same with me. I intended to be an anesthesiologist but this is what worked out for me and I'm glad it did. Kids are fun to treat most of the time. After my divorce and before I came to Lakeside Clinic I was doubting my choice a little, thinking maybe I should go back and become a pediatric anesthesiologist or specialist in something like pediatric oncology. Something to change my life. But that was all because

I'd lost Amy and she was like my compass in a lot of ways. Then I came here and realized I'm where I belong. No turning back. No changing."

"Well, it's never too late to change, if you're thinking about it. Nothing wrong with shaking things up."

He chuckled. "I think I've got a little too much water under my bridge to change my field at this stage of the game. Besides, I like what I do. General care is good. It's what I want to do because I like the interactions as well as the dynamics of the whole field. And in a day and age when so many people are specializing, or where so many family-care practitioners are seeing children, I think the place of the general-practice pediatrician is more needed than ever. Besides, kids are fun."

"Give it some thought, though, since it's still obviously on your mind. Lakeside has a good anesthesiology program. Then there are other hospitals with equally good reputations, as well."

"I've given it a lot of thought, but I'm where I want to be. Either in a clinic or in the ER."

"Well, you're good at what you do, and if you're happy there…" She quieted for a minute, then said, "Could you hang on for a second? I hear Charlie crying, and I'm not sure he's feeling so well this evening. I'll be back on in a minute."

"How about I let you go and I'll see you tomorrow?" he responded. "Charlie could take a little while, and I don't want to rush you."

"Tomorrow," she said, then hung up, smiling. It was nice having Simon for a friend. Although it did make her wish she had room in her life for something more.

* * *

For the first time in her motherhood experience, except for one brief exception, Charlie slept all the way through the night, which should have elated Del but actually it bothered her. He was restless, kept himself curled into a ball with his little legs drawn up to his chest, and didn't get the restful sleep she'd hoped he would. Then when by morning he was still fussy she knew he definitely wasn't feeling good. But another preliminary check showed him to be in good shape. No cough, no runny nose, no fever. Just grouchy again, and he definitely didn't want to be held, which was unusual. He also refused to eat. In fact, he threw his bowl of oatmeal on the floor, which was, perhaps, the most alarming thing of all as Charlie had a pretty hefty morning appetite and loved his oatmeal and bananas. So rather than taking him to day care first thing, she took him to the clinic to get an unbiased opinion of what could possibly be wrong since she had a suspicion she knew and it was best not to treat him herself. Not that she could, if she was right about this.

"Simon," she said on the way in, "would you mind looking at Charlie for me and seeing what you can come up with? He started acting fussy last night and, while I have my suspicions, I'd rather not be the one diagnosing him."

"Take him to Room One and I'll be right there," he said as he slung on his white lab coat and followed her into the exam room. "So what are his symptoms?" he asked, listening first to his chest, then his tummy.

"Fussy, won't eat, doesn't want to be held and he

balls up in a fetal position when I put him down. He was fine last night. Slept all night, was a little fussy when I put him down but he didn't display any overt symptoms."

"Knees drawn up to his chest?" Simon asked.

Del nodded.

"Has he ever had an intussusception?" This was a condition where intestine folded into another section of intestine, much like the way a collapsing telescope folded up into the section in front of it. In and of itself the condition was not serious in the first couple days but it did carry with it a risk of surgery if not treated soon enough. Especially if an intestinal blockage occurred.

Del sighed out loud and her hands started to shake. "No. Did we catch it in time or will he need surgery?"

"If his symptoms just came on him last night or this morning, he's probably a good candidate for treatment without surgery."

Del brushed back a tear. "I didn't miss it, did I?"

Simon shook his head. "You brought him in as soon as he presented with symptoms. Don't second-guess yourself, Del. Babies have no way of telling us what's wrong and if he's not showing symptoms, you can't just guess there's something wrong or you'd drive yourself crazy. You were observant and you did the right thing as quickly as you knew."

She brushed back another tear. "It's so difficult sometimes. So many things could go wrong."

"And so many things could go right."

"I guess so, but when it's your child…" She shrugged.

"You're a normal mom, doctor or not. And most moms would be scared by the diagnosis."

"So how are you going to treat him?"

"Conservatively at first. I'd like to start with an ultrasound followed by an abdominal X-ray just to make sure that the bowel hasn't gone necrotic. And we'll go from there. But he does need to be hospitalized for the procedures and to be watched for a day or two. You do understand that, don't you?"

She nodded. "He's going to be so frightened."

"He may surprise you. One of the reasons I like kids so much is that they take things better than we do. If someone told me my intestine was twisted up I'd be in a panic, but Charlie will just accept things as they come his way."

"He will, won't he?" she said, trying to muster up some conviction in her voice even though she was scared to death.

"Look, Del. You've seen this before and treated it. It's usually not a complicated procedure once the diagnosis is confirmed." He prodded Charlie's belly for a mass and sure enough, there it was. "You know the outcome is good in most of these cases. And if he does need to have surgery, it's a relatively simple procedure."

"I've treated it, but never in my child. He's always been so healthy."

"And he still is healthy," Simon reassured her. He was thinking back to when Amy was sent home from school with the measles. He'd been on call and hadn't seen much of her for a couple of days, then to see his daughter all covered with a rash the way she was—at first he'd been angry that her mother had allowed her to go to school that way, then he'd turned his concern to Amy, who had been one mighty sick little girl for a few days. He'd felt so helpless and vulnerable because there really had been nothing to do for her except sit with Amy and help her ride out the illness. Because of that, he knew how Del was feeling and his heart went out to her because she, too, was feeling so helpless and vulnerable right now. And blaming herself.

"So here's what I propose," he said to Del. "First we get him admitted to the hospital and get the diagnosis over with, then we discuss the options. And even though you know, it falls down this way. He'll be treated with either a barium or water-soluble contrast enema or an air-contrast enema, which will confirm the intussusception, and in the best possible scenario reduce it. The success rate is pretty good—about eighty percent. If this does recur, it should happen in about twenty-four hours, and that's when a surgeon will open the abdomen and manually squeeze the part that has telescoped. Or the surgeon may choose to reduce the problem by laparoscopy. Any way you go, it's going to be more stressful on you than it will be on Charlie. Best case scenario puts him in the eighty percent category and he'll be home in a couple of days. Worst case is surgery, which means he'll be here a little longer than that."

"I appreciate you going over this with me. Of course I know it, but right now I'd be hard pressed to tell you my name let alone anything else."

"It's Del," he said, smiling.

She smiled. "Will you be there during the tests and/or surgery?"

"If they let me. And if you request it."

"I'll request it," she said, "because I don't want him to be alone, and I know they won't let me anywhere near him while they're doing whatever it is they've got to do." She looked at her little boy lying there on the exam table all drawn up in a ball, then bent and kissed him. "I'm trusting you with my son, Simon. He's the best thing in my life and I'm handing his care over to you."

Simon swallowed hard. He knew what it was like to surrender your child. "I'll take good care of him, like he's my own."

"I'm counting on that," Del said as she reached out and took hold of Simon's hand and held on for dear life. "I'm really counting on that."

CHAPTER SEVEN

THE PROCEDURE TOOK longer than she expected and it was nice having Simon sit there with her, holding her hand at first, then holding on to her when her nerves finally got the best of her and her whole body started shaking. "It's so much worse when it's your child," she said, fighting back tears of fear and anguish. "Even though I know he's getting good care."

He ran his thumb over the back of her soft hand. "He'll be fine," Simon reassured her, even though she didn't feel much as if reassurances were going to work.

"Sure. But still, suppose this doesn't work and he has to move on to the next step, which is surgery?" She grabbed hold of his hand and clung tightly to him. "I don't know if I could get through it, the thought of them having to remove a piece of his intestine. That's so serious. And the risks so great it scares me to death. I mean, what if...?"

He stroked her cheek. "One thing at a time, Del. That's what I always tell the parents of my patients. We'll deal with one thing at a time, get through it and hope for the best. That's all you can do."

She exhaled a big, wobbly breath. "Easy to say when

the shoe is on the other foot. But when it's on your own…" She shut her eyes as the tears streamed down her cheeks. "When it's your own child it's different. He's my flesh and blood, Simon, and he's suffering. But there's nothing I can do to fix this. I'm the mother. I should be taking care of him."

"You can't just center your entire life around what he wants or needs. You need to have something in there for you, too, and that's your medical practice, no matter how hard it is to be a single parent as well as a full-time doctor. It's called balancing your life."

"But how did you do it?"

"It wasn't easy, and I'll be the first one to admit that. Amy came first, but my medical practice had its place in there, as well. I learned to balance it so we were both happy."

"How?"

"First, by realizing that I was happier having a life in medicine than I was without it. When I was happier, Amy was happier. I think by balancing myself I evened out everything for the both of us, which was difficult because the older she got, the more she recognized that her mother simply didn't care enough to be involved. Which made for some awfully moody moments. Except, she always had me and she counted on that. I just had to make sure I never missed out on the important things going on in her life. That was the tricky part, too, I'll admit. Amy needed me, my practice needed me and for a while even Yvette needed me. I suppose you can say I failed Yvette, but I think she set up the situation between us to fail." He shrugged. "There was nothing I could do about that, but I did have control over the rest of it, no matter how difficult it became. I just had to make sure that Amy never missed out because of anything else going on in my life."

"I admire that in you, Simon. I'm not sure my priorities are that clear yet. For me it's all Charlie and nothing else. Even my medical practice takes a backseat, which I know it shouldn't. But Charlie is so important to me that I'd love to retire and stay home with him. And I might for a while except I know I'd miss my practice and wouldn't be completely happy not working. It's a real dilemma."

"There were days I certainly hated walking away from Amy, so I understand."

"But you figured it out."

"After a while."

"When I had Charlie I was fiercely adamant that I could have it all, and I didn't count on the emotional turmoil I'm facing now. But there are days when I hand him over to day care that I'm literally so conflicted I don't know what to do."

"You do the best you can. That's all that can be expected from any of us. And the thing is, you can have it all. You already do...at least all that you want."

"What would I do if I did get involved with someone? Maybe even got married? There's not enough of me to go around. I couldn't do it."

"Sure you could, if that's what you wanted. You'd just have to marry the right person. The one who understands that you have this huge life going on already. He'd certainly have to be patient. You'd choose wisely." He smiled. "Because you've had what you know you don't want, I'm willing to bet you've put some think-ing into what you do want."

The surgery ward door pushed open and Del's heart doubled its rhythm, but it wasn't for her. Nothing to do with Charlie, but some other surgery waiters got a bit of good news judging from the round of cheers that went up.

After the noise of the happy waiters died down, she continued, "I've never really given it that much thought because I'm not sure anybody would want to handle my life, such as it is. It's so full already that I don't think I'd have room to add anything or anyone else. And I don't want to get involved when those are my expectations."

"But you could be missing out."

"Or not," she responded. "I mean, look at everything I've got. That's enough to keep me busy."

"But don't you get lonely when you go to bed alone every night?"

"Don't you?" she countered.

"I'd be lying if I said I didn't. But I've got different standards this time. And I'm going to be very careful if I get involved again."

"Let me guess. No women with children."

He arched his eyebrows. "I'm not opposed to chil-dren. In fact, I'd love to have a large family. But I don't want to be put in a position where the kids can be taken away from me. Next time I'm a dad, I want to be a dad for real."

"Poor child," Del said. "To count on someone so much then have him kicked out of her life."

Simon shrugged. "And not to know what she's doing. Sometimes I feel…lost.'

"But Amy lost, too, didn't she?"

"I hope not, but I can't help but think that she did. It keeps me up at nights sometimes wondering and worrying."

"I wouldn't do that to Charlie, which is why I'm happy just the way things are. But today...it's not what I bargained for, and that's stupid of me, considering how I'm a pediatrician. I mean, I know better. Kids get sick with all kinds of strange ailments and I guess I always thought I'd be exempt since I'm a professional in the field. But it doesn't work that way, does it?"

"Amy broke her arm once. She fell down a flight of stairs and the break was pretty substantial. Her mother was out of town, so that left me alone to deal with it and I don't know when I've ever felt more helpless than I did when she was getting it casted. But she came through it better than I did, just the way Charlie will come through this better than you do. I promise."

"Amy needs you as her father. Her mother did a really stupid thing taking her away from you."

"I agree with you on that. I would have done anything for that little girl." He shook his head. "Which is the reason I won't date another woman with a child because, if something should come of it, I stand a very good chance of having that child yanked away from me after I've formed an attachment."

"I can't blame you. If someone came and took Charlie away from me..." She brushed back a straying tear. "Just call me an overprotective mother. I know I am, and I'll admit it."

"Nothing wrong with that. Better to be overprotective than to be Amy's mother, who looks at her daughter as an inconvenience."

"Well, Charlie's not an inconvenience!" Del sniffed. "And I'd fight anybody who said he was."

Simon laughed. He liked that attitude of a mother lion, wished he'd seen it more in his own home with Amy. But Yvette had never cared that much and she was always glad to give up the chore of child care to someone else so she could have her life to herself. Honestly, had he seen that in her when they were married, they wouldn't have been married. But he'd been blinded by a great body and good looks, and back then he'd been too young to look any further. Now he knew, and he was on his guard against the type.

The thing was, Del could have been his type, as fierce as she was, but he wasn't about to put himself into that position again.

"You're a good mother," he told Del.

"With a sick son. I'm so worried, Simon. I know there was nothing I could do but it's still so easy to kick myself about it."

"If this is the worst he ever goes through you'll be one lucky lady. Kids get sick every day. If they didn't we'd have to find a new line of work."

She chuckled. "You're so good to me, Simon. You know exactly what to say and when to say it."

"Comes from practice. Years and years of practice. Just doing my job," he said, letting up a little on his grip around her for fear he was cutting off her circulation. Either that or creating a dependence he could ill afford to develop.

"This is going above and beyond the call," she replied, snuggling back into him. "And I appreciate it."

He knew he should pull away from her right now, but he liked the feel of her pressed tight to him, and it wouldn't take much for him to ask her out on a rightful date when this crisis was over. Of course, he wouldn't. She was a single mom and he'd promised himself he wouldn't do that. So as much as he liked Del, even cared for her, he wasn't going back on his word. Friendship was as far as he was taking it. Although, he wasn't quite ready to define the level of that friendship yet.

Another snuggle and he'd be lost, he was sure. Yet he didn't have it in him to pull back from her, especially not now when she needed him so badly. So he tightened up a bit, braced his back as well as his resolve and endured the feeling passing through him, the one that told him it would be very easy to develop feelings for Del. Whether or not they'd turn out to be serious feelings, he didn't know, but there was some kind of feelings there nonetheless.

They sat there together like that for the next hour, with her clinging and him regretting until the pediatrician on call came out and told them that Charlie's barium enema seemed to have worked out the kink just fine.

"I want to keep him here for a couple days to watch him," Dr. Knowles said. "But right now everything looks good."

"He's sleeping?" Del asked, pulling away from Simon and adjusting her white lab coat.

"Sound asleep, and I'd like to keep him that way for

a few hours, if we can, so when you go in to see him try and be quiet."

Del nodded. Then looked at Simon, who'd backed away from the whole scene. "You coming with me?" she asked him.

"No, I don't think so. The more of us in the room, the more likely the odds of disturbing him are. So I think I'll go back over to the clinic for now and catch up with you later on."

"I'm grateful for your support, Simon," she said, reaching out to take his hand. It was soft and gentle and large the way he was. "I couldn't have gotten through this on my own."

"Call me if you need anything," Simon said, then nodded to Dr. Knowles. "Thank you for what you did to help Charlie," he said, then turned and left the waiting area.

Brian Knowles smiled. "You make a cute family," he said.

"We're not a family. Simon's just a friend."

"Couldn't tell that from where I was watching."

"Then you were watching from the wrong spot because Simon and I have nothing going between us." Even though she wanted to, her feelings were growing so strong for him.

"Well, I've seen families with a whole lot less going on between them. All I can say is, you look good together, and Simon looks like he really cares."

There was no point in arguing the matter with the pediatrician. He'd already made up his mind and had her and Simon and Charlie posed together as a family. Of course, maybe that was what it looked like, the way she'd clung to Simon during the entire procedure. "When can I see him?" Del asked.

"Now. He's in Recovery, but you can go sit with him there, then after he's transferred to a regular room you can spend as much time with him as you want."

"Was there anything I could have done?" she asked nervously.

"Just what you did. It's a relatively rare condition and one that doesn't always get caught in time. I'd say, between you and Simon, you did an excellent job of catching and diagnosing it before it progressed too far. As for whether or not it's cured, time will tell, but I'm willing to bet it's probably a one-time incident. At least I hope it is." Dr. Knowles shook hands with Del and exited the room, leaving her standing there alone, feeling grateful and scared all at the same time. She didn't want to be alone just yet, but Simon had made it abundantly clear his involvement there was done. She was glad for as much of him as she'd gotten, but she wanted more just now. Wanted his comfort again, as she was still upset and his seemed to be the calming influence that had got her through.

It was three hours before Charlie was moved into a private room, and Del was right there with him every step of the way. Simon had called once, albeit a very brief and businesslike call. And Dr. Knowles had stepped in to have a look one time, pleased with the results so far. "It's looking good," he said to Del, as he hurried back out to see another patient. Leaving her and Charlie there virtually alone again, except for an occasional check by a nurse.

"You scared me to death," she told her son as she took hold of his hand and he gripped on for dear life. "But you're going to be fine. The doctor said you're making a good recovery so far."

"I understand you've arranged for more time off work," Simon said from the doorway. "I was going to put in the request for you, but you beat me to it."

"That's what I said I was going to do." She shrugged, secretly glad to see him, and trying to act aloof about her feelings all at the same time. "I'm used to doing things on my own."

"Well, I wasn't sure if that was you or a panic attack talking." He smiled as he walked over to the crib and looked down on Charlie. "Good-looking boy," he said. "He looks just like you."

She smiled. "I'm surprised you came back. I thought maybe I'd scared you off earlier, being so clingy."

"Your son was having a procedure. You were entitled to be clingy. So, what's the word?"

"So far it's all good. He can go home day after tomorrow if everything goes well."

"It will," Simon said confidently. "And in the meantime, I've ordered a pizza to be sent here to the hospital since I figured you haven't eaten all day."

"I hadn't," she admitted. "Too worried."

"Well, I ordered large because I thought I'd hang around and split it with you, if you don't mind."

"I'd welcome the company. And the pizza," she added, realizing how hungry she was now that the ordeal was over.

Dinner was neither fancy nor romantic, but she appreciated the gesture. In fact, had he not reminded her she hadn't eaten at all, she probably would have gone the rest of the day and maybe had some graham crackers from the nurses' station. But Simon had been so kind and thoughtful that she wondered why he was still single. Not every woman out there had a child and certainly he could have and probably should have attracted someone who liked him for all his endearing qualities. Maybe he just wasn't ready. Or he was mistrustful, which was certainly something she understood.

"This was awfully nice of you," she said, debating her second slice of pizza. "Does your ex-wife know what she let get away?"

"More like shoved out the door. She was all set for wealthy and I wasn't."

"Doctors aren't always wealthy," Del defended. "I'm comfortable, but you could hardly consider it wealthy."

"A lot of people don't understand that. Especially my ex. I had student loans to pay back, a family to support. It was a lot of responsibility."

"A lot of people don't count, but your ex should have in the manner in which she expected things from you. Personally, I'm not all that concerned with the material gains in my life. I want to make Charlie comfortable but I don't need to be wealthy to do that."

"So if the man you decided on was temporarily tapped out…"

"Wouldn't matter one way or another. I'm looking for character and integrity. Someone who'll be decent to my son and grow to love him. That's more important than anything else, at least in my opinion." Someone like Simon, she thought to herself. He would be the perfect man in her life, if he wanted to get involved. Of course, he didn't, which made her wary of her growing feelings for him.

"So would you ever find yourself in a relationship with someone who wasn't so tapped out as you are?"

"Depends on who she is, I suppose. My next go around, if there ever is another one, is going to be with someone who's down to earth, someone who values things other than financial gain."

"And her financial status wouldn't matter to you?"

He shrugged. "Get me to that point and we'll see. I'd like to think I'm more responsible than that but who knows? We all make our mistakes, I guess. Mine was thinking she'd change."

Del laughed. "That's what I thought, too. You know, you wake up one morning with the person you want who has magically changed overnight from the person you had."

"I stayed for Amy's sake and look where that got me." He sighed as he closed the pizza box. "None of it's predictable."

"Is that why you haven't gotten together with someone else?"

"Big mistrust factors on my part, and I'll admit it," Simon said. "I proved what kind of a bad choice I made the first time and I don't want to go there again. So for me it's easier being single."

"I get the mistrust factor. That's why I had Charlie with no one else involved. I wanted a baby but I didn't want someone else involved who might injure him the way I was injured during my relationship with Eric. Bringing up a baby alone was my choice and a good option for someone my age, I think."

"But don't you ever wish you had someone there to share parenting duties with? Another person who loves him as much as you do, who can help you when you need it?"

"I never thought I did, until today. But today was out of the ordinary."

"So what happens next time he gets sick and there's no one around to help you? I can tell you from experience it's easier raising a child with two parents than one. That's the kind of built-in support you need."

"But from the way you tell it, you had only you."

"I did. Yvette was more than happy to pass Amy off on me and it wasn't easy working and raising a child all at the same time. I really wanted things to be different, where she assumed part of the parenting chore, but she never did. I was the designated parent in the relationship and she was the one who was free and clear to do what she wanted without the involvement. In fact, if she hadn't met someone else I have an idea she would have still hung onto me because she knew how deep my feelings for Amy were."

"And you would have stayed?"

"Probably."

Del shook her head. "Sounds to me like I'm better off being a single parent than having someone else around who doesn't care as much as I do."

"The thing is, parenting is a tough job and the older they get, the tougher it gets. Charlie's just a baby right now, but what about when he's five or six and needs a man around?"

"What about when he's five or six and doesn't need

a man around?" she asked him. "Not all kids have two parents and most of them turn out just fine."

"But how do the parents turn out? What happens when you don't have someone to lean on?"

"Then I don't lean. It's as simple as that."

"You needed me today, Del."

"Because I was scared and this was Charlie's first real sickness outside a cold. And it wasn't about Charlie anyway. It was about my weakness. But I'll get better as I get more used to being a single mother."

"Maybe you will. Personally, though, I never got over needing someone else to help me raise Amy, and she had a mother."

"We all make our choices, Simon. You chose to raise Amy the way you did and I chose to have Charlie and raise him the way I am. Initially, I didn't get any support from my parents. They thought it was crazy. But once they saw their grandson…" She shrugged. "They changed, I changed and everything in my life changed all because of my decision. If you'd been allowed to stay and raise Amy your life would have been different, too."

"Which is why I won't do that again. It rips your heart out when the child isn't yours and you've got no legal claim."

"So we've both exercised alternately good and poor judgment that got us where we are today. What can I say?"

"That we're human." He stood and picked up the pizza box. "Look, I've got to go. I'll be working for two for a couple of weeks and I need to get to bed early tonight. If you need anything, give me a call… I assume you're spending the night here."

"I am. And thanks, but I'll be fine."

"Need some clean clothes? I can drop them by in the morning?"

"I was thinking about running home once Charlie's down for the night, grabbing a shower and changing my clothes, then coming back here and sleeping." She pointed to the bed next to the crib. "Not comfortable, but it will do in a pinch."

"How about breakfast in the morning? Or coffee?"

"Coffee would be lovely, but you really don't have to take care of me, Simon. I'm good on my own."

"Which is why you hadn't eaten today?"

She smiled up at him. "It would have come up at some point. I'm not a martyr to the cause."

"I think you are, but that's an opinion we'll save for another day since I really do need to get home."

"Thanks for everything you've done today."

"My pleasure," he said, thinking it was his guilty pleasure as he enjoyed his time with Del way more than he intended to.

"I'll... I'll see you around. Maybe I'll stop in the clinic when I know Charlie's one hundred percent."

"Or maybe I'll stop by your place one night and bring dinner. There's this great Chinese restaurant just down the street from me and..."

"Ming's?" she asked as her eyes lit up.

"Ming's," he answered. "Great—"

"Egg rolls!" she finished his sentence. "I like the vegetarian."

"And I like the pork."

"So we have a difference of opinion," she said, laughing as Charlie started to cry. He was strapped down with so many tubes and monitors it looked uncomfortable to her so she knew it had to be to him. She stood from her chair and picked him up gently so as not to disturb his IV or his NG tube.

"And on that note I'll say good-night and leave you two alone."

She'd gone home, taken her shower, changed her clothes and packed an overnight bag for both her and Charlie and headed right back to the hospital only to find him still sound asleep. It had been quite the ordeal for him today, and one for her, as well. Without Simon…well, she didn't even want to think how her day would have progressed without him. Going through all that alone just wasn't appealing. She had called her parents, who were on their way back from Costa Rica to help out, which she appreciated, but that help was a little too late, and for the first time ever Simon, combined with Charlie's illness, had showed her just how utterly alone she was as a parent.

It had never scared her before but now it unsettled her knowing she was in this all by herself without a nearby shoulder to cry on. Truth was, she didn't have a lot of friends—her job had taken care of that. And she had no brothers or sisters. Not even any cousins she could call on. So her backup plan was, well…no one. Which was why she was so glad to have Simon there with her for support. Not that she considered him her backup plan or anything like that. In fact, she wasn't even sure she considered him more than a casual friend yet. But things seemed to be leaning in a different direction, which made her glad he wasn't interested in anything more than a casual friendship because that would signal the end of things between them, since casual was all she wanted. Two peas in a pod, she decided. They both wanted the same thing for different reasons. How absurd was that?

He probably shouldn't have been so forthright with her about the way she was bringing up Charlie, as it was none of his business how she raised her child, whether that be alone or with someone else to help her. But he remembered how difficult it had been raising Amy without any help and the older she'd got, the more help he'd needed. It hadn't been easy, being a daddy without much of a clue, but he wouldn't have changed a moment of it because he'd loved that little girl. Still did. And he'd take her back in a heartbeat if her mother ever cared to give her up, which wasn't going to happen as Amy was a shining star who drew other people in. Yvette used that to her advantage. Took every chance she could to push Amy right on out there.

So he'd wanted to impart his wisdom, except his situation with Amy was nothing like Del's with Charlie. She'd made her choice and the one thing he knew for sure was that Del would never use Charlie as a pawn in her own schemes the way Yvette did with Amy. Del's love for her baby was true all the way.

Still, he didn't want to see things going so hard on Del and he knew they were right now, judging from the way she'd clung so desperately to him yesterday. It was as if he were the starch she needed to keep herself from collapsing, and if something ever happened to Charlie when he wasn't there to hold on to Del, he wondered how she'd manage to get through it. Her true colors as a caring mother had really shown through, but so had her frailties over being alone. Except, she wouldn't admit that was what he'd been seeing. One good, objective look was all it took, though. From him, even from her if she weren't so personally involved.

Admittedly, though, he'd liked being important for her in that time. Liked the way she'd held on to him, the feel of her hands grasping him, the way she wouldn't let go. It was nice being needed. Maybe even a little wanted. Especially by Del. But who was he kidding? It was a one-time event, born out of her need for comfort. That was all it had been, all it could be. After all, she had a child and he refused to put himself through that again. Once was too much. Probably for her, too, once she'd had time to think about it.

Simon sighed as he went to Exam Four to check out a youngster with type one diabetes. Both parents were there, both were equally concerned, even though they were newly divorced. That was the way a child should be raised, he thought as he knocked on the door then entered the room. Yes, that was definitely the way a child should be raised. Only he'd missed his chance and Del didn't want hers.

Weren't they the perfectly mismatched couple? he thought as he flipped on the computer screen in the room and took a look at the child's blood work. "Good job," he said to the little girl, who was about Amy's age. "Everything's in perfect order and it's all looking the way it should."

Everything but his life. And maybe a little bit of Del's life, as well.

CHAPTER EIGHT

IT WAS A week from the day of Charlie's successful procedure to the day when Del showed up at work. "Only a week off?" Simon asked her on his way in to examine a bug bite in Exam Three.

"My parents want some quality time with their grandson and that doesn't include me, I'm afraid. Besides, they're both retired doctors so who better to watch him for a few hours?"

"I talked to your dad on the phone the other night, when I was thinking about bringing dinner by. He's awfully protective of you. And of his grandson, too."

"So that's why you never came over?"

"They'd already eaten by the time I called. He seemed like a nice man, though. Reminded me a lot of you…straightforward, honest, overprotective of his child."

Del laughed out loud. "That's what a protective parent does. He watches after his kid even when his kid is thirty-five years old."

"And that will be you and Charlie in another few years. You won't exactly warn off the girls he'll want to date but you won't be overly friendly, either."

"Like father, like daughter, I suppose."

"Anyway, I'm glad you came back early. We're short staffed, as you already know. Dr. Kent went into early labor and Dr. Morgan is off with the flu. So we're really down on our numbers and we could use the help."

"Which is why I came in today. I'd intended to stay home with Charlie and my parents another week, but the clinic needs me even more than Charlie does since he adores his grandparents, so I was feeling a bit useless." She shrugged. "Meaning I'm back."

"How's Charlie?"

"Doing nicely. No flare-ups, no real disruption to his routine unless you could call grandparents a disruption. He had his incident and it was cured, and, even though the doctor wants to follow him for a couple of months, there don't seem to be any bad consequences."

"Good to hear that. Look, the board's full, and, even though you're one of the bosses and owners of the clinic, all I can do is tell you to take your pick of patients. We're busy today."

"And I was so looking forward to Ming's egg rolls," she teased as she took the first chart off the top of the stack then logged it into the computer. "At least now I know why you didn't bring them. My daddy scared you off." She almost strangled herself she laughed so hard.

"He didn't scare me. He just made it abundantly clear that my attention wasn't wanted or needed."

She reached up and ran her hand over his cheek. "I needed your attention."

"Well, just name the time and place and you've got it."

"Ming's tonight, after work. My parents won't mind.

In fact, I think they'll be glad to have extra time alone with Charlie. They don't get much time with him and it will be good for all of them."

"Allows them their time," he said. "Makes for good luck all the way around. That's what your fortune cookie will tell you."

It was sometime midafternoon, after Charlie's lunch, when Simon caught up to Del. "You look like you could use a cup of coffee or tea," he told her.

"I lost a patient today," Del said. "Not as in dying but as in yanking her kid out of the clinic, and it drained me. And I got pretty indignant with the girl's mother. Child's anorexic and the mom was pretty disgusted with the girl and I, in turn, got pretty disgusted with the girl's mom. And of course I couldn't say anything."

"For what it's worth, I think your indignation toward that girl's mother was righteous in every way. I know what it's like to deal with a parent who thinks it's all about them."

"Amy's mother," she murmured.

He nodded. "Trust me, there were plenty of times when I had a whole string of things I wanted to say to Yvette, but didn't because it wasn't in Amy's best interest."

"Is there a day that goes by when you don't think about her?"

"Not a day. Some days it's worse than others, though."

"I'm so sorry."

"Me, too. And thanks."

As the rest of the day pressed on, things settled down into a normal routine. Del saw a few regular patients, helped with the overflow, and nothing was out of the ordinary. Not the ailments, not even the minor emergencies. It was the kind of day everyone wanted and drove you crazy when you got it. But as the day progressed, she found herself looking forward to her dinner date at Ming's, and it wasn't the egg rolls that were stirring her. Del was actually excited about her date with Simon. Just the two of them in a quaint little hole in the wall. It had all the earmarks of being romantic, even though romance wasn't what she wanted from him. But she did like his company, loved his conversation, enjoyed their alone time together. It was amazing how in just a few weeks he'd become so important to her. And dinner at Ming's was just the icing on the cake as far as she was concerned.

Was there potential in their relationship? Possibly? Maybe even probably. Except he'd made it pretty darned clear he wasn't interested in getting involved with a woman who had a child. Who could blame him for that? Certainly, she couldn't, after the way his last relationship had turned out. Couldn't they have a casual fling though? One without commitments? One that could even be platonic if that was what he wanted in order to keep himself safe. Certainly, she wanted that safety net, too, and she'd made up her mind not to get so deeply involved that intense emotions came into play.

They took a seat by the front window, where they could look out over the lake, and if there ever was something that called for romance, this was it. The restaurant itself was tiny and intimate and the decor was like stepping back into old-world China, where a jade Buddha sat on a shelf, and beaded curtains separated the front from the back room. The room was bathed in reds and black and the smells coming from the kitchen were enough to make her mouth water the instant Simon opened the front door and she heard the quaint, old-fashioned door-bell jingle on entry.

And the lake… Del loved the vastness of it. Ming's sat on the other side of the busy Lakeshore Drive, opposite the lake, but because the lake itself there was so beautiful she didn't even notice the traffic up and down that stretch of road in front of it. All she could see was the sun setting over the water, casting it in the glow of golds and navy blues. And all she could hear was the faint strain of Chinese music playing in the background.

"I haven't actually been in here since, well, it was a long time before Charlie was born. This place always seemed like it was for couples and being a single in an establishment for two just didn't feel right. So I ordered takeout, or had it delivered. Made it less pathetic that way, I think."

"You think of being single as pathetic?" he asked her as he took the menus from the server's hand.

"In a restaurant that caters to romance, yes. In my normal day-to-day life, no."

"I've come in here alone before and eaten."

"Then you're braver than I am, Simon, or at least less self-conscious."

"But you've got nothing to feel self-conscious about. You made your choice and you don't regret it, so that should include dining out even if it is a romantic restaurant. Especially if you like the food."

"I love the food here. It's the best Chinese I've ever had. Everything prepared to order.'

"Like your life, where everything's prepared to order."

"And what's so different about your life?" she asked.

"I venture out of my comfort zone for one thing. I don't think you do."

"Maybe not so much, but I have Charlie to consider."

"And you couldn't bring him here with you?"

"Maybe when he's older." She looked up at the server, who was patiently awaiting drink orders. "I'll have unsweet iced tea," she said. "With a lot of lemon."

"And I'll have a beer. Whatever you have on tap is fine. And could you bring us a couple of egg rolls as appetizers, one pork and one vegetarian?"

The girl scrambled away to fetch the orders while Del and Simon continued talking. "I think the ambiance here would be lost on Charlie, anyway."

"But not on you, and you do count in the mother-son relationship. You can build your life around him to the point that you're suffocating him and I don't think that's your intent, is it?"

"Charlie goes out with me."

"Where?"

"To the park, and the grocery store. Sometimes we just go for a walk. He likes that."

"But where do you go for yourself?"

"Same places Charlie goes," she said, reaching across the table for a packet of sweetener. He laid his hand atop hers for a moment. "How long has it been since you've been on a real date?"

She thought a minute. "It's been about eight years.

I got tangled up with Eric for five, then I was recovering from that, then I got pregnant and next thing you know I had Charlie."

"Eight years? How could you deprive yourself for so long?"

"You were married, Simon. How long has it been for you?"

He winced. "About the same."

"So we're alike in that." She took the tea the server brought to the table and dumped the packet of sweetener in it while Simon took a swig of his beer, then sighed.

"We are alike in some ways, aren't we?"

"More than I like to think about," she said, pushing out her plate to take her oversized egg roll.

"So this is both our first dates in years."

"Except we're not dating," Del reminded him.

"Just having dinner for two in a romantic little hideaway. Sounds like a date to me."

Del shook her head as she cut off a bite of her egg roll and dipped it in sweet-and-sour sauce. "I accepted dinner, pure and simple. I wouldn't have accepted if you'd asked me out on a date. In fact, I'm fully prepared to pay for my own dinner, which makes this even more of a non-date."

"So I'm on a date and you're not. I suppose we could leave it at that."

"But I thought you didn't want to get involved with a woman with children."

"A date doesn't always mean an involvement. Sometimes a date's just a date and nothing more. Or less." He ate a large bite of his egg roll then picked up his menu. "So, do you want to order separately, or do you want to do the dinner for two, which starts with egg drop soup and goes from there?"

"They do have awfully good egg drop soup," she commented. "So if you want to go with the dinner for two..." She shrugged. "Why not? That could be my concession to our non-date date."

Simon chuckled. "You're stubborn. Did anybody ever tell you that before?"

"I wasn't for a lot of years. But when I broke clear of Eric that was one of the first things I worked on. I was in counseling and the doctor told me I had a lot of work to do on me and finding myself again. Which I did."

"You still in counseling, or is that too personal to ask?"

"Nope, not in counseling. I graduated from that when I decided I wanted a baby."

"How did that come up?"

"It didn't just come up. I've always wanted a baby and I thought—stupidly—Eric was the one. By the time I knew he wasn't I was in too deep. But that desire in me never changed. I still wanted a baby, just not his. So I jumped at the chance after we broke up. Actually, not jumped so much as gave it some long, hard thinking before I knew I could do it. And what about you and Amy?"

"I didn't know she was part of the picture when I married Yvette. Amy was never mentioned and at the time her father had custody. But he didn't want her so after we were married about six months there she was on the doorstep one day. A man with a toddler with a little suitcase of clothes, telling Yvette he was finished with the father things. Honest to God, that was the first time I knew of her existence and we'd been married for nearly six months. I suppose that's why I could never pin her down on having a family—she already had one she didn't want."

"That's rough."

"It was. But I think I grew into being a pretty good dad. Problem was, Yvette wanted someone more exciting than a dad, but Amy needed a parent." He sighed. "And life goes on."

"But you got hurt in the deal."

"Not as much as Amy did. That last day when I finally had to say goodbye she clung to me, crying, begging not to be taken from me." He sniffed. "I've never felt so helpless in all my life."

Their soup arrived before anything else could be said, followed by their chow mein, followed by deep-fried bananas and by the time they reached their fortune cookies, Del was almost too full to have the strength to open hers up. But she did.

You will have a lucky night.

Simon's said: *This will be a night to remember.*

"I think they have two different boxes of cookies—one with regular fortunes, and ones they give to the couple they believe will find romance." Del wadded up her fortune and tossed it on the table. "So much for that," she said, taking a bite of the cookie, then leaving the rest on her plate. "The only luck I'm going to have tonight is if I didn't gain five pounds eating so much good food."

"Well, mine's coming true as we speak because this is definitely a night to remember."

"But for how long? And for what reason?"

"Probably until I get senile, and the reason… I'm enjoying the company of my first date in all these years."

"Married years don't count?"

"Says who?"

"Says me," Del replied, looking at her crumpled fortune. "And that's all that counts."

"Whoa. You're the only one who's entitled to an opinion?"

She nodded. "In my life I am."

"But this is my life, too."

"And you're entitled to your opinion, however wrong it may be."

"Spoken like someone who was in a marriage-like situation for five years."

"Close to marriage, but not marriage. So it doesn't count. And for what it's worth, after we became a couple he never *dated* me again." She took out her credit card to pay her portion of the bill and Simon rejected it. "You can pick up the whole tab next time."

"It's a deal," she said, realizing suddenly that he'd taken the advantage here by getting her to commit to a second date. "If there is another time."

He arched wickedly provocative eyebrows. "There'll be a second time, if for no other reason than you owe me a dinner out."

"Aren't you the tricky one?" she said as they walked to her front door. It was a high-rise, its walkway lined with fall flowers and pumpkins. At the top of the five steps, she turned around and looked down at him. "Care to come in and meet my parents?"

"Um, no. They might think that we're...well, you know what I mean. And I don't want to give them any false hopes about their daughter."

"Coward!" She laughed. "They already know how I am, so there's no jeopardy involved."

"I've got an early morning," he finally conceded. "I promised to take early-morning duty at the clinic and work straight through to close."

"That's being quite the martyr, isn't it?"

"It gives a couple people the opportunity to be off and have the day with their families, including you, if you want it."

"But the clinic can be a madhouse on Saturdays because, outside the ER, we're the only practice that's open on the weekends."

Simon shrugged. "Weekday, weekend, it's all the same to me. Otherwise, I'd be spending my day at home, alone, which gets boring after the first hour."

"I might drop in, depending on my parents' plans," she said, then, standing on the top step while he was two below her, she gave him a gentle kiss on the lips. Nothing demanding, nothing deep and delving at first. Just a kiss between friends was the way she looked at it. Although the second kiss was more. It probed, and was a real kiss, not just a friendly one. And it went on forever, grew in intensity until she was nearly breathless. Her face blushed and her hands trembled as she tried to bid him a nonchalant good-night, which was nearly impossible to do given her rising feelings for him. So, he didn't want a woman with a child but she couldn't help the way she felt when she was around him, either, so what was she going to do?

"See you t-tomorrow," she stammered as her knees trembled on her way in the door. But before she could get inside he gave her a long, hard kiss.

This one deep and abiding. The kind of kiss reserved for dates and special occasions. The one that set her heart on fire.

Even though it was mid-October the chill in the air turned into a fiery blaze and it was all she could do to keep from fanning herself. But that would be too much of a giveaway. Too obvious a reaction to what should have been a simple kiss. So, instead she buzzed herself in and turned back to face him. "Oh, and, Simon, thanks for the lovely evening. I really did enjoy the time out with you." And the kisses. So very much the kisses.

"Glad you did," he said, backing away. One step down and he turned and sprinted to the sidewalk. "See you tomorrow...maybe."

She waited until he was out of sight before she stepped in and, once she'd greeted the concierge, she went on upstairs, which was where her mother practically pounced on her.

"He's quite a good looker," Mrs. Carson said.

"Were you looking out the window, Mom?" Del asked.

"Maybe for a minute. With your binoculars."

Del shook her head. "He's a friend. That's all. *A friend.*" Even though tonight he felt like more—so much more. And that second kiss was certainly for more than friends.

"He's a colleague," she said, feeling the blush rise

once again in her cheeks. "That's all." Except colleagues didn't kiss colleagues the way he'd kissed her, or the way she'd kissed him back. Especially the way she'd kissed him back!

CHAPTER NINE

SHE WAS QUIET around Simon for the next couple of days. In fact she avoided him—something that wasn't lost on him. When they did make contact it was about work and that was all. Nothing personal, no references to two nights before, definitely no small talk. But what had he expected from Del, anyway? She was the original no-contact girl, and he wasn't acting much differently himself. No contact, nothing personal. And there was nothing *not* personal about their kiss on her front step. In fact, as kisses went, it was right up there with the best he'd ever had. Which wasn't good at all as he didn't want the relationship to blossom. Of course, he was hanging on to the hope that she didn't want it, either. So that made it two against the odds, which he liked a lot. Except he was afraid that one more kiss and he'd fall hard, since he was already halfway down.

So the days went on and he alternately regretted and was glad for that moment of intimate contact because it showed him that he could move on. He was no longer so emotionally strung out from his previous marriage, which was a good thing. But the bad thing was the distance that kiss had put between Del and him and he regretted that enormously as he had to work with her, and he also enjoyed her friendship. But he was finding that he wanted more, and the more he resisted it, the more he wanted it and couldn't stop thinking about it. That wasn't to say he wanted some convoluted, drawn-out high-tension relationship that would lead him back to where he didn't want to go. But he liked the conversation, liked the companionship and most of all liked it with Del. Though, as it stood, that moment was done. They'd given in to the weakness and look where it had got them.

Simon sighed as he entered Exam Four to take a look at a little boy who had a bad cough and a runny nose. Cute kid with curly red hair and green eyes, and a look that told Simon he was in agony. "So, what can I do for you today?" he asked the boy, as he acknowledged the boy's mother.

"Can you make me better?" Billy asked. "I don't feel so good."

"And where do you feel bad?"

He pointed to his head then to his throat.

"How long you been feeling bad, Billy?" he asked the boy, who was about eight. He liked to make direct contact with his patients when he could as he found that they had great insight into their own ailments—insight outside what a parent might report.

"Since day before yesterday."

"So which came first? The runny nose or the sore throat?"

The child shrugged. "Runny nose, I think."

Now Simon deferred to the mother. "Is that right?"

"He was running a slight fever day before yesterday, and the sore throat came on last night."

Simon smiled. "Thank you for getting him here so quickly. You'd be amazed how long it takes some parents to react when their child is sick."

And so the conversation and exam went for the next fifteen minutes until Simon diagnosed Billy with a mild head cold, and prescribed something for the stuffiness as well as the sore throat. Then the exam was over. Just like that he was alone in the exam room thinking about Del again. So much for the power of a good distraction, he thought as he headed back to the hub to hand-deliver the applicable notes and prescriptions to the checkout clerk. In that brief lull he saw Del dash down the hall, white coat tails flying, and it all came back to him. The conflict, the resolve, everything.

Face it. He wasn't sure what he was going to do about Del yet and, so far, he hadn't given any thought to the fact that this might be the end of something that had never really got started. So he liked Del! More than liked her, cared for her! But as what? A friend, a possible lover? And what was the big deal anyway? They were two mature adults who knew exactly what they wanted. What was stopping them from taking their relationship to another level and evening it out there rather than leave it festering where it was?

Fear, that was what. They'd both spoken their minds, made their opinions, fears and vulnerabilities perfectly clear, and that was that. But why couldn't they work through those issues together? Or could they? It seemed a logical thing to do, having some help to get through. But Del was afraid of that help and, to be honest, so was he. Because there was no telling where it would go. Vulnerability was a strange thing. It caused people to do things they didn't want; caused them to break vows and promises and ignore the real heart. So maybe Del was correct in ignoring this whole thing.

But, damn it! Why did he want to pursue it anyway?

It wasn't the fact that it was awkward so much as that she was embarrassed by the whole episode. She'd kissed him. Started it, and welcomed the second and third kisses. Then she'd avoided him ever since because she didn't know where to go from there. They'd established some kind of chemistry, obviously. But it was nothing she wanted to admit. She wasn't ready. She had Charlie to think about. And a job. No time to be in a committed relationship. The list was long and she'd gone over and over it all weekend and hauled it out and went over it again each and every time she saw him. He had that irresistible charm she needed to keep away from or else next time the third kiss would lead to more, and she couldn't handle that. Didn't want to handle it. All she wanted in her life right now was her son. So it was time to back all the way away and simply be professional colleagues.

Except she remembered those kisses; they were on her mind all the time. So was the next thing and the thing that could come after that if she allowed it. Which she wouldn't. Of course. The kisses were it and no further. It was fixed in her mind like etched glass.

"Do you think talking about it would help us?" he finally asked her.

"Talk about what?"

"What we were leading up to."

She frowned. "We weren't leading up to anything. They were just simple kisses, that's all."

"But what they evoked wasn't so simple, was it? We've been avoiding each other like the plague for the past two days and I know it has everything to do with that last kiss."

"It was a mistake."

"You weren't acting that way Friday night."

"I was out of character for myself."

"Or maybe that was in character and now you're out of character," he returned. As they walked along the hall, each on his or her way to visit a patient, there was no way she could get away from him for the next thirty seconds, so he took hold of her arm, an intimate gesture in and of itself, and led her to Exam Three, to treat a rash. "You enjoyed the evening, Del, and there's no denying that."

"I'm not denying it," she said, looking around to make sure no one else could hear their private conversation. Luckily, that end of the hall was empty of employees, and all the patients back there were in their rooms and would have to have ears pressed to the door to hear them. "It was a nice evening and it was nice to get out and have some adult company."

"We could do it again."

"No," she snapped. "We can't. We both know where this thing could go if we let it, and neither of us want it."

"That's not what your lips were saying."

"Lying lips."

Simon chuckled. "Beautiful, kissable lips."

"And *that's* the problem. I don't want to be kissed. It

can lead to, well…other things. And I don't want that in my life right now. I'm doing good to manage everything I've already got without adding anything more."

"Would you even admit it if you wanted more?"

"Have you changed your mind, Simon? Have you suddenly decided that it's time to go out on the hunt again?"

"Not the hunt so much as I've decided it's time to move on."

She laid her hand on the door handle. "Well, I'm happy right where I am. And that's the difference between us. You can change your mind easily enough, but I can't. I'm on the course I want to be on."

"And you've never heard of adjusting the course?"

"Not in my life. Not since Charlie."

"Too bad, because I think we could have something." He bent low and stole a quick kiss, then left her standing all flushed and confused at her patient's door. It took her a few seconds to regroup before she went inside and was greeted by a mild case of the chicken pox. "Hello, Miranda," she said as she saw the little girl scratching away at the pustules on her arms. "I think I've got a cream that will help relieve the itching."

Too bad she didn't have a cream to relieve her of her growing feelings for Simon.

"Hello, dear," Del's mother said, greeting her at the door when she got home. "Your father's out for a stroll with Charlie. Oh, and those came for you a little while ago." Gloria pointed to the dozen long-stemmed red roses all bedded together in a spray of white baby's breath. "I don't know who he is—maybe the man on your door-step the other night—but he has good taste."

"He's one of the doctors at the clinic. Just a col-league."

"Colleagues don't send colleagues red roses if there's not something more attached to it."

"This colleague wants to take our friendship to the next level."

"Well," said her mother. "It's about time. Is he the one you went out with Friday night?"

"That was just a dinner among friends. That's all." OK, so it was a bit of a lie. But there was no reason to let her mother in on something that wasn't meant to be. She'd only get her hopes up that her stubborn daughter was giving in, which wasn't the case.

"And these are red roses among friends, too? Is he why you've been so grumpy these past couple of days? Honestly, that's why your father took Charlie for a walk over to the park. We're both aware of how grumpy you are when you come home from work, and he didn't want to deal with it this evening."

"OK," Del said, sighing. "I thought I'd found the perfect companion—someone who didn't want to get involved as much as I don't want to get involved. But things have changed. Now he...well. Let's just say that he wants to be the whole package when I'm still not in the mood to unwrap it."

"Because of Eric?"

"Because of Charlie and me. We have a good life."

"That could be so much better if you opened your-self up to letting someone in."

"That's your marriage, and maybe someday I'll find something like what you and Daddy have. But not now."

"And you're not the slightest bit interested in Dr. Red Roses?" her mother asked.

"I'm not saying I'm not interested. It's just that Simon wants to take things faster than I'm ready for."

"He's a man who knows what he wants."

"He wants me to fill a void left by his ex-wife and stepdaughter."

Gloria Carson took a step backward. "You didn't even read the card that came with the flowers." She grabbed it and handed it over to Del.

Del hesitated before she took it from her mother's hand. Suppose it spelled out some kind of term of endearment, or said something she didn't want it to.

"You're being silly, Del," her mother accused. "It's just a simple card. A small one. How many words could he have squeezed on it?"

"It's not how many, Mom. It's what they might say."

Her mother grabbed the card back and sat it down next to the flowers. "You're too stubborn for your own good. You know that?"

"It's just that I'm trying to do what's best for Charlie and me, and I don't think squeezing in a relationship is what either of us needs right now."

"Don't go using my grandson as your excuse. At his age he doesn't care one way or another. If there's something about this Simon that doesn't interest you, that's fine. There'll be another one come along. But you don't need any kind of excuse. If you want to, then do it. If you don't want to, then don't do it. But quit trying to fool yourself into believing that your son needs only you because he's at a perfect age to welcome others into his life. In fact, he's open to it much more than you are. So I'm not saying it has to be this Simon you work with, but at least keep yourself a little more open to the possibility that there's someone out there for you."

"It could be Simon," she heard herself admit, then wanted to kick herself for saying the words out loud.

Gloria arched her perfectly sculpted eyebrows. She was a striking lady—short blond hair, petite figure, eyes that told the whole story. "When I met your father I knew right away. No denying it for me as he was such a good catch I didn't want him single out there in the world for fear someone else would snap him up. But that's just me. I've always known what I wanted and gone out and got it."

"I know what I want," Del defended, as her gaze went to the flowers and the note sitting next to the vase.

"Doesn't sound like it to me. In fact, you sound a little lost."

"I'm not lost." Words spoken tentatively. "It's just that I'm not..."

"Found." Gloria crossed over and hugged her daughter. "Speaking of which, I'm going across the street to the park to find your father and finish off the walk with him. You're welcome to come along, or you can stay here and relax. And think of more excuses why you don't want to go after the one who could be the one." She patted her daughter on the cheek, then grabbed a light jacket and headed to the door. "And don't worry about dinner. Your father and Charlie and I will find something on our walk."

"Tell Daddy to make sure Charlie is warm enough."

"Your father doesn't need to be told how to take care of a child. The one he raised turned out just fine. Except for that little glitch…"

Del laughed. "I don't have a glitch."

"Then it's a blind spot. Call it what you want."

Del shook her head, and sighed impatiently. "How long will you be gone?"

"Long enough," her mother said, laughing. "And not a moment longer than that." With that she walked out the door, leaving Del alone in her condo. It was strange being there all by herself. She was used to having Charlie around, to talk to, to fuss over. "So it's just me," she said aloud, feeling silly for talking to the walls.

She looked at the card next to the roses, and it was getting larger and larger. Or maybe it was that her attention was becoming more and more fixed on it. Whatever the case, she picked it up, looked at it, then put it back down. Then picked it up again, and held it up to the light as if something were going to be revealed in the overhead studio lamp suspended from her ceiling. Talk about feeling silly. She was certainly going to teach Charlie to be more direct than she was.

"Charlie…" she murmured, as she picked up the envelope yet again and finally looked at the note Simon had enclosed. It simply read *thank you*. But that made her wonder what he was thanking her for. Was it dinner, or the kisses at the door? Was it for something on the job, or for listening to his plight with Amy? In fact, the card wasn't even signed so the flowers could have been from anyone, which left her feeling a little disappointed. No, she didn't want more sentiment, but she did want to know why he was thanking her. And if the flowers were, indeed, from Simon.

On impulse, she picked up her cell phone and called his number.

"Simon Michaels," he came on, sounding as if he was in a rush.

She found it strange he didn't identify her with the phone-number-recognition feature on his own phone but maybe he was in too much of a hurry to look at it. "It's me," she said, in a subdued voice.

"As in Del?" he asked.

She could hear the teasing tone in his voice. "As in Del."

"And what can I do for you this lovely evening, Del?"

Now he was toying with her, which caused her to relax a little.

"Were you the one who had the flowers delivered?"

"Flowers, you say?"

"Flowers, I said. Red roses, white baby's breath. Ring any bells?"

"Oh, *those* flowers. I seem to recall picking them out this afternoon on my lunch hour."

"Why, Simon?"

"I thought they were pretty."

"They're beautiful. But you're evading my question. Why did you send them?"

"I think the card says it all. You *did* read the card, didn't you?"

"You mean the one with the very vague thank-you?"

"I don't see that as vague. In fact, I think it's pretty direct. I was thanking you."

"But for what?"

"Ah, now comes the real reason for the phone call. The lady wants to know what I'm thankful for."

"The lady *is* curious."

"You're acting like nobody's ever sent you flowers before."

"I've had flowers before, even from you, but I usually know why they've been sent."

He chuckled. "Not knowing bothers you, does it?"

"Well, if it's for the kiss…"

"Which kiss, specifically, as we're beginning to develop a habit?"

"It's not a habit!" she exclaimed. "And the one this afternoon…"

"Stolen kisses are often the best, don't you think?"

"So that's what you're thanking me for?" She'd hoped it was for something more than a pure physical urge. Maybe in the grand scheme of things she did want him to admit that his feelings for her were growing stronger, and the roses signified that. But they were for that silly little kiss at the exam-room door? Yes, she was disappointed. The thing was, she seemed to be wanting some big romantic gesture on one hand, and on the other she didn't. Which clearly indicated she was confused by the whole prospect of the man called Simon Michaels.

"What I'm thanking you for is a whole conglomeration of things—your friendship, your kisses do have some play in there, for being a great colleague…"

"And for not firing you when you manhandled me in the hallway today?"

"You looked at that as manhandling?"

"I looked at it as inappropriate."

"Then you've never watched any of the medical

shows on television because they're always doing inappropriate things in empty rooms, halls, supply closets. X-ray is a particular hotbed of activity of that sort," he continued, then laughed. "Were you a woman of the world, you'd know."

"I am a woman of the world. I just didn't appreciate—"

"And here I was thinking you were calling me to thank me for the flowers. How disappointing that you turned it into an argument."

"You didn't even sign your name to the card."

"You've got that many men calling on you that it required my name?"

"You know I don't have *any* men calling on me. So what's this about, Simon?"

"Dinner tonight?"

She huffed an exasperated sigh into the phone. "You think food will fix whatever's ailing us?"

"What's ailing us, Del, is you. You're too suspicious. I invited you out for a simple dinner, and all that requires is a yes or no. Yet look what you go and do. You blow it up into something that it's not."

"But you're the one making advances."

"And you're the one rebuffing them. All I did was ask you out to dinner."

"You sent me flowers," she reminded him.

"For a totally separate reason, not to be confused with anything in the future."

"So you consider dinner tonight the future?"

"Well, it's certainly not in the past, is it? Especially since the evening is young. Oh, and I know you're alone because I ran into two people pushing a baby carriage with a baby in it who bears a striking resemblance to

Charlie. Nice people, by the way. They asked me to accompany them to dinner."

"So let me guess. You told them you hoped to have other plans in the near future."

"Actually, they told me to call you and ask you to come along."

"Which you didn't do."

"Which I'm doing now."

"Because you knew I'd call you."

"Something like that." He chuckled. "And for what it's worth, I'm willing to take romance off the table this evening, if that's what you want. In fact, since you're so darned suspicious of them, I'll even take the flowers back."

"I'm keeping the flowers. And I'm not going out with you to have dinner with my parents."

"Then where would you rather go? Over to Maria's Italian Kitchen? That's always good."

"What's always good is a night alone with Charlie."

"Which you can't have because he has other plans."

"So what are we fighting about, Simon?"

"Nothing, as far as I'm concerned. I sent you some flowers and asked you out to dinner. You didn't thank me for the flowers and you haven't accepted my invitation. Does that about sum it up?"

"Did anybody ever tell you that you can be frustrating?"

"I've heard that said a time or two."

"So then it's not just me who thinks that?"

"Why would I admit something like that to you? We all have our peculiarities, you know."

"Mine being?" she asked, not sure she wanted to hear the answer.

"Your attitude. You're so…evasive. And you're sure as hell one of the most doubting people I've ever known. I mean, I sent you flowers and look at the way you're acting about it. You'd think I'd sent you something toxic instead of roses."

"Yes," she said.

"Yes, what?"

"Yes, dinner."

"Seriously?"

"Didn't you ask me?"

"I asked, but I didn't expect you'd accept."

"Do you want me to turn you down? Because I can."

"No. No. I asked, and I wanted you to accept. But with the way we are…"

"How are we, Simon? Tell me, how, exactly, are we?"

"If you know, you tell me, because I don't have a clue."

"Well, then, should I have said no?"

"You should have said exactly what you said. But without all the bickering in between the question and the answer."

"How about we don't bicker tonight?" she asked him.

"No bickering. No romance. Anything else?"

"No more flowers."

"Then next time I should send chocolates?"

"I thought I'd order out and bring it home," he said when she arrived at his door later that evening. "Didn't know what you'd want so I have a sampler of several different dishes. I recalled you like Italian."

"I love Italian," she said, stepping into his condo. It was a converted warehouse, huge on space, and lacking furniture. But very esthetically pleasing. Immediately she began to decorate it in her head. Some easy chairs, a dining-room set, some bookshelves, a sofa... Right now all he had were a couple of chairs, a coffee table and a coat tree. "And I love this condo."

"Like I said, it's too much for me. I bought it with the intention of fixing it up for Amy, but now, since that's a no-go, I just haven't gotten around to doing anything with it."

"You could fit two of my condos in it. Charlie would love all the space."

"Really, at six months old? He's an advanced kid if he's that cognizant of the amount of space around him. Of course, babies are amazing little people, but I doubt the size of this place would really impress your son one way or another."

"Maybe in a few years."

He took her jacket and showed her to the counter in the kitchen, where he'd laid out his array of food. "You feeding an army?" she asked.

"Depends on how hungry you are."

"I can tell you right now that I'm not that hungry. Looks like you're going to be eating Italian leftovers for several days."

"You and Charlie can always drop by and help me."

"Or I can always stay at home and feed Charlie something less messy."

"At his age, is there anything less messy?"

She laughed. "He doesn't quite have his table manners down yet. But we're working on that."

Simon pulled two plates from the cupboard and handed one over to Del, who was busy deciding what she was going to eat. "I opted out of spaghetti because that's too messy. But if you want spaghetti I can run back over there and…"

She held up her hand to stop him. "What you have here is fine. I'm always good with penne and garlic bread." With that she dished up a plate then stood and looked at him. "Where do you propose we eat this?"

"On the floor at the coffee table." He held up a bottle of wine. "It's red. Hope that's OK with you. I know you don't drink much but you've got to have wine with a fine Italian meal."

"Red's fine. And I'll take half a glass."

"It really does affect you, doesn't it?" he asked, pouring the wine.

"When you've seen what I've seen…" She shrugged. "I spent my whole pregnancy being so careful, not eating or drinking anything that wasn't good for my baby, not engaging in risky activities. I know you can't prevent all the misfortunes that can happen in birth but I sure tried hard to be as good as I could be. And my resolve not to drink…well, let's just say that, while I'm not against it, I don't see enough people exercising wisdom when it comes to what goes into their bodies."

"I'm sensing all the carbs in the Italian might not be the best thing I could have done."

"Carbs are fine. We need them. But I saw a pregnant woman the other day and she was smoking and I really wanted to tell her what she could be doing to her unborn child, but I stopped myself before I caused a scene and remembered that it's her right to smoke if she wants.

It's not a good choice, in fact it's a lousy choice if you ask me, but she wasn't asking me."

"And the kids with FAS you treat—they're the reason you don't drink much."

"I got used to it in med school. My parents were never heavy drinkers—they'd have the occasional glass of wine but that was all. And as for me, the first time I saw a child with FAS I was glad I didn't drink too often as I would have given it up on the spot."

"I like a woman with conviction."

"I like a woman who controls her impulses," she said, on her way back to the living room, where she set her plate on the coffee table then sat cross-legged on the floor. "Or a man."

"You're referring to the kisses?"

"I might be."

"They were natural. A perfectly nice way to end the evening."

"What about the one you stole today?"

"I'll admit. I should have done better."

"You're kidding, aren't you?" she asked, reaching out to take her paper cup of wine.

"What if I'm not?"

"Then I probably shouldn't have come here."

He laughed out loud. "You're safe here, Del. Short of my getting drunk and manhandling you, you're going to be just fine."

"OK, so maybe that was a pretty strong word for what you did. I'm sorry that's the way I phrased what I think you see as a little innocent mauling," she said, then took a bite of her pasta.

"Mauling?"

She shrugged. "What else would you call it?"

"A kiss, pure and simple. A short, nearly circumspect kiss."

"Not circumspect enough."

"So it left an impression?" he asked.

"Not an impression so much as chapped lips."

"Whoa now. I wasn't there that long. If I'd really kissed you hard enough to chap your lips you wouldn't be eating tomato sauce with such gusto tonight. You'd be wincing between bites."

"I'm wincing on the inside."

"All this over one little stolen kiss. I wish now I'd made a production out of it. Swooped you into my arms, parted your lips with my tongue, run my hands over your…well, anything of yours would do fine."

She took another bite of her penne and shook her head. "You'd better not be running your hands over anything of mine," she said after she swallowed.

"Isn't that why you're here? To get a little adult stimulation?"

"Adult, yes. Stimulation, definitely not."

Simon held up his paper cup for a toast. "Here's to not stimulating you, even though you know you want it."

She pulled her cup back from his. "What I want is to eat my dinner without being verbally assaulted."

"But I'm not assaulting you."

"You said you weren't ready for a relationship. That's why I've been keeping company with you. Because I took you at your word. Thought you were safe." She tore off a corner of the garlic bread and popped it into her mouth.

"But I am safe. And whether or not I'm ready for a

relationship…honestly, I don't know. I tell myself I'm not, but when I'm with you…"

Del thrust out her hand to stop him. "No! Don't say it."

"Say what? That I'm attracted to you? Because I am."

"And I have a child."

"Which I'm fully aware of. That's the reason I'm not in this to commit to a serious relationship because I still mean what I said. No women with children. Not in the long-term."

"But short- or long-term, I'm a package deal and nothing about that's going to change."

"So we can't play at a flirtation?"

"Why bother?"

He set his paper cup down hard, and some of the wine splashed out on the hardwood floor. "Damn it," he grunted, jumping up to run to the kitchen to grab a rag to clean up his spill. When he got back, Del was shrugging into her jacket getting ready to leave. "What's this about?"

"We won't work. We can play at it, or play around it, but that's still not going to make it something it isn't."

"So that second kiss. When you kissed me back, and I might add it was pretty hard, it didn't mean *anything* to you."

"It meant we were getting too close."

"Which is your cue to run away. Right?"

"I'm not running. I'm just avoiding the inevitable."

"By walking out my door."

"Look, Simon. We haven't got our wires crossed here. We both know what the other wants, so why tempt fate and broken hearts?"

"Because we do know what the other one wants."

"How does that make sense?"

He shrugged. "I had it all worked out in my head before you came over tonight. Thought we could actually get through a semi-romantic evening and end our day on a good note."

"Well, the part you hadn't thought through is that you're getting too close. If and when I ever meet a man I want in my life, I don't want him conditionally, and that's all you can be—conditional. You don't want a woman who has children and that's a huge condition. And I'm not saying that I want to be alone for the rest of my life because that's certainly not true. But I want a man who wants Charlie in his life, too, and who'll love my son as much as I do. That won't be you. It's not your fault, though. The thing is, as much as you try to fool yourself into a relationship with me, it just won't work because I'm not who you ultimately want."

"Which makes me not who you ultimately want."

"Does that make sense?"

"You want to know what makes sense?" he asked, taking a step closer to her.

He was so close she could smell the tinge of garlic on his breath. "This won't make it right for us, Simon," she said breathlessly.

"Who the hell cares what's right or wrong?" he said, his voice so thick with need it was almost a growl.

Dear God, she wanted this, and she wanted him, too. Just one time. Like their stolen kiss, a stolen moment of intimacy. In that very moment all her resolve just melted away—she forgot all the reasons why this wasn't the sensible thing to do and just gave in to her desires. She wanted Simon. Now.

"Do you have a bed?" she asked, twining her fingers around his neck. So what if they hadn't defined their friendship in terms of how it was going to be? She was an adult and she could certainly be adult about a one-time fling. Or maybe it would be more than once. Who knew? Who even cared at this point? It wasn't as if they were a couple of kids groping around in the backseat for a fast slap and tickle. They could do this…she could do this without regrets because she genuinely cared for this man. Maybe she was even falling in love with the type she said she'd never have a relationship with. It didn't really matter, though. None of it did. She wanted him here and now and she could tell he wanted her just as much. So, all things considered, what was one night out of her life? Not much, that was what.

"King sized."

"With sheets?"

"Just put on clean ones because I was hoping…" He bowed his head down to hers and pried her mouth open with his tongue, and delved in urgently.

The kiss was rough and demanding, like the one she'd been waiting for and had never before had. It was so full of need as he explored the recesses of her mouth and pulled her so tightly to him she could feel his erection pushing against her belly.

"Are you sure?" he panted as he removed her jacket.

"One time only," she said as her own breaths started coming in short bursts. "Read nothing into it, Simon," she said, as he picked her up and carried her to the bedroom.

"Hell, reading is the furthest thing from my mind."
He threw her down on the bed and landed on top of her.
"Oh, and so you know, once is never enough."

CHAPTER TEN

DEL WAS NAKED, basking in the steamy spray of the shower with Simon, not anxious to leave his condo, torn between the knowledge that she wanted to stay and couldn't, when his cell phone went off.

"I should probably take this," he said, reaching over to the vanity top to grab it. "Simon Michaels speaking," he said, as he playfully rubbed the palm of his hand over her right breast.

He listened for a second then dropped his hand from her breast, and said, "When?" His voice was dead serious. "How is she doing?" He listened for a minute and finally said, "I'll be there in twenty minutes…No, you're not interrupting anything. I *said*, I'll be there." With that he clicked off his phone and stepped out of the shower abruptly, leaving the cold air to flutter in behind him.

Goose bumps raised on her body. "One of our patients?" she asked, grabbing a towel and wrapping it around her as she stepped out. Simon was already half-dressed.

"No. It's Amy. She was in an accident tonight and she's on her way to Lakeside right now. Yvette had her rerouted halfway across town so I could take care of her. Which I can't because I don't work in the hospital."

"Is it serious?" Del asked, running into the bedroom and dropping the towel to pull on her clothes.

"She's not conscious, and that's all I know."

She wanted to ask him if he needed her there, but that didn't mesh well with their new relationship—dragging a lover along to visit an injured little girl. So she followed him out the door, and down the flight of steps to the outside door, then onto the sidewalk. "If there's anything I can do..."

Simon shook his head. "I'll call you later." Then he was off in an abrupt run, no goodbye, no goodbye kiss. Nothing. She stood there for a second and watched him until he turned the corner, then she turned and walked toward her condo feeling quite...unresolved. Although it wasn't his fault. Amy was in trouble and his place was with her and Yvette.

Still, it was unsettling having him practically jump out of bed and into the arms of his ex-wife, no matter what the circumstances. Oh, well, she thought as she keyed herself into the building and said hello to the night concierge, who was sitting at the front desk reading a mystery novel. It was good while it lasted.

Very good. And best of all, come morning she wasn't going to kick herself because she'd wanted it just as much as he had. *I am human*, she thought, as she took one final appraisal to make sure every piece of her clothing was in perfect array before she entered her condo and was forced to confront her parents. Straightening her hair a little, and making sure her blouse was buttoned properly, she glanced at her watch. Two hours, all in. Not bad. Not bad at all. Especially for someone who'd started out the evening not even wanting a minute of it.

Del puttered around her condo for a while, folding Charlie's clothing, talking to her parents, all of it very restless energy. She knew where she needed to be and it certainly wasn't here.

"Why don't you go to the hospital and help your friend through this?" Her mother's suggestion was very much at the forefront of her thoughts, especially when she considered how he'd been there to help her when Charlie was sick. Simon hadn't left her side, and she wouldn't have gotten through it without him. But the thought that held her back was Yvette. She wasn't sure she wanted to see him with his ex, as that would remind her that Simon was at one time part of a happy little family group, even though she knew that wasn't the case now. But a badly injured child had a way of making people grow closer and, having just been in his bed, she wasn't sure she could go that route this soon after.

"He was a big help to me," she told Gloria, who was getting Charlie ready for bed.

"Then go to him, dear. I'm sure he'll be glad to see you."

But she felt a little strange running after him when just an hour ago they'd forgotten for a few minutes there was an outside world for them to worry about. But she had to behave maturely about this, didn't she? Simon might need her. And she was pulled toward him as she paced her condo, going back and forth from wall to wall. "Look, do you mind watching Charlie for the night? I think I need to be with Simon right now."

"Of course we don't mind watching Charlie, do we, Charles?"

Charles Carson smiled. "I'll walk you over to the hospital."

"I'll be fine on my own."

"You may be thirty-five, but you're still my little girl and my little girl gets her father's escort to the hospital even though it's only a couple blocks away."

Del nodded. Now wasn't the time to argue with her father. She just wanted to get to the hospital. So she threw on a lightweight jacket and waited for him at the front door. "I'm glad you're both here," she said, giving her mother a hug. "It makes life easier. And Charlie loves having you here."

"Not as much as we love being here with him," her mother said. "Now, you go on and take all the time you need. Charlie will be just fine with us."

Del's dad opened the door for her and took hold of her arm as they entered the hallway and went to the elevator to wait. "You like this fellow a lot, do you?" Charles asked her.

"We're friends."

"Last time we checked you were colleagues."

"Things change. And he's been a big support to me, especially when Charlie got sick."

The elevator door opened and they got in and rode down to the first floor. "He was there for me every step of the way. I didn't even have to ask him."

"And the two of you are dating now?"

Dating and so much more, but that wasn't something

she cared to discuss with her dad. "We've had a couple of dates. Nothing fancy. Just…nice."

"He's not like Eric, is he? Someone who'll string you along with his promises for years, and cheat on you every chance he gets."

"Simon and I don't have that kind of relationship. It's casual. If he dates someone else…" she tried to imagine Simon with another woman and her heartbeat increased a beat or two "…that's his business. Like I said, we're just casual friends."

"Well, casual or not, don't go getting yourself mixed up in another screwy situation like you had with Eric. He was no good for you."

That was putting it mildly. "What Simon and I have can hardly be called a relationship, Dad. So don't worry about me. I've got my head screwed on straight this time."

The rest of their two-block walk they talked about Charlie and the progress he was making. Then when they arrived at the hospital, Charles left Del at the admitting door and turned around and walked home, while Del's stomach knotted. This was where she got involved in a whole different way than she'd ever believed would happen and it scared her. But, this was about Simon and his stepdaughter, and they might need her help. At the least, Simon could use the support. So, turning toward the ward, she wandered down the hall, took a look at the admittance board in the emergency room and saw that Amy was in holding in Trauma Five. Which meant Yvette couldn't be too far away. Gulping, she slipped very quietly into Trauma Five and just stood pressed to the wall.

* * *

"Amy, honey, you're going to be just fine."

"I'll swear, that truck came out of nowhere," Yvette said. She was standing at the bathroom mirror fixing her hair.

Simon could smell the liquor on her breath and the stale cigarettes in her hair. So she'd picked up a new bad habit. Nothing like some secondhand smoke for Amy.

"What was she doing in the street in the first place? And at this time of night?"

"I was going to the store, and I had her run back to the house to get my purse. I'd forgotten my credit card."

"And she crossed the street alone?"

"She knows how to cross the street, Simon." Yvette slid into a chair and almost slid down to the floor, she was so *relaxed*. "I know you taught her."

"Of course I taught her, but I didn't teach her how to do it alone, after dark, on a busy street."

"It was an accident. And if that damn truck hadn't turned the corner when it did…" She waved a limp hand in the air. "It was all his fault. You should be talking to him."

"Did he stop after he hit her?"

"He stopped, and accused me of being a bad mother. Of all the nerve."

Simon shut his eyes for a moment. "Where's your husband?"

"Away on business," she said.

"Did you call him?"

"Why? Amy isn't *his* kid."

"And she's not my kid, either, but you called me."

"Because you can patch her up and see that she gets home."

"She's unconscious, Yvette. That's going to take a hell of a lot more than a patch."

"Maybe Yvette would like some coffee," Del said from the doorway.

Simon spun around to see her standing there with a paper cup full of coffee from the vending machine.

"I saw how she was and I thought…" She shrugged and held out the coffee. "Do you want anything, Simon?"

He shook his head no, then took the cup from Del and handed it to Yvette. "Drink it!" he ordered her.

"You know I like sugar in mine."

"I'll go get sugar," Del volunteered, and in a split second was out in the hall on her way to the bank of vending machines, with Simon on her heel.

"Why are you here?" he asked, his voice still hanging on to a shred of its accusatory tone.

"Thought you might need me. And I do have some clout here."

"What I need is information about Amy," he said, running a nervous hand through his still-mussed hair. He hadn't combed it after their shower together.

"She's going into X-ray right now. Still unconscious." She shrugged. "I looked at her chart before I came down here."

"She was hit by a truck."

"I know. And the police aren't holding the driver because it was an accident. Amy crossed against the light. Apparently her mother was across the street screaming at her."

"Damn," he muttered, fixing on the sugar packets in Del's hand. "She must have gotten confused."

"Or frightened, poor thing."

"Is Charlie OK?"

"He's with my folks. They'd put him to bed before I got home." She reached out and took his hand. "Look, Simon. She's in good hands here. It's a small hospital but the staff is top-notch all the way around and they'll take good care of Amy."

"I should have fought harder for her. Should have gone back to court another time."

"You did everything you could do. And when she's older I think Amy will understand that. But in the meantime, I think you'd better go take care of Yvette. She's not in very good shape." Del placed the sugar packets in Simon's hand and closed his hand around them. "I'll go see what I can find out and I'll be back to talk to you directly."

He bent down and kissed Del on the forehead. "Thank you for coming. I know I was a little abrupt when I left you on the sidewalk, but—"

"But nothing. You did what any good parent would do. And I don't blame you. We all have ups and downs, especially when your children are sick or injured." She turned and reentered the trauma wing while Simon went to the waiting area only to find Yvette sound asleep, her head on the shoulder of the stranger sitting next to her. He was drinking her coffee. No sugar.

"She's awake now and they said you can go in and see her for a minute," Del told Simon, who was standing out in the hall leaning against the wall.

"Did they give you her diagnosis?"

"No, I thought that it would be better if they talked to you *and* Yvette, since you can't make the decisions for Amy."

"Don't remind me," he grumbled as he walked through the trauma doors into the main hall, with Del walking shoulder to shoulder with him.

"She's in a serious condition, Simon," Del warned. "Pretty beat up on the outside with some internal injuries, as well."

He nodded, and greeted the doctor on call, who was looking at Amy's EKG tracing as Simon stepped into the cubicle.

"Daddy," Amy said weakly. "I'm scared."

"Daddy's here to take care of you now. No need to be afraid," Simon said gently, taking hold of Amy's hand. She was dwarfed by the chest tube, EKG leads, IV tubing and oxygen mask on her, and Simon's first reaction was to assess everything, including blood that was coming out of one of the tubes. "So what are we talking about here?"

"She needs emergency surgery," Dr. Ross said, "to remove her spleen. We also need to surgically repair her leg. Her head films are negative for brain damage and she's alert and reactive."

"Daddy?" Amy whimpered. "I don't feel so good. Is Mommy going to be mad at me for messing up her evening?"

"Mommy's not mad. She's worried."

"I didn't mean to get hit, and I didn't see that truck. Honest I didn't." Amy coughed and a little bit of blood trickled out her nose.

"I'll go wake up her mother and get permission for the surgery," Simon said.

"How about you stay here and I'll go wake her up?" Del offered.

"She can be pretty ugly when she wakes up from a drink."

"And I can be pretty insistent." Del smiled as she squeezed Simon's arm. "You stay here and comfort your little girl. She needs you more than Yvette does."

"Thanks," he said, hovering over Amy's bed as the child drifted off to sleep.

"Why's she drifting in and out?" Simon asked the attending physician.

"We gave her something for pain and she's pretty sensitive to it."

"So tell me the truth. Is she going to be OK?"

"I'd like to get her spleen out of her as soon as possible, to control the internal bleeding. We're not too worried about her leg. It should repair pretty easily once we get the orthopedics team in place."

"Will she be able to endure that much surgery all at once?"

"We'll have to evaluate that as we go along," Dr. Ross explained.

Damn, he felt helpless. He wasn't her real dad, and he didn't even feel much like a real doctor at the moment. The worst part was, he couldn't make the decisions. By all legal rights he shouldn't even be here since Yvette had a restraining order out on him. But he didn't care about that. If they rounded him up and threw him in jail for being at his daughter's bedside, so be it. This was about Amy now, and Amy needed him here. From the looks of Yvette, so did she.

Out in the hall, Del looked into the waiting room at the sleeping woman who was slumped all over the man sitting next to her. She knew they weren't together and could only surmise this was Yvette in her drunken-stupor, passed-out state. It wasn't going to be easy to shake her out of it. "Yvette," Del called from the doorway.

Yvette lifted her head for a moment, then crashed back down on the willing stranger, who didn't seem to mind having her there. Living vicariously, Del thought as she stepped inside the crowded room. "Yvette, wake up."

"I'm awake," she mumbled, opening her eyes.

"You need to get up and come back to Trauma with me. Amy needs you."

"Kid doesn't even understand a stupid traffic light," she said, her voice slurring.

"Amy needs you," Del repeated as all eyes in the room turned to her.

"Her dad is with her."

"No, Simon is with her and you made sure he's not her dad, so he can't sign off on what Amy needs."

The man next to Yvette pushed her upright. "Your kid needs you, lady," he said.

"Fine. Tell Simon to sign the papers for me."

"He can't!" Del crossed the room and physically pulled Yvette from her chair. "You have to do that."

"I faint at the sight of blood," she complained. "Never could understand Simon and his passion for medicine 'cause you get exposed to all kinds of nastiness."

Del steadied the wobbly woman, and pulled her out

into the hall. "She's in Trauma Five. Go down to the
nurses' hub and sign the papers then go down to see
Amy in Room Five. She needs to see you."

"And just who are you?" Yvette asked, straightening herself up.

"I'm a friend of Simon's."

"So he's got a girlfriend." She laughed a shrill laugh
that could be heard the entire length of the hall. "Well,
what do you know about that?"

"What I know is that you're wasting precious minutes of Amy's life. You need to go down there and sign
the surgery consent form."

"OK. OK. I'll sign it, but I expect Simon to stay here
with the kid while I go home and make myself present-
able for my husband. He's coming home tonight."

"Honestly," Del hissed, "I don't care what you do
after you sign the papers. In fact, I'll be glad to call
you a cab."

"I'll just bet you would." Yvette snorted as she
bobbed and wove her way down the hall, where she
stopped at the central hub to inquire about the paper-
work.

The unit secretary handed her a consent form, on
which she scrawled a signature halfway over the entire page, then she turned and staggered back to the
trauma doors.

"Your cab will be here in five minutes," Del told her.

"I don't suppose you're paying for it, too, are you?
See, I don't have enough cash on me right now to..."

Del huffed out an impatient sigh as she took hold
of Yvette's arm and led her to the door. The cab was
already there, waiting, so Del got Yvette inside and

handed the driver a hundred-dollar bill. "That's to make sure you get her up to her door," she said. Whatever happened after that, Del didn't care.

"How did you manage with Yvette?" Simon asked Del after Amy was taken down to surgery.

"Let's just say that she probably won't even remember any of it tomorrow."

"I appreciate everything you've done, up to and including sending her home."

"Amy doesn't need a drunken mother here."

Simon smiled as he took Del's hand and led her back to the cubicle where Amy had been treated. "She's going to spend the night in the ICU and if all goes well be transferred to a pediatric bed in the morning."

"Well, for what it's worth, I can see why you didn't stay with Yvette."

"Yvette does have her bad moments but she's not always so…oblivious. And she's not so cruel that she'd want to see her daughter hurt."

"But she's drunk!"

"Which means something's going wrong in her life."

He was much more lenient with Yvette than Del expected him to be. Did he harbor leftover feelings for her? Maybe part of him still loved her in some odd, convoluted way. It was obvious that Yvette still counted on Simon to see her through and Del felt confused by the emotional interplay she saw. Simon should have been livid with Yvette yet he wasn't. In fact, he was being awfully kind.

"She's worse now than she used to be. For all her faults, Yvette was never a real drunk."

"This new marriage must not be agreeing with her too well, then."

He shook his head. "And Amy's trapped in the middle of it."

"Might be a good time to revisit the custody issue. You'll have the records from the hospital to back you up." Del smiled sadly as he put his arm around her shoulder. "I'm sorry it turned out this way."

"So am I. Amy doesn't deserve this."

"Look, Simon. Let's go up to the doctors' lounge and sit there until Amy's out of surgery. I'll tell them at the desk where we'll be. They need to clean up this cubicle for the next patient."

Simon nodded his agreement and they walked, clinging to each other, to the elevator, where they boarded and went up one floor to the doctors' lounge. It was blessedly quiet in there. A couple of the docs there were dozing, one was eating a meal and another one was reading, with his reading glasses poised on the end of his nose. All in all, it was a peaceful place and Simon was glad for the quiet as he didn't feel like talking, he was so numb with worry. So he and Del sat on the couch, arms wrapped around each other, with Simon's eyes glued to the clock.

Every now and again he sighed and shifted, but he didn't let go of Del. It was well into the first hour of surgery when he finally spoke. "If I went after custody now, wouldn't it seem like I'm taking advantage of a bad situation? I'm afraid that would eventually hurt Amy. I should have had her with me, but the court has been against me every step of the way," he whispered, so as not to disturb the tranquil atmosphere in there.

Del nodded. "Sometimes life's just not fair. Tonight it's not fair for Amy."

He looked down at her and smiled. "Charlie's a lucky little boy having you for his mother. You were meant to have children, Del. I'll admit, I wondered why you wanted to do it, but now I know. You're a natural."

"Thank you," she said. "I love being a mother. I never gave it much of a thought while I was in med school, and even in the beginning of my practice, but being around babies every day…it's how I define myself now, even more than I've always defined myself as being a doctor. But I think you're a natural, too."

"A father without a child."

"Because the child's mother doesn't care enough about her to do what's right. I can't believe she wanted to go home before Amy's surgery."

"Believe it. That's the way the last couple years of our marriage were. She was out playing while I was at home taking care of Amy."

"Yet you still defend her."

"Because for all her faults, I know she does love Amy. It's just difficult for her because she doesn't have that natural mommy instinct like you do."

There he was defending Yvette again. She'd just made love with this man and here he was defending the woman she'd thought he hated. Perhaps it was her own judgment that should be called into question here, getting involved with a man who was distanced from the relationship because he still had feelings for another woman. Could she overcome that? Or did she even want to try?

"I'm just amazed that she wanted custody, when she clearly doesn't care about being a mother."

He shrugged. "I think having a child makes her appear more stable than she is. Yvette's a total mess. Worse tonight than I've ever seen her before."

"I can only imagine what her husband's like," Del commented.

"I've tried not to think about it," Simon said, sounding so discouraged his voice barely broke through the air around them.

"Simon, Del..." A scrub nurse entered the room. "Her splenectomy went fine. They're in for the leg repair now and Dr. Ross said to tell you he'll be up here in a little while to have a talk with you."

Simon heaved a sigh of relief. One surgery down, one to go. Which meant it was still a long night ahead of them. "Thank you," he told the scrub nurse, then turned to Del. "If you want, you can go home now. I'm fine here by myself. And little Charlie may be waking up wanting his mommy anytime."

"How about I call home and if I'm not needed there I'll stay here with you?"

"I'm really OK being by myself here. Especially since you did my dirty work and dealt with Yvette."

"Do you think you should call her with a progress report?" Del asked.

"How about I wait until she calls me?" he snapped.

"Because you're better than that."

"I know. And something's obviously wrong in her life or she wouldn't be acting the way she did. But I'd sure like to treat her the way she deserves."

"Except you won't, and you know it."

Simon sighed. "I'm not looking forward to calling

her, but maybe by now she'll be coherent enough to care a little."

While Del made her call, only to find out that everything was being managed quite well, Simon made his to a voice mail message, telling the caller to call back in the morning. *"If you're calling at night, call back in the morning when I'm awake. If you're calling during the day and I don't answer, leave a message and I'll get back to you as soon as I can."*

Damn, she sounded so sweet on the phone. He could see why he'd fallen for her. She had a way of turning it off and on to suit her needs.

"So, what did she say?" Del asked.

"Nothing. It rolled over to voice mail."

"Seriously? With her child in surgery? Maybe she didn't want to be here but you'd think she'd want to know what was going on."

"She doesn't care."

Del frowned. "I just don't understand it."

"And I hope you never do. People like that shouldn't have children, and Yvette certainly is one of those people."

"Well, for what it's worth, my parents said to tell you that Amy is in their thoughts and prayers tonight, and they're keeping a good thought for you, too."

"Are you going home?"

She shook her head. "I'm here for the duration. As long as you need me…"

"Daddy, where am I?" Amy asked.

"You're in the recovery room. The doctors had to operate on you tonight and you're going to be just fine."

"Is Mommy here?"

"Mommy had a headache and she had to go home."

"Oh," Amy replied, her speech thick with anesthesia. "I'm so sleepy."

"Then go back to sleep, sweetheart."

"Are you going to stay here with me?"

"I'm not going to leave your side," he promised. "And next time you wake up I'll be right here, holding your hand."

"Promise?"

"Promise." He bent over and gave her a kiss on her forehead, then looked at her tiny form lying under the blanket. The daughter he would choose…if the choice were his to make. Unfortunately, it wasn't and he was scared to death that once she was past this crisis Yvette would take Amy away from him again.

Simon didn't know how he'd survive that.

"She looks like an angel," Del said, stepping up behind Simon and putting her hand on his shoulder.

"She is an angel. Such a good child… Yvette doesn't know what she has or how lucky she is."

"Well, Yvette is out in the waiting room with a man I take to be her husband. He's older. Old enough to be her father, and he looks like a dude, with all his gold chains and rings. And he's wearing sunglasses even though he's inside the building at night."

"He brought her here?"

Del shrugged. "She seems more sober than she did when I sent her home several hours ago."

"I suppose I should go out and see her."

"Well, they won't let her in Recovery. I told her she'd have to wait until Amy went to the ICU, then she'd probably get ten minutes with her."

"Was she agreeable?"

"Her husband did all the talking for her. He wanted to know when that would be and I told him we have no way of knowing. He wasn't happy to hear that."

"I guess it has to be done." Frowning, Simon stood up and walked slowly to the door, then out to the surgery waiting room.

"How is she?" Yvette asked as she looked in a compact mirror and fiddled with her hair.

"Rough shape. She lost her spleen, and had to have orthopedic surgery. She'll probably be down about six weeks, and they'll get her up and start her on physical therapy as soon as possible so she won't get weak."

"Six weeks?" Yvette's husband shouted. "We can't have a sick kid hanging around that long. We've got things to do, and if she's laid up that means we'll have to get someone to watch her."

"You must be Mack Brighton," Simon said, without extending his hand to the man.

"Sure, this is my husband, Mack," Yvette said. "Mack, this is my ex, Simon. The one who was fighting me for Amy."

"So you're the one who wants the kid. Funny how that's going to work out for you, 'cause it looks like you're going to get her for a while, since we can't take care of her the way she needs. Or, I suppose we could put her in a nursing home of some sort if you don't want her the way she is now."

"Amy's not going to a nursing home," Simon said, fighting hard to hold his temper in check.

"Then you'll keep her?" Yvette asked hopefully.

"Of course I'll keep her. But you'll have to have the court revoke the restraining order against me."

"And you'll have to give him full custody so he can make all her medical decisions," Del said from behind Simon. She stepped around him and looked straight at Mack. "The way it stands now, Simon can't do anything to help Amy because of the way you've got him tied up. So untie him and give him a full-custody agreement, then you won't have to have him bothering you every time something has to be decided."

"Sure, whatever," Mack grunted. "I'll call the attorney first thing in the morning."

"You're taking my baby?" Yvette asked, as if she wasn't even paying attention to the conversation going on around her. "Does that mean you're going to pay for her, too?"

"Of course I'll pay for her."

"And he won't come after you at some time in the future if you agree to sever all ties to Amy now, and in the years to come."

"You mean you're just going to take my baby away from me forever?"

"That's exactly what he means," Del interjected.

"And I want to adopt her," Simon said. "Give her my name and become her legal father."

"That's being harsh," Yvette said. "Just because she had a little accident."

"An accident that almost killed her," Simon returned.

"Let him have the kid," Mack said. "If you don't she's going to cost you a fortune, and don't expect me to chip in for her care."

"Why do I feel like you're all trying to take advantage of me?" Yvette asked, putting on her pouty face.

"You think you can do better?" Mack asked.

"You know I can't do better than you, babe," Yvette answered him.

"Then give him the kid. You don't want her anyway. You told me so a dozen times."

"Yet you went after me and took a restraining order against me having any contact with her?" Simon almost shouted.

"That was purely a strategic move," Yvette said. "And you failed."

"You were going to extort money from him to see his stepdaughter?" Del asked. "Was that the plan?"

"Not extort money so much as just make him pay for the privilege."

"I sure as hell don't pay for that kid," Mack butted in. "And I made that perfectly clear when we got married that the kid was baggage."

"Baggage her mother thought she could make a buck on," Del argued.

"Who the hell are you anyway, lady?"

"She's the person who cares more about Amy than Amy's mother does," Simon told him.

"Your hook-up?" Mack asked.

"My friend."

With that Del stepped closer to Simon and slid her hand into his. "His very good friend."

"Then you tell your very good friend he can have the kid if he wants her, but it's going to cost him."

"It will cost me nothing," Simon said, squeezing Del's hand. "In fact it will save me another court battle where I go after child support from Yvette, which is what I could do since you're so willing to give Amy away. I'm sure the courts would agree with me that neither of you deserves to have her, and if it gets that far in the court system Yvette might be the one who ends up paying me child support."

"You wouldn't do that," Yvette said. "We were married five years and the one thing I know about you, Simon, is that Amy matters more than anything else to you. You wouldn't tie her up in a family court battle like one that is bound to hurt her."

"You're right. I wouldn't. But you would, and that's the difference between us, Yvette. You'd use Amy and I'd protect her."

Del smiled. "See, the thing is, Amy will be going where she's loved and wanted, and if you care for Amy at all, then you'd want that for her. Especially since you'll be getting Mack in the deal."

Yvette sighed. "Are you going to be around to help raise her?"

"I'll be around," Del said, then looked up at Simon. "One way or another."

"Could I at least see her sometimes, Simon?"

Del held her breath. This whole thing had been a gamble to start with, but it looked as if Yvette was about to give in to her husband's wishes. Here was hoping she had no more children in the bargain.

"Of course. Ideally, you'd even want to have a relationship with her."

"Except we're moving out of Chicago," Mack said.

"We are?" Yvette questioned.

"Yep. I've got a hot prospect coming up in Vegas

and I need to be closer to my work. Ain't no place for no kid, either."

"I could call."

"You can call," Simon agreed.

"And video conference," Yvette suggested.

Simon agreed to that, too, knowing full well that once Amy was out of her sight she'd also be out of mind. "So, I'll get an attorney. For my side of it, and—"

"Got one already," Del interrupted. "He's my next-door neighbor."

"Then it's set. I'll adopt Amy." It seemed so simple and almost civilized. Of course, they were talking money at this juncture and Yvette didn't have a say in that, apparently.

"And we won't be paying for the kid one way or another," Mack said, smiling as if he'd just won a great victory.

"And you won't be paying for the kid," Simon agreed, nodding. "Oh, and in case you're interested, Yvette, she did ask for you."

Yvette looked shocked. "You tell her Mommy's moving, that she'll be calling her as soon as she's settled in."

"You could see her before you go," Del suggested.

"Don't have time," Mack said. "We've got packing to do. Just make a lawyer's appointment before we leave town next week, and we'll get this all wrapped up."

"Dr. Michaels," one of the recovery nurses said, tapping Simon on the shoulder. "Just thought you'd want to know that Amy's coming round again and if you want to keep your promise to her…"

Simon took one last look at Yvette and, while he didn't regret their marriage because it had given him

Amy, he did regret that she'd let herself be trampled so low. But that was her life, and he had a brand-new life ahead of him. "Thanks," he whispered as Mack and Yvette walked away. Simon didn't know if it was his imagination, or if it was real, but as Yvette glanced back he thought he saw a look of regret on her face. He hoped, for Amy's sake, he did. But Yvette was pulled into Mack's embrace as they exited the hall, and she didn't look back again.

"Goodbye and good riddance," Simon said as he rushed back to the recovery room, pulling Del along with him. By the time Amy came around again, he was sitting next to her, holding her hand with his left, and holding on to Del for dear life with his right.

Things had worked out rather simply, Del thought as she stood there. But she still wondered about Simon. Would he commit to someone other than Amy? If, per chance, they got together, how would Charlie rate with him? Would Charlie always come in second? She pictured him adoring Amy while practically ignoring Charlie, and that bothered her. She couldn't be involved with a man who would do that. Time would tell, she supposed, and if there was one thing she had plenty of, it was time.

"That's all for the night," Del said as she and Simon walked away from the ICU viewing window. "You can see her again in the morning."

"This has been the longest night of my life," Simon said, stretching his arms as he turned and started down the hall. He reached over and took hold of Del's hand. "Congratulate me. I'm going to be a father."

"Since I've known you, you've never not been a father," she said.

"You got pretty feisty in the confrontation." They walked past the exit sign and on to the front door. "I've never seen that side of you before."

"That's the mother side of me fighting for a child. Tonight I was fighting for Amy."

"But you're not her mother."

"And you were in the position where you had to be more diplomatic than I was. One wrong word and Amy would have been chucked into a nursing home while Yvette and Mack went to Vegas. So as the innocent bystander..."

"You're not so innocent, Del. Let me tell you, I have a new appreciation for that side of your motherhood. Pity the poor idiots who try to get one over on Charlie, because you've got some wicked claws."

She laughed. "It's called a mother's defense mechanism."

They headed out into the parking lot and decided to spend the rest of the night next door in the clinic so they'd be close to the hospital in case Simon was called back. Not that there was much left of the night, as it was going on to four a.m.

"I wonder if I'll develop something like it."

"Oh, I think you already have. You stand up for Amy quite nicely. Nice enough that it got you a child tonight."

"I don't think that's sunk in yet. More than likely it won't until I see the signatures on the court document."

She stopped and pulled him over to her, and reached up and kissed him full on the lips. "That's for good luck."

"I've already had all the good luck I'll ever need,"

he said, putting his arm around her waist as they finished their walk over to the clinic. "And it's sure been
one hell of a night, you know that?"

"I know," she said, remembering how it had started
in bed. Just for a quickie was what she'd promised herself, except somewhere in there that quickie had been
extended into an emotional commitment. She realized
then that she did love Simon, and she didn't regret that
for a moment. Loved the way he took care of his child,
loved the way he was with her. Too bad he still wouldn't
commit to another woman with a child because she was
suddenly in the mood to be committed to him. But that
just wasn't to be and she knew that. Couldn't blame
him, either, after what he'd gone through with Amy.
Besides, Amy would be enough for him to deal with
for a good, long time.

Del sighed. Their timing was sure off, she decided.
Which didn't make them too much of a meant-to-be
proposition. It was on that note that she decided to leave
him alone at the clinic and go on home, where she was
supposed to be. At least in the morning she could see
Charlie, and he would renew her vitality. Because tonight she felt fully drained. Fully, completely drained.

"She's doing great," Simon said. "She's in physical therapy next door so I decided to run over here to the clinic
to see how things were going." He was on an extended
leave of absence, pending Amy's release from the hospital any day now. And although he was officially offf
call, he'd managed to drop in on Del at least once a day
for the past two weeks. Sometimes he had a legitimate
excuse, sometimes he just came to loiter and be near.

Either way, she always seemed glad to see him. Glad, yet back to the casual. So while they hadn't managed another night together yet, that connection was still there between them, ever clinging. But he felt it slipping away.

Besides, Del's parents had gone home to Costa Rica and she was back to her old schedule, which left her with very little time to herself. "I've checked in on her a few times when I've gone over to visit Charlie on my lunch hour and she's wonderful. So bright. So eager to work hard to get better because she wants to come home and live in her new daddy's condo."

Simon smiled. "I can see why you didn't want to leave Charlie. It's a hard adjustment to make."

"It's getting easier when I drop him off, but it's never totally easy."

"Have you ever thought about a child-care center here in the clinic? We've got a few parents here who could benefit from that."

"Actually, no. I'd never thought of it, but it might be worth considering."

"That would keep Charlie closer to you. And Amy closer to me before and after school."

"So you're really going to come back to us when she's better?"

"Yes. I'd never planned on quitting altogether. Somebody's got to support us. So unless I marry a rich woman who doesn't mind taking on all the responsibilities…"

"She can't have children," Del reminded him.

"About that. I think I've changed my mind."

"Changed your mind about what?"

"About someone with children. I think I could possibly manage to have a relationship like that in my life."

"How? When all I've ever heard from you is that you wouldn't get permanently involved with a woman who has a child. When did that change, or did it change?"

"It changed when I started using my head. And it's about finding the right relationship. Knowing that she would love Amy as much as I would love her child."

"So you mean a blended-family type of situation?"

"That's what they're calling it these days."

"But could you do that, Simon? Just walk into a family and love her children as much as you love Amy? Or would Amy always come first? Because that wouldn't be right. Children need love on their own terms, and they don't need it in a pecking order. Amy comes first, the other child comes second." She shook her head. "It wouldn't work."

"But what if I didn't have that pecking order? If I accepted all the children as they are and loved them in no particular order?"

"You've gone to hell and back for Amy. How could she not come first in your life? I mean, you bring with you, by default, a split family already."

"Not split. Just blended."

Del blinked hard. "Anybody in mind?"

"Just one person. But I'm not sure she wants a relationship with anybody other than her son."

"I think she does. Something tells me she had a change of heart somewhere along the way. But you scare her because of your close ties to your daughter. Can anyone else truly fit in or will there always be a division? And while we're on the subject, do you still have feelings for Yvette?"

"I'll always care about Yvette because she's Amy's mother. But does that mean I want her back? Hell, no! I want to stay as far away from the woman as I possibly can. As for that division, we wouldn't be divided, Del. I don't worry that you couldn't love Amy as much as I do because I know your heart. As I hope you know mine."

"It still scares me, Simon. I'd love to have a daughter and Amy's a wonderful little girl I've already grown to love. But you…you're the unknown to me. Could you ever love Charlie the way I do? Because you'd have to before I…committed to anything. And I just don't know."

"What tripped me up?" he asked.

"Your own words, that you won't have a woman who has a child. I know that's not playing fair using them against you at this stage of our relationship, and especially now that you have your daughter, but it scares me that Charlie will always run a distant second to Amy, and I can't have that."

"Yet you don't think that Amy will run a distant second to Charlie?"

Del shook her head. "I have room in my heart for many more children. Amy would just fill in one of those empty spaces."

"Yet you don't think I could do the same for Charlie?"

"Blending isn't easy, is it?"

"What if I were to adopt Charlie and give him my name as my legal son instead of my stepson?"

"You'd want to do that?"

"In a heartbeat, if you'd let me, and if it would prove to you that I could love him as much as I love Amy. Stop and think, Del. Amy is not my biological child, either, yet I'd defy anyone who said she's not my daughter. I fell for her just the way I'm falling for Charlie."

"Then that makes you a remarkable man," Del said.

"So if I'd ask you to move in to my much larger condo…"

"I might be willing to accept. Provided you really want to take on another woman's child again and maybe add two or three more to the mix."

"More kids?"

She shrugged. "I like being a mother."

"Well, Amy could use another child in the house. She'll make a super big sister, and I could certainly use a woman who would stand by me as staunchly as you do."

"That's a mighty tall order."

"From a man who's head over heels crazy in love with you?"

"And you're sure my having Charlie doesn't matter to you?"

"Oh, it matters a lot. I'd love to be the one to teach him to play ball when he's old enough."

"I think Charlie would love having a father."

"But would you love having a husband?"

"Depends on who it is, and since there's only one candidate on my list…"

"Want to go to Ming's tonight and discuss it?"

"I have a better idea. Let's go to your condo and discuss it. Because here's the thing. Now that I'm going to be the mother of two children, I'm dying to have another baby. So I could get a sitter and we could go to your condo and begin to work at making a baby of our own."

"Seriously?"

"You want to be a father, don't you? And I'm assuming it's to be a large family. So one or two more children should round us out nicely."

"Why, I'd love to make a baby with you, Del."

"And I'd love to make a baby with you, Simon." With that, she twined her fingers around his neck and pulled him closer for the kiss that sealed the deal. "I love you," she whispered to him, not caring that they were standing in the middle of the hall where anybody could see them."

"And I love you," he said back, his lips to hers.

"I love the family we have and the one we're going to make together, too," she continued, only this time in a whisper.

"Do we have to wait until tonight to start?"

"Just a minute," she said, then went to the doctors' board and wiped her name off it. "Now, we've got three hours until I have to pick Charlie up from day care."

"And I promised Amy I'd be back at the hospital to have dinner with her. This is our life now," he warned. "You do know that, don't you?"

"I know," she said, taking his hand as they hurried out the clinic door. "And I wouldn't trade it for anything."

As they walked hand in hand down the sidewalk to his condo, which was the closest by a block to the clinic, she looked out over the lake and smiled. Yes, this was her life now. The one she wanted. The one she needed. The one she loved.

* * * * *

*If you enjoyed this story, check out
these other great reads from Dianne Drake*

*TORTURED BY HER TOUCH
A HOME FOR THE HOT-SHOT DOC
A DOCTOR'S CONFESSION
A CHILD TO HEAL THEIR HEARTS*

All available now!

MILLS & BOON®

The One Summer Collection!

0616_MB523_OSA

MILLS & BOON®